PRAISE FOR DEBORAH CROMBIE'S

# AND JUSTICE THERE IS NONE

"Another hard-nosed piece of social criticism from Deborah Crombie."—*The New York Times Book Review*

"Wow!"—*Detroit News and Free Press*

"Artfully mixes aspects of British history with mystery . . . Absorbing."—*Forth Worth Morning Star Telegram*

"Masterly . . . a supremely satisfying traditional British mystery . . . essential for mystery lovers."
—*Library Journal*

"Anglophiles will cheer."—*Kirkus Reviews*

"Crombie keeps the action moving throughout . . . keeps the reader involved all the way to its conclusion."
—*Publishers Weekly*

"Crombie does an excellent job of pulling the reader into the heartrending lives of her characters . . . A great read."
—*Old Book Barn Gazette*

"Steady suspense, building to an explosive ending."
—*Booklist*

"A powerfully complex story . . . Crombie does a phenomenal job of plotting, combining a superb puzzle with an almost overwhelming poignancy."
—www.romantictimes.com

# A FINER END

"Crombie has laid claim to the literary territory of moody psychological suspense owned by P. D. James and Barbara Vine. Superbly creepy and melodramatic."
—*The Washington Post*

"Crombie . . . has evolved into a masterful novelist."
—*The Denver Post*

"Very richly written."—*Deadly Pleasures*

"A master of the modern British mystery . . . one writer who gets better with every book."—*The Patriot News*

"A really splendid book."—*Booknews* from The Poisoned Pen

"Intricately layered."—*The New York Times*

"Careful plotting, the development of characters and the evocation of place are hallmarks of Crombie's writing and the current book is no exception."
—*Mystery Lovers Bookshop News*

"A clever, cunning series."—*Old Book Barn Gazette*

# KISSED A SAD GOODBYE

"Atmospheric . . . absorbing . . . haunting."
—*The Washington Post Book World*

"Crombie never stumbles as she maneuvers her way through her complicated plot as skillfully as she handles

the ongoing romance between her two detectives.
The result is an Anglophile's delight."
—*The Sunday Denver Post*

"Deborah Crombie is an American mystery novelist
who writes so vividly about England, she might have been
born within the sound of Bow bells. [She] gets better
with each book.... Lyrical, biting, and evocative."
—*The Plain Dealer,* Cleveland

"Thanks to Crombie's ability to bring people and
places to life with a phrase, none of the seams show
as the story zips along."—*Chicago Tribune*

"An engaging, richly peopled, satisfying mystery."
—*Houston Chronicle*

"Compelling from start to finish. Another winner
from a dependable and gifted pro."
—*Kirkus Reviews* (starred review)

"[A] beautifully executed story of murder and revenge...
With each volume, Crombie grows in the understanding
of her characters and hones her writing and creative skills
with verve and elan."—*Booknews* from The Poisoned Pen

"Gripping. Highly recommended."—*Library Journal*

"Readers ... who loved Deborah Crombie's *Dreaming of the
Bones* will not be disappointed with *Kissed a Sad
Goodbye* ... Outstanding."—*Mystery Lovers Bookshop News*

"Crombie's plot is unpredictable, leaving a reader
guessing ... Her characters are well drawn."
—*Austin American-Statesman*

# DREAMING OF THE BONES

*Available from Bantam Books

# AND JUSTICE
# THERE IS NONE

## DEBORAH CROMBIE

BANTAM BOOKS

AND JUSTICE THERE IS NONE
A Bantam Book

PUBLISHING HISTORY
Bantam hardcover edition published September 2002
Bantam mass market edition / June 2003

Published by
Bantam Dell
A Division of Random House, Inc.
New York, New York

Thanks to Kensington and Chelsea Community History Group
(history@kcchg.org.uk) for permission to use quotations from its
publication *Portobello* by Whetlor and Bartlett.

*Notting Hill in the Sixties*
Photography by Charlie Phillips
Words by Mike Phillips
Lawrence and Wishart, London 1991

ISBN 0-553-57930-4

Manufactured in the United States of America
Published simultaneously in Canada

OPM   10 9 8 7 6 5 4 3

*For Nanny*

# ACKNOWLEDGMENTS

Many thanks are due, as always, to the *Every Other Tuesday Night Writer's Group:* Steve Copling, Dale Denton, Jim Evans, Diane Sullivan Hale, John Hardie, Viqui Litman, Rickey Thornton, and Milan Vesely, with added appreciation to Diane Sullivan Hale, RN, BSN, for her advice on medical matters. Thanks as well to Carol Chase and Marcia Talley for their inspiration and input; to Connie Munro for her astute copy edit; to Glen Edelstein for the book design; to Jamie Warren Youll for the jacket design; to Kate Miciak, my editor at Bantam, for simply being the best; and to Nancy Yost, my agent, for her long-standing patience and support.

# MILLENNIUM

*"The sun no longer shows*
*His face; and treason sows*
*His secret seeds that no man can detect;*
*Fathers by their children are undone;*
*The brother would the brother cheat;*
*And the cowled monk is a deceit...*
*Might is right, and justice there is none."*

— WALTHER VON DER VOGELWEIDE
c. 1170–1230

# AND JUSTICE
# THERE IS NONE

# CHAPTER ONE

Admiral Sir Edward Vernon, with a small fleet of ships
from the British Navy, captured the port [of Porto Bello] in
1739 . . . Bonfires were lit in all the major cities to celebrate
the victory . . . streets and districts were named after Vernon
and Portobello.

—Whetlor and Bartlett,
from *Portobello*

HE RAN, AS so many others ran, the black anorak protecting
him from the mist, the reflective patches on his trainers gleaming as he passed under the street lamps. The pattern of the
streets was etched in his mind, a living map. Down Portobello,
under the motorway, past Oxford Gardens, once the site of Portobello Farm, then back up Ladbroke Grove, past the video shop
and the Afro-Caribbean hairdressers, then into Lansdown Road
with its whitewashed Victorian austerity. He imagined that
the street's curve paralleled the track of the old racecourse that
had crowned Notting Hill a hundred and fifty years ago;
that his feet fell where the horses' hooves had struck.

Now, Christmas lights twinkled in front gardens, promising a cheerful comfort he could not share. Other joggers passed
him. He acknowledged them with a nod, a raised hand, but he
knew there was no real kinship. They thought of their heart
rates, of their dinners and their shopping, of home and children
and the demands of the holiday on their bank accounts.

He ran, as the others ran, but his mind revolved in a rat's
wheel of old things, dark things, sores that did not heal. Nor

*would they, he knew, unless he took the cleansing upon himself: There would be no justice unless he made it.*

*There, the spire of St. John's Church, rising disembodied above the mist-wreathed rooftops. The blood roared in his veins as he neared his destination; his breath came hard with the terror of it. But he could not turn away. All his life he had been moving towards this place, this night; this was who and what he was.*

*A woman with long, dark hair passed by him, her face in shadow. His heart quickened as it always did; it might have been his mother as he saw her in his dreams. Sometimes in his visions her hair twined round him, silken and cool, an elusive comfort. Every night he had brushed it with a silver-backed brush, and she had told him stories. Until she had been taken from him.*

*He ran, as the others ran, but he carried with him something they did not. History, and hatred, honed to a bright and blazing point.*

Portobello took on a different character once the shops closed for the day, Alex Dunn decided as he turned into the road from the mews where he had his small flat. He paused for a moment, debating whether to go up the road to the Calzone's at Notting Hill Gate for a celebratory pizza, but it wasn't the sort of place one really wanted to go on one's own. Instead, he turned to the right, down the hill, passing the shop fronts barred for the night and the closed gates of the café run by St. Peter's Church. Bits of refuse littered the street from the day's traffic, giving it a desolate air.

But tomorrow it would be different; by daybreak the

stallholders would be set up for Saturday market, and in the arcades, dealers would sell everything from antique silver to Beatles memorabilia. Alex loved the early-morning anticipation, the smell of coffee and cigarettes in the arcade cafés, the sense that this might be the day to make the sale of a lifetime. As he might, he thought with a surge of excitement, because today he'd made the buy of his lifetime.

His step quickened as he turned into Elgin Crescent and saw the familiar façade of Otto's Café—at least that was how the regulars referred to the place; the faded sign read merely *Café*. Otto did a bustling daytime business in coffee, sandwiches, and pastries, but in the evening he provided simple meals much favored by the neighborhood residents.

Once inside, Alex brushed the moisture from his jacket and took a seat in the back at his favorite table— favored because he liked the nearness of the gas fire. Unfortunately, the café's furniture had not been designed to suit anyone over five feet tall. Surprising, really, when you looked at Otto, a giant of a man. Did he never sit in his own chairs? Alex couldn't recall ever seeing him do so; Otto always seemed to hover, as he did now, wiping his brow with the hem of his apron, his bald head gleaming even in the dim light.

"Sit down, Otto, please," Alex said, testing his hypothesis. "Take a break."

Otto glanced towards Wesley, his second-in-command, serving the customers who had just come in, then flipped one of the delicate curve-backed chairs round and straddled it with unexpected grace.

"Nasty out, is it?" The café owner's wide brow furrowed

as he took in Alex's damp state. Even though Otto had
lived all of his adult life in London, his voice still carried an
inflection of his native Russia.

"Can't quite make up its mind to pour. What sort of
warming things have you on the menu tonight?"

"Beef and barley soup; that and the lamb chops
should do the trick."

"Sold. And I'll have a bottle of your best Burgundy.
No plonk for me tonight."

"Alex, my friend! Are you celebrating something?"

"You should have seen it, Otto. I'd run down to
Sussex to see my aunt when I happened across an estate
sale in the village. There was nothing worth a second
look in the house itself; then, on the tables filled with
bits of rubbish in the garage, I saw it." Savoring the
memory, Alex closed his eyes. "A blue-and-white porcelain bowl, dirt-encrusted, filled with garden trowels and
bulb planters. It wasn't even tagged. The woman in
charge sold it to me for five pounds."

"Not rubbish, I take it?" Otto asked, an amused expression on his round face.

Alex looked round and lowered his voice.
"Seventeenth-century delft, Otto. That's English delft,
with a small 'd,' rather than Dutch. I'd put it at around
1650. And underneath the dirt, not a chip or a crack to
be found. It's a bloody *miracle,* I'm telling you."

It was the moment Alex had lived for since his aunt
had taken him with her to a jumble sale on his tenth
birthday. Spying a funny dish that looked as if someone
had taken a bite out of its edge, he had been so taken
with it that he'd spent all his birthday money on its
purchase. His aunt Jane had contributed a book on
porcelain, from which he'd learned that his find was an

English delft barber's bowl, probably early eighteenth-century Bristol ware. In his mind, Alex had seen all the hands and lives through which the bowl had passed, and in that instant he had been hooked.

The childhood passion had stayed with him through school, through university, through a brief tenure lecturing in art history at a small college. Then he had abandoned the steady salary for a much more precarious—and infinitely more interesting—life as a dealer in English porcelain.

"So, will this bowl make your fortune? If you can bear to part with it, that is," Otto added with a twinkle born of long association with dealers.

Alex sighed. "Needs must, I'm afraid. And I have an idea who might be interested."

Otto gazed at him for a moment with an expression Alex couldn't quite fathom. "You're thinking Karl Arrowood would want it."

"It's right up Arrowood's alley, isn't it? You know what Karl's like; he won't be able to resist." Alex imagined the bowl elegantly displayed in the window of Arrowood Antiques, one more thing of beauty for Karl to possess, and the bitterness of his envy seeped into his soul.

"Alex—" Otto seemed to hesitate, then leaned closer, his dark eyes intent. "I do know what he's like, perhaps more than you. You'll forgive my interfering, but I've heard certain things about you and Karl's young wife. You know what this place is like"—his gesture took in more than the café—"nothing stays secret for long. And I fear you do not realize what you're dealing with. Karl Arrowood is a ruthless man. It doesn't do to come between him and the things he owns."

"But—" Alex felt himself flushing. "How—" But he knew it didn't matter how, only that his affair with Dawn Arrowood had become common knowledge, and that he'd been a fool to think they could keep it hidden.

If the discovery of the delft barber's bowl had been an epiphanic experience, so had been his first glimpse of Dawn, one day when he'd stopped by the shop to deliver a creamware dinner service.

Dawn had been helping the shop assistant with the window displays. At the sight of her, Alex had stood rooted to the pavement, transfixed. Never had he seen anything so beautiful, so perfect; and then she had met his eyes through the glass and smiled.

After that, she'd begun coming by his stall on Saturday mornings to chat. She'd been friendly rather than coy or flirtatious, and he'd immediately sensed her loneliness. His weeks began to revolve around the anticipation of her Saturday visits, but never had he expected more than that. And then one day she'd shown up unannounced at his flat. "I shouldn't be doing this," she'd said, ducking her head so that wisps of blond hair hid her eyes, but she had come inside, and now he couldn't imagine his life without her.

"Does Karl know?" he asked Otto.

The other man shrugged. "I think you would know if he did. But you can be sure he will find out. And I would hate to lose a good customer. Alex, take my advice, please. She is lovely, but she is not worth your life."

"This is England, for heaven's sake, Otto! People don't go round bumping people off because they're narked about . . . well, you know."

Otto stood and carefully reversed his chair. "I wouldn't

be so sure, my friend," he replied before disappearing into the kitchen.

"Bollocks!" Alex muttered, resolved to slough off Otto's warning, and he ate his dinner and drank his wine with determination.

His good humor somewhat restored, he walked slowly back to his flat, thinking of the other find he'd made that day—not a steal as the delft bowl had been, but a lovely acquisition just the same, an Art Deco teapot by the English potter Clarice Cliff in a pattern he had seen Dawn admire. It would be his Christmas gift to her, an emblem of their future together.

It was only as he reached the entrance to his mews that a more disturbing thought came to him. If Karl Arrowood learned the truth, was it his own safety which should concern him?

Bryony Poole waited until the door had closed behind the final client of the day, a woman whose cat had an infected ear, before she broached her idea to Gavin. Sitting down opposite him in the surgery's narrow office cubicle, she shifted awkwardly, trying to find room for her long legs and booted feet. "Look, Gav, there's something I've been meaning to talk to you about."

Her boss, a bullet-headed man with shoulders that strained the fabric of his white lab coat, looked up from the chart he was finishing. "That sounds rather ominous. Not leaving me for greener pastures, are you?"

"No, nothing like that." Gavin Farley had taken Bryony on as his assistant in the small surgery just after her graduation from veterinary college two years ago, and she still considered herself lucky to have the job. Hesitantly, she continued. "It's just, well, you know how many of the homeless people have dogs?"

"Is this a quiz?" he asked skeptically. "Or are you hitting me up for a donation to the RSPCA?"

"No . . . not exactly. But I have been thinking a good bit about the fact that these people can't afford care for their animals. I'd like to do some—"

She had his attention now.

"Bryony, that's extremely admirable of you, but surely if these people can afford a pint and a packet of ciggies they can bring a dog in for treatment."

"That's unfair, Gavin! These people sleep in the street because the night shelters won't take their dogs. They do what they can. And you know how much our costs have risen."

"So what can you possibly do?"

"I want to run a free clinic every week, say on Sunday afternoon, to treat minor ailments and injuries—"

"Does this have something to do with your friend Marc Mitchell?"

"I haven't discussed it with him," Bryony replied, her defenses rising.

"And where exactly did you think you'd hold this clinic?"

She flushed. "Well, I had thought Marc might let me use his place . . ." Marc Mitchell ran a soup kitchen for the homeless—"rough sleepers" the government liked to call them, as if they had voluntarily chosen to take a permanent camping holiday—down the bottom end of the Portobello Road. Of course there was the Sally Army further up, but in the business of providing for the needy there was no such thing as competition. There was never enough to go round. Marc gave them a hot lunch and supper, as well as whatever basic medical supplies and personal items he could get. But perhaps most important was his willingness to listen to them. There was an earnestness about him that encouraged the baring of ravaged souls, and sometimes that in itself was enough to start a person on the road to recovery.

"And how exactly did you intend to pay for the supplies and medications?" Gavin asked.

"Out of my own pocket, to begin with. Then maybe I could ask some of the local merchants for donations."

"You might get a bob or two," he conceded grudgingly. "I don't imagine having mange-ridden dogs hanging about outside one's shop draws in the customers. But say you can get this off the ground. What are you going to do once you form a relationship with these people, then they begin to show up here with a badly injured dog, or an animal with cancer?"

"I—I hadn't thought..."

Gavin shook his head. "We can't cover catastrophic care, Bryony. We just survive as it is, with the increase in rents and your salary. There's no room for noble gestures."

"I'll deal with that when I come to it," she answered firmly. "If nothing else, I can always offer them euthanasia."

"And pay the cost out of your own pocket? You're too noble for your own good." Gavin sighed with resignation as he finished the chart and stood. "I suspected that the first time I saw you."

Bryony smiled. "But you hired me."

"So I did, and I've not regretted it. You're a good vet, and good with the clients, too, which is damn near as important. But . . ."

"What?"

"It's just that we walk a fine line in this business between compassion and common sense, and I'd hate to see you cross it. It will eat you up, Bryony, this feeling of never being able to do enough. I've seen it happen to tougher vets than you. My advice is, you do the best job you can, then you go home, watch the telly, have a pint. You find some way to let it go."

"Thanks, Gav. I'll keep that in mind. Promise."

She mulled over his words as she walked the short distance from the clinic to her flat in Powis Square. Of course she knew where to draw the line; of course she realized she couldn't help every animal. But was she taking on more than she could manage, both emotionally and financially? And how much was she motivated by an unacknowledged desire to impress Marc Mitchell?

They'd become good friends in the past few months, she and Marc, often meeting for dinner or a coffee. But he'd never displayed what Bryony could really interpret as romantic intentions, and she thought she'd convinced herself that she didn't mind. Marc, unlike Gavin, had not learned to draw the line between work and home. His work was his life: Bryony suspected there was no room left for anything more demanding than friendship.

The pang of disappointment that thought caused her was so intense that she shied away from it. She just wanted to help the animals, that was all, and if it so happened that it brought her a bit closer to Marc, so be it.

• • •

Inspector Gemma James left the Notting Hill Police Station at six o'clock on the dot, an occurrence unusual enough to cause the desk sergeant to raise his eyebrows.

"What's up, guv?" he asked. "Got a hot date?"

"As a matter of fact, I have," she replied, grinning. "And for once I'm determined not to be late."

Kincaid had rung her from the Yard an hour ago and asked her to meet him at an address a few blocks from the station. He'd given her no explanation, only insisted that she be prompt, and that alone had been enough to arouse her curiosity. A superintendent leading Scotland Yard's murder inquiries, Duncan's schedule was as demanding as hers, if not more so, and they were both accustomed to working long hours.

Of course she had been trying to cut back, due to what Kincaid only half-teasingly referred to as her "delicate condition," but without much success. She had no intention of announcing her pregnancy to her superiors until she absolutely had to, and then she'd be even less inclined to beg off work.

And if an unplanned pregnancy weren't disastrous enough for the career prospects of a newly promoted detective inspector, Gemma suspected her unmarried state would garner even less favor with her superiors. At least when Toby had come along she'd been married to his dad.

Checking the address she'd scribbled on a scrap of paper, she walked down Ladbroke Grove until she reached St. John's Gardens, then turned left. The old church stood sentinel on the summit of Notting Hill, and even on such a dreary evening Gemma loved the calm of the place. But Kincaid's directions sent her onwards, down the hill to the west, and after a few blocks she began checking the house numbers.

She saw his MG first, its top buttoned up tight against the damp, and then across the street the address he had given her. It was the end house of a terrace, but faced on St. John's rather than the cross street. Porch light and street lamp illuminated dark brown brick set off by gleaming white trim, and a front door the vivid color of cherries. Through the trees that grew between the house and the pavement, she glimpsed a small balcony on the second floor.

Duncan opened the door before she could ring. "What, are you clairvoyant?" she demanded, laughing, as he kissed her cheek.

"Among my many talents." He took her damp jacket and hung it on an iron coat rack in the hall.

"What's this all about? Are we meeting someone here?"

"Not exactly," he answered. His grin made her think of her four-year-old son concealing a surprise. "Let's have a look round, shall we?"

The kitchen lay to the left, a cheerful, yellow room with a scrubbed pine table and a dark blue, oil-fired cooker. Gemma's heart contracted in a spasm of envy. It was perfect, just the sort of kitchen she had always longed for. She gave a lingering look back as Kincaid urged her into the hall.

The dining and sitting rooms had been opened into one long space with deep windows and French doors that Gemma presumed must lead to a garden. The dining furniture had an air of Provençal; in the sitting room, a comfortably worn sofa and two armchairs faced a gas fire, and bookcases climbed to the ceiling. In her imagination, she saw the shelves filled with books, the fire lit.

"Nice, yes?" Kincaid queried.

Gemma glanced up at him, her suspicions growing. "Mmmm."

Undeterred, he continued his tour. "And here, tucked in behind the kitchen, a little loo." When she had dutifully admired the facilities, he took her into the last room on the left, a small study or library. But there were no books on these shelves, just as there had been no dishes in the kitchen, no personal possessions or photographs in the dining and sitting area.

"I'd put the telly here, wouldn't you?" he went on cheerfully. "So as not to spoil the atmosphere of the sitting room."

Gemma turned to face him. "Duncan, are you giving up policing for estate agenting? I'm not going a step further until you tell me what this is all about!"

"First, tell me if you like it, love. Do you think you could live here?"

"Of course I like it! But you know what property values are like in this area—there's no way we could afford something like this even if we pooled our salaries—"

"Just wait before you make a judgment. See the rest of the house."

"But—"

"Trust me."

Following him up the stairs to the first floor, she mulled over her situation. She must make a change, she knew that. The garage flat she rented was much too small for another child, and Kincaid's Hampstead flat was no more suitable—especially since it looked as though his twelve-year-old son would be moving in with him over the holidays.

Since she had told Kincaid about the baby, they had talked about living together, combining families, but Gemma had found herself unwilling to face the prospect of such momentous change just yet.

"Two good-sized bedrooms and a bath on this floor." Kincaid was opening doors and turning on lights for her inspection. They were children's rooms, obviously, but again the walls bore pale patches where pictures and posters had been removed.

"Now for the pièce de résistance." Taking her hand, he led her up to the top floor.

Gemma stood riveted in the doorway. The entire top floor had been converted to a master suite, open and airy, with the balcony she'd seen from the street at the front.

"There's more." Kincaid opened another set of French doors and Gemma stepped out onto a small roof garden that overlooked the treetops. "That's a communal garden beyond the back garden. You can walk right into it."

Gemma breathed out a sigh of delight. "Oh, the boys would love it. But it can't be possible . . . can it?"

"It very well might be—at least for five years. This house belongs to the guv's sister—"

"Chief Superintendent Childs?" Denis Childs was Kincaid's superior at the Yard, and Gemma's former boss as well.

"—whose husband has just accepted a five-year

contract in Singapore, some sort of high-tech firm. They don't want to sell the house, but they do want it well looked after, and who better than two police officers vouched for by the Chief Super himself?"

"But we still couldn't afford—"

"It's a reasonable rent."

"But what about your flat?"

"I'd lease it for a good deal more than the mortgage, I imagine."

"What about child-minding for Toby? Without Hazel—"

"There's a good infant school just down the road from the station. And a good comprehensive for Kit not too far away. Now, any other objections?" He grasped her shoulders and looked down into her eyes.

"No...it's just...it seems too good to be true."

"You can't hold the future at bay forever, love. And we won't disappoint you. I promise."

Perhaps he was right...No! She knew he was right. When Toby's father had left her, alone with a new infant and no support, she had resolved never to depend on anyone again. But Kincaid had never failed her in any way—why should she not trust him in this, as well? Gemma let herself relax into his arms.

"Blue-and-yellow dishes in the kitchen," she murmured against his chest. "And a bit of paint in the bedrooms, don't you think?"

He nuzzled her hair. "Is that a yes?"

She felt herself teetering on the edge of a precipice. Once committed, the safety of her old life would be gone. There could be no turning back. But she no longer had the luxury of putting off the decision until she had exorcised the very last smidgen of doubt. With that realization came a most unexpected flood of relief, and an unmistakable fizz of excitement.

"Yes," she told him. "Yes, I suppose it is."


Moisture ringed the street lamps along Park Lane as the December dusk faded into dull evening. The air felt dense, as if it might collapse in upon itself, and the smattering of Christmas lights made only a pallid affront to the gloom.

*Bloody Friday traffic,* thought Dawn Arrowood. Suddenly claustrophobic, she cracked the window of her Mercedes and inched into the long tailback at Hyde Park Corner. She'd known better than to drive into the West End, but she hadn't been able to face the thought of the crowded tube, with the inevitable pushing and shoving and the too-intimate exposure to unwashed bodies.

Not on this day, of all days.

She had armored herself as best she could: a visit to Harrods before the doctor, tea with Natalie at Fortnum & Mason's afterwards. Had she thought these distractions could cushion the news she feared, make it somehow easier?

Nor had her old friend Natalie's ready comfort changed things one jot.

She was pregnant. Full stop. Fact.

And she would have to tell Karl.

Her husband had made it quite, quite clear, before their marriage five years ago, that he did not want a second family. Twenty-five years her senior, with two unsatisfactory grown children and a troublesome ex-wife,

Karl had firmly declared he'd no intention of repeating the experience.

For a moment, Dawn allowed herself the weakness of imagining he would change his mind once he heard her news, but she knew that for the fantasy it was. Karl never changed his mind, nor did he take kindly to having his wishes ignored.

The traffic light changed at last, and as she swung into Bayswater Road, she shook a cigarette from the packet in the console. She would quit, she promised herself, but not yet . . . not until she'd worked out a plan.

If she insisted on having this child, what could Karl do? Turn her out with nothing? The thought terrified her. She'd come a long way from her childhood in a terraced house in East Croyden, and she had no intention of going back. That Natalie had understood, at least. You have legal recourse, Natalie had said, but Dawn had shaken her head. Karl kept a very expensive lawyer on retainer, and she felt certain neither he nor his solicitor would be deterred by the small matter of her legal rights.

And of course this was assuming she could somehow convince him the baby was his.

The shudder of fear that passed through her body was instinctive, uncontrollable.

Alex. Should she tell Alex? No, she didn't dare. Alex would insist she leave Karl, insist they could live happily ever after in his tiny mews flat off the Portobello Road, insist that Karl would let her go.

No, she would have to cut Alex off, for his own sake, somehow convince him it had only been a passing fling. She hadn't realized when she'd begun the affair with Alex just how dangerous was the course upon which she'd embarked—nor had she known that she'd chosen the one lover her husband would never forgive.

The traffic picked up speed and too soon, it seemed, she reached Notting Hill Gate. The crush of evening commuters poured into the tube station entrance like lemmings drawn to the sea, newspapers and Christmas shopping clutched in their arms, rushing home to their suburban lives of babies and telly and take-away suppers. The image brought a jab of envy and regret, and with it the too-ready tears that had plagued her of late. Dawn swiped angrily at her lower lashes—she wouldn't have time to do her makeup over. She was late as it was, and Karl would expect her to be ready when he arrived home to collect her for their dinner engagement.

Appearances were Karl's currency, and she now knew all too well that she'd been acquired just as ruthlessly as one of his eighteenth-century oils or a particularly fine piece of china. What she'd been naïve enough to think was love had been merely possessiveness, she the jewel chosen with the setting in mind.

And what a setting it was, the house at the leafy summit of Notting Hill, across the street from the faded elegance of St. John's Church. Once Dawn had loved this Victorian house with its pale yellow stucco, its superbly proportioned rooms and beautiful appointments, and for a moment she mourned the passing of such an innocent pleasure.

Tonight the windows were dark as she turned into the drive, the blank panes mirroring her car lights. She had managed to beat Karl home, then; she would have a few minutes' respite. Turning off the engine, she reached for her parcels, then paused, squeezing her eyes shut. Damn Karl! Damn Alex! In spite of them, she would find a way to deal with this, to keep the child she wanted more than she had ever wanted anything.

She slid out of the car, keys in one hand, bags in the other, ducking away from the wet fingers of the hedge that lined the drive.

A sound stopped her. The cat, she thought, relaxing, then remembered she'd left Tommy in the house, despite Karl's strictures to the contrary. Tommy had been ill and she hadn't wanted to leave him out unsupervised, in case he got into a scrap with another cat.

There it was again. A rustle, a breath, something out of place in the damp stillness. Panic gripped her, squeezing her heart, paralyzing her where she stood.

Forcing herself to think, she clasped her keys more tightly in her hand. The house just across the drive suddenly seemed an impossible distance. If she could only reach the safety of the door, she could lock herself in, ring for help. She held her breath and slid a foot forward—

The arms came round her from behind, a gloved hand pressing cruelly against her mouth. Too late, she struggled, tugging futilely at the arm pinning her chest, stomping down on an instep. Too late, she prayed for the flicker of Karl's headlamps turning into the drive.

Her attacker's breath sobbed raggedly in her ear; his grip tightened. The carrier bags fell unnoticed from her numb fingers. Then the pressure on her chest vanished, and in that instant's relief, pain seared her throat.

She felt a fiery cold, then the swift and enveloping darkness folded round her like a cloak. In the last dim flicker of consciousness, she thought she heard him whisper, "I'm sorry, so sorry."

# CHAPTER TWO

Portobello was our family's shopping street. There were lots
of kosher butchers . . . eight or nine quite close, and Jewish
delicatessens where you could get lovely bagels and Jewish bread.

—Whetlor and Bartlett,
from *Portobello*

SHE SAT ON *the stoop, idly swishing her skirt between her
knees, listening to the faint sound of the new Cliff Richard
song drifting from the open window across the street. This was
not how she had imagined spending her twelfth birthday, but
her parents did not believe in making a big fuss of such occasions. Nor did they think she needed her own record player,
which was the one gift she desperately wanted. "A frivolous expense," her father had called it, and none of her arguments had
swayed him.*

*Sighing gustily, she hugged her knees and traced her name
on the dusty step with her finger. She was bored, bored, bored,
and hot, filled with a new and strange sort of discontent.*

*Perhaps when her mother came home from visiting friends,
she could wheedle permission to see a new film at the cinema, as
a special birthday treat. At least it would be cooler in the dark,
and she could spend her pocket money on sweets from the conces-
sionaire.*

*She was wondering if Radio Luxembourg would play the
new Elvis record tonight, when an engine sputtered nearby. A
lorry pulled up to the curb in front of the house next door. The*

lorry's open back held mattresses, an orange sofa, a chair covered with a bright flower print, all jumbled together, all blistering in the hot August sun.

The driver's door opened and a man climbed out and stood gazing up at the house. He wore a white shirt and a dark tie, and his skin was the deep color of the bittersweet chocolate her mother used for baking.

A woman slid from the passenger side, her pumps clicking against the pavement as she touched the ground. Like her husband, she was smartly dressed, her shirtwaist dress crisply pressed, and as she stood beside him she looked up at the house with an expression of dismay. He smiled and touched her arm, then turned towards the bed of the lorry and called out something.

From amid the boxes and bundles emerged a girl of about her own age with thin, bare, brown legs and a pink ruffled dress. Next came a boy, a year or two older, tall and gangly. It seemed to her that the family had blown in on the hot wind from somewhere infinitely more exotic than this dingy London neighborhood of terraced houses with peeling plasterwork; somewhere filled with colors and fragrances she had only imagined. They trooped up the steps together and into the house, and the street seemed suddenly lifeless without them.

When it became apparent that they were not going to reappear right away, she hugged herself in frustration. She would tell someone, then, but who? Her mother wouldn't be back for an hour or two, but her father would be at the café, his usual custom after a good morning's trading at his jewelry stall.

Leaping from the steps, she ran. Down Westbourne Park into Portobello, nimbly dodging the fruit-and-veg stalls, then round the corner into Elgin Crescent. She came to a halt in front of the café, pressing her nose against the glass as she caught her breath. Yes, there he was, just visible at his favorite *table in the back. Smoothing her dress, she slipped through the open door into the café's dim interior. The patrons sat in shirt-sleeves, men reading Polish newspapers and filling the hot, still air with a heavy cloud of smoke from their pipes and cigarettes.*

*She coughed involuntarily and her father looked up, frowning. "What are you doing here, little one? Is something wrong?"*

*He always thought something was wrong. She supposed he worried so because of his time in the war, although he never talked about that. In 1946, newly demobbed, her father had arrived in England with her mother, determined to put the war behind him and make a life for himself as a jeweler and silver-smith.*

*In spite of her precipitous arrival nine months later, he had done well. Better than some of the other men in the café, she knew, but still he clung to the things that reminded him of the old country: the smell of borscht and pierogi, the dark paneling hung with Polish folk art, and the company of buxom wait-resses with hennaed hair.*

*"No, nothing's wrong," she answered, sliding onto the banquette beside him. "And I'm not little. I wish you wouldn't call me that, Poppy."*

*"So, why does my very grown-up daughter come rushing through the door like a dervish?"*

*"We have new neighbors in the house next door."*

*"And what's so special about that?" he asked, still teasing.*

*"They're West Indian," she whispered, aware of the turning of heads. "A father and mother and two children, a boy and a girl, about my age."*

*Her father considered her news for a moment in his deliberate way, then shook his head. "Trouble. It will mean trouble."*

*"But they look very nice—"*

*"It doesn't matter. Now you go home and wait for your*

*mother, and stay away from these people. I don't want you getting hurt. Promise me."*

*Hanging her head, she muttered, "Yes, Poppy," but she did not meet his eyes.*

*She walked home slowly, her excitement punctured by her father's response. Surely he was wrong: nothing would happen. She knew there had been trouble when West Indian families had moved into other parts of the neighborhood, rioting even, on Blenheim Crescent, just round the corner from the café. But she'd known most of their neighbors since she was a baby; she couldn't imagine them doing the sort of things she'd heard the grown-ups whispering about.*

*But when she reached Westbourne Park, she saw a crowd gathered in front of the house next door. Silent and watchful, they stood round the lorry, and there was no sign of the new family.*

*For a moment she hesitated, remembering her father's instructions; then a dark face appeared at an upstairs window and the crowd shifted with a rumble of menace.*

*Without another thought for her promise, she pushed her way through to the back of the lorry, scooped up the biggest box she could carry, and marched up the steps. With a defiant glance back at the crowd, she turned and rapped on the door.*

As they descended the stairs from the top floor of the house, Kincaid heard the faint but insistent ringing of a telephone. The sound seemed to be coming from the vicinity of the coat rack, and Gemma swore under her breath as she crossed the room and plunged her hand into the pocket of her jacket, retrieving her phone.

From the stillness of her face as she listened, Kincaid

guessed that they would not be spending a romantic evening celebrating the beginning of a new era in their relationship.

"What is it?" he asked when she disconnected.

"A murder. Just up the road, near the church."

"You're in charge?"

She nodded. "As of now, anyway. The superintendent can't be reached."

"Any details?"

"A woman, found by her husband."

"Come on. You'll be quicker if I drive you up the road." His adrenaline had started to flow, but as they hurried to the car, he realized with a stab of disappointment that no matter how challenging the case about to unfold, he would be merely an onlooker.

He saw the flash of blue lights to their left as they crested the hill. Kincaid pulled up behind the last of the panda cars, then followed Gemma as she greeted the constable deployed to keep back onlookers.

"What can you tell me, John?" she asked quietly.

The young man looked a bit green about the gills. "I took the call. Gentleman came home and found his wife between her car and the hedge. He called the paramedics but it was already too late—she was dead."

"How?"

"Throat cut." He swallowed. "There's a lot of blood."

"Has the pathologist been called? And the scene-of-crime lads?"

"Yes, ma'am. Sergeant Franks took command until you arrived, ma'am."

Kincaid saw Gemma grimace, but she said merely, "All right, John, thank you. You'll get the area cordoned off before the SOCO's get here?"

"Yes, ma'am. Constable Paris has it in hand." As he spoke, a female constable appeared from behind the last of the patrol cars. She began unrolling the blue-and-white tape that would delineate the crime scene.

Following Gemma as she spoke to the young woman, Kincaid was the first to see the approach of a heavyset man already clad in the requisite white crime-scene coverall. This must be Sergeant Franks, whom Gemma had mentioned with dislike and a grudging respect. Balding, middle-aged, his face creased by an expression of perpetual discontent, Franks addressed Gemma without preamble. "You'd better suit up, then, before you go any further."

"Thanks, Gerry," Gemma replied smoothly. "Have you a coverall handy? Make that two." She glanced back at Kincaid, adding, "This is Superintendent Kincaid, from the Yard."

As they slipped into the coveralls Franks produced from the boot of one of the cars, Gemma asked, "What have you got so far, Gerry?"

"Husband arrived home, expecting his wife to be ready for a dinner engagement. Her car was in the drive, but the house was dark. He went in and called out for her, had a look round, then came back out into the drive and found the body. Tried to rouse her, then called nine-nine-nine."

"Did the paramedics touch her?"

"No, but the husband did. He's a right mess."

"What's his name?"

"Karl Arrowood. Quite a bit older than his wife, I'd say, and well off. Owns a poncey antiques shop on Kensington Park Road."

The well-off part was obvious, Kincaid thought,

glancing up at the house. The lower windows were now ablaze with light, illuminating the pale yellow stucco exterior and the white classical columns flanking the porch. In the drive, two dark Mercedes sedans sat side by side.

"Where is Mr. Arrowood now?" asked Gemma.

"One of the constables took him inside for a hot cup of tea, although I'd wager a stiff drink is more his style."

"Right. He'll keep for a bit. I'm going to have a look at the body before the pathologist gets here. What about lights?"

"Coming with the SOC team."

"Then we'll have to make do. What was her name, by the way? The wife."

"Dawn. Pretty name." Franks shrugged. "Not much use to her now."

Gemma turned to Kincaid. "Want to put your oar in?"

"I wouldn't miss it."

They pulled elasticized covers on over their shoes and made their way carefully along the edge of the drive nearest the house, assuming that to be the least likely area for the perpetrator to have traversed. As they passed the cars, they saw that a wrought-iron gate barred the end of the drive, meeting the hedge that ran down the drive's far side.

"There's no place to hide except in the hedge itself," Gemma murmured.

The body lay in front of the outside car, a dark heap that resolved itself as they drew closer into a slender woman in a leather coat. The thick, ferrous smell of blood was heavy in the damp air.

Kincaid felt the bile rise in the back of his throat as

he squatted, using his pocket torch to illuminate Dawn Arrowood's motionless form. As Gemma bent over, examining the corpse without touching it, he saw the sheen of perspiration on her forehead and upper lip. "You okay?" he asked softly, keeping the jab of fear from his voice with an effort. Gemma had almost suffered a miscarriage six weeks previously, the result of her harrowing rescue of a young mother and infant on the slopes of Glastonbury Tor. Although now under doctor's orders to take it easy, she had not been willing to take leave from work, and he found himself hovering over her like a broody hen.

"Shouldn't have had the curry for lunch." Gemma attempted a smile. "But I'll be damned if I'm going to sick it up in front of Gerry Franks."

"Not to mention it plays hell with the crime scene," he rejoined, feeling a surge of relief that it was merely nausea that was troubling her.

He turned his attention back to the victim. Young—perhaps in her early thirties—blond hair pulled back in a ponytail that was now in partial disarray, a delicate, high-cheekboned face that he suspected had been strikingly beautiful in life; all marred now by the savage gash beneath her chin. The torchlight picked up the white gleam of cartilage in the wound.

The woman's blouse had been sliced open and pulled back, and beneath the splash of blood from her throat, Kincaid thought he could make out another wound in her chest, but the poor light made it impossible to be sure. "There was no hesitation here. This bloke meant business."

"You're assuming it was a man?"

"Not likely to be a woman's crime, is it? Either

physically or emotionally. We'll see what the pathologist says."

"Did I hear someone take my name in vain?" called a
voice from across the drive.

"Kate!" Kincaid said warmly as another white-suited
figure came towards them. They had worked with Dr.
Kate Ling on several previous cases, and he thought
highly of her skill—not to mention her looks.

"Superintendent. Good to see you. Sounds like you've
got yourself a real media circus in the making here."

"Not my case, actually," he told her, cursing himself
for putting Gemma in such an awkward position.
"Inspector James is Senior Investigating Officer. I'm
just tagging along."

"Oh, *Inspector* is it now," Ling said, smiling. "Congratulations, Gemma. Let's see what you've got here."

Kincaid and Gemma stepped back as Ling knelt beside the body.

"Her blood's pooled beneath her body, so she hasn't
been moved," the pathologist said, as much to herself as
to them. "No obvious signs of sexual interference. No
hesitation marks on the throat. No readily apparent defense wounds." She looked up at Gemma. "No weapon?"

"Not that I've heard."

"Well, I'll be able to tell you a bit more about what
was used here when I get her on the table, but the
wound's very clean and deep." She probed the chest with
gloved fingers. "There seems to be a puncture wound
here as well."

"What about time of death?" asked Gemma.

"I'd say very recent. She's still warm to the touch."

"Bloody hell," Gemma whispered. "I walked right

by this house not more than an hour ago. Do you suppose..."

"Did you see anything?" Kincaid asked.

Gemma shook her head. "No. But then I wasn't looking, and now I wonder what I might have missed." She turned to Kate Ling. "When can you perform the postmortem?"

"Tomorrow morning, first thing," Ling said with a sigh. "So much for getting my nails done." She stood as voices heralded the arrival of the technicians who would photograph the body and the crime scene, and gather every scrap of physical evidence from the area. "Right, I'll get out of the way and let them do their job. When they get ready to bag the body, have them deliver it to the morgue at St. Charles Hospital. It's nearby, and convenient for me." Ling gave Kincaid a jaunty wave and disappeared the way she had come.

"And I'll get out of your way," Kincaid said as he saw Gemma glance at him and hesitate.

"Will you check on Toby, and let Hazel know what's happened? I've no idea when I'll get home."

"I'll stay with Toby myself. Don't worry." He touched her arm lightly, then made his way back to the street. But rather than getting in his car, he stood, watching from a distance as Gemma directed her team. As she climbed the front steps and entered the house, he would have given anything to be beside her.

"Bloody sodding hell!" Doug Cullen fumed, stomping into his flat and dropping his briefcase in the hall. He'd been reading his case files on the bus, as was his usual habit on his nightly commute home from the Yard, when he'd come across a scrawled note from Kincaid criticizing the conclusions he'd drawn after interviewing a suspect's associate.

*I think there's more here than meets the eye, Doug. This one warrants another interview. Be patient this time, see if you can get under his skin.*

"Like Sergeant James," Cullen mimicked Kincaid's unspoken parenthetical comment. The inestimable Sergeant Gemma James, who had apparently never made a mistake in her entire career at the Yard, and who had, as Kincaid so often reminded him, a special talent for interviewing people.

Cullen went into the kitchen and stared morosely into his barren fridge. He had meant to get off the bus a stop early and buy a six-pack at the off-license, but it had completely slipped his mind. Filling a glass with water from the tap, he gazed out the window at the traffic moving on the damp, greasy tarmac of Euston Road.

Of course he'd heard the scuttlebutt round the office about Kincaid's relationship with his former partner, and he was tempted to put Kincaid's veneration of her down to personal bias. But even if Sergeant James had been the most exemplary detective, did that mean he had always to be measured by her standard?

Cullen was introspective enough to realize that a good deal of his ire towards Gemma James had to do with his doubts about his own performance. Of course he was a good detective, he knew that, and he knew he'd never have landed this job at the Yard if his record hadn't spoken well of him. He was analytical, thorough, good at task management, but he also knew that his weakness lay in his impatience in interviewing witnesses and suspects. He wanted results quickly, and he wanted them in black and white—neither of which was very likely in police work.

Part of that he put down to his rather sheltered upbringing in suburban St. Albans, the only son of a City lawyer, part to an addiction to American cop shows on the telly, where the tough guys always got their man by the end of the hour.

But surely he could learn patience, just like anything else. And the fair, schoolboy looks that so plagued him gave him a ready advantage—people tended to trust him. If he could make himself sit and listen, even the most hardened criminals, he was learning, had a vulnerable spot for sympathy.

And wasn't that what his guv'nor was telling him, if he could get round his resentment of Gemma James? She was an ordinary mortal, after all, one who had probably muddled through her first few months as Kincaid's sergeant in much the same way he had. Perhaps if he were to meet her, see her as a person, it would lay the ghost of her perfection to rest in his mind. And he had to admit to a good measure of plain old-fashioned curiosity.

Wandering back into the sitting room, he tidied automatically, mulling over possibilities. It was not likely that a chance errand would send him to Notting Hill Police Station any time soon, nor could he foresee any upcoming social encounters . . . unless he were to manufacture an occasion. His girlfriend, Stella, was always on at him about his lack of enthusiasm for her dinner parties—but what if he were to suggest one?

Not here, though. He looked round his flat with distaste. At Bloomsbury's northern edge, the small flat in an ugly, concrete sixties building had been a good value for London but lacked any charm or comfort. To make matters worse, Stella, a buyer for a trendy home furnishings shop, had decorated it for him in neutrals and grays. She insisted that the color scheme and the boxy lines of the furniture harmonized with the building's architectural style. After her efforts, he hadn't the heart to tell her that he found it all extremely depressing.

Stella's flat, then, in Ebury Street, near the Yard. He would jolly her into it at dinner tonight, even if it meant the trade-off of committing himself to one of her friends' country-house weekends—and that was a fate he considered almost worse than death.

The house smelled of flowers, the sweetness of the scent a painful contrast to the acrid smell of blood. A console table held an enormous arrangement of fresh blooms, and glimpses into the rooms on either side showed equally sumptuous bouquets. Walls the color of goldenrod accentuated the richness of the dark furniture, the elegance of the silk draperies falling to pools on the carpets, the discreet lighting on the paintings that hung on the walls.

The touch of something soft against her ankle made Gemma gasp, but when she looked down she saw that it was only a gray cat, materializing as if by magic. She knelt to stroke it and the beast butted against her knees, purring gratefully. Was this Dawn Arrowood's pet? Gemma wondered. Missing its mistress—or perhaps merely craving its supper.

She heard voices from the back of the house, an intermittent murmur of conversation. Giving the cat a last pat, Gemma followed the sound down the corridor. The large kitchen was as elegant as the other rooms, lined with cream-colored cabinets and copper accessories. At a table in the breakfast area sat Constable Melody Talbot, and beside her a man in a white, blood-soaked shirt.

Gemma paused, halted in part by the unexpected sight of so much blood in such surroundings, and in part by her surprise at Karl Arrowood's appearance. "An older husband," Gerry Franks had said, and she had mentally translated that into "feeble elderly gentleman." But the man gazing at her across the kitchen was, she guessed, no older than his mid-fifties, lean and fit, with a strong, lightly suntanned face, and thick hair still as yellow as the walls of his house.

"Mr. Arrowood," she said, collecting herself, "I'm Detective Inspector James. I'd like to speak to Constable Talbot for a moment, if you'll excuse us."

When Talbot had followed her into the hall, Gemma asked, "Anything?"

Talbot shook her head. "Just what he told Sergeant Franks. And he has no inclination to talk to me. I suspect he considers me beneath his notice." She made the statement without rancor.

"Right. I'll tackle him, then. Go check on the search warrant, then let me know the status."

Returning to the kitchen, Gemma sat across from Karl Arrowood. His eyes, she saw, were gray, and without expression.

"Mr. Arrowood, I'd like to ask you a few questions."

"I don't know how I can help you, Inspector. I've come home, found my wife murdered in my own drive, and all your lot seem to be able to do is offer me tea."

"Our investigation is proceeding along normal lines,

Mr. Arrowood, and one of the necessary components is a detailed description of everything you remember about finding your wife. I'm sorry, I know this must be painful for you."

"I've already gone over it with your sergeant."

"Nevertheless, I need to hear it as well. I understand you were expecting your wife to be at home when you arrived. Is that correct?"

"We had a dinner engagement at the Savoy, with customers who come over regularly from Germany. Dawn wouldn't have been late."

"So you were surprised when you arrived home and found the house dark?"

"Yes, especially as I knew she'd taken her car, and it was in the drive. She was meeting a friend at Fortnum's, and she didn't care for public transport. I thought..." For the first time he hesitated, and Gemma saw that in spite of his apparent composure, his hands were trembling. "I thought perhaps she'd come in feeling unwell and fallen asleep, but when I checked the bedroom, there was no sign she'd been there."

"What is the name of your wife's friend?"

"Natalie. I'm afraid I don't recall her surname. She was an old school friend of Dawn's. I've never met her."

Gemma found that a bit odd, but let it go for the moment. "Then what did you do?" she prompted.

"I called out, had a look round the house. Then... I'm not quite sure why, I went back out into the drive. I suppose I thought she'd met a neighbor or...I don't know." He rubbed a hand across his forehead, leaving a tiny smear of red. "I saw something white in the drive, near the bonnet of her car. When I got closer I saw it was a carrier bag, from Harrods. And then..."

This time Gemma waited in silence.

"I thought she'd fallen . . . fainted, perhaps. She hadn't been feeling well lately. I tried to lift her . . ."

"Then you rang for help?"

"I had my mobile in my pocket. I couldn't leave her."

"Was there anything worrying your wife, Mr. Arrowood?"

"Good God! You're not suggesting suicide?"

"No, of course not. Only that she might have been approached by someone recently, or had an argument with someone. Anything out of the ordinary."

"No. I don't know of anything. I'm sure she'd have told me." He drummed long fingers on the table and Gemma saw that he had blood under his fingernails. "Look. Is that all? I've phone calls to make. Her family . . . I'll have to tell her family . . ."

A motion in the hall alerted Gemma to Talbot's return. Talbot gave her a nod of assent, then stood by for instructions.

"Mr. Arrowood, Constable Talbot is going to stay with you while we search the premises—"

"Search my house?" Arrowood scowled in disbelief. "You're not serious?"

"I'm afraid I am. It's the first thing we do in any homicide investigation. We'll need your clothes as well, for the lab. I'll have one of the technicians bring you some clean things from upstairs."

"But this is outrageous. You can't do this. I'm going to call my contact in the Home Office—"

"You're welcome to ring whomever you like, Mr. Arrowood, but the warrant's already been issued. I'm sorry. I know this is difficult, but it's normal procedure and we've no choice under the circumstances. Now, did your wife keep a diary of her appointments? Or an address book where I might be able to find the name of the friend she met for tea?"

She thought he might refuse, but she held his gaze and after a moment the fight seemed to seep out of him. His shoulders sagged. "In the sitting room. On the desk by the window."

"Thank you. Is there someone you can call to stay with you?"

"No," he said slowly, almost as if the thought surprised him. "No one."

Gemma found the address book and diary easily enough, just where Arrowood had said; small books, covered in floral fabric and smelling of perfume. A quick look showed her that Dawn Arrowood had written only one thing in her diary for that day, at ten o'clock in the morning: *Tommy to vet.* Was Tommy the gray cat she had met in the hall?

Gemma paged carefully through the neat script in the address book. With helpful feminine logic, Dawn had placed All Saints Animal Hospital under V for vet. Making a note of the number, Gemma continued searching for Dawn's friend Natalie. In the W's, she found a listing for a Natalie Walthorpe, but Walthorpe had been carefully lined through and Caine had been written in after it.

After writing an evidence receipt, Gemma tucked both books in her bag for later perusal.

"Anything upstairs?" she asked the technician.

"No bloody shoes tucked neatly in the wardrobe, if

that's what you're hoping," the technician returned cheek-
ily. "You can have a go, if you like."

"Thanks, I will."

As she climbed the stairs, she felt again the brush
against her leg, and looked down to find the cat padding
up the stairs alongside her. "Tommy?" she said experi-
mentally.

The cat looked up at her and blinked, as if to ac-
knowledge his name. "Okay, Tommy it is."

At the top of the stairs, she turned towards the sound
of voices. She was rewarded by the sight of the master
bedroom, and within it, two coveralled technicians going over every surface with tweezers and sticky tape.

"Afraid you'll have to observe from the doorway for a
bit longer, guv," one of them informed her. "Let us
know if there's anything particular you want to look at."

With that Gemma had to be content. She stood, taking in the atmosphere of the pale yellow room. It was a
gracious and elegant retreat, large and high-ceilinged,
with a draped four-poster bed. The floral print of the
drapes was matched by the coverlet and window cover-
ings, a show of expensive decorating that made Gemma
feel slightly claustrophobic.

Tommy the cat jumped up on the bed, curled himself
into a ball, and began to purr. When the technician
gave her the go-ahead, Gemma went into the room and
began to look round her.

The bedside table on the right held glossy copies of
*Vogue* and *Town and Country,* as well as a copy of the latest best-selling novel and a delicate alarm clock. Gemma
thought of her own bedside, usually endowed with a
stack of dog-eared paperbacks and a used teacup.

Peeking into the en suite bathroom, she found monogrammed, pale yellow towels, and an antique oak sideboard displaying expensive makeup and perfumes tidily arranged on lacquered trays. On the back of the door hung a fluffy toweling dressing gown. Where, Gemma wondered, was the hastily abandoned hairbrush, the jewelry taken off and left to be dealt with at a later time?

The built-in wardrobe revealed more of the same: neatly arranged women's clothes on one side, men's expensive suits on the other. Frowning in frustration, Gemma dug deeper. Shelves held handbags and stored summer clothes, the floor racks of shoes. It was only when she sat back with a sigh of exasperation that she saw the edge of the box behind the shoes. Moving the shoe rack, she pulled out the box—not cardboard, heaven forbid, but a specialty shop storage container—and removed the lid.

Here at last was some semblance of a jumble. Tattered volumes of Enid Blyton's children's books jostled against romantic novels and two dolls; a smaller, obviously hand-papered box held school reports and family photos labeled in a childish, yet recognizable, hand.

Gemma sat back, perplexed. These things had, at one time, defined the woman who had died that night. Why had Dawn Arrowood found it not only necessary to reinvent herself so completely, but to hide away the remnants of the person she had been?

Kincaid had tucked Toby into bed with a reading of Graham Oakley's *The Church Mice Adrift,* the boy's book of choice as of late, and now sat at Gemma's half-moon table, nursing a glass of the Chardonnay he'd found in her fridge.

As he looked round the room, he thought how deeply Gemma had stamped her presence on this space. It had given her safety and comfort when she had felt adrift in her life—Would he be able to provide her as much security as she'd found here? God knew they needed anchors badly enough in their jobs . . . and this case she'd landed tonight would test her resources; he'd known that from the outset. The media attention alone would be brutal, especially if she failed to produce a suspect in the amount of time the journalists deemed suitable.

Was he making the right choice in moving her into a house in her own patch, where there would be no escape from the presence of work, and in forcing her to do it so quickly? Yet he felt compelled to act; now that she'd agreed at last, he was afraid if he hesitated she might change her mind.

And then there was Kit to consider. His son's school term ended in a week, and when Kit made the move from Grantchester to London, Kincaid wanted them to begin as they meant to go on—as a family. He still harbored the fear that his ex-wife's widower, Ian McClellan, who remained Kit's legal guardian, might change his mind about leaving the boy in Kincaid's care when Ian took up a teaching post in Canada in the new year.

And then there were his ex-wife's parents, who felt they should have charge of their grandson. Eugenia Potts was both selfish and hysterical, and when forced to stay in her care, Kit had run away. Since then, Ian had allowed the grandparents only one supervised visit a month, which was coming up the Friday after Christmas. Eugenia had chosen the stuffy formality of afternoon tea at Brown's Hotel for their meeting—not the outing of choice for a twelve-year-old boy.

Nor would Eugenia be happy to see Kincaid, whom she despised, or to learn about Kit's new living arrangements. Over them hung the specter that Eugenia might actually undertake the legal action she threatened on a regular basis, and attempt to wrest Kit's guardianship for herself.

Well, they would just have to deal with that when the time came. If Kincaid's job had not taught him that there were few guarantees of stability in life, he should have learned it from his ex-wife's tragic death.

Thinking of the young woman they had seen that night, her life so unexpectedly snuffed out, Kincaid got up and poured the remains of his wine down the sink. He turned off all but the bedside lamp, then opened the blind and stood looking into the darkened garden. What worried him most was that he had seen a murder like this once before, less than two months ago.

# CHAPTER THREE

If you saw Notting Hill at the beginning of the sixties, it
would be hard to recognize it as the same place you can see
today. Nowadays Notting Hill is wealthy and gentrified.
Go back thirty years and the area is a massive slum, full of
multi-occupied houses, crawling with rats and rubbish.

—Charlie Phillips and Mike Phillips,
from *Notting Hill in the Sixties*

A WARM, MOIST current of dog breath woke her. Bryony
opened one eye and tried to focus on the lolling pink
tongue of Duchess, her golden retriever mix, inches
from her face.

"What is it, girl? What time is it?" Turning over, she
peered at her alarm clock. Was it seven already? "Shit,"
she muttered, rolling out of bed and giving Duchess a
hasty caress as she headed for the loo. She'd meant to be
at the café before now. Several of them had formed a
habit of meeting for early coffee and croissants before
the Saturday morning trading got into full swing,
and she was dying to tell someone about her project—
especially Marc, if the truth be told. Whether or not her
plan would work depended on him.

When she'd scrubbed her face and pulled on jeans,
boots and sweater, she took Duchess for a quick consti-
tutional in the postage stamp of Powis Square, then set
off for Elgin Crescent.

A blanket of cloud hovered over the rooftops, obscuring the light of the rising sun, but at least it had not yet begun to rain. Bryony's long strides devoured the distance from her flat to the café, and by the time she pushed open the door she'd worked up a rosy glow.

Her friends sat in the back, gathered round two tables: Wesley, his ebullient dreadlocks sedated by a cap; Fern Adams, whose punk dress and makeup belied her knowledge of the antique silver she traded in the market; Marc, who flashed Bryony the quick smile he seemed to reserve just for her; and Otto, apron-clad, coffee pot in hand. Only Alex Dunn was missing.

They all looked up at her with solemn faces as she came in, and no one offered a greeting.

"What?" Bryony joked. "Did someone die?"

When no one answered, she gazed at them with dawning horror. "Oh, no," she whispered, sinking into the nearest chair. "Has something happened? Not Alex—"

Otto upended a cup from the stack on the table and poured her a coffee, but it was Wesley who answered. "It's Dawn Arrowood, the lady that Alex was, um, seeing. She was killed last night. Murdered."

"Mrs. Arrowood? But that's not possible! She was just in the surgery yesterday, with her cat. Gavin saw them." The pretty blond woman, so devoted to her cat, was one of the hospital's regular clients. "I can't believe it. What happened?"

Marc shook his head. "That's all we know for certain. Although rumors have been going around the market like wildfire since daybreak."

"Alex—" Bryony glanced uneasily at Fern, whom she knew had been Alex's lover until recently. They had made an odd couple; Alex with his Oxford cloth shirts and Oxbridge haircut, Fern in glitter and camouflage, but their stalls were side by side in the market arcade, and Bryony had seen proximity make stranger bed-fellows.

"I told him," Otto rumbled. "I told him it was a bad business. But I thought it was he who would come to harm."

"Does he know?"

"No." Fern tugged nervously at the silver ring in her eyebrow. "He was setting up his stall when I left. There were whispers round the arcade, but no one dared say anything to him."

"But what if he comes in?" asked Bryony. "We'll have to—" She stopped as Fern's eyes widened. Turning, she saw Alex Dunn pushing open the café door.

"Morning, all," he called out. "It's going to be a bloody miserable day, but let's hope that won't dampen the Christmas shoppers' enthusiasm. Has anyone got a newspaper? I'd no change for the newsagent this morning—"

"Alex—" interrupted Wesley, then turned helplessly to Otto.

His face creased with distress, Otto said, "I'm afraid we have some very bad news. Dawn Arrowood was murdered last night."

Alex stared at him. "If this is your idea of a joke, it's not amusing. Just leave it alone, Otto. It's my business."

"I am not joking, Alex. When I heard the first rumor this morning, I went to the house. There are still police everywhere, and I knew one of the constables. He told me it was the truth."

Blanching, Alex whispered, "No. There must be some mistake."

"There is no mistake," Otto assured him grimly. "Karl Arrowood came home and found her in the drive."

Alex looked wildly from one friend to another. "Oh, Jesus, no!"

"Alex—" Fern reached out and touched his hand, but he jerked away as if burned. She huddled back into her chair, her eyes filling with tears.

"But why—How?" Alex whispered.

"That I don't know," answered Otto, but the big man didn't meet Alex's eyes and Bryony found herself unexpectedly wondering if he was lying.

"I don't believe it. I'm going to see her."

"You don't want to cross paths with Karl just now," Otto cautioned.

"Do you think I give a bloody piss about Karl?" Alex snarled.

Marc came out of his chair in one fluid motion and laid a restraining hand on his shoulder. "I know you're upset, but try to be reasonable, man—"

"Reasonable? Why the hell should I be reasonable?" Alex slapped Marc's hand away. "Just bugger off, all of you."

He stormed out of the café, and as the door swung closed behind him, Bryony saw that it had begun to rain.

The smell of disinfectant, laced with the faint but undisguisable odor of death, made Gemma clench her teeth against rising nausea. Morning sickness and morgues did not make a good combination, but she was certainly not going to announce her discomfort to Kate Ling. Something must have given her away, however, because when Kate glanced up from the postmortem table, she asked, "Are you feeling all right, Gemma?"

"Late night. Not enough sleep," Gemma offered in explanation. It was true enough. After leaving the technicians to finish their search of the Arrowood house, she had set up and staffed the incident room, arranging for the correlation of information in a database, and designed the questionnaire that would be used in the house-to-house inquiries begun this morning. Fortunately, they had been able to use Notting Hill Station itself because of the proximity of the crime, rather than having to set up a mobile incident room, an undertaking always beset with problems. She'd put Gerry Franks in charge, which left her free to conduct interviews.

And she had dealt with the press, refusing to release any details until Dawn Arrowood's family had been informed of her death. By evening, however, the tabloids would be in full cry, and she needed to make use of them, asking anyone who had seen anything odd in the neighborhood of the crime to come forward.

Only then had she allowed herself to go home and slip into bed beside Kincaid, where she had lain awake into the small hours of the morning thinking about the momentous decision she had made.

"Gemma," said Kate Ling, drawing her attention back to the matter at hand. "Here's something you might find interesting. Did anyone mention that the victim was about six weeks pregnant?"

"No." Gemma thought of the dolls and the Enid Blyton books, saved perhaps for a longed-for child? "Her husband did say she hadn't been feeling well."

"Perhaps he didn't know?" Kate raised an eyebrow.

"And if not, why not?" Gemma mused. "Have you come across anything else that might be helpful?"

"Well, it's as we thought last night; there's no evidence of any sort of sexual interference. So it looks like you can rule out sexual motivation for the crime."

"What about the chest wound?"

"A single stab, which penetrated the left lung. From the angle, I'd say it was done last, after she fell to the ground."

"Can you tell if the killer was male or female?"

"Male, I'd say. Or a very tall woman."

"Left- or right-handed?"

"Right."

"Any ideas about the weapon?"

"Something quite sharp and clean-edged. A razor, or possibly a scalpel."

"Oh, God. We can't let the press get hold of that."

"No. You'll have a Jack-the-Ripper panic on your hands, and that you don't need." Kate gave her another assessing glance. "You can take off now, if you want. I'll get the organs off to the lab, and let you know the results."

"Thanks." Gemma gave the other woman a grateful smile, sensing that they had connected for the first time on a personal level. But as she left the hospital, she also wondered just how much Kate Ling had guessed about her condition. Glancing down at her rapidly thickening waist, she knew she wouldn't be able to keep her secret much longer.

• • • •

"I'm going after him." Fern pushed her coffee away and stood up.

"It might not be a good idea to try to talk to him now," Marc advised her gently. "Especially not in front of the Arrowoods' house—"

"I'm not going there. He'll go back to his stall, when he's sure it's true. I know him." She turned away from the pity in their faces, and for a moment she hated them for it. She did know him, better than anyone, and she *could* comfort him, no matter what they thought.

Rounding the corner into Portobello Road, she ducked her head against the rain and battled the flood of shoppers coming down the hill as if she were a salmon swimming upstream, turning into the arcade where she and Alex had their stalls.

The narrow aisles offered some relief from the crowd, but she knew it wouldn't be long before the shoppers were packed shoulder to shoulder there as well. Already the air was redolent with cigarette smoke, and the familiar odors of grease and coffee drifted up from the basement café.

She unlocked the stall's protective screen and raised it up, slipped inside, and settled herself behind the glass case that held the silver spoons, magnifying glasses, and trinkets that were her bread and butter.

Making a pretense of business, she took out her cloth and began to polish the fingerprints from a Georgian teapot she'd got for a good price from a dealer at Bermondsey yesterday. It could mean a nice profit, if the right buyer came along, but Fern found she'd lost her enthusiasm for the sale.

The stall beside hers seemed ominously empty without Alex. She knew his stock almost as well as she knew her own, and it came as a relief when a woman stopped and admired a delicate Coalport cup and saucer on display. Fern unlocked Alex's stall—they each had the other's spare key—and took the cup and saucer down for the woman, holding it up to the lamp Alex kept for demonstrating the translucence of bone china.

Enchanted, the woman paid the sticker price without haggling, a definite sign of a novice. Fern tucked the money into the cash apron Alex had left behind the front display case, then stood looking round the stall, remembering the first time Dawn Arrowood had come into the arcade.

There had been something about her that had immediately drawn Fern's attention. Everything from the designer jeans to the perfect blond hair spoke of money, but Dawn's was an elegantly understated look that Fern knew she could never achieve. And yet, in spite of the woman's sleek veneer, there had been an appealing freshness about her, and Fern had flashed her a friendly smile.

But the woman had looked past her. Curious, Fern had turned, following her gaze, to see the woman meet Alex's eyes. He had stared back, transfixed, and Fern's heart had been pierced with a sudden and sure knowledge.

Oh, she had fought it! First his embarrassed excuses, then his irritated rejections, until at last Fern had given him no choice but to tell her outright that it was over between them. Even then she'd never quite given up hope that she might somehow win him back...and more than once she had wished Dawn Arrowood dead.

But not like this—not murdered! And Otto had hinted this morning that her husband might have killed her because of Alex.

Fern looked up, realizing the arcade had gone abruptly quiet. Alex stood in the street door. Water dripped from his sopping hair onto his collar; his face was blank with shock, his eyes expressionless. One of the other vendors spoke to him softly and he shook his head, then stumbled forward. Fern slipped out of the stall and went to him. "Alex! Are you all right?"

He moved blindly forward as if unaware of her, stopping before his stall as if he had no clear idea what he was doing there.

"Alex, let me help you," Fern urged. "You're soaking—"

"I have to get something." Pushing her aside, he went into the stall, bumping against the porcelain-laden shelves as if they held Brighton souvenirs. He fell to his knees and rummaged behind the display case, emerging with a brightly colored teapot Fern hadn't seen before. Wrapping it in a cloth, he shoved it into a carrier bag, then stood. His eyes fell on Fern and for the first time he seemed to register her presence. "You'll watch the stall for me, won't you?"

"Alex, what are you doing? You're soaked. If you don't look after yourself you'll catch your death—"

"I have to go, to get away." He started to push past her but this time she stepped resolutely in front of him.

"Where, Alex? At least tell me where you're going."

"Don't know. I just have to get away from here, that's all."

"You're in no fit state to look after yourself, much

less drive. Let me take you." An idea took shape in her mind. If Karl Arrowood had murdered his wife because he'd found out about Alex, might not Alex be next? But not if Karl couldn't find him. "Give me your keys," she ordered. When he handed them over without protest, she called to Doris, who traded antique toys from the stall across the aisle, "Watch the stalls for me, Doris, please. I'll make it up to you."

Taking his carrier bag and a handful of bills from her own stall, she quickly locked both screens, then shepherded him out into the street and up the hill to the mews where his Passat sat parked in front of his flat. Alex seemed to have given up all resistance; it was only when she'd bundled him into the passenger seat and buckled herself into the driver's that he mumbled, "Where are we going?"

"Somewhere safe," Fern assured him. "Somewhere no one will think to look for you."

The crowd of curious onlookers in front of the Arrowoods' house had grown since earlier that morning. Gemma saw familiar faces—the press was out in force, and the recognition was mutual. A whisper rippled through the gathering and half a dozen reporters surged to the front.

Putting up her umbrella against the persistent drizzle, she held up her free hand against the clamor of questions. "I'll speak to you at six this evening, in front of Notting Hill—"

"This house belongs to Karl Arrowood, the antiques dealer," interrupted Tom MacCrimmon from the *Daily*

*Star,* one of the least reputable tabloids. A woolly-headed man with a red bulbous nose like a Christmas ball, Gemma had found MacCrimmon's aggressiveness to be tempered by a sense of humor. "Was it someone in the Arrowood family who was killed?"

"The victim's family has yet to be notified, Tom. Please let us do that before you speculate in print—or on camera," she added, seeing the telltale red eye of another reporter's video camera. "I promise I'll give you as much as I can this evening." She turned away and the constable on duty quickly lifted the tape, allowing her inside the sealed perimeter.

Once out of the crowd's hearing range, she spoke to the officer. "Where's Mr. Arrowood?"

"Waiting for you at the station, as per your request. Sergeant Franks took him in, and was none too gentle about it."

"What about the forensics team?"

"Just finishing up. Haven't found anything obvious, as far as I know."

"Right. Just keep an eye on the crowd, will you? I need to know if any one person hangs about too long."

Karl Arrowood had been ushered into Interview Room A, where Gemma suspected he'd worn a path in the floor with his pacing. Fully dressed in a dark suit and tie, clean-shaven, his thick corn-yellow hair neatly brushed, he showed no sign of the shock Gemma had seen last night.

"Inspector, I do not understand why I'm being treated like a common criminal, dragged to the police station and then left to cool my heels in this revolting room."

"I know our decor leaves a bit to be desired, but do sit down, please, Mr. Arrowood. This won't take long." Gemma had asked Melody to join them, rather than Franks. She knew Franks would be miffed at the exclusion, but she didn't think his aggressiveness would be helpful at this stage of the interview process.

As she and Melody took their seats, she gestured towards one of the plastic chairs across the table.

"I can't think what I can possibly tell you that we didn't discuss last night—"

"What about your wife's family, Mr. Arrowood? Have you notified them?"

"Yes." He grimaced and sat reluctantly. "I'm meeting them at the mortuary this morning. I've told them there was no need, that I could arrange everything, but they insisted."

"Perhaps they need to feel involved? It does provide closure of a sort. You realize, of course, that the pathologist won't release your wife's body until she's completed her examinations."

"I've scheduled the funeral for Tuesday, at Kensal Green. Surely that's time enough."

"Tell me about your wife's family."

The grimace came again, fainter but unmistakable. "They live in East Croydon. Name of Smith."

"Any other children?"

"No."

"This must be quite difficult for them."

"I suppose so," Arrowood said, as if the idea hadn't occurred to him. "But I don't see—"

"I'll need to talk to them, as well as to Dawn's close friends."

"What can that possibly have to do with my wife's murder? She just happened to be in the wrong place at the wrong time, when some psychopath—" He swallowed, losing his composure for the first time.

"That may be the case. But even if your wife's killer had no personal connection with her, he may have been watching her, and someone she knows may have noticed something odd."

"Watching her?" Arrowood's skin paled beneath his artificial tan.

"It's a possibility we have to consider."

"My wife . . . was she sexually assaulted?"

"No. The pathologist found no indication of that."

Arrowood met Gemma's eyes, looked away. "Dawn . . . Do you think she had time to be frightened?"

Gemma thought of the few signs of struggle on the woman's body and answered truthfully, "I think it must have been very quick."

"I keep seeing—" Blinking, Arrowood gave a sharp shake of his head, as if discarding an instant of weakness. "There's no point dwelling on it. It's just that she told me once she thought she would die young. She was always worried about cancer, things like that. But this . . ."

"Mr. Arrowood, did you know your wife was pregnant?"

"What?"

"The postmortem revealed that your wife was about six weeks pregnant."

"But that's— No, I'd no idea. I knew she hadn't been

well lately, but that possibility never occurred to me. . . ." He seemed to wilt, his body settling into the curvature of the plastic chair.

"I'm very sorry." Thinking of her own case of prolonged denial, Gemma said, "Perhaps she hadn't realized herself."

Karl Arrowood contemplated this for a moment. "Perhaps not. But I rather hope she knew. She very much wanted a child."

Gemma thought again of the children's books and dolls, carefully hidden away. "And you didn't?"

"No. I've two grown sons already that are trouble enough." His lips had curled in obvious distaste.

Two grown sons who might be counting on their father's money, thought Gemma, and might not have appreciated a young stepmother mucking up their prospects. "I'll need their names and addresses, please. And their mother? Is she living?"

"Sylvia? There have been times I wished she weren't"—his smile held grim humor—"but yes, she's living. And living well, I might add, in Chelsea."

"Did you provide for your sons in a will, Mr. Arrowood? Or did Dawn inherit your estate?"

He glared at her. "I've poured money down those boys' throats since they were children, with no thanks and less result. Of course I've left the bulk of my estate to Dawn; she was my wife."

"And your sons knew this?"

"I never particularly discussed it with them. But what you're suggesting is absurd—"

"Absurd or not, these things happen, and we have to explore every possibility. Did Dawn work, Mr. Arrowood?"

"My wife had no need to work."

*How very antiquated of you,* thought Gemma, exchanging a glance with Melody, but she asked merely, "Then what did she do with her days?"

"She had the house to manage. She helped in the shop occasionally. She saw her friends."

"Any friends in particular, other than Natalie?"

"I didn't keep her social calendar," Arrowood answered so sharply that Gemma suspected he hadn't a clue what had filled the long hours of his wife's day.

"And yesterday, I believe you said you had just arrived home from a meeting when you found your wife?"

"I'd had drinks at Butler's Wharf with a European dealer."

"His name?"

Arrowood's eyes widened in surprise, but he shrugged and answered, "Andre Michel."

Gemma wrote down the man's name and London address, as well as the time Karl Arrowood claimed he'd left his friend, although she knew there was no way to prove how long the drive from Tower Bridge to Notting Hill would have taken in evening traffic; nor, once he arrived home, would it have taken Arrowood more than five minutes to murder his wife and call for help.

"Mr. Arrowood, did you notice anything odd about your wife's movements or behavior in the past few days? Did Dawn give you any indication that she might be frightened?"

"She did seem a bit distracted yesterday morning. But I thought it was just because the damn cat was off-color."

"That's Tommy?"

"Rotten little beast. I've told Dawn a thousand times

to keep that cat out of the . . ." Arrowood trailed off, as if realizing he'd have no more opportunities to chastise his wife. The muscles in his strong face sagged abruptly, and he rubbed a hand across his mouth. "I can't believe she's really gone."

Kincaid had risen with Gemma and seen her off in a gray dawn that presaged rain. She'd been pale and pinched with exhaustion, but he knew it would serve no purpose to nag her about getting more rest.

After fixing Toby his favorite breakfast of fried eggs, Kincaid deposited the boy at Hazel's and drove to his office through a steady downpour. He had always liked the Yard on a Saturday. Although the place was never truly quiet, the normal cacophony of activity was reduced to a hum, the ringing of telephones intermittent rather than constant, and he often took advantage of the opportunity to catch up on unfinished business. First, he called the prospective tenant he had lined up for his flat and arranged a viewing; then he rang Denis Childs, telling him they would be occupying the Notting Hill house as soon as possible.

Then, after a token shuffling of papers, he came to the conclusion that he could no longer delay acting on the disquiet that had niggled at him since the previous evening, despite his fear that Gemma would feel he was undermining her authority. Retrieving Marianne Hoffman's file, he read it from beginning to end. When he had finished, he picked up the phone and rang Denis Childs back, requesting permission to liaise with Notting Hill CID in the investigation of the murder of Dawn Arrowood.

*She just couldn't figure out what made her new neighbor tick. Betty, her name was, Betty Thomas. If you spoke to her, she smiled and answered in her soft Caribbean accent, but that was all. If you tried to continue the conversation, she'd dig her toe in the pavement and look away, and after a minute you'd give up.*

*The father was an upholsterer, she'd learned that much, and the family came from Trinidad, in the West Indies. They kept themselves to themselves, but sometimes on the warm evenings she could smell their cooking, so different from the food her own family ate.*

*The summer days were warm and long, the air filled with the smell of the moldering rubbish that piled up on the pavements, and the rats grew fatter than the neighborhood cats. She took to gazing out her window, elbows on the sill, making up stories to herself about the Thomases and a rather pimply boy across the street called Eddie Langley. Everyone else she knew had to share a bedroom with brothers and sisters or grandparents, sometimes even aunts and uncles, but that only made her feel lonelier. Her mother hadn't been able to have any more children because of some sort of female problem that was never properly explained, and her grandparents had died in Poland during the war.*

*She felt connectionless, as if her little family had failed to pass some basic but secret test. She began to imagine that she was adopted, that somewhere she had another family, not Polish, not Jewish, and much more glamorous than the family in which fate had chosen to place her. Taking refuge in the library, she devoured biographies of film stars and long romantic novels with invariably tragic endings. In that way the summer passed, and it was not until the start of school in the autumn that she thought much about Betty Thomas again.*

*The previous year the old school on Portobello Road had been reorganized as boys only and renamed Isaac Newton. Girls were shunted out of the neighborhood to the comprehensive in Holland Park, and she and Betty Thomas were placed in the same class.*

*It seemed only natural that the girls should fall in together on the long walk home that first day, silently at first, then in desultory conversation.*

*"She's all right, don't you think, the new teacher?"* Betty offered in her soft voice. *"But the subjects, we did them two years ago in Trinidad."*

*"What's it like there? Trinidad."*

*"Warm. Like this, but more so, all the time. But a lot of the folks are poor, and my daddy, he thought he could do better here. Now he says we shoulda stayed at home."*

*"Do you want to go back?"*

*Betty shrugged. "Not for me to say."*

*"There are some nice things here,"* she said, feeling a bit defensive. *"And school will be easy for you if you've already done the subjects."* It was a clear day, just hot enough to make the pleated woolen uniform skirt itchy on bare thighs, and as they walked on she began to perspire. *"It's not fair, the boys getting to stay at the old school. And my mother wouldn't give me bus fare, said she wouldn't waste the money when I had two good feet."*

*"My mother said I mus' be havin' a fever to even think such a thing."* Betty rolled her eyes in imitation, and both girls giggled.

*Emboldened, she asked, "Why won't you ever talk to me at home?"*

*"Your family don't like coloreds living next door. Though my daddy, he says the Polish Jews are better than some."*

*"It's not that they don't like it,"* she said, torn between

embarrassment and a desire to defend her parents. "It's just that they're afraid of trouble, like what happened over in Elgin Crescent last year. But I don't really see what that has to do with us."

Betty gave her a skeptical glance. "You don't mind if the other kids in the neighborhood won't talk to you?"

Shrugging, she answered, "I'm used to being alone. And besides, I'd rather talk to you."

They walked in silence for a bit, then Betty stopped and looked full at her, as if she'd come to a decision. "When I saw you, that first day, I thought you looked like the painting of an angel they had in our old church, in Trinidad."

"Me? An angel?" No one had ever said anything like that about her before. Her oval face was ordinary; her soft brown hair neither strikingly blond nor brunette; her eyes were too pale for beauty. A warm glow began in her midriff and spread outwards. "I wish I could see the painting," she said wistfully.

"Oh, she is that lovely, with her sweet face and the sky all blue and gold behind her. Of course," Betty gave her a sly smile, "I don't know if you wanna be that good. Or if your mother and father, they would let you go in a Catholic church."

"No, and no," she answered, laughing.

"I think I'm going to call you that. Angel. It suits you."

"Angel," she repeated, trying it out on her tongue, liking the sound, and the image of the painting in her mind.

And so she became Angel, to Betty, to Betty's brother, Ron, and to all the friends that came after. This small thing constituted not only the cementing of her friendship with Betty, but the beginning of an identity that would separate her finally from her family. What she didn't realize was that the image of the angel in the painting would stay with her long after she had lost touch with all who had known her by that name.

# CHAPTER FOUR

Opinions vary as to the start of the antiques trade in Portobello Road. One theory is that when the Caledonian Market, well known in prewar days as the place to buy a secondhand wardrobe or bedstead, closed in 1948, some of the displaced antique stalls set up in Portobello Road.

—Whetlor and Bartlett,
from *Portobello*

GEMMA CHECKED THE address of Dawn Arrowood's friend in the *A to Zed* she kept in her car, locating the flat near the South Ken tube station. Near enough that she thought she would drive there unannounced, and informal enough to justify her going alone.

The rain began to slacken as she pulled away from the station, and it seemed natural to her that she should drive down the hill and stop for a moment in front of the house on St. John's Gardens.

It looked larger than she remembered from the previous evening. More solid and prosperous. She thought of her parents' flat over the bakery, the cheap digs she had shared with a friend in her first days on the force, the tatty semidetached in Leyton she had bought with Rob, and now her tiny garage flat. Doubt flooded through her. Was she up to this house, with the expectations and commitment it represented?

Then she thought of her friend Erika Rosenthal's home a few blocks away, and of the sense of contentment and homecoming she'd experienced in those rooms. It came to her that with this house she was being offered a chance to create that life for herself; she would be a fool to pass it by.

She closed her eyes, gathering herself for her next task, and in that instant she had a vision. Distant and silent, as if viewed through the opposite end of a telescope: They were all together in the house, she and Kincaid, the boys, and a child whose face she could not see. The image vanished as abruptly as a bubble popping, but the sense of home and family stayed with her like a half-remembered dream.

Natalie Caine lived in a garden flat in Onslow Gardens. It was a chic address and the flat's entrance reflected it: shining paint and polished brass, flanked by perfect topiaries set in large Italian pots. The sound of a television came faintly from within. Gemma lifted the knocker and rapped lightly.

A woman opened the door so quickly that Gemma decided she must have been expecting someone else. Tall, slightly heavyset, with pale olive skin and a mass of frizzy dark hair pulled back with an oversized clip, she looked as if she had been crying. "Oh," she said, her brow creasing as she studied Gemma. "I thought you were someone come about the telly. But you're not, are you?"

"No, I'm afraid not." Gemma slipped her identification from her jacket pocket. "My name's Gemma James. Are you Natalie Caine?" When the woman nodded, Gemma continued, "I wondered if I might have a word with you about your friend Dawn Arrowood."

Natalie's face crumpled in a sob. She gestured Gemma into the flat, shaking her head in apology. "Sorry. I've been blubbing like a baby all morning. I just can't believe it's true."

Gemma sat opposite her in the sitting room. The velvet-cushioned Victorian love seat and chairs seemed incongruous with the sisal carpet and rattan blinds, but the effect was pleasing, if a little untidy—not unlike its owner. In one corner, a television gave out sound but no picture. "That's why I was trying to get the telly fixed," Natalie explained. "I thought I might see something on the news."

"Did someone ring you about Dawn?" Gemma asked.

"My mum, this morning. She heard from Dawn's mum. Poor Joanie... And Dawn was an only. Not like me." Natalie attempted a wavering smile. "When we were kiddies, Dawn always wanted to be at our house because she liked the hubbub, and I always wanted to be at hers because it was *quiet*."

"You've known each other a long time, then."

"Since grammar school. As much as Dawn wanted to get shut of anything to do with Croyden, she kept in touch with me. Even though we weren't exactly in her social league. I mean, Chris and I have done all right, but Dawn's husband wouldn't have given us the time of day."

"Did they get on all right, Dawn and her husband?"

Natalie looked uncomfortable. "Well, I don't want to be one to tell tales."

A sure sign that she only needed a bit of gentle encouragement, thought Gemma. "He's much older, isn't he? That must have caused some problems."

Natalie snorted. "*Trophy wife* might have been invented

for Dawn. But she couldn't see it at first. It was so romantic. All this *'I vill take you away from thees sordid life'* stuff."

Gemma suppressed a smile. "Did you tell her what you thought?"

"Even with your best friend, you can only go so far. . . . But now I wish . . . I don't know. Maybe I could have done something, changed things somehow."

"Why? Do you think her husband might have had something to do with her death?"

"Oh, no! I didn't mean that. It's just that, if she hadn't been married to Karl, Dawn wouldn't have been where she was, would she? And it wouldn't have happened."

"The-wrong-place-at-the-wrong-time theory," Gemma muttered, as much to herself as to Natalie. "So you can't think of any personal reason why someone would have wanted to harm Dawn?"

"Oh, no. She was . . . lovely. Luminous. You'd have to have known her." Natalie looked as if she might break down again.

Gently, Gemma probed, "Did you know your friend was pregnant?"

Natalie hesitated a moment, then shrugged. "I suppose there's no need to keep secrets now, is there? She wasn't sure until yesterday. She had an appointment with her doctor before we met for tea."

"How did she feel about that? About being pregnant?"

Again, Gemma sensed hesitation, then Natalie said slowly, "She was pleased about the baby, I think . . ."

"But?"

"She didn't know how Karl would react. He'd told her from the beginning he didn't want children."

"That seems a bit unfair. Surely he'd have accepted the situation. And he'd not have had much choice, unless she was willing to have an abortion?"

"Well, it's a bit more complicated than that." Natalie's olive skin colored. "He'd had a vasectomy—at least that's what he told Dawn."

*The missing ingredient,* thought Gemma. *A lover.* Now they were getting somewhere. "So Dawn was seeing someone else. Was this a casual affair, or something more serious?"

"She wouldn't have just, you know, gone off with anyone." Natalie spoke defensively. "I think she loved him. But she said there was no hope for them, because Karl would never let her go."

"How could he have stopped her?"

"That's what I said. Why couldn't she just walk out, file for divorce? But she said it was more complicated than that. And then I told her not to be so bloody materialistic, that she could do without Karl's money. She was pretty—more than pretty—she was smart, capable. She could make it on her own. I even told her I'd help her get her job back; we both worked for the BBC before she married Karl, and I'm still there. I could just kick myself now for being so hard on her! I didn't know I'd never get to see her again."

"Was she angry?"

"No. That would have been easier. But she just shook her head and kept saying that I didn't understand, that there were things I didn't know. She looked almost... frightened. You don't think... when you asked did I think Karl had something to do with her death..."

"We haven't ruled out the possibility of anyone's

involvement, but it's early days yet. What can you tell me about Dawn's boyfriend?"

"Not much. I know his name's Alex, and that he sells porcelain in Portobello Market. I've never met him."

"It's a small world, the market. He shouldn't be too difficult to trace. Did he know about Dawn's pregnancy?"

"I doubt Dawn had said anything to him. She didn't know what she was going to do."

Glancing at her watch, Gemma saw that it was just after noon. The Portobello Market would still be in full swing, giving her a good opportunity to track down Alex the porcelain dealer.

As she thanked Natalie for her help and took her leave, Natalie stopped her with a touch, her eyes filling again with tears. "Could you let me know when you find out who did this? I don't want to hear it on the news."

"It's a promise," Gemma answered, and vowed to keep it.

Bryony stood beside Marc at the serving table, ladling hot vegetable soup into bowls. He added wheat rolls and apples to the trays before passing them on to the hungry and indigent waiting patiently in the queue. Clients, he preferred to call them, as he was providing them a service, and feeling the term identified them in a more positive way than saying "the homeless" or "the needy."

How like Marc, she thought, to show such sensitivity to the delicate nuances of self-respect. Here, he was in his element, always ready with an interested expression, or a kind word. And they responded, these "clients." For many he provided the first step towards rejoining mainstream life, but he had no less patience for those who would never leave the streets and the meager existence they provided.

Through the glass-fronted doors, Bryony could see those shoppers who'd been resolute enough to make it to the bottom end of the Portobello Road, and now milled round the graffiti-decorated pedestrian mall that had been built adjacent to the Motorway flyover. Marc's soup kitchen was only a few doors from the old Portobello School, with its two entrances marked separately for girls and boys.

"You're quiet today," he commented, when the last person had moved through the queue, a withered woman who favored him with a beatific toothless smile. "I'm sure we always have a bigger crowd on Saturdays when you come."

"Sorry. It's this business about Dawn Arrowood and Alex."

"I know," he replied somberly. "I haven't quite taken it in myself. But you know what really worries me? Fern. Now poor old Fern thinks she's going to save the day with Alex, and I doubt very much that's going to happen. And I'm not sure how convincingly sympathetic she can be, considering the fact that she despised Dawn Arrowood."

"I can't say I blame her, under the circumstances. And she never had a chance to get to know Dawn—not that I knew her well, but she seemed a really nice person."

"I doubt that would have mattered to Fern. I only hope Alex won't slap her down too hard."

"Fern's a grown woman—there's no law that says she can't make a fool of herself." Bryony heard her words hit a bit too close to home and flushed. The memory of Gavin's dig yesterday about her efforts to impress Marc still stung. "I just can't believe that Dawn is dead. She was right there in the clinic yesterday morning, worrying over her cat, with Gavin putting on his usual dog-and-pony show for her—you know how he is with pretty women—"

"An ordinary day, then."

"Except that Dawn always tolerated Gavin; she managed to ignore his advances graciously, if you know what I mean. But yesterday she seemed a little edgy, and when she came out of the examining room she looked like thunder. Didn't even hear me when I said good-bye."

"Maybe Gavin finally went too far."

Bryony shrugged. "I've always assumed Gavin's all bark and no bite."

"Could she have been upset about the cat?"

"It was just the usual abscessed bite. Tommy gets in fights, the little bugger." Bryony filled a second bowl of soup for a frail young man whose retriever looked in better shape than he did.

"Marc," she said slowly, "I've been meaning to ask you something, then with everything that's happened this morning it flew right out of my mind." She glanced at him, trying to gauge his responsiveness, then forced herself to go on. "Could I set up a weekly clinic for your clients' animals?"

"Here?"

She nodded. "I thought maybe on Sunday afternoons."

"But, Bryony, you know they couldn't pay."

"Of course not. But I could fund it myself in the beginning—it's my time that's the most expensive factor—then, if it takes off, I thought I could solicit donations in the neighborhood."

"But Bryony, it's too much—"

"I could only do vaccinations and minor injuries and illnesses, I know that, but surely that's better than no care at all."

"No, I mean it's too much for you. I don't think you realize how much of your time and energy this could take—"

"How can *you* say that to *me*? You live and breathe for this place; you sleep on a mattress upstairs; you barely have enough money to buy the occasional coffee—" Bryony felt the color stain her cheeks as she realized she'd gone too far. "Oh, Marc, I'm so sorry. I'd no right to say those things—"

"No, you're absolutely right. I sounded a self-righteous prig, telling you you weren't up to the task, and I owe you an apology." One of his rare smiles lit his face. "I think it's a splendid idea, and that you're equally splendid for thinking of it. When shall we start?"


Gemma left the car in the police station car park, knowing that the likelihood of parking anywhere near Portobello Road on a Saturday would be nil. As she walked along Ladbroke Road towards the market, she found that although the rain had stopped it was bitterly cold, and the bare branches of the trees were pearled with droplets.

By the time she reached the top end of Portobello Road, she was shivering, and she looked in envy at the one-way tide of shoppers, their brisk steps and bright eyes revealing an insatiable appetite for a bargain. But here the narrow, curving street held only flats and a few posh shops; they had a ways to go before reaching the stalls and arcades packed with imagined treasures.

She came to a complete halt in front of the entrance to the Manna Café, run by St. Peter's Church. Why not have some lunch and a hot drink to warm her up? Edging her way through the milling pedestrians, she crossed the pretty little courtyard and pulled open the café door, relaxing instantly as the warmth and cooking aromas enveloped her.

A half hour later, having devoured a hot bacon sandwich, she nursed a cup of tea and thought about what she had learned. Karl Arrowood was certainly shaping up odds-on favorite for prime suspect, and that was without taking into account the statistical likelihood that he had murdered his wife. If he'd had a vasectomy, and he'd suspected or discovered that his wife was pregnant, that certainly gave him motive. Opportunity was a given; he could even have been waiting for Dawn when she arrived home. What Gemma needed was corroboration, and if Arrowood had threatened his wife, Dawn might have told her lover.

When her waitress, a woman with pale Fräulein-like plaits wrapped round her head, brought her bill, Gemma said, "Do you by any chance know a porcelain dealer called Alex? Youngish, I think, and nice-looking?"

"That'd be Alex Dunn," the girl said in an accent

nearer East London than East Germany. "I know he lives up the road, in one of the mews, but I've no idea which flat."

"Do you know where he trades in the market, then?"

"Um, I think his stall's in the arcade just down the road on the left, before you get to Elgin Crescent. Just ask anyone in the arcade. They'll point him out for you."

Gemma thanked her and left, feeling fortified to continue her search. As she walked on, the crowd grew ever thicker, and music drifted towards her. Reaching the intersection of Portobello and Chepstow Villas, the official beginning of Portobello Market, she paused to listen to the string quartet that was busking on the corner. A past acquaintance having made her kindly disposed towards buskers, she fished a pound coin from her bag and tossed it in the open violin case.

Continuing onwards, the strains of Mozart faded into the rhythm of a steel drum. A mime in painted face and costume enthralled watchers. In spite of herself Gemma found the cheerful, carnival atmosphere infectious. She would have to bring the children here, she resolved, one Saturday soon.

With reluctance, she left the bustle and color of the street for the more crowded and smoky confines of the arcade. At least, she thought, it was warm. Stopping at the first stall, which held a miscellany of small objects from pocket watches to penknives, she spoke to the vendor, a shriveled, heavily made-up woman with hennaed hair. "Do you know where I might find Alex Dunn?"

"His stall's right in the back, if that's what you mean, but you won't find him there today." The woman shook her head. "A terrible business, his friend being murdered and all." She leaned forward confidentially, wafting the smell of smoke and sour coffee into Gemma's face. "They're saying it's a regular Jack-the-Ripper killing. I don't know how I'm going to sleep in my own bed tonight."

There might be some others not sleeping in their own beds tonight, Gemma thought furiously, if she found out who had leaked that particular snippet. "I'm sure there's no need for you to worry," she soothed, forcing a smile. "Would you happen to know where Alex went?"

"Left this morning with young Fern Adams. Looked ghastly, he did—it was all poor Fern could do to keep him on his feet. But I've not seen hide nor hair of either of them since."

"Who's Fern Adams? Is she a friend of Alex's?"

"She's a silver vendor, has the stall next to his. Fern's family's had a stall or a barrow in the market since after the war; grew up in Portobello Courts, she did. She's a good girl, Fern, in spite of her looks." The natural suspicion that had been held in abeyance by the thrill of gossip suddenly asserted itself. "And why might you be asking all these questions, ducks?"

Gemma produced her warrant card. "It's just routine inquiries. Do you know where I could find Fern now?"

"I'd not be one to say," the woman told her, turning her attention to a waiting customer. Caution had obviously set in.

"Do you know anyone else I might speak to?" Gemma persisted, refusing to be ignored. "Friends of Alex who might know where he's gone?"

The woman scowled at her in annoyance. "I suppose you could try Otto's Café just round the corner in Elgin Crescent. I know Alex goes there, and some of the others."

As Gemma turned to leave, the woman relented and called out, "Mind you, there's no sign says Otto's. It's just that everyone knows it by that name. You can't miss it."

She recognized the café by the yellowed menu posted in the window. A babble of sound met Gemma as she opened the door. The café was packed with animated shoppers, but she spied one empty table near the back and made for it quickly. Once settled, she ordered a coffee from the young black man who appeared from the kitchen. He smiled at her when he came back with her drink, and as their eyes met, she felt the sort of instant connection she'd only experienced a few times in her life. There was nothing sexual about it; it was purely emotional, or even spiritual, as if they'd known each other in another context.

"What's your name?" she asked, as if it were the most natural thing in the world.

"Wesley Howard."

"Mine's Gemma James. I've been told that Alex Dunn comes in here. Do you know him?"

Wesley's smile vanished. "Sure I know Alex. What you want wiv him?" When she showed him her warrant card, he gazed at her in surprise. "You the Bill? I would never have credited that. But you still don't tell me what you want wiv Alex."

"We'd like to interview anyone who knew Dawn Arrowood well."

"Can't say I ever met a Dawn Arrowood." Wesley was not a convincing liar.

"Alex was having an affair with her. And if you're his friend I don't believe for a minute that you didn't know about it."

"And what if I did?"

"She was killed last night, and I don't believe that news hasn't made the rounds, either."

"You're not saying as Alex had something to do wiv her murder?"

"Why? Do you think he did?"

The young man's dreadlocks trembled as he shook his head. "Man, Alex would never 'ave hurt Mrs. Arrowood. He was crazy 'bout her."

A large, bald man in a white apron came through from the kitchen, his face registering alarm as he came towards them. "Wesley, is there a problem?"

"She the Bill, Otto. I only tell her Alex would never have hurt Mrs. Arrowood."

"I am Otto Popov. How can I help you?"

"Did you know Dawn Arrowood, Mr. Popov?"

As Wesley excused himself to attend to the customers, Otto sat, the chair creaking under his weight. "I had seen her about—a lovely creature—but no, I was not personally acquainted with Mrs. Arrowood."

"But you knew about Alex's relationship with her?"

"We knew because we are his special friends. It was never really discussed, even among us, until we heard this morning of the poor lady's death."

"Have you seen Alex today?"

"It was we who had to break the news to him this morning."

"How did he take it?"

"Hard. Quite hard." Otto shook his massive head. "We all felt for him very much."

"Do you know where Alex is now?"

"I have not seen him since he left here this morning. Have you tried his stall in the arcade?"

"A vendor there told me he'd left with a young woman called Fern Adams." Seeing Otto's surprise, she added, "You know her?"

"Of course," Otto answered. "Since she was a child. She's very fond of Alex. She will look after him."

"Do you know where they might have gone?"

"No. But perhaps these people can help you."

A couple had entered the café. They stood awkwardly, as if unsure whether they should cross the room and join the conversation. The woman was tall and slender, with deep auburn hair pulled back in a plait, and strong facial bones. Gemma would have called her handsome rather than beautiful; this masculine quality was emphasized by her jeans, jumper, and heavy boots.

The man was less distinguished, tall, with short-cropped hair, and spectacles that lent him a studious air. Otto motioned them over.

"This is Bryony Poole," he told Gemma. "And Marc Mitchell. Marc runs the soup kitchen just down the road."

"Oh, I know your place," said Gemma. "By the old Portobello School. You provide a great service for the neighborhood."

"This lady is from the police," Otto continued, "and is looking for our friend Alex. She says he left the arcade this morning with Fern."

"Is this about Dawn Arrowood?" Bryony Poole asked. "It's just dreadful."

"Alex was in a terrible state this morning." Marc pulled over chairs for himself and Bryony. "And Fern seemed determined to offer help and succor."

"Was there something unusual in that?" asked Gemma.

"It's just that they hadn't been on good terms lately," volunteered Bryony. "Fern and Alex had a thing going, until he met Dawn Arrowood. So of course Fern wasn't best pleased with the whole affair."

"Do I take it that Fern hasn't given up?"

"I don't think anyone thought Alex's relationship with Dawn Arrowood would last—could last," Bryony corrected. "I mean, either her husband was going to find out, or she would decide to call it off before he did."

"Perhaps he *did* find out," suggested Otto. "Is it not usually the spouse in these cases?"

"You think Karl Arrowood had something to do with his wife's death?" Gemma asked, and heard the sharpness in her voice.

"That man is capable of anything," Otto growled, but when Gemma pressed him, he merely shook his head and clamped his lips together. Before she could question him further, two small girls ran in from the kitchen. They wore matching hair ribbons and dresses, and their round faces marked them immediately as Otto's progeny. He wrapped his arms around both.

"These are my daughters, Anna and Maria. I have promised them the cinema. Something about spotted cows, I think?" he added, twinkling at them.

"Dogs, Daddy. Dalmatians," they chorused. "And we'll be late if we don't go."

Groaning, he let them pull him to his feet. "If you have more questions, you might speak to Wesley."

As Otto and his daughters disappeared into the kitchen, Bryony stood as well, and Marc joined her. "We've not got time for coffee, after all, I'm afraid," she said apologetically. "We—I hope you find whoever did this."

Gemma gave them each a card, asking them to ring her if they thought of anything that might help.

When they had gone, Wesley came back to her table, although he kept an experienced eye on the remaining customers. "You don't want to take what Otto says about Karl Arrowood too seriously," he told her quietly. "There's some sort of bad blood between them that goes way back. Otto thinks Karl's the devil himself."

Gemma noticed with amusement that all traces of his West Indian accent had vanished. "What sort of feud?"

"I really couldn't say. Something to do with Otto's dead wife, but that's all I know."

"An affair?"

"Could be. But it was before I came to work here, and Otto doesn't talk about it."

"I take it you do a bit of everything around here."

Wesley smiled. "Cook, bottle washer, waiter, and child minder. I like helping out with the girls."

"How old are they?"

"Seven—that's Anna, and nine—that's Maria. They're good kids."

"When did their mother die?"

"It was before I came, and I started four years ago." He looked curiously at Gemma. "Do I know you from somewhere? You seem awfully familiar—and it's not because you've thrown me in the nick."

"I used to walk a beat here, but you'd have been a mere babe," Gemma teased in turn, glad to know the feeling of past acquaintance was mutual. "Now I've been posted back to Notting Hill," she added, finding herself inexplicably confessing, "and I'm moving here as well, into a house near St. John's."

Wesley whistled. "Poncey address for a police lady."

"Terrifying." Gemma grinned. "But my kids will love it. Now, before I go, can you give me Alex Dunn's address?"

Only when she had thanked Wesley and left the café did she realize that for the first time, she had claimed Kit as her own.

"The victim's name was Dawn Arrowood," Gemma told the press gathered on the steps of Notting Hill Police Station at six o'clock. "If anyone saw anything suspicious or unusual in the vicinity of St. John's Church, Notting Hill, yesterday evening, please ring the police at this number." She gave out the number of a special line manned in the incident room. Ninety-nine percent of the calls would be cranks, but there was always a possibility that someone had actually seen something useful.

She fielded a few questions with "I'm sorry, we can't disclose that information just yet," then ducked into the station to retrieve her bag while the crowd cleared away.

Although she was leaving the station, her workday was not over. Penciled in her notebook was the number of Alex Dunn's flat in a mews just off Portobello Road. She'd already stopped there twice since getting his address, but had found the flat dark and apparently uninhabited, as were those of his neighbors.

Picking up her car from the station car park, she drove to the flat again, but Alex still hadn't returned.

Gemma let the car idle for a moment, gazing at the now lit flat next door.

Should she interview Alex's neighbors now? No, they would keep, and she needed to speak to Karl Arrowood's business associate before any more time passed. She could stop on her way home, sending a constable to take a formal statement later. Turning the car round at the bottom of the mews, she headed for Tower Bridge.

The Brewery at Butler's Wharf was a very posh address, especially for what she assumed was only a part-time London accommodation. The old brewery had been converted into elegant flats with a view of the Thames at Tower Bridge. She searched for a parking space in the warren of streets near the river, her frustration mounting. By the time she found a spot and walked back to the brewery she had little patience for the building's gilt-and-green-marble lobby. Taking the lift up to the second floor, she found the flat number Arrowood had given her and rang the bell.

Within moments, a ruddy-faced, handsome man in his fifties opened the door and beamed at her as if she were a long-expected relation. " 'Ullo. You must be the inspector from the police." His accent was heavily French but understandable, and Gemma found herself unable to resist smiling back.

"I'm Gemma James. Mr. Arrowood must have rung you."

"Yes." Andre Michel ushered her into the flat and closed the door. Tower Bridge, stunning and immense, filled the windows. "Such terrible news. Here, please sit down. Can I offer you something to drink?"

Drawing her eyes away from the view, Gemma saw that a tray on the coffee table held wine and several glasses. "Nothing for me, thank you. But you couldn't have known I was coming just now—"

"No." Michel laughed. "I would like to claim that level of clairvoyance, but alas, it is merely that I'm expecting friends this evening." The delicious aroma of garlic and herbs wafted from the kitchen Gemma could just glimpse through a door on the far side of the sitting room. "A little coq au vin, a family recipe," Michel added, seeing her glance.

"Then I'll take up as little of your time as possible, Mr. Michel." Gemma took the seat he indicated, facing the windows, but she was sorry to look away from the display of oil paintings she had noticed on the walls. "I understand you had drinks with Mr. Arrowood yesterday."

"If you don't mind?" Michel glanced at her before pouring himself a glass of red wine. "Yes, and we parted with good cheer. If I had known I was sending him home to find his poor wife, murdered...I think it a good thing sometimes that we cannot foresee the future."

"Did Mr. Arrowood seem as usual to you yesterday?"

"Karl? Karl is always business. I think he grows impatient with our French philosophy of enjoying all parts of life."

"What exactly is it you do for Mr. Arrowood? I believe he said you were a dealer?"

"A dealer, a collector, among many other things." Michel gestured back towards the paintings. "I have a knack for finding eighteenth- and nineteenth-century landscape oils, whether at auction or under sacks of turnips. It is a gift, like a pig's nose for truffles, not something for which I can take credit."

"And you sell these paintings to Mr. Arrowood?"

"Karl is one of my clients, yes. He then sells the paintings to his clients, for a much greater price." Michel gave a Gallic shrug. "That's the way the antiques business works; a little profit for everyone. But Karl is definitely at the top of the pyramid."

"Have you known Karl—Mr. Arrowood—for a long time?"

Michel laughed merrily again. "For many years. But in those days, Karl had much less finesse. He always knew what he wanted, however, and even then he made it a point to meet the right people, get invited to the right places." Sighing, he added, "London parties were something to see, then, or perhaps it's just that I was young enough to prefer that life to a good bottle of wine with friends."

"And yesterday, Mr. Michel, did Karl buy anything?"

"Two paintings, in fact, which he took away. He was particularly pleased with them."

"What time did he leave you?"

"Ah, now it gets difficult." Michel frowned in concentration. "I know it was just getting dark. The bridge lights had come on. I would say around five o'clock, but I had no reason to check the time."

Gemma made a careful note, her pulse quickening. If Michel's estimate was accurate, even taking into account Friday-evening traffic, Arrowood could have got home in time to kill his wife.

"But you know I cannot swear to that," Michel added, and Gemma heard an apology in his tone.

"Is that because you're not certain? Or because Karl Arrowood is too important to cross?" she pressed.

"The antiques business is a small world, Inspector, but Karl's ill will would not damage my business to any great extent. Nor would I protect anyone who had committed such a terrible crime. Why do you believe Karl would do such a thing?"

"Perhaps his wife had a lover?"

Michel shrugged again. "Where I come from, that is not a matter for murder."

"But it wouldn't surprise you."

"Dawn Arrowood was young and very beautiful. And she had a certain . . . gravity . . . about her . . . some quality that made you want to know her."

Natalie Caine had called her luminous; Otto Popov, a lovely creature. Gemma suddenly felt a stab of regret that she'd not had a chance to know the young woman. "Thank you," she said, standing. "You've been very helpful."

Michel took her outstretched hand, holding it just a moment longer than necessary, and the look he gave her was frankly appraising. "Are you sure you won't stay and sample my coq au vin? If you don't mind my saying so, you are much too lovely to be doing a policeman's work."

Gemma felt herself blushing furiously. "I'm very flattered, Mr. Michel. But I'm . . . um . . . otherwise engaged." As would soon be all too obvious, she thought, with a glance down at her barely disguised belly.

She must tell Hazel first. Toby's four-year-old exuberance would not allow him to keep the momentous news of the move to himself, and as much as she owed her friend, Gemma would not have her hear it secondhand.

The street was quiet as she parked in front of the tiny garage flat in Islington. The flat was still dark—Toby would be in the main house with Hazel, and she had not heard from Kincaid. She got out of the car, shivering against the sudden chill, and went through the wrought-iron gate into the garden that separated the flat from the main house.

She found Hazel in the kitchen with Toby and her own daughter, Holly, who was the same age as Toby, and his boon companion. "Where's Tim?" she asked as Hazel greeted her with a hug.

"Catching up on paperwork at the office. I wish he wouldn't do that on a weekend, but needs must. The children have had their tea"—Hazel indicated the remains of sandwiches on the table—"let me make you a cuppa before you take Toby home."

"Please," said Gemma gratefully, then added quietly, "Hazel, we need to talk."

Hazel's startled glance held a hint of alarm, but she put the kettle on without comment. Enticing the children into the sitting room with a promise of a Christmas video, Gemma glanced at the piano and sighed with regret. Hazel had allowed her to practice on the old instrument to her heart's content. Now she would have no opportunity to play— Would she have to give up her lessons as well?

When they were seated at the kitchen table, Gemma cradled her steaming mug for warmth and met her friend's eyes.

"You're all right, aren't you, Gemma?" Hazel asked. "The baby—"

"The baby's fine. It's just that— Well, it's obvious we're going to have to make some changes. There's no room in the flat for the baby, not to mention the burden it would put on you. And Duncan's found a house, in Notting Hill. He wants to move in right away, to get Kit settled before the holidays."

"Right away?" Hazel repeated. Much to Gemma's surprise, Hazel's eyes had filled with tears. She couldn't remember ever having seen Hazel cry.

"I'm so sorry, Hazel. I know I'm not giving you proper notice, but this has all been so sudden—"

"Oh, no, it's not that. And it's not that I haven't been expecting this—it was inevitable. It's just that I'm going to miss you. And Holly will be inconsolable without Toby."

"We'll visit often, I promise." Gemma found herself in the unexpected position of comforting the friend who had always provided such comfort for her. "And you and Holly can come to Notting Hill. The kids can play in the garden while we catch up on things."

"I know. Now you're going to be the one with the big house full of kids," Hazel said, teasing, but Gemma detected the wistfulness in her voice.

"Hazel, why don't you and Tim have another child?" she asked, wondering why it had never occurred to her before.

Hazel looked down, lacing her sturdy fingers round her cup, and for a moment Gemma thought she had gone too far. Then Hazel shrugged and murmured, "As much as I'd like that, it doesn't seem to be in the cards just now." Then, smiling, she abruptly changed the subject. "Tell me about the house."

"Oh, I can't wait for you to see it. It's absolutely

lovely," Gemma told her, and proceeded to describe it room by room as they finished their tea.

When Tim came in, Gemma collected Toby and took him home to bed. But as she tucked in her son, she couldn't help feeling that something was troubling her friend, and that she had missed a chance to learn what it was.


Alex had squeezed his eyes tight shut as Fern drove south, as if he could close out reality, and Fern didn't disturb him. It was not until she left the M25 for the M20 West that he stirred and looked around.

"You're going to Aunt Jane's." It was a statement, not a question.

"It seemed a good idea. No one would think to look for you there."

"Why should anyone look for me?"

Fern glanced at him before focusing on the road again. "You know what Otto said."

"Otto's full of crap. And what would Karl Arrowood want with me, now that Dawn's gone?"

"What if he killed her, and now he means to kill you, too?"

"I don't believe that. No sane person would do—" His voice cracked. "No sane person would do something like this." He stared straight ahead, not meeting Fern's eyes. It came to her that Alex couldn't allow himself to believe that Karl Arrowood had killed his wife because of her affair with him, because that would make Alex responsible for her death.

"Why are you doing this?" There was no gratitude in

Alex's voice—not that she had expected any, and yet his coldness shook her.

She shrugged. "You're my friend. I wanted to help."

"There's nothing you or anyone else can do to help."

What answer could she give to this? When she glanced at him a moment later he had closed his eyes again. She drove on, struggling to find comfort in the fact that he had not, at least, told her to turn around and drive back to London.

Although it was not yet noon, clouds had rolled in from the west, bringing a twilight gloom and the promise of more rain. When the ancient town of Rye appeared on the horizon, perched on its sandstone bluff overlooking the marsh, Fern slowed and began looking for the turning she only vaguely remembered from the one time Alex had brought her here.

"Next on the right," he told her, his eyes open again.

She followed his instructions, down one lane and then another until she reached the house tucked in a wooded close at the edge of the downs. Behind the house rose the dark hill, both protecting and threatening; before it stretched the wide, flat expanse of Romney Marsh. The house had been an oasthouse, its twin kilns, with their odd tilted caps, long since converted to living quarters.

Fern coasted to a stop in the drive and killed the engine. When Alex didn't stir, she got out and went to find his aunt, Jane Dunn.

There was a light in the front window, and smoke curling from the chimney, but a brisk knock on the door brought no answer. Fern had raised her hand to knock again when she saw Jane coming round the corner of the house, wearing an Arran jumper and mud-streaked wellies, her dark, chin-length hair beaded with moisture.

"I thought I heard a car," Jane called out. "Fern, whatever are you doing here? Have you got Alex with you?"

As Jane took her hand in a welcoming clasp, Fern blurted, "I *have* brought Alex. But something terrible's happened."

Jane gazed at her in surprise. "What do you mean?"

"I don't know if you knew—Alex was seeing someone else. She was married, and now she's dead. I mean someone murdered her, last night."

"But that's dreadful!" Jane looked from Fern to the car. "I'm not sure I understand, though, why you've brought Alex here."

"I—" In the face of Jane's competent manner, Fern suddenly felt her fears might sound silly. "I was worried about him. I didn't know what else to do."

"In a bad way, is he? I'm sure you did the right thing." Jane gave Fern's arm a reassuring squeeze and started towards the car.

Alex got out and came slowly to meet her. Fern saw Jane speak to him and start to put an arm round his shoulders, but he flinched away from the contact. This Fern found gratifying—at least she wasn't the only one he couldn't bear.

Jane led the way into the house. The two hop-drying kilns had been combined into a pleasant, open-plan living area, with small, high windows that failed to make the most of the existing daylight.

After standing for a moment as if unsure what to do

with himself, Alex slumped down on the sofa nearest the fireplace.

When Jane had the fire going and had brought them all coffee in earthenware mugs, she sat down beside Alex. "Do you want to talk about it, love? Fern says a friend of yours was killed last night."

His face contorted. "I told Otto it was a lie. She couldn't be dead. So I went there, to the house. There were police all round, and one of the neighbors said Karl came home and found her in the drive. Her . . . her throat had been cut."

Fern gave a small cry of surprise, but Jane remained calmly watching Alex. "Do you know anything about this?" she asked. "Who might have done this? Or why?"

"How could anyone hurt her?" Alex protested. "I can't go on, you know, not without her. I can't bear it."

Unable to listen any longer, Fern went out. She walked round in the drive, taking in Jane's greenhouses and the spade left standing against the house when Jane had been interrupted at some gardening task. Gazing out across the marsh, she breathed the damp earthy-smelling air and tried to blot out Alex's grief. When Dawn had been alive, Fern had been able to fantasize that Alex's affair with Dawn was merely a passing infatuation, that he would come to his senses and return to her. Now there was no questioning the depth of his feelings for Dawn Arrowood. Her death had not given Alex back to Fern, but had taken him from her in a way she could never have imagined. And if Alex was unable to go on, how then could she?

At the sharp click of the front door closing, she

turned back to the house. Jane came across the drive towards her.

"I've persuaded him to stay," Jane told her. "Not that it matters much to him where he is, at this point."

"I don't think he should come back to London. If Dawn Arrowood was killed by her husband because he found out about Alex, Alex could be next."

"Surely you can't be serious."

"That's what our friend Otto says, and he's known Karl Arrowood for a long time. Is it worth taking a risk?"

Jane seemed about to argue with her, then she sighed. "I suppose you're right. What about you? Will you stay with him?"

With sudden resolution Fern said, "I'll take the train back to London, if you'll run me to the station. If anyone asks, I'll say I haven't seen him. And the sooner I go, the better."

"I think you're overreacting, but I don't see what harm it can do. I'll just get my keys while you say goodbye to Alex."

"Why don't you tell him for me?" Fern asked, suddenly feeling that she would rather face a murderer herself than the look in Alex's eyes.

# CHAPTER FIVE

In the nineteenth century Notting Dale was still known as
the Potteries after the area's gravel pits and the Norland
Pottery Works on Walmer Road. It was also known as the
Piggeries—the district had 3000 pigs, 1000 humans, and
260 hovels.

—Charlie Phillips and Mike Phillips,
from *Notting Hill in the Sixties*

THE INSISTENT BURRING of the phone finally penetrated Gemma's consciousness. "Mummy," she heard
Toby say, very near, very seriously. "The phone's ringing." Forcing her eyes open, she found her son staring at
her intently from a few inches away.

"Uh-huh. Get it for me, would you, sweetie?" She
propped herself up on the pillows as Toby obediently
trotted over to the table and lifted the cordless phone
from its cradle. A glance at the clock told her it was not
yet eight. Taking the phone from Toby, she had just
time to think *oh God, not work, please,* when she heard
Kincaid's voice.

"Not still asleep, are you?" he asked with annoying
cheerfulness.

She didn't dignify that with an answer. "What happened to you last night? I waited up for ages."

"Sorry about that. The prospective tenant I had lined
up for the flat came round for a viewing. Apparently, he
was so enthralled with the place that he couldn't bring

himself to go home. By the time he left, I was afraid I'd wake you if I rang."

"Very considerate of you," Gemma said grumpily, unmollified.

"I'll make it up to you. How about if I bring over Sunday breakfast? I can stop at the bakery down the road. Bagels and cream cheese?"

"The sort with everything on them?"

"If you'll provide the coffee."

"You'll have to live with decaf."

"If I must," he said with an exaggerated sigh.

"Deal." Gemma rang off, her temper considerably improved, and pulled Toby to her for a hug.

By the time Kincaid arrived, Gemma had showered, dressed, set the small table, and made fresh coffee in the *cafetière.* Once they'd settled at the table with their bagels, she said, "I take it the prospective tenant accepted, then?"

"Formally. Signed a contract. And he wants in the flat right away."

Gemma eyed him warily. "What do you mean by 'right away'?"

"Next Sunday we'll be having breakfast in our new home. I've arranged the house-moving for Saturday, not that either of us has much to move."

"Saturday?" She heard the squeak of panic in her own voice.

"It'll be all right, love, I promise. The sooner the better."

Looking up from the jam-and-cream-cheese puddle he'd made on his plate, Toby asked, "What new house?"

Kincaid glanced at Gemma, eyebrows raised, and she gave him a nod of assent. "We're all going to move into a new house together, sport," he explained to the boy. "You, your mum, Kit and me. What do you think about that?"

Toby considered this for a moment. "Will Kit get to bring his dog?"

"Of course Tess can come. The house has a big garden, with a swing."

"And Sid?" Sid was the black cat Kincaid had inherited from a friend who had died. "Can he go out in the garden?"

"Sid will love the garden. He might even be able to catch a mouse."

Toby's small brow creased in a frown. "What about Holly? Can she come live with us, too?"

"No," Gemma answered quickly. "Holly has to stay with her mummy and daddy. But she'll come to visit often."

"Can I take my trucks?"

"We'll make a special place for them. Do you want to pack them now?"

"Okay," her son said with great equanimity. Leaving his bagel half finished, he scrambled down from his chair and disappeared into the tiny box room that served as his bedroom. When Gemma peeked in on him a few minutes later, she found him methodically stowing his collection of miniature lorries into his *Star Wars* backpack.

"What about Kit?" she asked Kincaid as she returned to the table and refilled her mug. "Have you arranged things with him?"

"Ian will drive him up from Grantchester on Saturday."

"And you're sure Ian won't change his mind?"

"As sure as one can ever be with Ian McClellan. But he seems to have pretty well burned his bridges this time. He told me he'd already booked his flight to Canada, and that the university has arranged a small apartment for him."

"As in 'bachelor pad'?"

"So I suspect. Gemma..." Kincaid scrubbed at his fingers with his napkin, avoiding her eyes. "There's been a development, with your investigation."

"Dawn Arrowood?" she asked, puzzled.

"In a way, yes. Do you remember the case I was working on a couple of months ago, before we went to Glastonbury? An antiques dealer named Marianne Hoffman was found dead outside her shop in Camden Passage. Her throat had been cut, and she had been stabbed in the chest. When I saw Dawn Arrowood's body—"

"Why didn't you say anything?"

"I wanted to check the details in the files, make sure that I wasn't just manufacturing coincidence."

"But—you're talking serial killer!"

"I think it's too early to use the term, but I also think the similarities can't be ignored. Especially considering the choice of weapon. And there's something else— it seems to me that the second murder was executed more expertly."

"As if the killer's skill is improving with practice?" Gemma shook her head. "I don't buy it, coincidence or not. I think that whoever murdered Dawn had a very personal connection with her."

"Then maybe we should be looking for a connection between Dawn Arrowood and Marianne Hoffman."

"We?"

Kincaid seemed to hesitate. "I'll be working with you and your team."

"Officially?"

"Yes."

"You've cleared this with Chief Superintendent Childs? Without discussing it with me first?"

"I'd not have consulted any other officer in charge of the Arrowood case. Did you want to be treated differently?"

Gemma glared at him, furious. "You're twisting it! You could have at least let me know what you were doing. Is that why you didn't come by last night?"

"No. But you're right, of course. I should have told you before I spoke to the guv'nor. I suppose I was afraid you might not want me messing about on your patch."

"You're bloody right!" Gemma hissed at him, careful to keep her voice lowered on Toby's account. But Kincaid looked so crushed that she felt some of her anger evaporate. "It's not that, really. It's that you'd never have done something like that without discussing it with me when we worked together."

"It would never have come up. I handled this badly, love. I'm sorry."

She folded her arms across her chest, considering him. It would be nice to work as a team again, but she didn't want to risk damaging her still tenuous authority with her staff. "What about my team?"

"You'll communicate with them directly. And I'll try not to step on your toes."

"I still don't like it."

"Can't you think of me as a bonus? A good resource?"

He always knew when to be diplomatic, she thought grudgingly, but then that was one of the things that made him good at his job. "All right. I'll hold you to that. First you can tell me everything you remember about that earlier case. And then you can go with me to see Dawn Arrowood's parents."

"Here we are." Gemma stopped the car in front of a terraced house of dark brick in East Croydon. It was an ordinary neighborhood, a universe away from the elegance of the Arrowoods' house in Notting Hill.

Gemma's face was set as she climbed from the car. Kincaid knew she was dreading this interview, but it was a necessity they couldn't avoid. The street was quiet as he rang the bell, the air filled with the scents of Sunday lunches in the oven.

The man who came to the door was in his fifties, graying, slightly heavyset, and dressed in shirt and tie as if he had just come back from an ordinary Sunday church service.

"Mr. Smith?" asked Gemma, showing her warrant card. "We'd like to talk with you and your wife, if you feel up to it."

The man nodded without speaking and led them through into the sitting room, saying, "Joanie, it's the police." Sorrow was palpable in the air. A Christmas tree in the corner and a string of cards across the mantel seemed cruelly and inappropriately cheerful.

Dawn's mother rose from the sofa, and Kincaid saw that she had been looking through a photo album. Kincaid could see that until yesterday Joan Smith might have had a shadow of her daughter's beauty; her thinness might have been expressed as elegance. But grief had sucked her dry, left her gaunt and brittle and looking more than her age.

"Have you found him?" she demanded. "The monster that killed our daughter?"

"No, Mrs. Smith, I'm sorry. I know this must be difficult for you, but we hoped you could tell us a bit about Dawn." Gemma was at her most gentle, and Kincaid was content to listen, and watch. "Could we sit down?" Gemma asked, and Mrs. Smith sank obediently back to the sofa, clutching the photo album. Kincaid saw that the crowded room was filled with pictures of Dawn from babyhood on, an adored only child.

"Could you tell us when you last saw your daughter?" Gemma directed the question towards them both, but it was the mother who answered.

"Two weeks ago. She came for Sunday lunch. She didn't often come on a weekend, because *he* didn't like it, but he was away on some sort of a business trip."

"Karl didn't like your daughter to visit you?" Gemma clarified, her brow creased in a frown.

"Weren't good enough, were we? Clarence manages a supermarket, and does a good job of it, but that meant nothing to Karl Arrowood. He wanted nothing to do with us."

Her husband sat beside her, watching her, and every so often he gave a slow, wounded shake of his head as she spoke, as if he were depending on her to express what he could not.

"Do you know that he never came here once? And we were never invited to their house? Not even for Christmas or holidays! Oh, Dawn would make excuses, saying he'd planned a business dinner, or that they had to go to France or to some posh country house. And she'd promise the next time would be different, but we learned she didn't mean it, that Karl would never allow it. He took our daughter away from us, and now she's dead."

"How did she meet Karl?"

"At some swank London party. She'd taken a job at the BBC, her and her friend Natalie, and they were living the high life. She'd come home and tell me about it in those days, what everyone was wearing, what was served, the latest gossip.

"We couldn't believe it at first, when she said she was going to marry this man twice her age. But we thought, well, she's a grown woman, we'll make the best of it, and at least he can afford to give her a proper wedding." Mrs. Smith pinched her lips together in renewed anger.

"But he didn't?"

"Took her away. To Nice or some such. We never even had a photo." She hugged the album to her chest, as if that lack created a physical void. "And now he's planned her funeral without consulting us. We'd thought to have a service at the crematorium here, where she grew up, where our friends and neighbors could come. But, no, he's arranged it all. A burial, in Kensal Green, on Tuesday."

"I suppose he does have that right, as her husband," said Gemma. "And as you say, he can afford it. But it does seem insensitive of him not to take your feelings into account."

Dawn's mother nodded and sniffed, as if gratified by Gemma's support.

"Did Dawn seem any different the last time you saw her?"

Mrs. Smith looked at her husband as if seeking confirmation. "Now that you mention it, she did. Sweeter, I guess you could say. She even hugged us when she left, and our Dawn was never a demonstrative girl. It seemed to me—I told Clarence so that day, didn't I?" She didn't wait for a response, but went on, "It seemed to me that she was apologizing somehow."

"Did your daughter ever talk to you about children?"

"No. She knew how we felt, though. She was an only child. If she didn't give us grandchildren, we'd have nothing. Not that *he* would have let us see them," she added bitterly.

"Did Dawn tell you that Karl didn't want children?"

"No, but we suspected as much. After all, they had been married for five years . . ."

"Mrs. Smith . . ." Gemma hesitated. She didn't wish to cause Dawn's parents further distress, but she knew they had a right to know. "Your daughter was expecting a baby. She'd just had the pregnancy confirmed that afternoon."

"Oh, no," the woman whispered. "Not that, too. How could someone take that away from her—from us?" She fastened her gaze on Gemma. "Did *he* know?"

"Karl? He says not. Mrs. Smith, did you ever have reason to think Karl mistreated your daughter?"

"You mean, did he hit her?" Mrs. Smith's surprised expression seemed to indicate that this was one evil she hadn't attributed to her son-in-law. "No. She never . . . You're not thinking she told him about the baby and he—"

"We haven't ruled out any possibilities at this time," Kincaid told her. "Do you think your son-in-law could have—"

"No." Mr. Smith drew himself up, his mouth working in agitation. "No one who knew Dawnie could have done such a thing. And besides, the man was too... clean. You can't imagine him mussing his hands, or his shirt. Do you see what I mean?"

"I think so, yes," Kincaid answered soothingly. "Mrs. Smith, did Dawn have friends other than Natalie that she kept in touch with?"

"No. Natalie was her closest friend. It was only that kept him from driving them apart."

"And Dawn didn't mention anything else to you, something worrying her, or someone new in her life?"

"No." Mrs. Smith's eyes glistened with unshed tears, as if the lack of her daughter's confidences had added to her grief.

Gently, Gemma said, "If you remember anything else, Mrs. Smith, just give us a ring. We won't disturb you any further." She gave both parents her card, and thanked them.

But when she and Kincaid reached the car, she said, "You know, if Karl did abuse Dawn, she'd have kept it from her parents at all costs. To tell them, or let them see it, would have been to admit what a mistake she'd made."

Gemma arrived at work on Monday morning to find a copy of the previous day's *Daily Star* prominently displayed in the center of her desk. The headline screamed, "Slasher Strikes a Second Time in the Heart of Notting Hill."

"Bloody hell," she muttered as she skimmed the lurid account of Marianne Hoffman's and Dawn Arrowood's murders. "I'm going to kill the man."

"Had you not seen it, boss?" asked Melody Talbot, who had been passing by her office door. "I brought you my copy—thought you might want to have this MacCrimmon bloke drawn and quartered."

"It wouldn't do any good. The Hoffman case didn't attract all that much notice, but the record was available. All MacCrimmon had to do was put two and two together, and he's obviously quite adept at that. But I had hoped we could keep the details on the Arrowood case out of the papers for a few days."

"The throat-cutting went round the neighborhood like wildfire. I suppose the press were bound to latch on to it."

"Yes, but Tom MacCrimmon wouldn't have printed a rumor without some confirmation. Someone in the department must have given him the nod. I've heard he's free with the drinks." Gemma peered at the paper again. "There are similarities in the two cases, I have to admit." She'd spent the previous evening going over the Hoffman file. "But I'm not convinced that the Arrowood murder was random."

"What connection could there possibly be?"

"I've no idea. But I'm going to start by interviewing anyone who had recent contact with Dawn Arrowood. According to her diary, she took her cat to the vet on Friday morning. That seems as good a place to start as any."

Having found the address in Dawn's book, she presented herself at Mr. Gavin Farley's veterinary surgery on All Saints Road shortly after opening time. All Saints Road was the heart of the Notting Hill Carnival, but on this cold morning in mid-December it was hard to imagine the existence of the summer's color and activity. The surgery, its exterior painted the color of orange sherbet, provided a bright spot in otherwise drab surroundings.

A bell tinkled as Gemma pushed open the door. "Be right with you," a female voice called from behind the reception desk, then an auburn head appeared. "Sorry, receptionist's a bit late this—"

"It's Bryony, isn't it?" said Gemma. "I met you at Otto's on Saturday. Whatever are you doing here?"

"I'm Gavin's—Mr. Farley's—assistant." The young woman gazed back at her with equal surprise. "What are you doing here?"

"I've come to see Mr. Farley. According to Dawn's diary, she brought her cat in on the day she died."

"Oh, Tommy, rotten little beastie. Always getting in spats. Yes, she did bring him, and it was Gavin who saw him, not me. But what has that to do with her death?"

"I thought it possible she might have said something to Mr. Farley, confided something unusual she'd seen or heard, for instance. Could I see him?"

"Not in yet," Bryony replied with a grimace. "Doesn't take his first appointment until nine o'clock. Because I live just up the road, in Powis Square, Gavin tends to take advantage a bit."

"Were you here when Dawn came in on Friday morning?"

"Yes, but I was in and out with clients myself, so I didn't really—Oh, sorry," she broke off as the door chimed and a woman came in with two Dalmatians straining at their leads. Bryony expertly shepherded client and dogs into an examination room, then popped back out, saying to Gemma, "Look, I won't be a moment. Make yourself at home."

Gemma had never had much occasion to visit veterinary surgeries, having never owned a pet. Her parents had been adamant that animals and bakeries didn't mix—"Can't have customers worrying about dog or cat hair in their scones and buns, now can we?" her mother had responded cheerfully whenever Gemma or her sister had pleaded for a puppy or a kitten.

She found the surgery's atmosphere reassuring, with its faint smell of dog and disinfectant, leatherette-covered banquette seating along the walls, displays of the pet foods offered for sale, and posters of raining cats and dogs decorating the walls. A photo taped to the side of the reception computer caught her eye; she moved closer to examine it.

*Geordie,* the caption beneath the photo read. *Two-year-old neutered male cocker, blue roan. Needs good home.* The dog's coat was a pale, mottled blue-gray, with dark gray patches. A blaze in the lighter color divided the dog's alert, intelligent face, and his long, silky ears were dark. He seemed to gaze back at her, head tilted, the expression in his eyes, Gemma could have sworn, one of instant recognition. The dog reminded her of the spaniel in the painting Duncan's cousin Jack had recently given her, a memento of their time in Glastonbury.

"Lovely, isn't he?" asked Bryony, coming up behind her.

"Finished already?" Gemma looked round for the Dalmatians.

"I'm going to have to x-ray one of them—seems he's

eaten all the glass balls off the Christmas tree—amazing what dogs can digest—and for that I'll need Gavin's help." Bryony tapped the photo with her fingertip. "Are you interested in a dog, by any chance?"

"Why does the owner want rid of him?" Gemma asked warily.

"She's just married a man with a dreadful allergy to dogs—sends him to hospital with asthma. I think it was a close call between the dog and the husband," Bryony added, grinning, "but in the end she decided to keep the husband. But she won't let the dog go to just anyone."

"I'm just moving into a house in the area," Gemma heard herself saying. "With a garden."

"Geordie's a sweetheart. Owner's taken him through several levels of obedience classes. Do you have kids?"

"Two boys. Twelve and four."

"Perfect. Look, why don't I bring Geordie along to meet you one day this week? I've got your number from the other day—I'll ring you and make arrangements."

"But—" The chime of the front door cut Gemma off, and with a pang of regret, she realized she'd allowed herself to be maneuvered into a corner.

"Gavin," said Bryony, "this is Inspector James from the police. She'd like to have a word with you about Dawn Arrowood." Was there a touch of satisfaction in her voice?

Turning, Gemma saw a short, stocky, dark-haired man, his appearance made more solid by his white clinical tunic. He hung his overcoat on a peg, then faced her. "Such a tragedy. I couldn't believe it when I heard it on the news." He shook Gemma's hand warmly, but the glance he gave her was shrewdly assessing. "Anything I can do to help."

"Is there somewhere we could talk, Mr. Farley?"

"Come into the office, why don't you?" Gavin Farley ushered her inside, then closed the door of the small space, which contained a desk and files. Gemma slipped notebook and pen from her bag.

"Was Mrs. Arrowood a regular client, Mr. Farley?"

"More than regular, you might say. Her husband wouldn't allow her to keep the cat in the house, so the animal was always getting in scrapes—and coming off the worst in them, I suspect. Every few weeks he'd be in with an abscess, a torn ear, an infected eye. Not that we minded seeing Dawn, of course."

"Did you know Mr. Arrowood, as well?"

"No. He never came in with her, even the few times the animal was badly hurt. Seemed rather an unsympathetic character, if you ask me."

"And did you ever see Dawn outside the clinic?"

"No. I live in Willesden, so our paths weren't too likely to cross." If Farley was aware of any inference other than a casual social encounter, he disguised it well.

"And on Friday, did you notice anything unusual in her behavior?"

For the first time, Gemma sensed hesitation. "She did seem a bit more upset about the cat than usual, although it was a minor injury. In fact, I remember asking her if she was feeling all right."

"And?"

Farley's eyes flicked towards the door, then he looked back at Gemma and shrugged easily—too easily. "She said she was fine. Thanked me for asking, in fact. I still can't believe she's dead, or that someone would do such a terrible thing."

"I'm sure it must be difficult for everyone who knew her, Mr. Farley. So why do I have the feeling you're not telling me the truth?"

"I've no idea what you're talking about. Why would I lie about such a thing?"

"I don't know," answered Gemma. "But I can assure you I will find out."

Kincaid allowed the worst of the Monday-morning traffic to die off before he and Doug Cullen signed out a Rover from the Yard motor pool and headed north. Cullen drove, giving Kincaid the luxury of observing the London morning's ebb and flow. Daybreak had brought fitful sun, but Kincaid suspected the break in the weather would not hold.

They picked up the M1 just south of Hendon and were soon bypassing the cathedral town of St. Albans. "Didn't you tell me your family was in St. Albans?" Kincaid asked his companion. "It looks a nice place."

"Suburban hell," Cullen replied with a grimace. "Bridge nights and dinner circles and absolutely sod-all to do if you're under the age of forty. I can't imagine that my parents not only chose to live there, but considered it a great accomplishment."

"Still suffering from a bit of rebellion, I take it?"

Cullen glanced at him, as if to ascertain whether he was being teased. "I assumed most people felt that way about their parents' lifestyles."

"I don't know," Kincaid mused. "I rather envy my parents theirs. But twenty years ago, I couldn't wait to put the dust of the provinces behind me."

"And now, would you go back?"

"To live, maybe. To work in a small-town police force, after the Met—Now, that would be a bit more difficult." Kincaid thought again of taking Gemma and the children to Cheshire, sometime soon—perhaps this summer, to show off the new baby. His mum and dad were beside themselves with anticipation.

City and suburbs dropped away, revealing the rolling, winter-bleached farmland of Herefordshire. The power of the English countryside to assert itself never failed to amaze Kincaid, although he knew all too well it was more than ever under siege.

By mid-morning they had reached Bedford, a pleasant county town with a generous share of parks and the Great Ouse River running through its center. Eliza Goddard lived along the Embankment in a comfortable, semidetached Victorian house, a far cry from the tiny flat her mother had occupied above her shop in Camden Passage.

Goddard answered the bell quickly, calling back over her shoulder to quiet her children. Kincaid saw her surprise as she turned back to them, then the unconcealed mixture of wariness and distaste. "You've come about my mother, haven't you?" She did not invite them in. "Have you found out something?"

"Not exactly, Mrs. Goddard. But we would like to speak to you, if you could spare us a few moments," Kincaid said, at his most diplomatic. This woman surely had no reason to look fondly on the police: They had not only given her the terrible news of her mother's death, but had failed, after a lengthy investigation, to find her killer.

"All right." She said it reluctantly. "Just let me get the girls settled in the kitchen."

As Kincaid and Cullen followed her into the sitting room, Kincaid wondered, as he had the first time they'd met, about her parentage. Marianne Hoffman had been a slight, fair-skinned woman—her daughter had the lovely café-au-lait coloring and dark eyes indicative of mixed race. The twin daughters Eliza was shepherding into the kitchen took after their mother, each with dark hair neatly plaited into two pigtails.

"Let's get some colored paper, and you can make paper chains for the Christmas tree," he heard Eliza say. A moment later she rejoined them in the sitting room.

"How old are your daughters?" Kincaid asked her.

"Five. Going on fifteen." Eliza rolled her eyes, but her smile was indulgent.

"Identical?"

"Yes. All the child psychology books say you shouldn't dress them alike, but the authors apparently didn't consult my girls. They throw fits if I try to put them in different outfits. Maybe next year when they start school..."

Sensing Cullen's impatience, Kincaid gave him a quelling glance. "You've a great place here," he told Eliza, admiring the room's soft sage-and-cream paint-work and fabrics. Woven baskets held the children's toys neatly, and although the furniture looked casually worn, Kincaid suspected it was valuable. Gesturing at the oak sideboard, he said, "Eighteenth century?"

"Yes. My mother's passion, eighteenth-century farm-house furniture. She never bought it to sell; she said that would've taken the joy from the hunt. But she loved finding these pieces for me, and she's the one put the room together." Eliza sat down at last, and Kincaid and Cullen followed suit.

"She traded only jewelry in her shop?"

"Oh, sometimes she'd take in a table or a lamp, but she preferred to stick with the small things." Eliza brushed at her skirt and finally met Kincaid's eyes. "Look, what is this about?"

"I'm afraid there's been another death," Kincaid answered. "Similar to your mother's. But this time in Notting Hill—the wife of an antiques dealer."

"I don't understand. What has that to do with me?"

"There might be a connection."

"You mean the same man who killed my mother might have killed this woman, too?"

"It's possible, although we hope not."

"But how can I help you?" She sounded more bewildered than angry.

"Did you ever hear your mother mention the name Karl Arrowood?"

Eliza shook her head.

"Nor Dawn Arrowood? Or Dawn Smith?"

"No."

"What about Alex Dunn?"

"No. I'm sorry."

"Do you know if your mother had *any* connections in Notting Hill?"

"Not that I know of specifically, although people do get around in the antiques trade. But Mum never talked about her past. Sometimes I used to imagine that her life started with me."

"What about your dad? Could he help us?"

"I never knew my dad at all."

"His name was Hoffman?"

"That was my stepdad. Greg was okay; he even officially adopted me. But Mum divorced him when I was fifteen. I still see him sometimes. He sends Christmas and birthday cards to the girls."

Kincaid had run a check on Greg Hoffman after Marianne's murder in October. A textiles salesman, he'd been out of the country at the time of his ex-wife's death, and Kincaid had never interviewed him. "Do you know why Greg and your mother broke up?"

"Mum just said she didn't want to be married anymore. I missed him," Eliza added unexpectedly, glancing towards the sound of an escalating row in the kitchen. "I hope my girls never have to be without a dad."

"What do you remember about your childhood? Anything before your mother married Greg Hoffman?"

"We lived in York when I was little. Mum had a small shop there. She only moved back to London after I married and came to Bedford."

"Mummy!" came a cry from the kitchen. "Suki tore my loop!"

"I did not. Sarah made it too big. I was fixing it!"

"Excuse me." Eliza got up with a soft sigh and went to sort out her children.

Kincaid stood and gazed out the window at the river and the park running along beside it. Three swans glided by, unperturbed by human commotion.

"Not making much progress, are we?" Doug Cullen didn't bother to hide his exasperation.

"Too soon to say," Kincaid rejoined. He turned back

to Eliza Goddard as she reentered the room. "What about your mother's things, Mrs. Goddard? Did she leave any keepsakes? Or photos?"

"I haven't touched her personal effects." Eliza's eyes sparkled with sudden tears. "I just couldn't, not this time of year. I'm not even sure yet how we're going to get through Christmas... I don't think the girls understand their grandmother isn't coming back. They keep asking what Nana's giving them for Christmas."

"I'm truly sorry, Mrs. Goddard, and sorry to have to dredge all this up again. But if you could bring yourself to go through your mother's things, there might be something that would connect her with this latest murder." He couldn't recall having seen anything connecting Hoffman with either the Arrowoods or Alex Dunn, but he wanted to be absolutely sure he hadn't missed vital evidence.

"There is one thing," Eliza said hesitantly. "My mother always wore a heart-shaped silver locket. But it wasn't in the things you returned to us, and we didn't find it in the shop. I know you told us at the time there was no evidence of burglary, but—Might her killer have taken the locket?"

Melody Talbot sat down across from Gemma's desk and kicked her shoes off, stretching out her legs and examining them with a frown. One of her tights had ripped in the toe and she tugged at it in annoyance. "My feet will never be the same. This is the first time I've got off them in three days."

"Found anything worthwhile?" From the discouraged

expression on Melody's face, Gemma had not much hope of the answer. Gerry Franks had been in earlier with an equally discouraging report. He'd pressed her to talk to Karl Arrowood again, but she was determined to wait until she'd spoken to Arrowood's first wife.

"Surely there must have been joggers round St. John's at that time of the evening, but so far we haven't turned up anyone," Melody told her. "And none of the neighbors remember seeing anything out of the ordinary."

"Nor did I," Gemma murmured, but when Melody raised a questioning brow, she shook her head.

Melody winced and wiggled her feet back into her shoes. "Anything from forensics yet?"

"No. It's early days. But try telling the media that." Gemma pushed away the remains of a packaged sandwich and tepid tea. "If Karl Arrowood came home earlier than he said, he could have simply pulled up in the drive and attacked Dawn when she came home." Had she seen one car? Gemma wondered. Or two? But even if she had seen two cars, she might have passed by while Karl was looking for his wife in the house. None of the neighbors had reported a second car in the drive, but they had better double-check. "Why don't you go round the neighbors again, make sure no one saw Karl's Mercedes."

Melody groaned and stood up. "Yes, boss." At the door she turned back. "You might want to talk to the lady next door yourself. She didn't report seeing anything particular, but she's a friendly soul. And she's taken in Dawn Arrowood's cat."

·     ·     ·

Mrs. Du Ray lived just the other side of the Arrowoods' hedge. The house was semidetached, and Gemma saw that although the paint round the trim and windows was peeling, the garden was neatly tended and the door brass gleamed. Any lack of care must be due to insufficient funds rather than neglect, and lack of funds in this neighborhood was enough to arouse her curiosity.

A neat, gray-haired woman greeted Gemma with a friendly smile. "Can I help you?"

"Mrs. Du Ray? I'm Inspector James from the Metropolitan Police." Gemma bent to stroke Tommy, who purred loudly and butted against her legs.

"I see you two know each other," said Mrs. Du Ray as she led Gemma through the house and into the kitchen. "I'll just put on some tea."

"My constable said you were very hospitable."

"Most people are too busy rushing about these days to take the time. Especially the young mothers chauffeuring their children about. Gymnastics and ballet lessons and piano and martial arts. It's all very well, but when do they have time to be children? But you probably have young children yourself and think I should mind my own business. I admit I'm hopelessly old-fashioned."

"Not at all," Gemma assured her. "And I'm afraid I don't have the luxury of chauffeuring my children around, nor did my parents."

"Quite." Mrs. Du Ray spooned tea leaves into a delicate flowered teapot and covered them with boiling water.

Gemma relaxed in her chair, as Melody must have done before her, glad of the respite. It was a pleasant room, clean and well kept if a bit run-down, like the house's exterior. "Have you lived here long, Mrs. Du Ray?"

"Thirty-five years. My husband bought this house when we were first married. Now that's he's gone, and the children are all grown up and married themselves, I suppose I could set myself up nicely in a little bungalow somewhere if I were to sell. But it's hard to contemplate leaving such familiar surroundings, and so many memories."

Gemma found it difficult to imagine such a settled existence. Had Dawn contemplated living a good portion of her life in the house next door, perhaps raising children there? Through the wide window over the sink she could see its pale stucco walls rising above the hedge.

"Did Mr. Arrowood ask you to look after Tommy?" she asked when Mrs. Du Ray had handed her a teacup of the same delicate china as the pot.

"No. But by yesterday the poor creature was begging at my door, and it was obvious he hadn't been fed. I let him in and picked up some tins of food at the market. I don't know what Dawn fed him, but he doesn't seem fussy." Mrs. Du Ray made a little face as she sipped at her tea. "As for Karl Arrowood, I went round yesterday evening. I didn't want him to think I was taking liberties by caring for his wife's cat. But when I told him, he just shrugged and said, 'Do as you please.' It wasn't that he was rude exactly, just indifferent. I suppose that's understandable under the circumstances."

"It's kind of you to take in the cat."

"It's just decent," rejoined Mrs. Du Ray. She stroked Tommy, who had made himself at home on the dining chair beside her and was industriously washing a paw. "You'd have done the same."

"Did you know Dawn well?"

"Perhaps not as well as I should." At Gemma's questioning look, Mrs. Du Ray went on more slowly. "Beautiful, young, wealthy . . . it didn't occur to me that the girl might need friends. But now that I think about it, she spent a good deal of time in that house alone."

"How could you tell? You can't see their drive from your house, can you, because of the hedge?" As Mrs. Du Ray began to bristle, Gemma added hurriedly, "I don't mean to imply that you were prying. I'm just wondering what you would notice in the normal course of your day."

Mrs. Du Ray went back to petting the cat, relaxing again. "You're right. You can't see the drive from the downstairs windows. But I can see it when I'm working in the front garden, and I can see it from the bedroom windows upstairs. And I did notice, just the way you do, without really thinking much about it."

"You didn't happen to be upstairs on Friday, a few minutes after six?" But she saw instantly from the woman's face that she was going to be disappointed.

"No, dear, I'm sorry. I don't usually go upstairs that time of day. I was here in the kitchen, preparing my supper. A boiled egg and toast, I remember, as I'd been out to lunch with a friend."

"And you didn't hear anything?"

"Not a sound. Until the sirens, of course, and then I went out to see what had happened."

"Did you ever hear them arguing, Karl and Dawn?"

"Oh, no, nothing like that. They seemed the perfect

couple, always off to parties and dinners, and she was always dressed to the nines. But surely you don't think that Karl Arrowood had anything to do with Dawn's death? That's just not possible!"

"I know sometimes it's difficult to accept, but that is often—"

"No, no, that's not what I meant. I mean I don't believe Karl is physically capable of such a crime. I know how she died, you see. It's been whispered round the neighborhood."

"I don't understand."

"Karl is terrified at the sight of blood. He can't help it, I'm sure. My husband was the same way, from his childhood."

"How do you know?"

"I cut myself badly in the garden one day—a shard of broken glass had somehow worked its way into the front border—just as Karl and Dawn came home. I must have cried out, because Dawn came over to ask if I was all right, and Karl followed her. I thought the man was going to faint when he saw the blood running down my arm. Went white as a sheet and Dawn had to hold on to him. She took him inside, then ran me to the casualty ward at the hospital. She stayed with me, too, and brought me home again when they'd bandaged me up."

"That was kind of her. Did she confide in you at all? One tends to, in that sort of situation."

"No. Nor did she ever. You'd have this lovely conversation, and then later you'd realize you hadn't learned anything about her."

"That makes her an ideal candidate for sainthood, doesn't it?" reflected Gemma softly.

"You mean it allows people to make her into any-thing they want? I suppose I may have done that my-self. But no. There was something genuine there, I'm sure of it. And it's a great loss to everyone who knew her." For the first time, Mrs. Du Ray showed a hint of tears.

"Karl Arrowood, faint at the sight of blood? You're jok-ing." Kincaid glanced at Gemma, then focused his at-tention once more on the Kensington traffic. He'd dropped Cullen at the Yard before taking the motor pool Rover to pick Gemma up at Notting Hill.

"She was positive," answered Gemma. "And it's not the sort of thing you'd mistake."

"But an elderly lady—"

"Not elderly," she corrected. "Older. And sharp as a tack. And although Arrowood does seem an unlikely candidate, I've seen stranger things."

"If it's true, his phobia didn't prevent him from lift-ing the body of his dead wife."

"Shock might account for that. What I wonder is if he could have brought himself to cut her throat, and so decisively. There were no hesitation marks."

"Maybe he paid someone else to do it," Kincaid sug-gested.

"In that case, knowing what he would find, would he have touched her?"

"Has this turned you into an Arrowood apologist? I thought you were dead set on him as Dawn's killer."

"No," Gemma answered, a trifle crossly. "I mean no, I'm not ruling him out. I'm just playing devil's advo-cate."

"Well, let's see what the former Mrs. Arrowood has to say about him." They had reached Lower Sloane Street, a bastion of elegant and expensive red brick town houses, just below Sloane Square. Kincaid whistled under his breath. "He certainly set her up in style."

Gemma had rung ahead, suspecting that it might be difficult to pin down Karl's former wife without an appointment. Sylvia Arrowood must have been watching out for them because she opened the door before they rang the bell. She was tawny, slender, and extremely well preserved for a woman he guessed to be in her fifties. It intrigued Kincaid that she was the same physical type as Dawn Arrowood—had Karl been guilty of trading in the old model for the new?

"You must be the police," she said. "Can we do this as speedily as possible? I've an appointment." Her tone clearly said that her time was important and theirs was not.

Kincaid put on his most bland expression to hide his irritation. When he asked if they could sit down, she did not conceal hers. "We'll try to inconvenience you as little as possible, Mrs. Arrowood," he began as he took quick stock of the room.

It was filled with what he judged to be expensive antiques and objets d'art, but this was a room to be looked at, not lived in. There was something oddly off balance about it, and after a moment he realized what it was. The room was just slightly overcrowded, and he sensed this was due not to a love of the objects acquired, but to greed. Why have one priceless Georgian table, or Sèvres vase, when you could have two?

"...lovely flat," Gemma was saying.

Mrs. Arrowood perched on the edge of one of her gilded armchairs, watching them, her only acknowledgment a nod.

"You do realize why we're here?" Kincaid spoke a bit more sharply than he'd intended. "Your ex-husband's wife has been murdered."

"And why do you think that should be of particular concern to me? I never met the woman. I haven't seen Karl in years."

"How long have you been divorced?" asked Gemma with just a hint of sympathy in her voice.

"Thirteen years. Karl left me when Richard was eleven, and Sean, nine. Have you any idea what it's like to bring up boys that age on your own?"

"I can imagine," Gemma replied. "Mrs. Arrowood, we've been told that your husband had a vasectomy during his marriage to you. Is that true?"

Sylvia Arrowood stared at her. "Why on earth do you want to know that?"

"It's relevant to the case. I'm afraid I can't give out any details."

Shrugging, Sylvia said, "Well, I can't see any harm in telling you. I wanted another child after Sean, and the bastard went out, without discussing it with me, and got himself fixed. 'Just to make sure,' he said, 'that there won't be any accidents.' I never forgave him for that."

"No, I can see that." Gemma glanced at her notebook. "Mrs. Arrowood. Was your husband upset by the sight of blood?"

"How do you know about that? A shaving nick would make Karl swoon, as giddy as a girl." Sylvia smiled, but

Kincaid didn't get the impression that it was in fond remembrance. "You're not thinking the bastard murdered his little wife, are you? That's absurd!"

"Why?"

"Not just because he couldn't bear anything to do with blood. Karl's much too cruel for something so clean and quick. He likes to torture his victims slowly. And why would he do such a thing...unless she was having an affair?" Sylvia seemed to read confirmation in their expressions. "I see. Well, I can tell you, he'd have made her pay, all right, if he found out. But he'd have drawn it out—it's much more likely he'd have turned her out in the street with nothing, sent her back to whatever grotty suburb she came from. By the time he married her he didn't need money," she added bitterly. "He could afford to go slumming."

"Maybe he loved her," Gemma suggested.

Sylvia looked at her as if the comment were too absurd to deserve an answer.

"Mrs. Arrowood," Kincaid interjected, "are your sons close to their father?"

"No. Why do you ask?"

"Let's see, the elder, that would be Richard? He must be twenty-four now, and his brother, twenty-two?"

"I congratulate you on your math, Superintendent."

"And has either of them followed in their father's footsteps?"

"If by that you mean the antiques trade, no. They both work in the City. Richard's in insurance. Sean's in banking."

"Could you give me their addresses? Just routine," he added, seeing her instant wariness. No point in getting the wind up her any more than necessary at this point.

When she had complied, with obvious reluctance, he thanked her and they said good-bye.

"If one of the sons did it, they'd have to have known, or at least suspected, that Karl hadn't made any provision for them," Gemma observed when they were back in the car. "And what about Marianne Hoffman?"

"Maybe he left money to her, too," Kincaid suggested, and Gemma gave him a quelling look. "Okay, that's a bit far-fetched, I admit. But I think it's certainly worthwhile having a word with Arrowood's sons."

# CHAPTER SIX

Then in 1833, in response to a crisis caused by the scandalous overcrowding of graves in London's churchyards, fifty-six acres of land between the canal and Harrow Road to the west of the lane were purchased to create Kensal Green Cemetery, the first burial ground to be specifically built for the purpose in London.

—Whetlor and Bartlett,
from *Portobello*

BY THE WINTER of 1961, Angel could hardly remember a time when she hadn't been friends with Betty and Ronnie. Although Ronnie, she had to admit, had seemed different since he'd turned sixteen and left school. For one thing, he'd started referring to her and Betty as "little girls"; for another, he'd stopped listening to American pop music with them and started talking a lot of high-sounding nonsense about jazz and the black man's influence on the development of music. This in particular hurt Angel's feelings, making her feel as if she'd been deliberately excluded.

But Ronnie was smart, there was no doubt about that. He'd been taken on as an assistant at a local photographer's, and he roamed the streets of Notting Hill with the camera he'd bought with his wages. He intended to make something of himself, he told the girls, and he swore he'd never do manual labor like his dad.

"I wouldn't exactly call upholstering furniture 'manual

labor,' " Betty had snapped back. "It's a skilled trade. You make him sound like a navvy."

But Ronnie had no patience with her or with his parents, and saved every shilling he made towards the day when he could move into his own flat. The girls shrugged and learned to amuse themselves without him, although Angel missed his teasing and his bright smile more than she had imagined possible.

That autumn, she had finally badgered her father into buying a television, and the novelty helped a bit to fill the gap left by Ronnie's absence. They were one of the few families in the neighborhood to own such a thing, and it held pride of place in the sitting room. The girls huddled in front of the grainy black-and-white screen, watching the latest pop idols on Oh Boy! as Angel imagined herself older, glamorous, moving in the same exalted circles as the stars on the telly.

A moan from her mother's bedroom brought her swiftly back to earth. Her mother suffered more and more often from what she called "one of her headaches." She would vomit from the pain, and only darkness and quiet seemed to bring her any relief. Her father fussed about as helplessly as a child on her mum's bad days, and Angel coped with the household tasks as best she could.

Whenever possible, she escaped to Betty's. Although Betty's family had to share a bathroom on the landing with two other families, the flat was always filled with the scents of good things cooking and the cheerful sound of Betty's mother's singing. It was Betty's mum who taught Angel to prepare West Indian dishes, and to buy yams and aubergines and the strange, slimy okra pods from the stalls in the market. "Who goin' to teach you to cook if your own mother don't, girl," she'd said, shaking her head in disapproval.

But it had never occurred to Angel that there might be

*anything terribly wrong with her mother until the leaden
February day she came home from school and found the doctor
in the sitting room, his black bag by his side.*

"What is it?" she asked her father, her heart thumping
with sudden fear.

"Your mum's had quite a bad headache today." Her dad
looked exhausted, and for the first time she saw the deep lines
scoring his cheeks. "Even worse than usual. The doctor's given
her something for the pain."

"But why— What's wrong with her?"

"We don't know," answered the doctor, a portly, bald man
whose patient voice belied his stern expression. "I think we
shall have to take some pictures, Xrays, of your mother's brain.
Then we shall see."

"Will she have to have an operation?"

"That's one possibility, but it's too early to say."

"I'm sure she'll be fine," her father told her, sounding as if
he were trying to reassure himself as much as her. But Angel
somehow knew, in a moment of gut-squeezing terror, that her
life was about to change forever.

Anthony Trollope was buried here. And William
Thackeray," Kincaid told Gemma as she bumped the
car through the gates of Kensal Green Cemetery. It was
just before eleven o'clock on Tuesday morning, and they
had been told that Dawn Arrowood's remains were to be
interred in a graveside service.

"My God." Gemma stopped at the first junction of
roads and tracks that traversed the place. "It's immense.
I'd no idea." Kensal Green lay at the northern edge of
Notting Hill, tucked against the slow curve of the
Grand Union Canal on one side and the Harrow Road

on the other. A sign at the gate had informed them that this was a wildlife refuge, which meant that the grass was not mown nor the graves tended unless specifically directed by the owners of a plot. Desolate and shaggy under the gray December sky, the place had an air of comfortable decay. The bouquets of plastic flowers placed on the occasional grave looked pathetic and inadequate against the rank wildness of nature.

"It was a business. By the 1830s Londoners had run out of places to bury their dead. The churchyards were all full. So they formed a corporation to find land and build cemeteries. This was the first one, and very successful it was. It was quite the rage to be buried here." Seeing Gemma's dubious glance, Kincaid added, "Honestly. I'm not joking."

"And how do you know so much about it?"

"I've been here before," he replied, but didn't elaborate.

"Do you know how to find Dawn's gravesite, then?"

"Um, I'd go to the right, and look out for cars."

"That's very helpful," she said sarcastically, but did as he suggested. She followed the road for some way before she saw a dozen cars pulled up on the verge, empty. Away in the distance she glimpsed a knot of people in dark clothes, but the track leading in that direction was barred to motor traffic.

"Looks like we walk from here." Stopping the car, Gemma looked down at her shoes and grimaced. She'd been expecting something far more civilized. "Let's just hope it doesn't rain."

"I wouldn't tempt it," Kincaid warned, laughing, as he took her umbrella from the door pocket.

They walked along the track in silence. New headstones were interspersed among the older graves and monuments, but the newer markers were of shiny black marble and lacked the grace of their older counterparts.

"Now the Victorians," Kincaid remarked softly beside her, "they knew how to celebrate death."

Never had Gemma seen so many angels: angels weeping, angels on guard, angels reaching heavenwards. The quiet of the place began to seep into her and she found herself taking a long, deep breath. Nor was the landscape as desolate as she had first thought. The gnarled trees and thickets were alive with birds of every kind, and squirrels ran busily in the long grass. To the right she began to glimpse a building through the trees, a large structure with white, classical columns.

"The Anglican chapel," Kincaid told her. "Although *chapel* seems a rather meager term for such a grandiose affair. I don't think it's in use."

They approached the cluster of mourners, out of courtesy stopping a few feet away. An ornate coffin rested beside a dark hole in the earth, and at its head a black-robed cleric intoned the burial service. Karl Arrowood stood beside him in a black suit and overcoat, his head bowed, his gold hair glittering with drops of moisture. Dawn's parents stood opposite, as if trying to avoid contact with the widower. Gemma also recognized a softly weeping Natalie Caine, propped up by a stocky, cheerful-faced young man that Gemma assumed must be her husband; the remaining mourners appeared to be friends of Dawn's parents. "No unusual suspects lurking about," Kincaid murmured. "Worse luck."

The priest finished, closing his book. Karl Arrowood stepped forward and laid a single white rose on the coffin. Dawn's mother burst into anguished sobbing and her husband turned her away. Several people stepped up to Karl and shook his hand. With obvious reluctance, Natalie did the same, then gave Gemma a nod of recognition as she and her husband started back towards the cars.

Gemma and Kincaid waited until everyone had paid their respects. Arrowood stood as they approached, his hands in the pockets of his overcoat.

"Mr. Arrowood," said Gemma, "this is Superintendent Kincaid, from Scotland Yard."

"Do I take it this means the Yard has been called in? Perhaps you'll make some progress now in solving my wife's death."

"I'm investigating a different murder, Mr. Arrowood," Kincaid answered. "It took place two months ago, in Camden Passage. A woman named Marianne Hoffman was killed in the same manner as your wife. Did you know her?"

"No," said Arrowood, but he had paled. "Who was she?"

"Mrs. Hoffman sold antique jewelry from her shop in Camden Passage. She lived above the premises. Do you know of any connection your wife might have had with this woman?"

"You say this woman sold jewelry? I bought all Dawn's jewelry for her. She'd have had no reason to frequent a shop like that."

"When we spoke on Saturday, Mr. Arrowood," Gemma said, "and I told you your wife was pregnant when she died, you didn't happen to mention that you'd had a vasectomy prior to your marriage." She saw a small tick at the corner of his mouth, swiftly controlled.

"And why should I have thought such a personal matter was any of your business?"

"Because if you'd learned of the pregnancy, you would naturally have assumed that your wife had a lover. In my book, that makes an extremely strong motive for murder."

"If you are suggesting that *I* killed Dawn, Inspector, you had better be very careful. I loved my wife, although you seem to find that difficult to believe, and I had no reason to think her unfaithful. These procedures are known to fail, and *that* is what I naturally assumed."

"And you'd no idea before Mrs. Arrowood's death that she was pregnant?" Gemma asked.

"No. I've told you before. I knew she hadn't been feeling well, but that possibility didn't occur to me at the time, for obvious reasons. But now that I know, I will *not* entertain the idea that the child was not mine."

His face was set so implacably that Gemma wondered whom he most wanted to convince—them or himself? "Speaking of children, Mr. Arrowood, have you seen your sons lately?"

"My sons? What have my children got to do with this?"

"You told me the other day that you'd made it clear to them not to expect anything from you."

"I was fed up with them begging money for this and that. I never told them specifically—Surely you're not accusing them—"

"Money can be a powerful motivator. If they thought that Dawn's death would assure them of an inheritance—"

"No! That's absurd. I know my sons. They like things to come easily because their mother has spoiled them all their lives, but neither is capable of murder." Arrowood was visibly shaken.

"Nevertheless, our near and dear ones can sometimes surprise us," Kincaid commented.

Narrowing his eyes, Karl Arrowood retorted, "If you mean to intimidate me by badgering my family, Superintendent, it won't work. I'll be in touch with my solicitor as soon as I get back to my office."

"Both your sons are of age, Mr. Arrowood. We don't need your permission to question them. But this is simply a matter of following routine lines of inquiry, and the more cooperative everyone is, the sooner we can move on."

"Are you saying I should encourage my sons to talk to you?"

"Assuming they have nothing to hide, it would make the process easier for everyone."

Arrowood's smile was bitter. "You're assuming I have some influence over my children, Mr. Kincaid. Unfortunately, that's not the case."

"I thought they might be here today," Gemma put in mildly.

"They aren't here because I didn't invite them!" Arrowood snapped at her. "Why should I have given them the opportunity to disrespect Dawn in death as they did in life?"

"Perhaps they regret their behavior—"

"With their mother's constant poison in their ears? Highly unlikely."

"I'm assuming Dawn had nothing to do with the breakup of your marriage." Thirteen years ago, Dawn would have still been at school. "In which case, why did your ex-wife dislike her so much?"

"Because Sylvia is a spiteful bitch," he countered with grim amusement. "Does that answer your question, Inspector?"

Although Gemma felt inclined to agree with his assessment, she didn't say so. "What about your colleagues, Mr. Arrowood? Surely they might have come to support you today?"

"I didn't notify anyone at the shop. I meant this occasion to be private—or as private as possible," he amended with a glance at Dawn's parents and their friends, talking with the priest some distance away.

Gemma was suddenly furious with his callous disregard of the Smiths' feelings. "It's the least you could do for them!" she snapped. "You're not the only one who has suffered a loss."

Arrowood gave her a surprised look, then said slowly, "No, I suppose you're right."

"What do you have against your wife's parents?" Gemma asked. "I understand you've only met them briefly."

His eyes had gone cold again. "The fact that they are utterly and tiresomely middle-class."

"And you blame them for that?" she retorted. "As if it were a matter of choice?"

"Isn't it?" he asked. "Dawn chose to overcome her upbringing. So did I, for that matter," he added quietly, gazing at the nearby headstones as if seeking something familiar. Then he looked back at Gemma with a crooked smile. "If you'll excuse me, I had better pay my respects to my in-laws."

"There is one more thing, Mr. Arrowood," interjected Kincaid. "Do you know an Alex Dunn?"

"Of course I know Alex. I trade with him frequently. What has he to do with anything?"

"According to several sources, your wife was having an affair with him."

If Gemma had wished to see Karl Arrowood lose his infuriatingly tight control, she was now amply rewarded.

"Alex? An affair with Dawn? That's impossible!" Arrowood reached out for the nearest support, a block of lichen-stained granite.

"Why?" Gemma asked.

"Because—because Alex wouldn't—She couldn't—I won't even consider such a thing! Nor will I discuss it with you any further." His face was pinched with shock; the knuckles of the hand grasping the stone were white with strain. He turned away from them. "For God's sake . . . go."

"We will be speaking to you again, Mr. Arrowood," Gemma said, but he made no acknowledgment. Glancing back as they walked away, she saw Arrowood still standing over his wife's coffin, his head bowed, his shoulders sagging.

"Is he telling the truth?" Kincaid asked Gemma when they were once again ensconced in the warmth of the car. True to his prediction, the rain had begun again as they left the graveside.

"Which time?" Gemma's cheeks were pink from cold, her skin glowed, and damp tendrils of copper hair had escaped from her plait to curl round the edges of her face. It seemed to Kincaid in that moment that she was achingly beautiful, and he was about to tell her so when she added, "I'd swear he didn't know about his wife and Alex Dunn— Of course, that's assuming that what we've been told is true."

Disciplining himself into a professional state of mind, Kincaid wrenched his gaze away from her. "He didn't like the idea that his sons might be involved, either. If the thought had occurred to him before now, he's a bloody terrific actor."

Gemma frowned, tapping her fingertips on the steering wheel as the car bumped along towards the cemetery exit. "A good actor, yes. But somehow I think there's a vein of real grief for his wife in there somewhere."

"The human mind is a complex thing. It *is* possible that he could have killed her and yet still truly grieve for her."

He saw Gemma shudder as she said, "That's a hell I'd rather not contemplate. What about Alex Dunn, then? Everyone we've talked to says how much he loved her, but that doesn't mean he couldn't have murdered her. We've no idea what might have happened between them. . . . Maybe Dawn told him she was pregnant but that she wouldn't—or couldn't—leave Karl, and Alex lost it. . . . And if he wasn't involved in Dawn's death, why the hell has he disappeared from the face of the earth? His friends at the café and the woman in the arcade said he was terribly distraught—"

"You've requested a search warrant for his flat?"

"Melody had it in hand as we were leaving for the funeral."

"Then you'd better have her meet us there."

"Still no sign of Dunn's car," Melody had told Gemma when she'd rung the station.

As well as requesting all police forces to be on the lookout for Dunn's Volkswagen, Gemma had checked the previous address on his lease: a small flat in Kensington now occupied by someone who had never heard of him. His birth records had yielded as little. Alexander Dunn had been born in 1971 in a London hospital, to a mother listed as Julia Anne Dunn. No father was given, and the address of record, in the nether regions of Notting Hill, would have been a squalid bedsit in the early seventies. No one in the area remembered Julia Dunn, or her child.

Had he gone to university? she wondered. Would anyone know? Who had been close to Alex Dunn, except Fern and Dawn Arrowood?

She turned into the narrow mews, mentally congratulating herself as she pulled into a rare parking space. Alex Dunn's Volkswagen had not reappeared, nor was there any answer when she and Kincaid rapped on the flat's door.

There was a twitch, however, at the next-door flat's front window. "Ah, an interested neighbor," Kincaid murmured, and without consultation they retraced their steps and knocked next door. The window box was bare and the pavement round the door littered with wind-blown rubbish, but the door opened immediately.

The flat's occupant was a tall, rabbity man with stooped shoulders and thinning hair. He wore a meticulously darned cardigan the color of mud, liberally flecked with dandruff. "Can I help you?" he asked with an air of eager expectation.

Kincaid showed his warrant card. "We were wondering if we could have a word with you about your neighbor—"

"My tenant, actually. So what's young Dunn done?" He giggled at his own humor. "Oh, forgive me, I'm Donald Canfield. Do come in."

The murky flat smelled sourly of cabbage and un-washed flesh. Although Canfield seated them on a sofa facing a large television, Gemma could see an armchair carefully positioned by the front window, and her hopes rose.

"We wondered if you might know where we could find Mr. Dunn," Kincaid said, after refusing Canfield's offer of refreshments, much to Gemma's relief.

"It's about that woman, isn't it? The blonde, the one that got her throat slit. I saw her picture in the news-papers."

"Dawn Arrowood. Had you seen her with Mr. Dunn?"

"Oh, yes. She came here to his flat for months, almost always in the daytime. I did wonder if she was married. I heard them, too, if you know what I mean," he added, with a sly glance at Gemma. "Walls in these old houses aren't what they should be. And she was very... enthu-siastic." He giggled again.

Repelled, Gemma scowled and looked away.

Kincaid had no such scruples. "Did you ever hear them arguing, as well?"

"No, no, I can't say as I did. Although that's not true of the other one."

"What other one?" asked Gemma.

"The little girl with the streaked hair. Oh, they had some terrific rows, she and Alex, when Alex first started seeing the blond woman. But she hasn't been around for months, until the other day."

"The other day?"

"Saturday. The day after the murder. The girl came here with Alex. Then they got straight into his car and drove away. Funny thing was, *she* was driving."

"Did you see them come back?"

Canfield pursed his lips in disappointment. "I left just after that, I'm afraid. A visit to my sister in Warwickshire. I just returned last night. I didn't know, you see, that it was the blond woman who had been murdered. I'd have stayed here, otherwise, even if it did get up my sister's nose."

"What about the evening before, Mr. Canfield?" asked Kincaid. "Were you here then?"

"Yes, yes, I was."

"Did the blond woman visit Alex that afternoon or evening?"

Again came the little moue of disappointment. "Not that I saw. But I'm a busy man, of course, and I might have missed her."

"Of course," Kincaid agreed. "What about Alex? Did you see him coming or going that evening?"

"I know he came home around five: I looked out when I heard his car. Then he left again just as the news came on the telly, but walking this time."

"What were you watching?"

"Channel One. I always prefer Channel One."

That would have been half past six, then, if the man was to be relied upon, thought Gemma. And if Dawn had died a few minutes earlier, it seemed unlikely that Alex Dunn could have killed her.

"Do you know anything about Alex, Mr. Canfield?" she asked. "Who his friends are, or if he has family?"

"No. He tends to keep himself to himself," Canfield said stiffly, and Gemma read the history of rejection in his expression.

"Is he a good tenant, then?" she pressed, daring him to find something good to say about Alex Dunn. "Neat? Timely with his rent?"

"Well, yes." Canfield admitted it reluctantly. "Although I don't know as I want a tenant in my property that's been involved in a murder..."

"We don't know that he is involved in Mrs. Arrowood's death, Mr. Canfield," she said, knowing perfectly well that the man wouldn't miss the excitement for the world. A flash of black and orange outside the front window heralded the arrival of a panda car and Melody Talbot.

Kincaid stood and thanked Mr. Canfield, shaking his hand, but Gemma pretended not to see the limp digits proffered in her direction.

"Nasty little pervert," she muttered, knowing Canfield was watching them avidly from the window. It made the hairs rise on the back of her neck. "Maybe he developed an obsession with Dawn, watching her coming and going next door and knowing what they were up to—"

"He could have followed her easily enough and learned where she lived," Kincaid agreed. "Then lain in wait for her that evening—"

"Right," replied Gemma, rolling her eyes. "Canfield doesn't look fit enough to have attacked a kitten. And if he was out murdering Dawn, how would he have known what time Alex left his flat? Still, I suppose it wouldn't hurt to run a check on him."

Melody, having been obliged to turn the panda car round and seek a parking space outside the mews, reappeared at the top of the road. "I've got the warrant," she called out as she neared them. "And a locksmith coming."

"I'd assume Mr. Canfield has a key," Kincaid told her.

"But let me give it a try." He carried a small set of professional lock picks, and Gemma knew he enjoyed an opportunity to practice his skills.

"I don't think it's very likely we'll find him here," he said quietly as he bent over the lock. "As Canfield saw him leave in his car, and the car hasn't been returned. Besides, there's no smell."

Gemma grimaced at his reassurance. "Might have topped himself somewhere else, though," she offered.

"Then what happened to the girl who was driving? The one with the interesting hair?"

"Fern Adams."

Kincaid glanced up at her, one ear still tuned to the sound of the tumblers he was manipulating.

"His ex-girlfriend. The one his friends at the café said was determined to help. And a witness saw Alex leave the arcade with her."

"Then where are they now?" asked Melody. "Do you have an address for her?"

"No. I know she lives nearby, but Dunn's car hasn't been spotted anywhere in the district."

"Got it!" Kincaid exclaimed as the door swung open.

He entered cautiously, calling out and turning on light switches with his handkerchief. There was no reply, and it was soon apparent that the flat was unoccupied.

The bedroom was at the front, sharing a wall with Mr. Canfield's sitting room, Gemma realized with distaste. A pair of trousers lay across the unmade bed as if they had been carelessly tossed; the dressing table held a hairbrush, a bowl of pocket change, and two lovely blue-and-white vases; the two bedside tables held stacks of antiques magazines and Christie's catalogues. In the wardrobe, Gemma found two suitcases and a duffle bag along with neatly folded and hung clothes. There was no indication that Dunn had packed for a trip. Nor could any room have looked less like the scene of an illicit love affair.

A dark, glossy green tile surrounded the tub, men's toiletries were ranged round the sink, and the bath gave off the faint but unmistakably masculine scent of soap and aftershave. There was no sign of regular occupation by a woman.

"He uses an expensive electric razor," Kincaid commented. "You'd think that if he'd meant to go away, he'd have taken it."

Everything in the sitting area had been painted a warm cream, including the cabinets in the kitchen at one end. Gemma wondered if Alex had been trying to wipe out any trace left by his landlord, as she couldn't imagine the decoration being the product of Donald Canfield's imagination, but the most practical reason for the vanilla hue of the walls and carpet was obvious: It displayed Alex's collection at its best.

Lovely examples of blue-and-white porcelain were scattered about the room on small tables, shelves, and desk, and one wall held a glass display cabinet filled with colorful Art Deco pieces that made her gasp in delight.

French doors led out to a small enclosed garden. A flagstone patio held pots of now withered geraniums and a white iron table with two chairs. Gemma imagined Alex and Dawn sitting there on a warm evening, engrossed in one another, and felt a twinge of sadness.

"Another dead end," Melody said with a sigh of discouragement.

"Not entirely," countered Gemma. "It at least lets us rule out the possibility that Dunn came back here and killed himself in despair over Dawn's death."

"Dunn didn't disappear until Saturday morning," Kincaid pointed out. "If he killed Dawn on Friday night, then returned to the flat, he certainly hasn't left any obvious evidence."

"We'll get forensic in, just in case. But in the meantime," Gemma added, "I'm going to find Fern Adams."

Gemma combined an information-seeking stop at Otto's Café with a belated lunch, served to her by the cheerful Wesley. Kincaid had returned to the Yard to begin background checks on Karl Arrowood's sons.

Otto, Wesley told her as he served her a bowl of steaming lentil soup, was out for the day. He didn't elaborate. Was he regretting his forthrightness when they had spoken before? Gemma wondered.

"Perhaps you can help me," she said when she'd finished her soup and he'd come to take away her dish. "Have you seen Fern Adams since she left here on Saturday?"

"No. That's a bit odd, too. She's usually in here every day for a coffee."

"Nor Alex?" Gemma knew that constables inquiring after Alex would have asked here, but she wanted to hear for herself what Wesley had to say.

Wesley shook his head, his mobile face portraying worry. "You'd think the man had vanished into a bloody great hole. No one's heard a thing from him. Do you think— He wouldn't— He was that upset . . ."

"I'd be more concerned if he hadn't left his flat with

Fern—we've a witness who saw them. It's Fern I'd like to talk to now. Do you know where I could find her?"

"She lives in Portobello Court. I don't remember the flat number, but I can tell you where it is." He gave Gemma detailed directions. "Don't mistake me," Wesley added, "Miz Arrowood's murder was a terrible thing, only I didn't know her. But if anything's happened to Alex or Fern . . . They're like family."

"Do you have family of your own?"

"My mother." Wesley's face split in a brilliant smile. "She lives down Westbourne Park." Sobering, he added, "My dad's been gone a few years now. Heart attack."

"You stay with your mum?"

"Can't afford nothing else, you know what it's like," answered Wesley with no hint of complaint. "But even if I could, I'd not want to leave my mum on her own. She's a good woman, my mother."

Gemma said good-bye and walked thoughtfully back up Portobello Road. Would her children have such care for her when they were grown?

Portobello Court was the first modern block of flats built by the Council after the war, containing such sought-after amenities as indoor plumbing and separate kitchens, and she knew that many flats had been occupied by the same families since the fifties.

Following Wesley's directions, she climbed the stairs to the first floor and knocked on what she hoped was the right door. A door across the corridor opened and an elderly lady peered out at her, shaking her head.

"You looking for that girl? Rings in her nose, and

Lord knows where else. Don't know what the world's coming to."

"Do you know where she is?"

"Been holed up in the flat for days, far as I know. Don't know how she expects to make a living if she doesn't get out and scour the countryside. That's what it takes to turn a profit, you know. My husband was in the trade, had a stall next to her daddy."

With some assurance that Fern was at home, Gemma turned and knocked again, more loudly, and this time she was rewarded by the sound of shuffling and the click of a latch.

The young woman who gazed out at her did indeed have a ring through her nose, and another through her eyebrow, but her small, pale face was devoid of makeup, and the multihued strands of her hair looked flattened and neglected.

"Miss Adams? I'd like to talk to you about Alex Dunn."

"What about him?" The sight of Gemma's warrant card had not prompted the woman to open the door wider.

"Do you happen to know where he is?"

"Why should I?"

The door of the flat opposite creaked open an inch.

"Do you think I might come in?" Gemma gave a pointed glance at the obvious eavesdropper.

"Yeah, I suppose. Old cow," Fern added under her breath, but she stepped back, allowing Gemma into the flat. Boxes and tag-ends of furniture cluttered the space. Gemma could see no rhyme or reason for the arrangement of items—a set of mahogany side chairs faced a wall, a matching settee had its back cozily against the television, side tables stood adrift among lamps and pictures. A glimpse out the glass balcony doors revealed an equally unprepossessing view; large men's underclothing hung out on a makeshift clothesline, and there were a few drooping potted plants.

Gemma gestured at the boxes. "Are you moving?"

"No. My dad travels—the auction circuit. He brings things home, and so do I. This is about as sorted as we get." Fern cleared a chair of several old tasseled lampshades, which Gemma took as an invitation to sit.

"Have you been traveling this week?"

"Yeah." Fern rubbed at a spot on the back of her hand, a liar's gesture. When Gemma didn't speak, she added, "Estate sales, country markets, you know the sort of thing."

"What about Alex? Is he traveling as well?"

Fern shrugged with great casualness. "Dunno. Haven't seen him."

"But you have seen him since Dawn Arrowood died. The two of you left the arcade together."

The girl's startled glance met Gemma's, then she looked deliberately away. "I took him home for a cuppa. He was a bit wobbly and all. Why do you want to know about Alex, anyway?"

"I understand he and Dawn were quite close. She might have told him something that would help us find her killer."

"You mean, like, if someone had been bothering her?"

"Exactly. Or maybe he noticed someone hanging round her. Or, say if her husband had threatened her, she might have told Alex." When Fern nodded without comment, Gemma added, "Would Alex have told you?"

"Not likely. Dawn Arrowood wasn't exactly a topic of discussion between us."

"Not even on Saturday morning? You must have talked about her murder."

"He wouldn't believe it at first, when Otto told him. But then he went to her house. It was crawling with coppers and one of the neighbors told him her throat had been cut. After that he was, like, a zombie or something."

"And after you brought him back here for a cup of tea?"

Fern shrugged again. "I suppose he went home."

"You let your good friend go home alone in a terrible state of shock?"

"I offered to stay with him, but he didn't want me."

Gemma studied her for a moment. "All right, Fern, that's enough of the games. Alex's landlord saw the two of you leave in Alex's car that morning, with you driving. Where did you go?"

"Don't know what you're on about," Fern retorted, but Gemma had glimpsed the flash of fear in her eyes.

"Yes, you do. Do you also know that you could face charges for interfering with a police investigation?"

"I don't know where he is!"

"I don't believe that. You left together in Alex's car on Saturday morning, and neither Alex nor his car has been seen since. We've put out a bulletin on his car registration; we *will* find it, but the sooner we talk to Alex the better for him."

"But he hasn't done anything—"

"Why would he disappear like this, unless he had something to do with Dawn's death?"

"Because he's in danger!" Fern scowled at Gemma, but her lip was trembling.

"Alex? Why should Alex be in danger?"

"Otto knows Karl Arrowood, and he says that if Karl killed his wife, Alex could be next."

"If Alex has some evidence that Dawn was murdered by her husband, he needs to give it to the police as soon as possible. Tell me where he is."

"No. I can't tell you because I don't know. I took him for a drive, then I took him back to the flat." Fern's hands were balled into fists now, and in spite of her frustration with the girl, Gemma found something about her defiance endearing.

With a sigh, she said, "I hope Alex appreciates your loyalty."

Something flickered in Fern's face—an instant of doubt? Hesitation? Then it was gone and her lips were clamped in a stubborn line. "I'm telling you, I don't know where he is."

"All right, Fern." Gemma stood, tucked her notebook in her bag, and handed Fern her card. "But I'll be back. And in the meantime, you think about whether you really want Alex to go to jail for evading the police and impeding a murder inquiry."

As soon as she reached the station, Gemma organized a twenty-four-hour watch on Fern Adams's flat and requested access to Fern's phone records. She had absolutely no doubt that Fern knew where Alex Dunn was, and that the young woman would contact him.

When her own phone rang with a summons to Superintendent Lamb's office, she thought nothing of it; her super regularly called her in to discuss cases in progress.

But to her astonishment, Lamb cleared his throat and said, "Gemma, Sergeant Franks has been to see me. I thought you should know that the sergeant has expressed some concern over your progress on this case. He feels that not enough pressure has been put on Karl Arrowood, as the obvious suspect in the murder of his wife—"

"Sir. You know that we don't have one single bit of concrete evidence. I can't confront Karl Arrowood with nothing but dicey forensics and supposition, and I certainly can't make a case to the CPS—"

"I realize that, Gemma. I'm not questioning your judgment. In fact, it seems that as well as being wealthy, Arrowood has quite a reputation for supporting charitable causes like helping the homeless. The Commissioner has had calls from a friend of Mr. Arrowood's in the Home Office, and from two prominent MP's, expressing concern for Arrowood, and he has in turn been breathing down my neck. We're certainly not going to make any rash charges at this point, although our clearance rate is under scrutiny—" He stopped and waved his hand in a dismissive gesture. "But you know all that, and that's not why I called you in here. My immediate concern is your communication with Sergeant Franks—"

"But sir, you must know that Franks resents all the female officers. He's done his best to undermine my authority since I started here."

"I also know that Gerry Franks is an experienced and able officer, and you're not doing yourself any favors by allowing personal—or gender-related—differences to sabotage your working relationship. He could be a valuable resource to you, and I don't have to tell you that we need this department to run as efficiently as possible. See what you can do to remedy the problem, eh?" It was clearly a dismissal.

"Right." Gemma stood. "Thank you, sir. If that's all—"

When Lamb nodded, she left the office, her cheeks flaming with embarrassment. She had gone out of her way to defer to Gerry Franks, trying to allow him to retain some of his dignity, and this was the thanks she got. Of course she'd been aware of his thinly concealed insubordination, but this was absolutely the last straw. She would have to find a way to deal with him. And then her own doubts flooded over her.

*Had* she done everything possible? *Had* she let her concern with her pregnancy and her future cloud her judgment? And if that were the case, how could she repair the damage?

# CHAPTER SEVEN

When the Caribbeans began to arrive in the fifties and early
sixties Notting Hill was still depressed and underdeveloped.
This was the sort of London no one cared for, or cared about.
Its devastation wasn't the result of bombing, so the mythol-
ogy which the wartime and post war propagandists assem-
bled around the East End passed it by; and unlike the East
End's acres of crumbling Victorian warrens, it contained a
stock of large well-built homes.

—Charlie Phillips and Mike Phillips,
from *Notting Hill in the Sixties*

*SHE WATCHED HER mother fade away, day by day, month by
month. The doctor's X rays had revealed a tumor in the front
part of her brain, growing down into her nasal passage; surgical removal was deemed impossible. There were medications, of
course, that might slow the tumor's growth, but as they made
her mother violently ill and did not appear to affect the tumor,
they were quickly stopped.*

*And yet, her father refused to give up hope. "Maybe today
there will be some improvement," he would say every morning,
long after Angel knew that the only possible improvement to her
mother's condition was death.*

*She did the necessary sickroom nursing without complaint,
but she loathed it. She hated the dark bed, the heavy brown-
and-rose wallpaper, the smell of sickness, her mother's silent acquiescence. Most of all, she hated her mother. How could her*

*mother abandon her, and with so little fuss? Did her mother not love her at all? Didn't parting from one's only child deserve a bit of drama, at least some railing at God?*

*But her mother only smiled her gentle smile, drifting in and out of her morphine-induced dreams, and when she began to fret from the pain, the doctor would increase her dosage.*

*As the tumor pressed its way forward, her face began to sag as if it were a plastic mask left too long before the fire; one eye socket slid down and canted sideways, her nose twisted, her forehead bulged. The pain intensified then; a simple touch would make her cry out, so that Angel could hardly bear to bathe her.*

*And then came the day when there was no flicker of recognition in the damaged eye, and the sole response to Angel's entreaties a soft, continuous moaning.*

*Angel fled next door, into Mrs. Thomas's comforting arms. Sobbing, she demanded, "Is she still in there somewhere? Or has her soul gone to God already and her body's just waiting?"*

*"I don't know, child," answered Mrs. Thomas, wiping her own tears with the tip of her apron. "Seems to me she's somewhere in between, still connected to her poor body but reaching out for the next place."*

*"But can she hear me?"*

*"I suspect she can, but she don't have the strength to answer. So you keep talking to her, child, tell her you love her, that she's goin' to be all right."*

*Angel went back, resolute, but try as she might, she could not bring herself to say those words to the unfamiliar thing her mother had become. She sat in silence, and gradually the fear came on her that God had frozen her tongue as well as her heart. When her father came home at last, she'd huddled in the same position for so long that he had to lift her and carry her from the room like a baby.*

*After that, the end came soon, and on a bitter January day,*

Angel walked in procession to Kensal Green. It was the coldest winter in memory; snow lay grimy in the gutters, and Angel's wrists and knees were blue beneath the sleeves and hem of the coat she had outgrown. There had been no one to notice, no one to help her shop for a new one.

The Thomases were there, dressed in their best but standing a little apart, and some of her father's friends from the antique stalls and the café. The service was of necessity brief, and it was too cold for weeping. Her father had made a temporary marker, in lieu of the granite stone that would take several months to carve. Miriam Wolowski, it read. Went to Sleep January 9, 1963. Many of the other headstones said the same, Angel noticed, and she felt a hot anger that people couldn't speak the truth. "Asleep" implied that a person would wake up, would come back to you: That was something her mother would never do.

Her father had managed to provide a few cold meats and tea for the mourners, but no one stayed long. When the last guest had left, Angel looked round the neglected flat, at her father, gaunt and hollow-eyed, collapsed in his chair, and wondered how she would bear it.

She did the washing up, mechanically, and when her father fell into a doze in front of the television, she slipped out the door.

All the Thomases were home, even Ronnie, which was unusual these days, and they, too, were gathered round the television. As Mrs. Thomas patted the sofa beside her, Betty made an awkward attempt at normality. "There's a new group from Liverpool on tonight. They're supposed to be super."

But Angel had more important things on her mind. "Mrs. T, could I talk to you?"

"Of course, child."

"I mean, in the kitchen?"

"*I suspect you could use a proper cup of tea, after this afternoon,*" said Mrs. Thomas, rising and leading Angel to the scrubbed, square table. To the others, she called back, "*Now, you tell us when those boys come on.*"

When she'd made Angel a steaming cup of milky tea, she sat and picked up the sewing that was her constant companion. "*Now, what's worrying you, child?*"

Angel swallowed hard. "*Mrs. T, now that my mother's gone, could I come and live with you?*"

Mrs. Thomas stared at her. "*What you be thinkin', girl? That's the craziest thing I ever heard!*"

"*I could share with Betty; she wouldn't mind. And I don't eat mu—*"

"*That's got nothing to do with it, Angel. We feed you mos' the time as it is, and that's never been a burden. But you have to think about your poor father. Who would look after him in his time of need? And what would people say, a nice white girl boarding with a black family?*" She shook her head in dismay. "*You have to think on your place in life, girl, and that's something that's jus' not done.*"

"*But—*"

"*You know I love you like my own child, and so does Clive. You were the first person who ever showed us a kindness when we came here, and we've never forgot that. But that doesn't mean you don't have to do what's right, and you know it, too.*"

Angel could only nod, desperately trying to keep the tears at bay. Of course, Mrs. Thomas was right; she had known it in her heart, but the rejection bit deep, and with it, her last small flicker of hope winked out.

Jane Dunn put down the phone and stood staring at the glass ornament she still held in her hand. She'd bought a Christmas tree that morning from a local nursery, one of her customers, choosing the largest fir available. Now it rose bravely towards the kiln roof, hung with a multitude of tiny white lights, and decorated with the hand-blown glass ornaments she'd bought Alex on a trip to the Black Forest when he was ten. Did she hope the tree would cheer him? Or her?

What it had done was bring back a rush of memories of his childhood; Alex as a solemn yet charming little boy, possessing the gravity of those children who are brought up in the company of adults. Jane had had no experience with mothering, after all, had not known how to treat him except as a friend and companion.

Her sister, Julia, had appeared without warning one day at her door, holding the small, towheaded boy by the hand. Julia had left years before, after a blazing row with their father over her irresponsible behavior. She'd slammed out of the house, taking nothing with her, vowing never to come back.

Their parents had died of grief. Jane knew this as well as she knew herself, even though the coroner's certificates had read heart failure and stroke. The loss of their volatile, favored, younger daughter had been more than the Dunns could bear.

They had left Jane the house, the land, and a little money. She had set out to find a way to support herself—and she had vowed she would never love anyone, or anything, as much as her parents had loved Julia.

Jane hung the ornament on the tree, watching it swing until it fell still. Was this how she had failed Alex? For she had come to feel, in the last three days, that she *had* failed him, that she had not given him the core of emotional strength he needed.

Or was this his mother's legacy, the fatal crack in the porcelain not seen until now? Years ago, Julia, hollow-eyed and emaciated, had pushed her frightened child away from her, promising Jane she'd come back for him in a few days. For months afterwards, Alex had stood every day at the end of the drive, watching, waiting, but his mother never returned.

Jane had spent much time and money at first trying to trace her sister, but gradually it had seemed less urgent. She and Alex settled into their life together, and by the time he started school she had given up the search altogether. When Alex questioned her as he grew older, she'd told him his mother was dead.

With a last look at the Christmas tree, she left the sitting room and went out into the drive. The early December dusk would settle in soon, and Alex had not returned. Every day he left the house after breakfast, walking as if he could escape his grief, returning only as it grew dark. In the evenings he ate whatever she'd prepared for supper without seeming to notice what it was, and then he began to drink.

As Alex had enjoyed his wine but had never been more than a moderate drinker, this worried Jane greatly, but she didn't know how stop him. Unable to sleep, she began checking on him in the middle of the night. Once, near dawn, she'd found him poring over his boy-hood collections, as if he found some solace in touching the birds' eggs, the nests, the bent and tarnished spoons; and once, asleep, his body wrapped around a pot-tery teapot as if he were cradling a child.

During the day, her every attempt at conversation or confidence had been met with the same blank stare, as if she spoke a language Alex could no longer comprehend. But now she knew she must try to reach him.

Fern had rung from London, saying that the police were looking urgently for him, and that they had even threatened her with arrest if she didn't reveal his whereabouts.

Whatever Alex had seen, or done, or knew, she must convince him to go back to London and face up to it. If she let him go on in this way, she would be compounding her own failure. Nor could she go on watching him disintegrate before her eyes. It came to her, with the cold breeze that eddied off the marsh, that time and familiarity had betrayed her, concealing the fact that she had long ago broken her own vow.

Gemma rang down to the incident room and summoned Gerry Franks. When he appeared, his sneer more apparent than usual, she settled back in her chair and laced her fingers together.

"I've just had a word with the guv'nor, Gerry," she began conversationally. "He tells me you're unhappy with my handling of the Arrowood case. I'd like to know why you didn't come to me first if there was something you thought needed to be addressed."

"Figured you had more important things to do than listen to your sergeant," he said. Watching the swift calculation cross his face, she knew that diplomacy was not going to be enough. "What do I have to offer compared to Scotland Yard?"

"You're a good, experienced officer and I depend on you more than I've let you know," she replied. "I'm sorry if I've made you feel you were left out of the loop. We've no hope of solving a case this difficult without working as a team, communicating and cooperating, and I intend to do a better job of both. What about you?"

"What about Arrowood, then? We've danced round him like butterflies on a bloody daisy."

"Karl Arrowood is a powerful man, and we'd be mad to antagonize him more than absolutely necessary. Not to mention the fact that we have half a dozen other strong leads that need following up, including finding Alex Dunn, and we cannot leave out the possible connection with Marianne Hoffman's murder. If you don't feel you can work within those parameters, I can ask to have you transferred off the case." Pausing to let the threat sink in, she added pleasantly, "But I'd like you to stay, Sergeant. You're an asset to this investigation, and I'd be hard put to replace you."

She saw him struggling between his anger with her and the salve to his vanity. When he cleared his throat and sat up a bit straighter, she knew vanity had won. "This Hoffman woman. Might help if I had a look at the file."

"I'll send a copy down to you. In the meantime, I'd like you to go through the house-to-house reports once more. Someone has *got* to have seen something that we've missed."

When he left, he stopped at the door and gave her a brusque nod. It seemed a token of grudging respect, and she thought it might be a while before he realized he'd been assigned to paperwork Siberia.

Reaching for the phone to ring Melody Talbot,

Gemma realized her hands were trembling. It was then that the pain struck. A radiating web, it encircled her abdomen, squeezing, making her gasp for breath. How long it lasted she didn't know, but at last it receded, leaving her shaken and sweating.

She waited, deliberately slowing her breathing, alert to the slightest sensation, but the cramping didn't come back. She moved, gingerly at first, then ran her hands over the gentle swell of her abdomen. Had she felt a flutter, a faint tickle of movement? Surely it was too soon, she thought, but the sensation reassured her.

She was all right, the baby was all right, everything was going to be all right.

Melody came into her office balancing two Starbucks cups. "Decaf latte," she announced. "Just the way you like it."

"You must be able to read minds." Gemma wrapped her hands round the cup gratefully.

Sitting with her own coffee, Melody studied her. "You okay, Gemma? You seem a bit pale."

"I'm fine. Really. Melody, do you know Otto Popov, the man who runs the little café on Elgin Crescent?"

"A nice bloke. Russian, but that you must have gathered. First generation, as I think his parents came over after the war, when he was a child."

"Any idea why he would want to see Karl Arrowood blamed for his wife's death?"

"None...but..."

"But what? Out with it, Melody. I need to know."

"Um, I don't know why it would have anything to do

with Arrowood, but I have heard vague rumors about Otto.... Something to do with the Russian Mafia. I wouldn't give any credence to that sort of talk. In my opinion, it's just prejudice combined with idle gossip."

"Know anyone who'd know more?"

"As in 'off the record'?" Melody thought for a moment. "Yeah. Maybe. I'll see what I can do. And in the meantime, you've got media vultures waiting in the anteroom for their afternoon bulletin."

"We are still pursuing multiple leads," Gemma told the gathered reporters, sensing their disappointment in the lack of new developments. She plowed on, looking directly into the eye of the Channel 4 video camera and ignoring Tom MacCrimmon's probing gaze. "If anyone in the neighborhood of St. John's Church last Friday evening saw anything out of the ordinary, please ring this number." Her hope of a response was dwindling; it had been two days and not one legit call had been received.

Excusing herself, she pushed through the group and out the front entrance, but MacCrimmon was right behind her.

"Buy you a drink, Inspector?" he asked, looking as innocent as a puppy.

"You think I'd have a drink with you after that headline the other day?"

"Just doing my job. Surely you're not cross with me for that? Come on"—he gestured towards the pub across the street—"you look like you could use a break."

"Thanks very much," she replied acidly, although it was hard to stay angry in the face of his good-natured cheek. Still, she wasn't about to be seen in the pub with a tabloid journalist. "Look, Tom, I don't have anything more for you than I've said. But I promise I'll let you know when I do, if you keep a civil pen in your head in the meantime."

"That's a hard thing to ask of me, Inspector," he said with a grin. "But I'll do my best."

"I'm sure you will," Gemma muttered, leaving him on the steps. She hurried on to the car park and locked herself in her car, starting the engine with a sigh of relief. Her interview with the super and her meeting with Gerry Franks had affected her more than she cared to admit; she was glad of the refuge.

Her phone rang and she answered swiftly, seeing that it was Kincaid. "I'm so glad it's you. You won't believe what happened to me this afternoon—"

Static cut them off. When she could hear him again, he was saying, "—reason for ringing. Doug Cullen and his girlfriend have invited us for dinner on Saturday night—"

"Saturday? We're *moving* on Saturday!"

"All the better. Kit can watch Toby, and we won't have to cook. A nice gesture on Cullen's part, I thought. I'll tell him about seven, all right? See you tonight, love."

The phone went dead, but Gemma sat for a long moment with it pressed to her ear, thinking thoughts of murder.

He walked around the edge of the little town of Rye, perched on its sandstone cliff, as he had for the past three days. Here three rivers met, and at one time the sea had lapped at the town's base, but the courses of the rivers had changed and the sea had retreated, now a silver thread on the southern horizon.

Between the town and the sea lay the marsh, sheep-dotted, thick with seabirds. Alex knew every footpath through its reaches; it was the territory of his solitary childhood and of his dreams. If he stumbled occasionally as some memory of Dawn pierced the connection between muscles and brain, his body seemed to right itself and plod on of its own accord.

But to his surprise, it was Karl's face he saw vividly now. In spite of his reputation as a sharp businessman, Karl Arrowood had always seemed to treat him fairly—had, in fact, gone out of his way to share his knowledge of antiques and to refer business to him. Alex realized that he'd never seriously allowed himself to contemplate his betrayal of a friend, or Karl's reaction if he'd learned the truth—nor had he paid attention to Dawn's increasing uneasiness about her husband. How could he have been so stupid? So blind?

In the distance he could see the cloverleaf towers of Henry VIII's Camber Castle, floating like a mirage, and beyond that rose the low green hill that hid the ancient Cinque Port of Winchelsea in its folds.

When he reached Winchelsea Beach he stood, looking out over the gray, rolling water, unaware of the cold until his hands and feet lost all sensation.

Then he turned back the way he had come, reaching Rye as dusk settled over its cobbled streets and red tile roofs. Feeling invisible in the dying light, he climbed up into the town. From the lookout on Watchbell Street he could see lights wink on along the quay and the Channel, and somehow his very isolation gave him strength.

At last the cold and dark drove him down again, and

he made his way home, drifting through the footpaths as insubstantially as a ghost. Smoke curled from Jane's chimney, and as he stepped into the house he smelled something savory baking in the oven, but when he called out there was no answer. Jane must be in the greenhouse, tending the potted cyclamens and azaleas she had carefully nurtured for the Christmas market.

Another scent drew him forward, into the sitting room, something green and sharp and fresh. Alex stood rooted, gazing at the tree that filled the room, the glass star at its tip sparkling against the dark vault of the kiln. His life seemed to telescope before him, compounding his loss. There was Dawn, his childhood, and something beyond memory that even now he could not bear to look at directly.

Alex fell to his knees before the tree, overcome by great, wrenching sobs that tore at his throat and pierced his chest.

Suddenly Jane was there, smelling of cold and earth. "Oh, Alex," she whispered. "I'm sorry. I'm so sorry." She tried to put an arm round him but he pulled away.

"No. *I'm* sorry." His mind felt suddenly clear again, as if the static that had fogged it for days had vanished. "I've got to go back. There are things—"

"Fern rang this afternoon. She said the police are looking for you, they've even put out an alert for your car—"

"The police? What do they want with me?"

"I'm sure they hope you know something about the murder. The sooner you talk with them, the sooner you'll be able to clear things up."

It hadn't occurred to him that the police might think

him a witness—or a suspect. Well, he would go back to London first thing the next morning, and he would talk to them. But his purpose had become clear, and he'd no intention of letting the police or anyone else interfere with his agenda.

# CHAPTER EIGHT

Saturday street market has existed in Portobello Road since the 1860's. Selling meat, fish, fruit, vegetables, and flowers during the day, the costermongers were joined on Saturday nights by numerous street sellers and entertainers.

—Whetlor and Bartlett,
from *Portobello*

GEMMA LAY IN bed, staring at the partially opened slats of the blinds and hoping for the faint gray streaks that would presage dawn. Kincaid slept with his back to her, his breathing comfortingly steady. From the next room she could hear Toby's occasional snort; he was getting over a slight cold.

At last she gave in and tilted her head so that she could see the luminous face of the bedside clock; she groaned. It was only bloody five o'clock. Daylight was still a good two hours off, and it looked as if sleep had deserted her for the night.

Nor had they gone to bed at a reasonable hour the previous evening. Still furious with Kincaid over the business of Doug Cullen's invitation, she'd turned on him as soon as he arrived to help her pack.

"How could you? How could you accept a dinner invitation in the midst of moving house? We'll be tired, and filthy, and I've only so much time to get the new house sorted—"

"But I thought it would give you a break—"

"It's our first evening in the new house as a family!"

His face fell. "Of course, you're right. It was really stupid of me. I'll ring Doug straight away and say we can't come." He flipped open his phone and stepped outside.

Gemma knew she should be pleased at his capitulation, but her face flamed as she imagined his conversation with Cullen. When he returned a moment later, she spat, "Now I feel a right bitch. They'll have made arrangements already—"

"Gemma, they'll understand." He frowned at her. "It's not like you to be unreasonable—"

"So now I'm unreasonable?" She turned away and began rolling a wineglass in a sheet of newspaper, her fingers trembling.

"That's not what I meant, and you know it." He came to stand beside her, placing a tentative hand on her shoulder. "What's wrong?"

She hesitated, then the words boiled out in a rush. "The super called me in today. Gerry Franks complained to him that I'd been too soft on Karl Arrowood."

"Surely Lamb didn't take him seriously?"

"Not really. But he told me my management skills could use some improvement."

"So what did you do?"

She took another glass from the kitchen shelf. "At first I was going to rip Franks to shreds, but then I decided that wasn't the most helpful tack. I told him he was welcome to get off the case, but that he was a valuable asset and I'd rather we tried to work together, and that I hadn't meant to exclude him from portions of the investigation."

"Very diplomatic of you." Kincaid raised a quizzical eyebrow. "Was it true?"

"Oh, I suppose the super's right," she admitted, grimacing. "Franks is a good officer, especially with detail—he has that sort of bulldog mentality, worries at things until he gets them right. I should've managed the situation better."

"It sounds as though you've made a good start at improving things," Kincaid had said reassuringly, and thus, harmony had been more or less restored.

Now, lying awake in the predawn darkness, she found herself thinking of her ex-husband, Rob, who would have seen her confidence as an opportunity to tell her just how *he* would have handled things. Kincaid's supportiveness, she realized, was rare, and a trait to be appreciated—so why the hell couldn't she bring herself to tell him so?

Three hours later, hunched over her desk at the station, she'd pored over every note, every communication from the incident room, every file, wondering what she could possibly have missed. Exhausted, she groaned and dropped her head in her hands.

At the soft rap on her door, she looked up, blinking. It was Melody, carrying two coffee cups and a bag that smelled suspiciously of fresh carrot muffins.

"Latte, again? And breakfast? You must be the coffee fairy, Melody. Or coffee angel, I should say."

A blush stained Melody's plump cheeks. "I get off the tube at Notting Hill Gate. So it's no trouble to pop into the Starbucks on my way here. I know how much you like it, boss, and it seemed, especially today...I mean, I heard about Sergeant Franks talking to the super, and I think it's bloody unfair."

"Thanks. But I suppose he had a point. We don't seem to be making much progress, do we? Here, sit down, eat your muffin."

Melody sat obediently and peeled the paper wrapper from her breakfast. "Remember you asked me if I knew why Otto Popov was so certain Arrowood was guilty? Well, I went round the pubs last night, some of the more fringy ones, if you know what I mean."

"Not dressed like that?" Gemma gestured at Melody's neat skirt and jacket.

"Not on my life. I wore my leather trousers—you'd never have recognized me."

"I take it you weren't looking for a date?"

Melody grinned. "Well, I did chat up some okay-looking blokes. But I got a name, in the end, someone who might know something about Popov. A little Cockney named Bernard. I found him in a pub near the flyover, and after a couple of pints he agreed to have a chat with you, for the price of a pint and some readies."

Gemma's interest quickened. "When? Where?"

"Lunchtime today, in the Ladbroke Arms. Said he wanted to meet someplace no one would notice him. But, as Bernard has a face like a monkey and smells like he hasn't bathed for years, I don't think he'll be exactly inconspicuous."

Gemma tensed when the phone on her desk rang, fearing a repeat of yesterday's summons to the superintendent's office. But it was the officer on duty in reception.

"There's a young man to see you, Inspector. Says his name is Alex Dunn."

"Dunn?" Gemma repeated, before swiftly collecting herself. "Right. Put him in an interview room. I'll be down in a second." Hanging up, she said to Melody, "Come with me. I'll need backup on this."

Alex Dunn rose as they entered the room, holding his hand out as if it were an ordinary social occasion. He was about Gemma's age, good-looking in a tidy sort of way, and on first impression it seemed to Gemma that his was not the sort of appeal likely to make a woman risk a marriage.

When she had introduced herself and Melody, she switched on the recorder and gestured for him to sit again.

"Is that necessary?" he asked, with a shocked glance at the recorder. His ready confidence seemed to ebb a little.

"Oh, I think so," Gemma replied evenly. "We've been looking everywhere for you for five days. That tends to make us feel a bit official."

"I didn't know. Honestly. I was down at my aunt's in Sussex—a friend drove me there on Saturday—and it never occurred to me that anyone wanted to talk to me. I wasn't..." His voice trailed off. "Myself," he concluded.

"How could you *not* realize that the police would want to question you? Your mistress was murdered—"

"She was not my mistress! I mean—I suppose technically she was—but I never thought of it that way. That makes it sound—makes her sound—cheap."

"Well, however you thought of it," Gemma kept her

tone tart, "you were still the person closest to her, barring her husband. Did Dawn talk about him?"

"She never talked about Karl. I think, when she was with me, that she liked to pretend Karl didn't exist. If I pressed her about it, I mean about leaving him, she would just...withdraw. Shake her head and get this closed look."

"Did she ever give you the impression that she was afraid of her husband?"

"No. And she would have told me," he insisted, but he sounded less than certain.

"And she never told you that Karl suspected she was having an affair?"

"No."

"Did you see Dawn on the day she died?"

"No. I rang her mobile from a phone box several times. But she didn't answer."

"From a phone box? Isn't that a bit cloak-and-dagger for a woman who wasn't worried about her husband?"

Alex colored. "It was to ensure my number never showed up on her itemized calls."

"Very cautious of her," commented Melody.

"Dawn was...thorough. About everything. That's just the sort of person she was."

Gemma thought of Dawn Arrowood's careful blotting out of her background, of her family, and of her neat and characterless bedroom. "Did Dawn ever talk about herself, where she came from, that sort of thing?" she asked, curious.

"Yeah, she did. Clapham, or Croyden, something like that. Her father ran a supermarket."

"He still does," Gemma murmured, but she saw that Alex didn't understand. "Go on. What else?"

"Oh, the silly things you do as a kid. Sneaking cigarettes, kisses on the playground, that sort of thing. And she talked about her friend Natalie, and how she always wanted a family like that, big and noisy and busy." He frowned. "But I don't think it would have suited her, somehow."

"Did she mention any friends other than Natalie?"

"No. There didn't seem to be anyone other than Karl's business associates. And me."

"Did she talk about wanting children?"

"Only once. When we'd—when she'd had a bit too much wine. She cried. Then, when I tried to comfort her, she got angry. Said I didn't understand, that Karl would never let her have children. I said—Well, you can guess what I said. But it was no use. And she was always very careful about that, too."

"Birth control?" When he nodded, Gemma added, "Apparently not careful enough."

"What do you mean?"

"You didn't know? She didn't tell you?"

"Tell me what?" His voice rose. "You're not saying—"

"She was pregnant. The doctor had confirmed it that afternoon."

Dunn's eyes were dilated with shock, his face the hue of parchment. "But . . . I don't . . . How could she not tell me?"

"Maybe she meant to. But she never had the chance. Or maybe it wasn't your baby; maybe it was Karl's. His vasectomy could have failed; that's what he claims, after all. Or maybe it was someone else's altogether—"

His face bleached whiter still, and Gemma feared she might have pushed him too far.

But he shoved back his chair, shaking with rage, and

stabbed a finger at her. "She wasn't seeing anyone else. You make her sound like a slag, and it's not true! If I know anything about her, it's that she loved me. She would have left him, we would have worked something out—"

"Okay, point taken. Sit back down, Alex, please. Constable, could you get Mr. Dunn some water?"

He obeyed her, reluctantly, and when he was seated again and had sipped at the water Melody brought him, Gemma said, "Look, I'm sorry. Let's start over. Why don't you tell me about last Friday. Were you supposed to see Dawn that day?"

"No. We'd met the day before, but she'd said she had a doctor's appointment on Friday—a routine checkup—and that she was meeting Natalie for tea. And I was planning to visit my aunt, as well as getting ready for Saturday market, so . . . If I'd insisted she come by the flat, maybe—" He looked stricken.

"Then you'd be assuming her murder was happenstance, and we don't believe that. I believe that whoever waited for Dawn that day would have waited longer, or come back another time." As Gemma spoke, she realized how strongly she meant it.

"But—if it was Karl—And if she had left—"

"Karl might have changed his mind? From what I know of the man, that seems unlikely. And we've no proof that he killed his wife. It seems to me that you and your friends—particularly Otto—have made an awfully big assumption."

"But—Otto said—Otto was sure that it was Karl. I didn't want to believe him—"

"It always comes back to Otto, doesn't it?" Gemma glanced at Melody. "Alex, what else did Otto say?"

His stare was defiant. "Otto said Karl would kill me, too, if he found out. But that's crap, isn't it?"

"Is that why you went to Sussex?"

"It was Fern's idea. She meant well, but I feel a fool now for going along with it. As I said, I wasn't myself."

"Do you know how your friend Otto comes to know so much about Karl Arrowood? Has he told you?"

"Otto doesn't talk about himself much. But he's lived in the neighborhood a long time, knows a lot of people."

"You don't know anything about Otto's dead wife?"

"Dead?" Alex looked puzzled. "No. I just assumed they were divorced or something, I mean, you never know these days, do you?"

"Do you know someone called Marianne Hoffman?"

"Never heard of her. Why? Is she a friend of Otto's?"

Was it possible, Gemma wondered, that Otto could be the link between the Arrowoods and Hoffman? The café owner knew many people in the trade, as Alex had pointed out. And he was a powerful man, skilled, she assumed, as were most cooks, with a knife.

"Let's go back to Friday. You were getting ready for Saturday market. What does that entail?"

"Setting things out in my stall in the arcade, arranging, pricing. I'd been to an estate sale in Sussex, near my aunt's, so I had a good deal of new stock."

"And then?"

"I went back to the flat. I'd had a good day, and I wanted to celebrate, so I went to Otto's for an early dinner."

"What time was this?"

"About half past six, I think. I really wasn't paying attention."

"Was Otto at the café when you arrived?"

"He served me himself."

"Everything as usual?"

"Of course. Except..." Dunn hesitated, then went on. "We had a little disagreement. I wouldn't exactly call it an argument."

"About what?"

"He warned me about Karl. I'd found a lovely piece of porcelain I thought I might sell him, and Otto said not to take Karl for a fool. I didn't realize until then, you see, that everyone knew about Dawn." He crumpled the paper cup Melody had given him in his fingers. "How could I possibly have been so flaming stupid?"

Kincaid listened as Gemma related her interview with Alex Dunn. He'd picked her up at Notting Hill for a quick run into the City, where they had appointments with Karl Arrowood's sons. Kincaid had debated surprising them, but decided there was no point in risking possible inconvenience to himself and Gemma. He had no doubt the boys' mother would have got the wind up them already.

He had arranged to meet the elder son, Richard, in a well-known Fleet Street pub at eleven o'clock, and the younger, Sean, in the same place at half past.

They had no trouble finding a table, as the pub was just gearing up for its lunchtime business. When Richard Arrowood walked in the door at the stroke of eleven, they recognized him instantly, a pale and less substantial copy of his father.

"Mr. Arrowood," Kincaid called out.

"What is this about?" Arrowood asked as he sat

down, adjusting his perfectly creased trouser leg at the knee. "I don't have much time."

"You are surely aware that your stepmother has been murdered? Brutally, I might add."

"So? What has that to do with me?"

"Did you know Dawn well?" Gemma asked pleasantly, but Kincaid saw the tick in her jaw that meant she was clenching her teeth.

"My father had us round for drinks a few times when they were first married, and once for a meal. *She* didn't cook, of course, just had something brought in." From the contempt in Richard Arrowood's voice, she might have served them fish and chips.

"And your mother cooks, I take it?" Gemma's smile was vicious.

"My mother has nothing to do with this," Arrowood retorted.

"I wonder," Kincaid interposed. "Is there a particular reason why you disliked your stepmother so much? I understood that your mother and father had been divorced for several years before he married Dawn."

"That didn't make her any less of a money-grubbing bitch," said Arrowood, sniffing, and Kincaid revised his estimate of the young man's character. Not only was Richard Arrowood arrogant, rude, and unpleasant, he was astoundingly stupid.

"I would have thought your father had enough to go round."

"Not once the fair Dawnie got her paws on it. I had some debts." The young man's cheeks flushed with remembered anger. "You know, the sort of thing anyone starting out in the City encounters. But Father wouldn't lift a finger. He said helping me would threaten Dawn's security."

"Does one *encounter* debts, Mr. Arrowood? I always rather thought one acquired them." Kincaid watched him realize he'd been insulted, and bridle.

"Look here, you can't speak to me this way—"

"I can, you know. May I remind you that this is a murder inquiry, and that you may be under suspicion?"

"Suspicion? But that's absurd." His bravado seemed to evaporate suddenly. "I haven't seen Dawn in ages—"

"Would you mind telling us where you were last Friday evening?"

"Friday? I—I was at a drinks party. A bloke from work had several of us round to his flat in Borough Market. My brother was there, too."

"What time was this party?"

"We went straight from work. Half-five, maybe."

"And how long did you stay?"

"Until a group of us went out to dinner. Around eight, I suppose."

"And you were there all the time?"

"Of course I was bloody there! Look, you can't—"

"We'll need your friend's name and address. And of course we'll confirm this with your brother."

Richard looked from Gemma to Kincaid. His forehead was damp with sweat, and he sniffed again, brushing the back of his hand across his nose. "I don't think you can speak to me like this without a solicitor," he said, but without much conviction.

"You are, of course, entitled to a solicitor at any time, Mr. Arrowood. But this is just a friendly conversation, a routine inquiry, and I don't think you'd want it to look as though you'd something to hide. Just a bit of advice."

"I—" A look of relief flooded Arrowood's face, and following his gaze, Kincaid saw that his brother had arrived, a few minutes ahead of schedule. Again, the resemblance to their father was unmistakable, but Sean Arrowood was a bit stockier, a bit darker, and he came to the table with a smile and an outstretched hand.

"I'm Sean Arrowood. I know I'm early, my meeting finished ahead of schedule—is that a problem?" The quick glance he gave his brother showed concern.

"Not at all," Kincaid reassured him. "We were just finishing up with your brother." He nodded at Richard in dismissal, and the elder Arrowood made his escape with a look of relief. "Perhaps you can confirm some things for us," Kincaid continued to Sean. "I understand you were not on the best of terms with your stepmother?"

Sean looked pained. "That's not exactly true. You have to understand that we didn't dislike Dawn—and that we were very distressed to hear what had happened to her—but her marriage to our dad made things particularly...difficult...with our mother. She worries about our futures, although we've told her often enough that she needn't. And Mother would have interpreted any friendliness towards Dawn on our part as...disloyal."

"She did seem to have a bee in her bonnet," Gemma said, and she and Sean shared a small conspiratorial smile. "When did you see Dawn last?"

"Um, I saw her quite recently, in fact, a few weeks ago. She rang and asked me to meet her for a coffee."

"Was this usual?"

"No," Sean admitted. "I was a bit taken aback, but curious."

"She asked to see only you? Not you and Richard?"

"Dawn and I got on better. And my brother sometimes has a tendency to . . . overreact."

"I take it this was a delicate matter?"

"She was concerned that Richard and I might think she had encouraged our father to treat us unfairly."

"Did she tell you that Karl meant to cut you and Richard out of his will?"

Sean met her eyes steadily. "Apparently, Richard had been a bit intemperate in his demands, and Father was angry. I can't say I blame him."

"And did you tell your brother what your father meant to do?"

"I didn't need to. Father had made his intentions quite clear, the last time Richard saw him."

"What I don't understand," said Gemma, when they were back in the car, "is why Dawn would have wanted to intervene on Richard and Sean's behalf. They had treated her badly—or at least Richard had—Why not just say 'to hell with them'?"

"Perhaps it wasn't so much a desire to benefit them as to ease her own conscience—"

"She couldn't deal with Karl leaving her all his money when she knew she was betraying him?" Gemma considered the idea. "But if she meant to leave him, he'd have changed the will back in his sons' favor anyway—"

"We don't know that she meant to leave him," Kincaid interrupted. "But our immediate concern is Richard Arrowood. If he knew his father meant to change his will, he had a good motive for killing Dawn. We need to check out that alibi." Opening his phone, he dialed Sean and Richard Arrowood's friend Charles Dodd.

After a moment's conversation, he rang off and told Gemma, "He's out of the office on business all afternoon, according to his assistant. We'll have to try him at home later on. Um, about this lunchtime meeting you've got . . . I could come with you."

"To see Bernard?" She didn't know whether to be touched or aggravated at the note of concern in his voice. "He's expecting only me, and I don't want to take a chance on scaring him off. I'll be fine. Melody says the man's a dreadful lecher, but harmless—and after Alex Dunn's landlord, a bit of straightforward lechery sounds like good, clean fun."

She spotted him the moment she walked into the Ladbroke Arms. He sat in a corner, wearing a cap that she guessed had once been houndstooth but was now merely a mottled gray, his brown, wizened face half concealed by his pint glass. Drawing nearer, she saw that his attire was completed by a thin, grease-spotted tie and an ancient tweed jacket. She slid onto the bench, sitting no nearer to him than absolutely necessary for conversation. If his clothing was any indication, Melody had been correct about his personal hygiene.

"You must be Bernard. I'm Inspector James." She started to show her warrant card but he waved it away.

"No need to flash that thing about in here, luv. I'll take your word for it." He looked her up and down. "Young Melody said you was a good looker, and you've not proved her wrong."

Gemma nodded at his glass, ignoring the compliment. "Can I get you another?"

"I wouldn't mind, luv, wouldn't mind a bit." He lifted the glass to his lips and reduced the level by several inches.

She fetched another pint from the bar, adding an orange juice for herself. When she returned to the table Bernard took a suspicious sniff in the direction of her glass.

"Not some kind of a teetotaler, are you?" he asked.

"Oh, no, no. It's just that I have to go back to the station, and they frown on that sort of thing. No amount of peppermint can get you past our desk sergeant."

"Ah." Bernard seemed mollified. "Bet I could teach you a thing or two."

"Another day?" Gemma awarded him her most winning smile. "Bernard, Constable Talbot said you knew a bit about Otto Popov."

"I might." He looked pointedly at her handbag. "Young Melody said as how you might be inclined to make it worth my while."

Gemma opened her wallet and removed a ten-pound note. Bernard's gaze didn't waver. After a moment she sighed and pulled out another ten. "That's all the department's resources will allow, I'm afraid."

His hand moved and the bills disappeared faster than Gemma's eye could follow. "Right," he said. "I suppose that's enough to be going on with. Now, where were we?" He settled himself more comfortably, cradling his glass. "You want to know about Otto, you have to go back a ways, you have to know how things fit together. You see, I've been round these parts a long time, though

I was born in Whitechapel. Jack the Ripper territory, that. Makes yer think, don't it, what with this murder—"

"That's an old chestnut, Bernard. It has nothing to do with this."

"All right, all right, don't get yer dander up." He cackled, then siphoned another inch off his pint.

Gemma sighed again, sure that he meant to get his beer's worth out of this discussion—although how his shriveled little body could hold more than a pint or two, she couldn't imagine.

"So what brought you to Notting Hill?" she asked.

"It was the business, you see. I started out doing little odd jobs for dealers in Bermondsey, and during the course of things I got to know folks in Notting Hill. Now *this*"—he made an expansive gesture—"was the place to be in the sixties, luv. The antiques trade was just beginning to boom—"

"But we're not talking about the sixties." Gemma was determined to nip extended reminiscence in the bud. "Otto can't have been more than a child."

"Big fer his age, weren't he? Sixteen, seventeen, maybe, old enough to know better. But the point is, luv, that's where it starts. Otto's family was right off the boat from Russia, not a word of English. So they move into a street with some other Russian families, and they keep themselves to themselves. As did the Poles, and the Germans, and the Jews. They all had their own shops, their own cafés, and nobody mixes with anybody else.

"Until the blacks come along, late fifties, early sixties. And all of a sudden the Poles and the Germans and the Russians find something in common, and it's the blacks that nobody else mixes with." He fixed Gemma with beady eyes that were surprisingly sharp and blue. "A combustible situation, you might say. Then along comes young Karl Arrowood—"

"Arrowood? I thought we were talking about Otto."

"I'll be getting to that. Where's yer patience, luv? As I were saying, along comes Karl Arrowood. Now he's a few years older than Otto, an up-and-coming boyo with a finger in more than one pie, and he figures that Otto's Russian relatives maybe have some connections he needs, so he hires him."

"Karl hired Otto?"

"Righto, luv. Not that Karl doesn't have a few connections of his own, mind you, German relatives that just happened to know the whereabouts of objects liberated during the war. Karl puts two and two together and before you know it, he's got a nice little import business going."

"So that's how Karl got started?"

"Also how he made the acquaintance of some less than savory characters, Russian bigwigs, if you know what I mean. Now young Otto—still a kid, really—having been raked over the coals by everyone from his mum and his dad to his aunt Minnie for consorting with a bad boy like Karl, decides he wants no more to do with this business, and disappears from London for a while.

"But Karl, now, he sees this as an act of desertion, and Karl has a memory like a bloody elephant. So years later, when Otto's come back to London and set himself up a nice little business, got married and all, Karl finds a way to make Otto work for him again."

"How?"

"Now, that I couldn't tell you, luv." Bernard finished the last of his pint and wiped his lips. "Thirsty work, all that talking."

Gemma fetched another pint from the bar in record time, sloshing beer as she slid it across the table to him.

"Careful, luv," he admonished her. "Like spilling gold, that is."

"You must have some idea what sort of leverage Karl used on Otto," Gemma prompted him.

"Well, Otto'd gone and made himself vulnerable, hadn't he?"

"His wife, you mean?"

"A pale little thing, Otto's wife, always looked a bit sickly. Didn't surprise me when she snuffed it."

"You're saying Karl had something to do with the death of Otto's wife?"

"Now I wouldn't go that far," Bernard answered cagily, tempting Gemma to throttle him with his greasy tie. "Some sort of illness. Heart, I think they said. But I didn't know the poor mite myself, and I wasn't exactly in Otto's personal confidence."

Gemma glared at him. "I don't believe you, Bernard, and I definitely don't buy that you don't know what happened to Otto's wife. Why won't you tell me?"

Bernard put his finger to the side of his nose, looking for a moment like a wizened Saint Nick. "God didn't miss me when he went to handing out the brains, luv. Now, there's conversation, and then there's stupidity, and I reckon as 'ow I know the difference 'tween the two."

Having had a few things to attend to at the new house, Kincaid decided to stay in Notting Hill and grab a sandwich in the station canteen. As he sat down, he noticed Sergeant Franks at a nearby table. The man nodded at him, his knowing look verging on a sneer, before getting up and leaving the room.

It was obvious from his behavior that Franks was aware of Kincaid's personal relationship with Gemma, causing Kincaid to wonder if there was more to Franks's complaint than she'd let on. But if that were the case, why hadn't she told him?

He debated whether he should have a word with Superintendent Lamb, an old mate of his from police college, but he was concerned that his interference would only make Gemma's situation more difficult in the long term—not to mention the fact that Gemma would kill him if she found out.

He felt frustratingly handicapped, not least by his inability to understand Gemma's emotional swings. There was, for instance, the matter of Cullen's dinner party. After he'd rung and canceled, she had decided she wanted to go after all and had had him call back and accept.

If he failed to understand her reasoning in this or any other matter, how could he predict what would help her to cope? Walking on a minefield would be easier, he sometimes thought. Then he looked up and saw her standing in the doorway, and knew that she was worth whatever it took.

She smiled at him and came across to his table.

"Have a seat," he said. "I got you a prawn mayonnaise in case you hadn't eaten."

Gemma made a face. "I've gone off prawn mayonnaise."

"I thought that was your favorite."

"Last week. But I'll manage, thanks." She opened the plastic container and nibbled at a corner of the sandwich.

"I take it you survived your encounter unscathed?"

"I rather liked him, actually. Though I would send him out to the dry cleaners, clothes and all." She related Bernard's story while she ate, taking an occasional sip of Kincaid's cold tea.

"It sounds as though we've enough now for a useful conversation with Otto Popov," Kincaid remarked as she finished.

"And Karl Arrowood?"

"Otto first. The more pieces we can fill in before we tackle Karl, the better. Russian Mafia?" He raised a dubious eyebrow.

"I assume that's what Bernard meant, cagey old devil. And that would go a ways towards explaining why everyone's so bloody terrified of Karl."

They found Otto wiping down tables after the last of the lunchtime customers. He smiled when he saw Gemma, but she noticed that his expression became neutrally wary as she introduced him to Kincaid.

"Otto, this is Superintendent Kincaid from Scotland Yard. He's working with me on this investigation."

"Please, sit." Otto pulled out two chairs for them. "Anything I can do. A coffee on the house?"

"No, we're fine, really," Gemma replied. "Could you join us for a moment?"

Otto sat, his bulk balanced with surprising grace on the small chair. "Young Alex is back, have you heard?"

"He came to see me this morning. Apparently, Fern took him to his aunt's in Sussex for a few days, but she was afraid to tell anyone where he was. Otto, both Alex and Fern have said that you warned them Alex might be in danger from Karl Arrowood. Why did you think that?"

"Karl is a dangerous man. Everyone knows that. One hears stories."

"I think it's more than that," Gemma probed gently. "I think you've had personal experience with Karl. First, a long time ago, when you put him in touch with some Russian, um, colleagues. Then, more recently, before your wife died."

Otto stared at them, his dark eyes unreadable.

"Did you work for Karl in his importing business?"

"Importing, pah!" Otto spat, stung. "He cheats people, Karl Arrowood. That is all he has ever done. I swore I would never again work for such a man!"

"Then you must have had a very good reason for doing so. Did it have something to do with your wife?"

His eyes were like pebbles now, cold and flat. "You will please leave my wife out of this."

Gemma met his gaze evenly. "You had nothing to do with Karl for what, twenty years? You made a life for yourself, a good business, you married, then all of a sudden you connect again with a man you obviously despise. We *will* find out why, eventually, but I would rather hear it from you."

Otto stared at Gemma, then at Kincaid, as if assessing them both. At last he said, "I have nothing to hide. For myself I do not care, only for my wife's name and my daughters' memories of her. You understand?" When they nodded assurance, he went on. "Karl Arrowood is an evil man. He hated me, merely because when I was a boy I decided I no longer wished to be involved in his...activities. He waited for years, like a spider, until he saw his opportunity. My wife, Katrina, was never strong. She had problems with drugs when she was younger, but she had been better, much better, for a long time. Then after Anna was born, and then Maria, Katrina was depressed, and Karl saw his chance. He made available to her little gifts, and soon she was back to her old ways.

"Of course I did not know at first, and then when I realized what was happening, it was some time before I learned the source. I thought I would kill him, then, but he was too smart for that. Who would take care of Katrina, and the girls, he asked me, if I went to prison? And then he told me that if I didn't do as he wished, he would cut off Katrina's supply. He didn't need me to make his contacts by then, he wanted merely my compliance. And I had no choice. My Katrina was more and more desperate.

"What would have happened eventually, I do not know. But Katrina died, an overdose, and Karl had no more hold over me. Now do you see why I warned Alex to beware? Karl is ruthless. If he had found out about Alex, he would not have let it go unpunished."

"Heroin? Arrowood?"

"But of course. His business is the perfect vehicle. He buys antiques for cash, which are then sold legitimately. Even if his profits are only on paper, it doesn't matter. He has laundered his money."

"Mr. Popov," Kincaid leaned forward, "if Karl Arrowood did such a terrible thing to you, to your wife, why didn't you go to the authorities?"

"My girls know nothing of this, of their mother's problem. They *will* know nothing."

"But what if you found a way to make Arrowood suffer as you suffered, and no one need ever know?"

"You mistake me, Mr. Kincaid. First of all, I do not think Karl Arrowood cares enough for any living thing to suffer at its loss. Secondly, I would never harm an innocent such as Dawn Arrowood, never. Although I will not lie to you—If I had the opportunity to kill Karl without my daughters being harmed in any way, I would do it in an instant."

"Otto," Gemma said, "you realize we will have to check your alibi for that night. Were you here in the café?"

"On a Friday night? Of course."

"And Wesley?"

"Yes, he was here. I suppose you will have to ask him, but how can you be sure he is not protecting me?" His brow creased as he considered the matter. "There is always the dishwasher, of course. Although his English is somewhat lacking, he can vouch for us both."

"Is Wesley here now?"

"No, he has gone to the produce stall to replenish a few things for tonight's menu, then he will walk the girls home from school. If you go now, perhaps you can catch him before he meets them. And of course, you would not want to give me the chance to fit him up ahead of time." Although a faint twinkle had returned to Otto's eyes, Gemma reminded herself that he was a capable man with the most powerful of motives, and that very few alibis were foolproof.

·  ·  ·

"Why don't you go back to the Yard?" Gemma suggested as she and Kincaid left the café. "Talk to your mates in the drug squad, see if they know anything about this. I'll find Wesley."

"Right, then. I'll ring you if I learn anything. Otherwise I'll see you tonight." He lifted his hand in a wave and disappeared round the corner into Kensington Park Road.

Gemma headed the other way, down Portobello, keeping an eye out for Wesley's dark dreadlocks. She spotted him soon enough, coming out of the fishmonger's, his arms laden with carrier bags.

"Wesley!"

He crossed the street to join her. "Police ladies have to be doing their own shopping, now?" he asked, grinning.

"I was looking for you." She fell in beside him. "Wesley, last Friday evening, did Otto leave the café for any reason?"

"On a Friday? No way he would do that. Even early, we have plenty customers. Some regulars, they like their dinners early, before the evening-out business starts."

"Including Alex?"

"Sometimes he comes early. That night he did."

"And there's no way Otto could have slipped out for a few minutes without your noticing?"

Wesley laughed aloud. "Otto, he's a little hard to miss, 'case you hadn't noticed. Especially in the kitchen, he be slammin' and bangin' and swearin' at the pots. Gives things more flavor, he says."

"You're absolutely certain?"

" 'Course I'm certain! You're not thinking Otto trotted out in his apron and murdered Miz Arrowood, then came back to finish off his veal osso bucco? That's downright daft!"

"No, I admit it's not very likely."

"Part of the job, accusing people who have shown you hospitality?"

"That's unfair, Wesley," she retorted, stung. "I'm not accusing Otto of anything, just ruling him out. And I don't like it any better than you do."

He glanced at her, frowning. "Why all of a sudden you think Otto would have done such a thing?"

"I'm afraid I can't say. But you could ask him yourself."

"Like the confessional, is it, conversation with the police?"

"Something like that, yes."

"That's good, then," said Wesley, apparently mollified, and they continued walking in companionable silence.

Suddenly Gemma spotted a few wrapped Christmas trees at one of the flower stalls. "Oh, my gosh! I completely forgot about a tree!"

"A Christmas tree? This be for your new home?"

"Yes. We're moving in on Saturday."

"I'll find you a good tree, if you want, and bring it to you. A big one." He chuckled. "A black Father Christmas, how you like that?"

# CHAPTER NINE

Much of the housing around Portobello remained poor up
to and beyond the Second World War, when it was still not
unusual for homes to have a shared lavatory, no bathroom,
and cooking facilities on the landing.

—Whetlor and Bartlett,
from *Portobello*

PORTOBELLO HAD ALWAYS been a road of mixed use, the
antiques shops and arcades tucked in among flats and
cafés and ordinary businesses. Borough, on the other
hand, was an old dockside warehouse district made
fashionable by its proximity to the river and, except
when the Friday-morning produce market was in session, there was nothing in its dark brick buildings and
narrow streets innately friendly to the casual pedestrian. Kincaid and Doug Cullen found the address the
Arrowoods had given them easily enough, however: a
loft in a converted warehouse.

Charles Dodd was young, balding, with a plain, intelligent face. His black jeans and turtleneck made an
interesting counterpoint to the glass-and-greenery airi-
ness of the loft behind him.

"Charles Dodd?" Kincaid presented his warrant card.
"I'm Superintendent Kincaid, and this is Sergeant
Cullen. Could you spare us a few minutes?"

"What's this about?" Dodd inquired, but his manner
seemed friendly enough. "I've just got home from work

and I've guests arriving in a few minutes." As Dodd led them to a pair of matching white sofas, Kincaid noticed that a section of floor had been done in glass blocks that allowed a view of the high-tech kitchen on the lower floor.

"This won't take long," he assured Dodd. "Terrific flat you've got here. Good for entertaining, is it?"

"As a matter of fact, it is, and cooking's my stress relief from work."

"Last Friday evening, I understand you gave a drinks party here?"

"I did, yes. All perfectly legal, I assure you. Nothing served but wine."

"And Sean and Richard Arrowood were among your guests?"

"Those wankers?" Astonishment warred with amusement in Dodd's face. "What are they supposed to have done?"

"Their stepmother was murdered on Friday evening," said Cullen. "We need to ascertain the whereabouts of anyone who had a connection with the victim."

"You can't seriously think those two had anything to do with their stepmother's death? I read about it in the paper, a dreadful thing. But Sean and Richard couldn't slaughter a chicken between them if it meant the difference between eating and starving to death." Dodd lit a cigarette. "Oh, Sean's not so bad, really—or he wouldn't be if you could keep him away from his mother and his brother—but Richard's a parasite."

"Why invite them to your party if you dislike them?"

Dodd grimaced at Kincaid. "Work. Richard's in the

same office; Sean comes along gratis. Gets awkward if you invite everyone else and leave Richard out."

"What time did they arrive on Friday?"

"Between half-five and six. We all came straight from work."

"And they stayed until what time?"

"About eight. A few of us went out to dinner then, but not Sean and Richard."

"Can you be sure they were here the entire time?"

"There were fewer than a dozen of us. I'd have noticed if they'd nipped out for a murder. Besides, Richard was hitting the wine even more heavily than usual, and I was wondering if I was going to have to chuck him out. Sean saved me the bother, in the end."

"Richard was difficult?"

"Obnoxious would be a better description. Coming on to a lady who didn't fancy him at all. Possibly a bit of overcompensation for not admitting that he prefers boys."

"Would you say Richard's behavior seemed worse than usual? Did he seem nervous, upset?"

Dodd took a moment to put his cigarette out in an art-glass ashtray. "Hard to say, really. He was certainly fretful, but then he's rather an emotional sort."

Kincaid recollected Richard Arrowood's pallid countenance and incessant sniffing. "I suspect that Richard is not unacquainted with drug dealers. Do you by any chance know who supplies his coke?"

"Not a clue. Couldn't afford this flat if I did that sort of thing," Dodd added, but his smile had become strained.

"We'll need to have a word with the other guests at

your party, if you could jot their names and addresses down for us."

Dodd complied, although not happily. "This is going to do wonders for my reputation as a host," he grumbled as he gave them the finished list.

"You never know," Kincaid told him as they said good-bye. "It might add a bit of excitement to the prospect. Good food, good wine, a visit from your friendly copper."

When they reached the street, Kincaid handed Cullen the list.

Cullen groaned. "Does this mean what I think it does?"

*In the year following her mother's death, Angel slowly realized that she had lost her father, as well. Gone was the gruff man who had joked and teased with her; in his place a ghost wandered about the flat, eating the meals she prepared for him in silence, sitting vacantly in front of the television.*

*At first she made every effort to get his attention, talking to him, asking questions, begging for stories. But gradually she learned to exist in silence, as he did, and they moved through their days as if in two parallel but unconnected universes. So it was that when she came home from school one January afternoon to find him sitting motionless in his chair, it was half an hour before she realized he was dead.*

*A stroke, the doctor said, shaking his head and clucking in dismay. But as soon as he'd notified the undertaker, he had taken his bag and gone on to the more rewarding job of ministering to the living.*

*Mrs. Thomas offered to help with the funeral arrangements, while Betty and Ronnie, stunned by another death, avoided* her eyes. "It's not contagious, you know," Angel hissed at them, but she soon learned that their behavior was the least of her worries.

"You'll have to know how much you can afford before we talk to the funeral director," Mrs. Thomas advised her. "You had better see the bank manager, first."

Angel knew the bank manager from the days when her father had frequented the Polish café. A heavy man given to perspiring and wiping his bald scalp with a handkerchief, there was none of the jollity Angel remembered in his manner. He, too, shook his head and clucked, making her want to scream, but she merely sat quietly and waited.

"Your father was not the best with financial matters, Miss Wolowski," the bank manager told her reluctantly. "Especially since your mother's death. Whatever savings he had, he spent on her treatment, and I'm afraid that this past year he's brought little in."

This didn't come as a great surprise, as Angel had become accustomed over the past few months to the coldness of the flat and the scarcity of the money her father had given her to buy food. Nor had he spent much time trading at his stall in the market. "But surely there must be something?"

"Perhaps enough to settle a few minor accounts. The butcher, the greengrocer. But that's all. And I'm afraid your landlord has a reputation for moving quickly on these things, so you'll need to vacate as soon as possible."

"Vacate?"

"I'm afraid so."

"But I have nowhere to go."

"Your father must have appointed a guardian of some sort for you?"

"No."

The bank manager looked distressed, whether on her behalf

*or his own for having to deal with her, she couldn't tell.* "Well, how old are you, my dear?"

"Sixteen."

"You're of school-leaving age, then," he said with apparent relief. "I suppose you'll have to find work of some sort. I'll be more than happy to give you a reference. And there is one other thing. At the time of your mother's death, your father bought the adjoining plot at Kensal Green for himself, so that's one expense you needn't worry about."

"A burial, then, but no marker?" Angel said to Mrs. Thomas as they walked back to Westbourne Park.

"No. They're quite expensive, even the plain ones," Mrs. Thomas agreed. "But you can always add something later." Her dark eyes shone with concern. "Angel, I want you to know you're welcome to stay with us as long as you need. I'm sure your father never meant to leave you like this."

"I'll be all right, thanks. I'll find somewhere close by." It was not only that she still felt the hurt from last winter's rejection, but that things had changed and she no longer felt so at home at the Thomases'. Betty, having inherited her mother's skill with a needle, had left school to take a job with a milliner in Kensington Church Street. With the job had come new friends, a new life that did not include Angel. And Ronnie had little time for either of them. When he wasn't working at his job as a photographer's assistant, shooting weddings and family portraits, he roamed the streets with his camera, developing the black-and-white prints in the flat's bathroom and ignoring his family's complaints about the chemical odors. Angel found the Notting Hill street scenes and portraits fascinating, but felt the distance he had put between them too keenly to tell him so.

The day of her father's funeral, unlike that of her mother's, dawned clear and unseasonably mild. There was a hint of *softness in the air, as if spring might be hiding round the corner, but Angel knew it for a false promise. This time she and the Thomases were the only mourners. She had made no announcement of the service because she could not afford to entertain anyone afterwards. When Ronnie took her arm as the coffin descended, she felt an unexpectedly dizzying rush of pleasure.*

*Within the next few weeks, with the help of the bank manager's recommendation, she found a job as a cashier at the grocer's on Portobello Road. She also found a cheap and shabby bedsit in Colville Terrace, hoping her meager wage would cover the rent.*

*Carefully, she sorted through the flat, knowing she could not take much with her. Her own small bed, the best armchair, her mother's antique bureau, the television, a few kitchen utensils. The rest she arranged for one of her father's friends to sell in the market, but she didn't expect the things to fetch much. She could not, however, bring herself to sell the few bits of antique jewelry left in her father's stall at the arcade, whatever their cash value. The heart-shaped silver locket she fastened round her neck; the rest she put carefully away in the bureau.*

*When the day came, Ronnie offered to borrow his father's van to help her move the larger items the few blocks south to Colville Terrace. They rode amicably in the front seat, arguing the merits of a new band from Tottenham that had temporarily displaced the Beatles from their number one spot on the charts.*

*"The Dave Clark Five?" Ronnie said contemptuously. "What sort of name is that? I'm telling you, six months from now you won't remember what they were called. The Beatles, now, they've got some potential as musicians."*

*That he deigned to approve of any pop band surprised her: he usually extolled only the virtues of jazz artists like Thelonious Monk and Chet Baker. "What about the Rolling Stones, then?" she suggested, aiming for a sophistication she didn't feel.*

Ronnie's face lit up. "Now they've studied the old blues masters—they know their stuff," he said enthusiastically, and the relaxed atmosphere between them lasted the few minutes until they reached their destination.

"Here?" he asked incredulously as he pulled the van up in front of the new flat. By the time he had followed her up to the top-floor room, he was livid with anger.

"Angel, what you thinking of? This is a pit, a hole. A West Indian family right off the boat wouldn't be desperate enough to take this—"

"It's all I can afford, Ronnie, so just leave it—"

"Don't you know this is one of Peter Rachman's properties? He'll send his frighteners round if you don't pay your rent on time. And his dogs. And if your water goes out, or your heat, he's not known for taking care of his tenants—"

"I'll be fine," Angel insisted, fighting back tears.

"Those patches on the walls are damp, did you know that? And there's only a paraffin heater, for God's sake. You'll be lucky you don't set yourself alight—"

"Ronnie, either you can help me move this furniture, or I'll do it myself. But there's no point in you standing there criticizing me, because I've no choice."

Their glowering match lasted a full minute, then Ronnie shrugged. "All right. It's your funeral."

But by the time they had humped her things up the stairs, his anger seemed to have evaporated. He sat on the edge of the newly positioned chair, rotating his cap in his hands. "Look, Angel. I'm sorry for what I said a moment ago. It was . . . considering your father . . . anyway, I didn't mean it. I just don't understand why you can't stay with us until you work something out."

"And what exactly am I supposed to work out? I can't be a permanent parasite on your family, Ronnie. I'm grown up *now—I've got to learn to manage on my own."* She hoped he couldn't hear the tremor in her voice.

He stood. *"All right, then. But don't say I didn't tell you."*

Suddenly she felt she couldn't bear for him to turn and walk out the door. She put her hand on his arm. *"Ronnie. I am grown up now. You could stay if you wanted."*

She saw the naked flash of desire on his face, saw it swiftly replaced by horror.

*"Angel, you're . . . you're like my sister. I could never . . . you shouldn't even think such a thing."*

He did turn away then, clattering down the stairs, leaving her alone in the cold and damp-ridden room. Carefully, methodically, she lit the paraffin heater and curled up beneath a blanket on her narrow bed. Then she wept as if her heart would break.

Gemma spent the first part of Thursday morning reviewing the reports that had come back from computer forensics. There was no evidence, either in E-mail or personal files, that Karl Arrowood had intended to murder his wife—or that he had suspected her affair or her pregnancy.

Nor was there any evidence that Dawn had used the computer at all, which Gemma found interesting, but not surprising, considering Dawn's carefulness in other matters.

Unfortunately, they had not begun the investigation looking for financial discrepancies in Karl Arrowood's accounts, and she would now have to ask the computer team to go over everything once again. They would also have to look at his business computers, which she expected he would not take kindly.

"If what Otto says is true, that Arrowood sells drugs," Melody said thoughtfully, "mightn't Dawn's death be a professional matter? An irate customer? A dissatisfied partner?"

Gemma had requested that Melody go to Arrowood's shop with her as backup, first having made sure that Sergeant Franks was well buried in paperwork. "But in that case, where does Marianne Hoffman come in?" she countered.

"There is that," Melody agreed. "What about the blood work, then? Any progress there?"

"Not yet. Christmas slowdown at the Home Office. I've nagged them again." Gemma found a parking spot on Kensington Park Road, across the street from Arrowood Antiques. The shop was unobtrusively elegant, blending easily into the residences situated opposite the classical town houses of Stanley Gardens.

From the window dressing alone it was apparent the shop served an equally elegant clientele. As they entered, the door chimed melodiously and Gemma's feet sank into the plush pile of a Wilton carpet. The front room was small, holding a few choice pieces of antique furniture, objets d'art, lamps, and ornately framed watercolors, but other equally rich rooms opened out from it.

A woman—blond, middle-aged, perfectly coiffed and manicured—sat at a writing desk in view of the door. She gave Gemma a half-wattage smile. "May I help you?" she asked, and Gemma heard the unvoiced "Not that's there's anything here you can afford."

Gemma had to agree—if the lack of price tags was any indication. "Is Mr. Arrowood in?" she asked, and saw the flick of the woman's glance towards the back of the shop.

"He's just stepped ou——"

"I think he'll see us."

The woman's smile disappeared altogether at the sight of Gemma's identification. "Just a moment, please."

They waited only a few minutes before Karl Arrowood appeared, as immaculately groomed and suited as she had seen him at his wife's funeral. "Inspector James, and Constable Talbot, is it? What can I do for you?"

"We'd like a word with you, Mr. Arrowood. Your office?"

He took them into the back without demur, seating himself behind a polished, claw-footed desk and motioning them to plush-covered chairs. "I take it you haven't come to tell me you've found my wife's murderer?"

Gemma ignored the question. "Since we spoke last, Mr. Arrowood, it's come to our attention that some of your profits may come from areas other than antiques."

His gaze remained unwavering, slightly amused; his hands rested casually on his blotter. "I've no idea what you're talking about, Inspector."

"Drugs. According to our sources, you've long-standing connections with drug trafficking in the area."

The amusement grew stronger. "Sources? And what exactly are these sources? Comic books? I might be angry if I could take you seriously, Inspector." The gray eyes now held an unmistakable glint of steel. "However, I would remind you that I have a successful business here, and I would not appreciate having my reputation damaged among my customers."

"Good." Gemma smiled. "Then you have everything to gain by cooperating fully. It's not my job to follow up these allegations. I'm only interested in what bearing this new information may have on your wife's death. Could one of your customers, or your suppliers, have attacked her because of some grudge against you?"

"This is an absurd fantasy." His hands tightened, and Gemma saw him make an effort to relax them. "Which you are obviously indulging to mask your own incompetence. I'm not going to continue this discussion without a solicitor."

"You don't have to. I do have a warrant for our technicians to have a look at your office computers, however—I hope that won't be too much of an inconvenience." She glanced at her watch. "They should be here any minute."

"You can't do that!" He gripped his desk, no longer bothering to control his anger.

"I'm afraid I can." Gemma stood, followed by Melody. "Mr. Arrowood, did your wife know about your activities?"

"I've told you, there was nothing for her to know."

"And your sons, do they know? Surely you don't supply your own son with cocaine?" she asked. Kincaid had told her what he suspected about Richard Arrowood's drug habit, and she was inclined to agree.

"My son? What the devil are you talking about?"

"Didn't Richard come to you for a loan to pay off his drug debts?"

"Richard? Yes, he came to me for money, but he always needs money. I don't believe—"

"What did he tell you, when he came to you a few weeks ago?"

"Investments. He said he'd made a bad investment at work. He needed to recover the damages before it came to light."

"And you refused him?"

"Of course I refused him. He'll never make anything of himself if he doesn't learn to deal with his own mistakes."

A good theory, thought Gemma. Unfortunately, she suspected Richard Arrowood was long past benefiting from it.


Kincaid had left several messages on Eliza Goddard's answering machine, asking her to ring him back, but she had not. He urgently needed to see Marianne Hoffman's papers again, and he hoped that persuasion would be enough to convince Eliza to turn over her mother's things. If his attempt failed, however, he'd have to issue a warrant for the collection of the items.

But first, he had one more avenue to explore. He drove to Islington, leaving the car near the twisting alleyways of Camden Passage. Here, Marianne Hoffman's body had been found slumped against the door of her shop, two months earlier.

They had interviewed all the nearby shopkeepers and residents, but Kincaid remembered that the man who owned the shop next door to Hoffman's had been a particular friend. It took him a moment to pinpoint the exact location, as Christmas decorations altered the look of the shop fronts. Marianne Hoffman's premises had been taken over by someone selling antique dolls, but he recognized the cricket bats and leather golf bags in the window next to it.

Edgar Vernon sold antique sporting equipment, with the addition of old suitcases, globes, walking sticks, or anything else that might tickle the fancy of those dreaming of better Edwardian times. Today Kincaid saw a new addition carefully displayed in the front window: a set of beautifully preserved lead soldiers.

He went in, breathing in the sweet mustiness of old wood and leather. Vernon looked up from his desk, his expression momentarily puzzled, then gave a smile of recognition.

"Mr. Kincaid, isn't it? What can I do for you?" He was a trim man in his fifties with a small mustache and wire-rimmed spectacles.

"Mr. Vernon, if you have a few minutes, I'd like to chat with you about Marianne Hoffman again."

"I was just about to make some coffee. If you'll have a seat, it will only take me a moment."

"I'd rather poke about, if that's all right." It occurred to Kincaid that between the case and the move, he had altogether neglected his Christmas shopping. He caught sight of a silver-handled walking stick that he thought might suit his father admirably, but what about his mother?

By the time Vernon returned with a tray and *cafetière*, Kincaid had found the ideal thing—a badminton set, complete with original net and birds. Not exactly a seasonal gift, he supposed, but come spring he could imagine his mother setting it up between the apple trees in her back garden.

"Now sit, please." Vernon pulled a horn-and-hide chair up to his desk. "A souvenir from a safari," he explained. "And surprisingly comfortable. You said this was about Marianne? Have you discovered her killer?"

"I wish I could tell you that we had. And unfortunately, there's been another murder. In Notting Hill, the wife of an antiques dealer."

"Ah. I did wonder if there was a connection when I read about the case in the papers. Do you think it was the same killer?"

"We think it very likely. The victim's husband, Karl Arrowood, has quite a prosperous antiques business in Kensington Park Road. Do you know him?"

"I know of him, but merely by dealers' word of mouth. I've never done business with him personally—not my line."

"Do you know if Mrs. Hoffman knew him? Or his wife?"

"Not that I remember her mentioning. But, then, Marianne didn't talk much about herself."

Kincaid settled back rather gingerly into the horn curve of the chair. "Can you remember anything she *did* tell you about herself, or her background? I had the impression when we spoke that you were quite good friends."

"Yes." Vernon sipped at his coffee. "In fact, on reflection I'd say that Marianne was probably my closest friend, and vice versa. Not only because neither of us had anyone else, but because we were congenial spirits."

"Nothing of a romantic nature?"

Vernon smiled. "That was a complication spared us. My lover died five years ago of AIDS, you see."

"I'm sorry," Kincaid replied.

"There's no way you could have known. Anyway, the point was, Marianne had a way of letting you know she understood your feelings without making a fuss—a remarkable sort of quiet empathy. Although we saw each other off and on in the course of the day, over the years we developed a ritual of having take-away curry together on Friday nights. We would watch the telly, share a bottle of wine. I know it seems a small thing, but it astonishes me how much I miss it. And now, here I am talking your ear off just to lubricate my tongue."

"That's exactly what I hoped you'd do. Did Marianne ever say anything about her family—her parents, her background?"

"She never spoke directly of her parents, but I somehow had the feeling that her childhood was difficult—perhaps because she didn't share the usual reminiscences. Except . . . It's funny, now that you mention it. One Friday evening, not long before she died, we'd had a bit more wine than usual. There was this program on the telly about the sixties—pop icons, fashion, you know the sort of thing. And we began to make a game of it, bragging about who remembered most, or had done the most outlandish thing."

"One-upmanship."

"Exactly. Who crammed the most people in a mini, who waited in a queue for five days to see the Rolling Stones . . . Then she started to tell me about all the people she'd known, like Robert Frazer, the gallery owner, and models, artists, fashion designers. When she saw I was a bit skeptical, she got up and dug through a bureau drawer until she found this. I asked her if I could keep it." Vernon opened his desk and removed a photo he obviously treasured, handing it to Kincaid.

In the black-and-white image, a girl in a slip of a black dress gazed back at Kincaid. She was slender, with delicate features and large dark eyes enhanced by the makeup of the time. Her platinum hair was cut short and shaped to her head, giving her the irresistible appeal of the waif. And yet Kincaid could see the unmistakable resemblance to the older woman he had known only in death.

"She was stunning," he said, looking up at Vernon.

"Yes. Very much in the manner of Edie Sedgwick."

"Edie Sedgwick?"

"One of Andy Warhol's Factory girls; his lover, in fact. Edie left Warhol for Bob Dylan, who promptly abandoned her for someone else. The beginning of a tragic end."

"And you're saying that Marianne moved in the London equivalent of those circles? It *is* odd that she never spoke about it before that night."

"There's something else that's just occurred to me," Vernon added, frowning. "I often go to Portobello early on a Saturday, to see what I can pick up for the shop, but Marianne would never go with me, in all the time I knew her. She'd make some excuse or other, and sometimes she'd ask me to look out for something for her, so that it was obvious she knew the area, and the market, well. After a while, I stopped asking her to go, just took her little quirk for granted."

"An interesting aversion. What about her ex-husband, then? We never interviewed him. I believe he was in Thailand at the time of her death."

"A nice chap. They stayed good friends. I believe Greg's back in London at the moment; he stopped in for a bit not too long ago. He was quite devastated by Marianne's death."

"Have you any idea why they divorced?"

"She told me once that she was better off on her own. But I always suspected that she had lost someone very special to her, the way I had."

"You've been extremely helpful, Mr. Vernon. Could I borrow this photo for a short time? I'll have someone run it back to you as soon as I've made a copy. And now, if you don't mind, I'd like to do some Christmas shopping."

Kincaid bought the walking stick and the badminton set, wondering briefly how he was going to get them to Cheshire in time for the holiday. Then he hesitated, gazing at the lead soldiers in the window. "I didn't think you sold militaria."

"Toy soldiers are a particular passion of mine, and I can never pass up a good set. That one's a beauty."

"I'll take it," Kincaid decided impulsively. "For my son. He's twelve."

"A perfect age. You won't regret it."

As Kincaid took his tidily wrapped packages and bid Vernon a happy Christmas, he congratulated himself on his purchases. That left Toby, for whom he intended to buy a new Church Mice book, and Gemma.

For Gemma he had something entirely different in mind.


Gemma's mobile phone rang as she and Melody returned to the station. Expecting Kincaid with a report on his morning's activities, she was surprised to find Bryony Poole on the line.

"Gemma? Remember I said I'd ring about the dog? Could you come by the soup kitchen on Portobello Road? I've brought Geordie round for a lunchtime visit. The clients get a kick out of it."

"Right. I could use a break." Gemma had been wanting to talk to Bryony again, and this would give her a good opportunity.

Leaving Melody at the station, she drove the short distance to Portobello Road, finding a spot to put the car south of the point where the fruit-and-veg stalls lining the bottom half of the road made parking impossible. Walking on from there, she reached the double entrance to the old Portobello School. The soup kitchen was just to one side, in a nondescript building.

Gemma opened the door and peered in a bit gingerly. She'd been in the Sally Army facility up the road, of course, when she was on the beat, but she'd no idea what sort of place this was. What she saw reassured her. In the front of a clean, spare room, an assortment of people sat eating at long wooden tables. Towards the rear, Bryony and her friend Marc served a few stragglers from a buffet line. Bryony waved. "I'm on my lunch break," she explained as Gemma came up. "I tell Marc I come to help out, but it's really his food I'm after."

"Right," agreed Marc. "And I'll be moving on to the Savoy any day. Would you like something, Gemma?"

Gemma saw that it was not soup, but a thick vegetable-and-bean stew. It smelled delicious and she suddenly remembered that she had once again neglected breakfast. "Yes, please."

"Let me introduce you to Geordie, first," said Bryony. "So that you can be getting acquainted." She motioned Gemma round the buffet table. The cocker spaniel lay near Bryony, his head on his paws, watching her intently. But when Gemma knelt down beside him, he stood, his stump of a tail wagging.

"That's what I love about cockers," Bryony told Gemma. "Their entire bodies wriggle. No dissembling."

"Hullo, boy," Gemma said softly, holding out her

hand. Geordie snuffled her fingers, gave them a lick, his tail wagging harder, then looked up at her expectantly, as if to say, "What's next?"

Laughing, Gemma stroked his head and rubbed his silky ears. The dog promptly curled up with his head against her knee and gazed up at her devotedly.

"I'd say you've made a conquest." Bryony's pleasure was evident.

"He is lovely," Gemma admitted. "But I couldn't take him until the weekend," she heard herself adding. "We'll be moving on Saturday. And that's if his owner agrees, of course." Surely she had completely lost her mind, she thought, but she found she didn't care.

"I'll vouch for you," said Bryony. "If you come back to the clinic with me after lunch, we'll fill out the adoption paperwork. I'll ring you on Sunday and we can make arrangements."

Geordie followed Gemma as they settled at a table near the buffet with their bowls of stew, settling himself near her feet with a sigh. "I've never had a dog before," Gemma confessed. "I mean, not personally. My older son—stepson—has a terrier, but he hasn't lived with us until now. I mean my son, not the dog—Oh, it's too complicated to explain!"

"The dog is much simpler," Bryony answered, laughing. "Feed him, walk him, give him regular baths and lots of attention. That's all there is to it."

"Essentials," said Marc, looking round at the people finishing their meals, several with dogs at their feet. "Food and care. That's what keeps a good many of these folks on the street—they simply can't cope with anything more complicated than that."

"No cell phones and computerized banking?"

"Right. Overload. Their circuits just can't handle it."

A black woman stood and carried her dishes to the washing-up stack. She wore green wellies and what must have once been an expensive business suit beneath a worn man's overcoat.

"Take Evelyn, for example," said Marc. "She was in insurance. An executive of some sort. One day she just quit."

"Thank you, Mr. Marc," Evelyn called out as she collected her bundles from the pile by the door. "Lord bless you."

"See you tomorrow," Marc answered.

As Gemma ate her stew, Marc pointed out some of the other regulars to her. Some had simply lost jobs and not been able to meet their commitments, some had fallen victim to drugs, others were mentally ill.

"You know them all?" Gemma asked, pushing her empty bowl away.

"Most. Some—especially those with families—have a good chance of getting off the streets. Others, like Evelyn, have found a niche and have no intention of leaving it."

"But that's dreadful."

"It is and it isn't." Marc shrugged. "Again, it's down to basics, and their perspective is quite a bit different than yours. It depends on whether they can manage to sleep warm and dry, and get enough to eat. I try to take care of their minor medical needs, the things they absolutely won't go to hospital for. And Bryony—did she tell you what she's doing?"

Bryony colored. "It's just an idea I had, a free weekly clinic to treat the animals. Minor things, of course, as Marc said; that's all you can do." Glancing at Marc, she added with a grimace, "I'm going to have to be really careful about accounting for my supplies after that incident at the surgery a couple of weeks ago. Gavin was on at me again about it this morning."

"What happened?" asked Gemma.

"When I got to the surgery that morning, the door was unlocked. There were some things missing—not drugs, just small items: instruments, bandages. Some flea-control preparations, which bring a good price. Gavin said I must have left the surgery unlocked when I closed up the day before, although I know I didn't. He's taking the loss out of my paycheck."

Gemma raised an eyebrow. "Seems a bit unfair. Bryony, I know you said you were in and out with clients when Dawn came in last Friday, but did you see her when she left? I just had the impression, when I was talking to Gavin yesterday, that perhaps something had gone on between them."

Bryony looked uncomfortable. "It's not good politics to tell tales on one's boss."

"So there was something."

"I don't know what; I didn't actually hear anything except raised voices through the cubicle wall. But when Dawn left she looked furious. When I said good-bye, she didn't even notice."

"But you must have a theory as to what caused the row. Was there something going on between them?"

"Only in Gav's dreams! He always flirted with her and she took it good-naturedly enough, you know, without encouraging him. My guess is he went too far. Either that or she was less tolerant that day and told him she'd had enough."

Dawn had certainly had good reason to be less tolerant

that day, thought Gemma, facing a doctor's appointment she must have dreaded, not to mention the sick cat—

"Sid!" she exclaimed. "I completely forgot about Sid!" Realizing how daft she must sound, she amended, "Sid's our cat. Will Geordie be all right with him?"

"I'm sure he'll be fine," reassured Bryony. "So far, I haven't seen anyone or anything that Geordie *didn't* like. I'd say the future of the relationship is entirely up to the other party."

"The kids will be thrilled, I'm sure, but I don't know what Duncan will say," Gemma confessed to Melody.

"Tell him the dog's a Christmas present. Then he can't complain without looking like Scrooge."

"You're devious," Gemma said, laughing. "Remind me to come to you for advice more often." She nodded at the sheaf of papers in Melody's hand. "Have you got something else for me?"

"The blood work's come back, boss."

"Anything helpful?"

"Inconclusive. More on the negative side than the positive, if you ask me. It looks like Arrowood picked up his wife, just like he said, but that doesn't prove incontrovertibly that he didn't hold her from behind first, until she bled out."

"Difficult to do without getting some blood spatter on his clothes. And if he'd dumped some sort of protective covering anywhere in the neighborhood, we'd have found it by now." Gemma tried to keep the discouragement from her voice—this was no more than she'd expected. Six days and virtually no progress.

"So what do we do now?"

"We keep working on the drug angle with Arrowood. Which means we talk to Alex Dunn again."

They found Alex Dunn at home, packing bubble-wrapped china into a box. He seemed tired, and edgier than he had on Tuesday. Gemma suspected that he'd come into the station buffered by a surge of adrenaline that had since worn off.

"This is a Sèvres dinner service I found for a client in Nottingham," he told them. "That's a good deal of my business, selling to private clients. I keep an eye out at auction for them, or pick up things from other dealers that I know they want."

Gemma found her eye drawn once again to the bright dishes she'd noticed on her first visit. "Is that pottery, or china?"

"Pottery. Made by a woman named Clarice Cliff, mainly in the twenties and thirties, the heyday of Art Deco. She started work in the potteries at thirteen, and by the time she was in her late teens she was designing her own wares."

Moving closer to study the pieces, Gemma saw that although they all had the same bright, bold look, there was infinite variation in the patterns.

"It's not really my field," Alex continued, "but I fell in love with the first piece I saw and I've been collecting it ever since. And Dawn loved it. I was going to give her that teapot"—he nodded towards a piece dominated by red-roofed houses against a deep yellow ground—"for Christmas."

"Is the pottery expensive?" Gemma asked, with a private sigh of regret.

"Very."

"Would Karl have noticed?"

"Yes. Anything to do with antiques, Karl noticed. And he would certainly be aware of the value of Clarice Cliff pottery, even if it's not the sort of thing he stocks in his shop."

"So Karl is successful because he's good at what he does?"

Alex gave her a puzzled look. "The antiques trade is no business for fools, and Karl has a particularly good eye for finding pieces that will bear a huge markup. Not to mention the connections with clients who can *pay* the markup."

"We've been told Karl has other clients—and other uses for his business—as in laundering the money he makes in drug transactions."

"Drugs? You're joking." Alex's bark of laughter died as he read their faces. "But that's daft! Why would Karl need to do something like that? He's got more money than God."

"Maybe you're putting the cart before the horse. Maybe the drugs came first, or at least simultaneously. Did Dawn never mention anything like that to you?"

"Are you saying Dawn was aware of it?"

"We don't know. That's why we're asking you."

"I'm the last person you should've come to. Apparently there were a lot of things Dawn didn't tell me." He stuffed a wrapped teapot into the box so violently that Gemma repressed a gasp.

"You knew her better than anyone," she said. "How

do you think she would have felt about Karl's involvement in drugs?"

"A week ago, I'd have thought she'd have left him in horror if she found out." Alex said it savagely. "Now I'm not so sure. It's not the sort of thing we sat around and discussed. 'Oh, by the way, dear, how do you feel about drug trafficking?'"

"So what *did* you talk about?" Gemma asked. She needed to penetrate the bitter shell the young man had erected.

"Whatever you talk about with your significant other, assuming you have one. Food, music, movies, stupid television programs, the state of the world."

"But the problem with an affair is that you *don't* talk about the ordinary, everyday things, because you don't share them. What to have for dinner, the size of the gas bill, your child's cough."

"Do you think I don't know that?" Alex told her hotly. "Do you have any idea what I'd have given for even one day of conversations like that? You don't appreciate it, do you? Either of you?"

Gemma said softly, "No. You're right. I'm sorry."

"The funny thing is . . . She was so beautiful, the kind of woman men dream about. But it was the ordinary things I loved most about her. She had a passion for ginger ice cream. And flowers. They had a fortune in flowers delivered to the house every week, but she could go bonkers over a geranium in a pot on the patio, or a late rose blooming beside the pavement."

"But that's a good thing, isn't it?" said Melody. "That she had that capacity for enjoying life?"

"Is it? I'm not so sure." He stared at them belligerently. Then his anger seemed to dissipate and he knelt again beside his packing box. "Of course you're right. If I were a good person, I'd wish her every bit of joy given her by anything—or anyone—instead of envying what she might have shared with someone else.

"And what I said before, it was just the doubt eating at me. I *knew* her. Even if she didn't tell me she was pregnant, I'm absolutely certain that if she found out Karl was selling drugs, she would have left him in an instant."

# CHAPTER TEN

Funny thing, history. Since the sixties, all sorts of people, moral reformers, right-wingers, left-wingers, politicians, feminists, male chauvinists, law-and-order campaigners, and censorship freaks of every kind, have invented a straight-laced, well-behaved public life from which the country somehow strayed with the invention of permissiveness.

—Charlie Phillips and Mike Phillips,
from *Notting Hill in the Sixties*

ALTHOUGH NEVER VERY *substantial, Angel lost weight rapidly after she moved into the Colville Terrace bedsit. This was in part from lack of funds, as her wage did not stretch as far as she'd expected, and in part because the single gas ring in her room didn't encourage more than heating soup or stew from a tin. She took up smoking, finding that tobacco both dulled hunger and eased boredom, not to mention the fact that her boss gave her a discount on cigarettes.*

*She grew her hair long and straight, with a fringe that brushed her eyebrows and, unable to afford the new fashions, hemmed her skirts above her knees with clumsy stitches that would have made Mrs. Thomas cringe. Her lashes were heavy with mascara, her skin pale with the latest pancake foundation.*

*There were boys, of course, to impress with her newfound sense of style. As soon as word got round that she was on her own, they came into the shop in pimply droves, wanting to take her to the cinema, or out for a coffee.*

At first she was flattered, but she learned soon enough what those invitations meant. After the first few disappointing encounters, she decided she preferred to stay in her room in the evenings, watching the telly and listening to 45s that scratched and hissed on her father's old phonograph. Posters of the Beatles now covered the damp stains on her walls—their smiling faces watched over her like medieval saints.

These small comforts kept her going until a bitterly cold night in March, when she came to the end of her wages, her food, and paraffin for the heater. It was two days until payday and, shivering beneath a swath of blankets as her stomach cramped from emptiness, she wondered how she was going to manage. Her employer, Mr. Pheilholz, was kind enough, but she knew he had nothing extra to give her. She could go to the Thomases, but the thought of Ronnie's pity and contempt made her decide she'd rather die than give in to that temptation.

Prompted by the thought of the Thomases, however, a memory came to her unbidden. She had been ill once, as a child, and her mother had soothed her with tinned chicken soup and fizzy lemonade. The recollection brought tears to her eyes. She shook it off, as she did most reminders of her former life, but the thought of her mother had triggered another vivid flash.

She got out of bed and scrabbled in the bureau. She didn't remember throwing away the last of her mother's tablets—were they still there? When her mother had been too fretful to sleep, the tiny morphine tablets had given her ease. Could they help her daughter now?

Her fingers closed on a smooth round shape, right in the back of the drawer. She drew it out—yes, it was the same brown glass bottle she remembered. Unscrewing the cap, she shook a few of the tablets into her hand, then, with sudden resolution, took a kitchen knife and cut one in half. Gingerly, she swallowed the tiny crescent moon.

*She regretted it instantly. Her heart thumped with fear as she waited, wondering how she would feel dying, poisoned, unable to call for help.*

*After a few minutes, something began to happen. First came a cold numbness in her mouth, then warmth spread through her body and she felt a strange sort of separation from the cold and hunger. She was still aware of the sensations, she knew that they were a part of her, and yet she was somehow outside them.*

*Forgetting her terror, she relaxed, snuggling deeper into the blankets. It was all right...It was going to be all right. A rosy contentment possessed her. The light from her single lamp seemed to coalesce into a luminous halo, and she hummed to herself as disconnected bits of songs floated through her brain. At last, she drifted into a deep and blissful sleep, the first in days.*

*After that, she hoarded the little white tablets, saving them for the times when things seemed more than she could bear.*

Summer came at last, and with it her seventeenth birthday. The day passed unremarked except for a card sent by Betty and her mother. It was hot, even for August, and as the afternoon wore on, the shop became more and more stifling. Angel was minding the place on her own, as Mr. Pheilholz had declared it unbearable and departed for the day. She stood at the cash register, aware of every breath of air that came through the open door, watching the hands on the big wall clock move like treacle.

The young man came in for cigarettes. She barely noticed him at first, as there was a faint buzzing in her ears and her vision seemed to be doing strange things.

"Are you all right?" he asked as he took his change. "You're pale as a ghost."

"I...I do feel a bit odd." Her voice seemed to come from a long way away.

"It's the heat. You need to sit down, get some air," he told her decisively. "Here." Dumping the apples from one produce crate into another, he turned over the empty one and placed it in the doorway. He then led her to it, holding her by the arm. "Sit. Put your head down." He pulled a newspaper from the display and fanned her with it.

After a few minutes, he asked, "Feeling better?"

"Yes, thanks." Lifting her head, she took in the blond hair brushing his collar, the clear, gray eyes, the smart, uncreased jacket he wore even in the heat, and the giddiness that washed over her had nothing to do with the heat. She thought that he was the most beautiful thing she had ever seen.

"Come on, then," he ordered. "I'll take you out for something cold to drink."

"Can't. Not until closing. I'm minding the shop."

"Then shut it. It's too hot for anyone to buy groceries, much less cook them."

"I can't!" she protested, horrified. "I'd lose my job."

"And that matters?"

"Of course it matters!" she told him, but she was partly convincing herself.

He studied her, and she gazed back, as mesmerized as a rabbit facing a snake.

"How long till you can close, then?" he asked.

She glanced at the clock and was surprised to find that half an hour had passed. "An hour. It's my birthday," she added, inexplicably, feeling a fool.

"Is it? Then I suppose I'll just have to wait." Leaning against the produce case, he crossed his arms, looking about the shop with evident disdain. "What are you doing working in this lousy place, anyway?"

"It's all I could get." She was ashamed, seeing it through his eyes. "And it pays my rent."

"*You haven't told me your name.*"

For a moment she hesitated, then she lifted her chin. "*Angel.*"

"*Just Angel?*"

Excitement surged through her. He knew nothing of her, her parents, her background; she could reinvent herself as she chose. "*That's right. Just Angel.*"

Two weeks later, she lay beneath him in her narrow bed, the rumpled sheets pushed back, the window open as wide as it would go. "*Tell me what you want, Angel,*" he urged, his breath catching in his throat. "*I can give it to you. I can give you anything—fame, fortune, glory.*" He had pursued her as if nothing else mattered in the world, waiting at her flat every day after work, taking her out for meals and to the cinema, buying her trinkets . . . and staying every night in her room. The wonder of it took her breath away. What could he possibly see in her, when he could have anyone?

His skin, glistening with perspiration, slid effortlessly against hers as he moved inside her. A sultry breeze lifted the curtains; the light from the street lamp silvered his corn-yellow hair.

She was lost, and she knew that he knew it, but she didn't care. "*I want you to love me.*" Digging her fingertips into his shoulders, she whispered against his cheek, tasting the salt like blood. "*I want you to love me, just me. More than anyone, or anything, ever.*"

Kit McClellan loaded the last of his boxes into his dad's—make that his stepdad's—Volvo. He had learned, since his mum had died the previous April, that the man he had always known as his father was actually not his dad at all, and that his real dad had not known of his existence until his mum's death. It was all quite confusing, but he had gradually got used to it, and now everything was going to change again.

His stepfather, Ian, was taking a teaching post in Canada, and Kit was going to live with his real father, Duncan, Duncan's girlfriend, Gemma, and her son, Toby, in a house in a part of London Kit had never even seen. It was what he had wanted, to be a real family, and Gemma was going to have a baby in the spring, a new brother or sister for him.

It was also terrifying, and it meant leaving the pink cottage in the little village of Grantchester where he had spent his whole life, and where he had last seen his mum.

That morning he'd said good-bye to his friend Nathan Winter, who had been his mother's friend as well, and who had fostered Kit's love of biology. Much to Kit's embarrassment, Nathan had given him a crushing hug, and it had been all Kit could do to keep from blubbing like a baby. "You know you can come visit any time the pavement gets too much for you," Nathan had teased, and Kit thought with a pang of the long, slow days spent by the river that flowed past his back garden.

"Are you ready, Kit?" called Ian.

Swallowing hard, Kit took one last look at the cottage, its "For Sale" sign already posted in the front garden. "All set."

He opened the car door and summoned Tess with a whistle. "Ready for a ride, girl?" he asked the little terrier who had been his constant companion since he'd found her hiding in a box behind a supermarket, just days after his mum's death.

Tess bounded into the car, licking his face excitedly as he climbed in beside her.

They made the drive in silence, Kit watching out the window with avid interest as they reached London and drove west along Hyde Park. He could bring Tess to the park, Duncan had said, whenever he liked, so they must be getting close to the house.

He had a fleeting impression of ugly, square buildings round the Notting Hill Gate tube stop. They swung to the right, entering streets lined with sedate rows of terraced houses. Next, a church, its brick dark with age; then they were running down a hill and drawing to a stop before a solid-looking brown brick house with a red door and white trim.

"You'll come to Canada on your summer break," Ian reminded him. "I'll make all the arrangements."

Kit nodded absently, for Duncan had come out the front door, and Toby stood at the garden gate, calling excitedly to him. His new life had begun.


Hazel had helped her pack with such cheerful competence that Gemma decided she must have imagined that her friend was distressed over her leaving. But Gemma herself found it hard to say good-bye to the tiny flat: It was the first home she had been able to call entirely her own. And then there was Hazel's piano—when would she ever be able to play again? Making an excuse for a last trip into the big house, she dashed into the sitting room and stood for a moment gazing at the instrument, then touched the keys briefly in farewell.

"Don't worry if you've forgotten something," Hazel assured her as Gemma squeezed into the car with the collected bundles. "Holly and I will come over tomorrow and help you get settled."

"I'll need it, I'm sure," Gemma called out as she waved and drove off. Duncan had taken Toby with him in the van he'd fixed to transport the things from his flat—and Sid the cat. They would meet her at the new house.

After a week's relentless drizzle, Saturday had dawned clear and unseasonably warm, a perfect day for moving, and as Gemma neared Notting Hill she found herself singing along with the old Crosby, Stills, Nash & Young tune "Our House" on the radio. She laughed aloud with sudden, unanticipated joy.

They were all waiting for her—Duncan, Toby, and Kit, with Tess bounding round and barking madly.

"I take it she likes the house." Gemma gave Kit a welcoming hug.

Toby tugged at her, his cheeks flushed with excitement. "Mummy, Mummy, have you seen the garden? Have you seen my room? Sid's shut in the loo." The poor cat must be utterly traumatized, thought Gemma, but before she could check on him, Toby grabbed her hand and yanked her towards the stairs. "Come see my room, Mummy. Kit's going to share with me!"

"Okay, okay," she said, laughing. "We need a plan. First we tour the house, then we start on the boxes. I'll take the kitchen, you boys can start on your bedrooms, and Duncan can take the sitting room."

"Yes, ma'am. I take it we save our bedroom for last?" Kincaid grinned and winked at her over the boys' heads.

By mid-afternoon Gemma had made a list of essentials they would need to buy, including new linens for the boys' beds and a set of dishes for the kitchen. Her few mismatched bits and Duncan's bachelor plates were not going to do for a real kitchen, and she had seen exactly the thing in a catalogue: a blue-and-yellow French farm-house design, perfect for the blue-and-yellow kitchen.

She was humming happily as she confronted the oil-fired cooker, thinking she would make them all a pot of tea, when her cell phone rang.

It was Melody Talbot, calling from Notting Hill Police Station. "Sorry to interrupt your moving day, boss, but we've had a call that might add up to something. A Miss Granger, who lives near the Arrowoods, was out jogging the night Dawn was killed. She's been out of town on business and just now saw the media appeal."

"Go on," Gemma encouraged as she filled her chipped teakettle. Not expecting much, she only half listened, mentally adding "new kettle" to her shopping list.

"Well, it seems Miss Granger passed another jogger that night, going the opposite way on Ladbroke Grove. That would mean he was going north, away from St. John's Gardens. His hood was up, which she thought was a bit odd because it had stopped drizzling, and when she looked back she saw that he was leaving a trail of dark footprints. She shrugged it off at the time, thinking he must have run through a puddle or something, but now . . ."

"Jesus . . ." Gemma set the kettle down on the very

edge of the stove, then grabbed it as it tipped. "Blood? You're thinking it was blood?"

"His shoes would have been soaked, wouldn't they, if he stood behind Dawn?"

"And his hood was up to conceal his face. Could this Miss Granger describe his clothes?"

"Ordinary jogger's things; a dark nylon tracksuit."

"Did you get a full statement?"

"I'm going to her flat myself, right now. Boss, does this rule out Karl?"

They'd assumed that if Karl had murdered his wife, he had parked in his own drive, killed Dawn, then rung the police. But what if he had parked his car elsewhere, changed into jogging clothes, run to the house where he waited for his wife and killed her, then run back to his car, disposing of his bloody outer garments and weapon before driving to the house and calling for help—and all in the few minutes' leeway the traffic between Tower Bridge and Notting Hill might have allowed him? Implausible, improbable, and bloody unlikely.

"I'd say so," Gemma responded grimly, "unless he's Superman."

By evening Gemma was happy enough to have a soak in the roll-top tub—the highlight of their new bathroom— and ready enough to leave the boxes behind for a civilized dinner. They'd ordered pizza for the boys, a treat, apparently, of royal proportions, and assured Kit that he could reach them on their mobile phones.

"Have you met Cullen's girlfriend?" Gemma asked Kincaid as they drove towards Victoria. "And what is she doing with a flat in Belgravia?"

"Her father owns the building, I think Doug said."

"Oh, charming."

Kincaid snorted. "Your prejudices are showing. I'm sure she's perfectly nice. Doug says she works for a home furnishings shop."

"Worse yet," Gemma muttered.

But when they reached Ebury Street, she found she was actually a little nervous about meeting Doug Cullen. "What's he like, really?" she asked, tucking her arm through Kincaid's as they climbed the stairs to the first-floor flat.

"A nice chap. Don't worry, you'll like him."

And indeed she did, at first sight. Cullen exuded a sort of perpetual naïveté, his fresh-faced, public-school looks made only slightly more severe by the wire-rimmed spectacles he kept pushing up his nose.

In contrast to Cullen's comforting ordinariness, Stella Fairchild-Priestly wore a cropped pink angora top and black capri trousers that bared her rhinestone-studded navel—or at least Gemma assumed the sparkling gems were rhinestones. The girl's pale hair was expensively and trendily cut, her makeup salon perfect, her nails a frosted pink that matched her sweater. "Hi, I'm Stella," she said with a brilliant smile, and Gemma felt instantly frumpy, fat, and ancient.

Nothing could have been better designed to make Gemma feel even more uncomfortable than being forced to ask for mineral water while the others drank martinis. Stella had a drinks tray ready, and as the others discussed the merits of olives and shaken versus stirred, Gemma looked round the sitting room she instantly dubbed Fifties Chic.

The room had two sets of French doors giving on to a balcony that overlooked Ebury Street. Around evergreen topiaries Stella had wound strings of tiny Christmas lights, and these were reflected in mirrors on the flat's interior walls, adding sparkle to the long, low shapes of the furniture.

The table Stella had arranged at the room's far end gleamed with silver and starched white linen, and as Gemma moved closer she saw that there were even tiny silver place card holders. "Bloody hell," she whispered, wondering if she had wandered into a magazine set.

"Dougie promised me you weren't vegetarian," Stella said a few minutes later as she served Gemma's plate with perfectly prepared veal scaloppini, fresh asparagus, and a saffron rice timbale—at least that's what Gemma thought it was, having seen something similar on a cooking program once.

"Dougie" blushed to the roots of his hair. "Stella, you know how much I hate it when you call me that."

"Sorry." Stella smiled at him over the candles, unrepentant. "But we are among friends, after all. Gemma, tell me about your new home."

As Gemma launched into a description of the house's attributes and furnishings, Stella interrupted with, "You'll need linens, won't you? You'll have to come to our shop. Two-hundred-thirty-thread count, from Portugal. They're yummy. You'll have to iron them, of course, but we have lavender linen water, just the thing for it."

"Um, where is the shop exactly?" Gemma murmured. Even if she could afford Stella's sheets, where on earth did the silly woman think she would find time to iron them? Stella began on the virtues of Portuguese lace, but Gemma listened with only half her attention, as Kincaid had begun filling Cullen in on the day's developments.

"So if this jogger was indeed the killer," Cullen was saying earnestly, "he'd have had to dispose of the bloody clothes a good distance away—we've searched the immediate neighborhood with a fine-tooth comb—and that would have meant changing socks as well as shoes, and not leaving a smidgen of trace evidence in his car."

Out of the corner of her eye, Gemma saw Stella pale.

"If this development makes Arrowood a less than likely prospect," Cullen continued, "where does that leave us?" He seemed oblivious to his girlfriend's growing discomfort.

"Alex Dunn has a fairly watertight alibi, and so does Otto Popov, unless everyone in his café is conspiring to cover up for him, including Alex." Gemma pushed the rice around on her plate as she thought. "But what about the Arrowood boys? You've been working on that angle, haven't you, Doug?"

Cullen gave an exaggerated sigh that Gemma suspected was for Stella's benefit. "I've interviewed every guest at the party they attended that night. The only way Sean or Richard Arrowood could have murdered Dawn would have been by hiring a professional killer. And as for that, I can't see Richard having the nerve, or Sean the motivation."

"No evidence of drugs or debt on Sean's part?" Kincaid asked.

"Just a long history of cleaning up his brother's messes. But I can't see his loyalty to Richard extending to murdering his stepmother to get Richard out of a scrape."

Into the discouraged silence that followed this

pronouncement, Kincaid said, "There must be something we've missed—someone else whose path crossed Dawn's—"

"There is the vet," interrupted Gemma. "Gavin Farley. Remember my telling you that Farley's assistant, Bryony, said he had a row with Dawn the day she died?"

"And Bryony had no idea what the row was about?"

"None, other than the fact that Farley liked to flirt with Dawn, although Dawn didn't encourage it. When I interviewed the man, he denied arguing with her at all."

"So either Bryony or Farley is lying?"

Gemma nodded. "I'd put my money on Farley. It's at least worth seeing where he was on the night of Dawn's murder."

"You're leaving out Hoffman, again." Doug pushed his spectacles firmly up. "What connection could a veterinarian possibly have had with the Hoffman woman? She didn't even have a pet."

Kincaid expertly balanced the last bite of his veal on his fork. "We know nothing about the man at this point. I say we start by seeing what we can dig up on him. Doug, you can make that your project—"

Depositing her silverware on her plate with a clatter, Stella pushed away her half-eaten dinner with a brittle smile. "I must say, this evening *has* exceeded my every expectation—educational and pleasant. Anyone for dessert?"

Fern cursed as she tripped over something bulky and hard on her sitting room floor. She edged forward, fumbling for the light switch.

Illumination revealed a box containing old children's toys, a tricycle, and—was that really a weathervane?—set down willy-nilly in the center of the room. That meant her father had been and gone again, no doubt to squander the proceeds of his day's trading at the pub. For a moment she considered leaving the box where it was, but decided she couldn't risk his falling over it when he came in. Instead, she shoved it to one side, then retreated to her room and slammed the door.

Once inside, she sat on the edge of her bed, looking round at the neat shelves and storage boxes with her usual sense of relief. This was her island in the storm of her father's chaos; here her silver was arranged and catalogued, and nothing was ever, ever out of place.

She could have moved out years ago, of course, as her mum had done, and left him to his own devices. It wasn't that she couldn't afford to live on her own; she made a reasonable living with her trading, enough for a little studio or maisonette, maybe not in Notting Hill itself, but at least on the fringe.

But then who would get her dad his tea, or look after him when he'd had a night on the tiles? Or make certain the rent and the rates got paid? As much as she liked Marc Mitchell, she'd no desire to see her dad frequenting Marc's soup kitchen, and she had no doubt that was where he'd end up.

Of course, if she ever got into a serious relationship, she'd have to come up with another solution, and it had occurred to her that her refusal to give up on Alex gave her an easy out. Unrequited affection required no action, nor any tough decisions. Had she loved him as much when she thought he loved her?

Shying away from the question, she got out her laptop and began entering the day's transactions. She liked keeping track of her merchandise, and of what sold and what didn't. "Prissy accountancy," her dad called it. She argued that it was merely practical, but the truth was that it made her feel secure.

Tonight, however, nothing kept her mind off Alex. She was worried about his safety and frustrated by the fact that she could do nothing to remedy the situation—nor could she talk to him about it, as she had discovered that morning in the arcade.

They'd always been comfortable together; even after Dawn came on the scene, they had still managed to get through Saturday trading with a certain amount of shoptalk and banter. But today had been awful, a long, awkward day of aborted conversations and unaccustomed silences, after which Alex had locked up on the stroke of five and hurried out as if he couldn't bear another moment of her company.

Then, an hour later, he had rung her at home, hesitantly asking if she'd come round to his flat.

Baffled by his behavior, but determined not to jump at his beck and call, she'd made a date for nine o'clock. But as the time passed she grew increasingly uneasy, and as she walked up the hill to his mews, she had to make herself slow her pace. When she arrived to find him looking just as usual, she felt a ridiculous surge of relief.

"Coffee?" he asked cheerfully. "No alcohol for me, I'm afraid, but if you'd rather I can give you a glass of wine."

"No, coffee's fine." She wasn't sure she wanted to

know why he wasn't drinking, and he didn't volunteer any explanation. She stood silently as he made the coffee in his drip pot, then watched in shock as he put one of his treasured Clarice Cliff coffeepots and two matching cups on a tray. This was not stuff you *used,* for heaven's sake—breaking just one of the cups would cost you a month's wages.

"Alex, what are you thinking of? You can't seriously mean to drink out of those?"

"And why not? I distinctly remember you serving punch out of a Georgian bowl at your friend Alicia's wedding."

"Yeah, but that's different. You can't really hurt silver. But this stuff..."

"So what do you suggest I save it for? Isn't this special occasion enough?"

"Oh, please. I seem to recall us having coffee out of polystyrene cups this morning. Since when is having a cup of coffee with me an occasion?"

"Now."

Staring at him, she said, "Okay, cut the bullshit, Alex. What's this really about?"

"It's not bullshit. I mean, you don't know, do you? When something might—Anyway, there is something I wanted to say, and it's... awkward. I never thanked you for what you did last Saturday. I don't know what I'd have done if you hadn't... You've been a good friend, Fern, and I've behaved abominably. To Jane and to you."

Considering this, she said slowly, "Yeah, I suppose you have. But under the circumstances..."

"I wanted you to know, in case... Well, I've learned it's better not to leave things unsaid."

"What do you mean, 'in case'? In case what?" Her heart was hammering.

"It's just an expression. I could walk in front of a bus, that's all."

"Alex, are you okay now? I mean really okay?"

"Honestly?" This time his eyes met hers. "I don't know. I've never done this before. I don't know how I'm supposed to feel."

"Maybe you should talk to someone. You know... a professional."

"A shrink?" He laughed sourly. "What would that fix? Look, there's something else I wanted to ask you. Have you ever heard anything about Karl Arrowood selling drugs?"

"What?" Her voice rose to a furious squeak. "Don't tell me *you're* giving me the she's-got-green-hair-she-must-know-about-drugs bit?"

"Of course not! God, Fern, I didn't mean to offend you. But you've lived in the area your whole life. You know things, hear things, in a way I never will."

"I suppose that's true." Her anger abated a little. "Well, you know how Otto talks about Karl, but he's never said anything specifically about drugs. But... I have heard a few vague whispers over the years. You know, that maybe some of Karl's money was ill-gotten. But it's not like he's gone around selling heroin to the kiddies at Colville School."

"You knew this, or suspected it, and you didn't tell me?"

"Like you'd have believed me! *'Oh, by the way, Alex, your new girlfriend's hubbie's a major drug kingpin.'* Besides, I don't even know if it's true."

They glared at one another over the forgotten coffee, a standoff.

It was Alex who broke it. "All right. Maybe I wouldn't have believed you. But what if . . . What if Dawn found out, and threatened to leave him? Or threatened to expose him?"

"And he killed her? First of all, I don't buy her being married to the guy for years and not realizing what he was up to—if he was up to anything. She'd have to have been living in never-never land. And second, I don't buy that for motive. I think you're just trying to find some way around the fact that he killed her because he found out you were—"

She had clamped her mouth shut on the words, but it was too late.

She'd left after that, cursing herself all the way home. What the hell sort of damage had she done because she couldn't control her stupid temper?

Setting her laptop aside in disgust, she pulled over the box of items she'd brought home from the stall display case and began to sort through them. She needed to rotate some of her stock before next Saturday; the regulars got tired of seeing the same things week after week.

Spoons, thimbles, magnifying glasses; cigarette, card, and needle cases; snuffboxes, sugar nips, tea scoops, and paper knives—

Wait. She knew she had put in a lovely, engraved Victorian paper knife, with a razor-sharp edge. She went through the box again, taking each item out and setting it on the table. No paper knife. Was she losing her mind? No, she distinctly remembered transferring the knife, because she always had to be careful with the blade.

With growing horror, she remembered that just before closing, she had asked Alex to watch her stall while she went to the loo. Surely he wouldn't . . .

Methodically, refusing to entertain the unthinkable, she placed every item back in the box. But the image of Alex's face as she returned to the stall remained with her. At the time she'd put it down to the discomfort between them, that and her overactive imagination, but he had looked—there was no other word for it—furtive.

# CHAPTER ELEVEN

> By about the middle of the decade the Grove was changing
> rapidly. The affair of Christine Keeler and Stephen Ward
> had finally dampened down the fine Bohemian frenzy with
> which the bad boys moved among the district.
>
> —Charlie Phillips and Mike Phillips,
> from *Notting Hill in the Sixties*

"WE *WERE* TERRIBLY rude," Gemma said as they got into her car in front of Stella's flat.

"I did my best to make up for it." Kincaid had apologized to their hostess, then given her a peck on the cheek. Stella had looked surprised, then she'd smiled—a real smile, not the frosty, pasted-on equivalent she'd been wearing for the past hour.

"You're a charming sod," Gemma agreed now. "Poor Doug would've given rubies to keep us there. I imagine she's pouring boiling oil over him as we speak."

"Doug's all right." Although he said it as a statement, Gemma sensed that her approval mattered to him.

"Yes."

"The best of the lot, since you left. It helps a bit." He glanced at her. "I shouldn't say this. But in a way I'll be sorry to see this case finished. It's been good to be together again."

She touched her fingers to his cheek. "Don't worry. I'm sure you'll be fed up with me soon enough."

. . . .

At first, she worried about the bedroom's distance from Toby, who was now an entire floor below, when she was used to hearing his breathing from the next room. But she told herself he was safe and sound, sharing with Kit, and Kincaid soon took her mind off anything but decreasing the space between them.

She slept, in *their* bed for the first time, deeply and luxuriously, and she awakened early with a tremendous sense of energy and a determination to put her house in order.

By early afternoon, by force of will, she had reduced the still-packed boxes to a meager half-dozen. And she'd been to the supermarket, stocking pantry and fridge with necessities as well as treats for the children. The boys had organized their room, Toby with considerable assistance from Kit, and when they'd finished sandwiches in the kitchen, she'd sent them out to the garden to burn off some energy. An arctic front had dipped down from Scotland during the night. There was the smell of snow in the cold, gray air, and to Gemma it finally felt like Christmas.

Kincaid had been shelving books, hooking up the stereo system, and, last she heard, hanging his beloved London Transport posters. The hammering had recently stopped, however, so she went into the sitting room to see what he was doing.

He stood with his back to the hearth, looking quite pleased with himself. He'd managed to get the gas fire going, "White Christmas" played on the sound system and, above the mantel, he had hung the oil painting of the soulful-eyed hunting spaniel. Until now, they'd had no place to display the portrait. It made her think of Geordie, the cocker spaniel, and she wondered if she should tell Duncan about the commitment she'd made. No, she'd wait, she decided, at least until she heard from Bryony.

Instead, she said, "Oh, it's lovely.... Everything's lovely." With books and posters and baskets of the children's toys, the room looked infinitely inviting. The only thing missing was the Christmas tree, and Wesley hadn't rung her. She realized she'd no way to contact him, and chided herself for not getting his phone number.

As if summoned by her thought, Wesley arrived three minutes later. Beside him stood not Bryony, but Marc Mitchell, holding the cocker spaniel in his arms.

"What—" Gemma stared at them. "But I thought you were going to ring—both of you, I mean."

"Bryony's holding her first clinic this afternoon," explained Marc. "And the dog's owner brought him round, so Bryony asked me if I'd bring him to you as a surprise. Heavy beastie," he added, setting Geordie down.

"And as I was lending a hand at the clinic," said Wesley, "I thought I'd bring your tree." He nodded towards a white van sitting at the curb. "Otto's contribution—he loaned the van."

Gemma recovered enough to say, "Oh, come in, please. Forgive my manners." Kincaid had appeared behind her, a hand on her shoulder. She introduced him, then gave him what she hoped was a coherent explanation of their visitors' burdens.

"Geordie, eh?" Kincaid dropped to one knee to fondle the dog's silky ears. "The kids will be thrilled."

"You don't mind, do you?" Gemma asked softly. "He was meant to be a Christmas surprise . . . for the family."

"I think he's lovely." He gave the dog a last pat and stood up. "Now, what about this tree?"

The three men managed to unload the tree from the van and lean it against the wall in the corner of the sitting room before the children, red-cheeked and bright-eyed, came trooping in from the garden.

It was the dog they noticed first, Kit wide-eyed with surprise, Toby his usual vocal self.

"What kind of doggie is he, Mummy? What's his name? Is he ours? Can we keep him?"

Gemma was accustomed to answering sequential questions. "Well, he's a cocker spaniel, his name is Geordie, and we'll have to see how he gets along with Tess and Sid before we're certain he can stay."

Tess was sniffing the spaniel cautiously, while Geordie stood, alert and quivering. Gemma watched anxiously, terrified the dogs might snap, but after a thorough investigation, Tess gave a playful bark and Geordie, his stump of a tail wagging furiously, sniffed back. Gemma breathed a sigh of relief.

"That just leaves Sid," she said, "though heaven knows where he is." Sid the cat had been released from the downstairs loo yesterday evening and had promptly vanished under the furniture, but his food bowl had been empty that morning. "Now he'll be even more upset."

"He was rescued from a rubbish bin when he was a kitten, so I imagine he can deal with another dog in the household," Kincaid reassured her.

"Do you mind if I nip out to the van for a minute?" asked Wesley. "I left a couple of things."

He came back with a paper bag from which he removed several boxes of tiny white fairy lights. "I didn't know if you had any, and I thought it would be rather a letdown if not..."

"Oh, Wesley, I don't know what to say. I bought a stand for the tree at the supermarket this morning, but I completely forgot lights." She retrieved the stand from the pantry, and Marc lifted the heavy tree into it with one apparently effortless heave.

"Can we put the lights on the tree now?" asked Kit, with the quiet intensity Gemma was learning meant he was either very excited or very happy.

"There is one more small thing," said Wesley. He pulled what looked like a pasteboard shirt box from the bag and opened it. A dozen little nests of white tissue paper held what at first glance looked like bright birds. But when Gemma examined them more closely, she saw that they were angels, their faces delicately painted on cloth, their robes and wings exquisitely sewn from colorful scraps of silks, brocades and organdy.

"But—"

"A housewarming gift from my mother. She makes them, and when I described you— Anyway, she said a new household needs its own set of angels." He shoved his hands in his pockets, and Gemma wondered if he were blushing. It was the first time she'd seen him discomfited.

"Wesley, they're gorgeous. Thank your mother for me. Where on earth did she learn to sew like this?"

"My grandmother was a crack seamstress—"

"Why is your hair like that?" interrupted Toby, pointing at Wesley's head. "Can I touch it?"

"Toby!"

"No, it's all right," said Wesley, laughing. He knelt down. "Put your fingers right in. They're called dreadlocks. White people can have them, too, but they have to work harder at it."

The doorbell rang again. This time it was Hazel, with Holly in tow and arms laden with carrier bags. Gemma did what any good hostess would do in such circumstances: She made tea.

Bryony packed her few remaining supplies into her case. The last of her clients had gone, and Marc had not yet returned from delivering the cocker spaniel to Gemma James.

Her task finished, she sat back in contentment, recalling each of the dozen or so dogs and the two cats she'd treated, and their owners. Sore paws, skin conditions, minor infections, fleas; there'd been nothing she wouldn't see in a normal day's work. But the owners' gratitude had been completely out of proportion to the seriousness of the animals' condition, and the work had given Bryony the greatest satisfaction she could remember experiencing.

Of course, there had been frustrations as well, things she'd been unable to treat, and she'd used most of the medicines and bandages she'd brought from the surgery. If she were going to continue this, she'd have to find some other means of financing—her bank balance wouldn't hold up long at this rate. And Gavin had been a right prat yesterday, standing over her, making sure she noted every item against her account. Did he think her dishonest?

It seemed to her that Gavin had been more difficult

than usual this past week, making her wonder if Dawn Arrowood's death had had more than a casual impact on him. Could there have been more to their relationship than Gavin's flirting? She couldn't imagine a woman like Dawn taking Gavin seriously.

But then, who was she to say? She'd been attracted to Tom, after all, and had not seen him for the complete rotter he was until he'd waved it in front of her like a red flag.

A niggle in the back of her mind asked her if she could be wrong about Marc, too, but she refused even to entertain such an idea. The real question, the one she'd been avoiding for a good bit now, was where their relationship was going.

She'd invited him over for dinner the previous evening, as she often did, and although she couldn't compete with his cooking, she'd done her best with wine, candles, and atmosphere. For a moment, as he was saying good night, she'd thought something might happen. But then he'd given her his usual quick peck on the cheek and left.

Had it been her imagination, that instant of chemistry? Or did he truly believe that men and women could simply be friends, in which case her feelings for him could only lead to her complete humiliation. What if she were to slip up, say something blindingly obvious, and be kindly, politely rejected?

Just the thought made her face burn with anguish and embarrassment, and at that moment Marc walked in.

"Bryony? Are you all right?" He came closer and peered at her. "You're as red as beetroot."

"I'm fine," she lied. "I'm absolutely fine."

· · · ·

Toby had commandeered Hazel and Holly for an immediate tour of the house and garden, while Marc helped Kincaid and Kit level the tree in its stand.

Gemma glanced at Wesley as they waited for the water to boil in the kitchen. "You're good with the kids. Didn't you say you help Otto out a bit? I remember you were picking his girls up from school the other day."

"Poor mites. At least their dad's around all day, but Otto doesn't have a clue about little girl things, you know what I mean? Plaiting hair and choosing dresses, stuff like that. Now me, I grew up with five sisters, so I know about girls."

"Five? One was bad enough in my case," Gemma said with feeling. Having nothing that matched, she put an odd assortment of mugs on a tray. "You've worked for Otto for a while—are you planning to stay in the restaurant business?"

"No way. It just pays my school fees. I can only afford to go part-time."

"University?" When he nodded, she asked, "What sort of degree?"

"Business." Wesley said this with no great enthusiasm.

"That sounds very practical. So what is it that you really want to do?"

He grinned. "You don't miss much, do you? I'd like to go into photography, like my uncle, but there's no money in it. So in the meantime I just shoot for fun, you know? Your little one, he'd be a treat to photograph some time, if you wouldn't mind. His face is transparent; it shows everything he's thinking."

"Devil or angel," Gemma agreed, chuckling. "But

you might have to sit on him to hold him still long
enough," she warned.

When the lights had been threaded on the tree and the
handmade angels hung, Wesley and Marc said good-
bye, to much protest from the children. Kincaid took
the children and the dogs out into the communal garden for a game of football before the light faded altogether, leaving Gemma and Hazel curled up before
the fire. Gemma had substituted Italian carols for old
Christmas standards, and the ethereal voices filled the
room.

The coffee table was littered with empty teacups and
crumby biscuit plates that Gemma pushed aside to
make room for her feet.

"I've brought a little housewarming gift," said Hazel,
removing a book from her capacious handbag and giving it to Gemma.

"*The Secrets of Aga Cookery?*" Gemma asked, studying
the cover.

"If you don't learn how to manage the thing, you'll
be living on take-away pizza."

"You're not expecting me to turn into some sort of
gourmet cook, are you? This"—Gemma's gesture took
in the house—"is quite overwhelming enough. I'm still
pinching myself. This can't be me, this can't be *my* life."

"And why not? There's no reason to limit yourself.
And I don't know anyone more deserving. You've done
a good job, bringing Toby up on your own." Hazel
wagged an admonitory finger at her. "Not that I think
this blended family of yours will be easy, mind you, but

the point is, you don't have to do everything by your-self."

Gemma felt the too-easy tears stinging her eyes, and swiped angrily at them. "Damn it, I feel like a bloody fountain these days. It's maddening."

"It's your hormones, remember. You might as well resign yourself to it for the next few months."

"It wouldn't be so bad if it weren't for this damned case. Every avenue turns out to be a complete dead end."

"But surely it's only been—what? A little more than a week? You don't normally expect a resolution in that short a time, do you?" Hazel frowned. "Tell me you won't have to miss Christmas dinner. No case is worth giving up Christmas turkey—"

"And Christmas wouldn't be Christmas without any turkey," Gemma chimed in, laughing.

"I've made the pudding, if you'll bring the brandy. You know," Hazel added more soberly, her dark eyes in-tent, "I didn't realize how accustomed I'd become to having you in the garage flat. Even when you weren't home, it still felt occupied. Now I find myself trying not to look across the garden."

"Will you let the flat again?"

"I don't think so," Hazel answered slowly. "I'm con-sidering going back to work, actually, and using the space as an office. Now, with Toby gone, there's no rea-son Holly can't start infant school."

"I thought you'd be glad to be rid of me, get your life back. Now I feel I've left you in the lurch."

"Oh, forgive me for whining." Hazel reached out to pat Gemma's arm. "I'm just being selfish, and I'll get over it. You did absolutely the right thing—and I'd have been furious with you if you hadn't. Although I have to admit the house isn't the same without you banging on the old piano."

"I never banged!" Gemma protested, laughing, then sighed. "The only good thing I can say about this case is that I've been too busy to miss playing."

"How's Kit, by the way?" asked Hazel, as the sound of the children's shouting and the dogs' excited barking came from the garden. "It must be hard for him, leaving Grantchester, not to mention his dad—I mean, Ian—sodding off without a care in the world."

"If he misses Ian, or the cottage, he hasn't let on. But he seems happy." Gemma thought of all Kit had endured in the past year. "This will be his first Christmas without his mum, of course. I just hope we don't let him down."

*By November, Mr. Pheilholz's grocery had closed its doors, unable to compete with the new Tesco on Portobello Road.*

*But it no longer mattered to Angel: she'd left her job the previous month. Karl had rented a flat in Chelsea, in a tiny Swiss-cottage mews just off the King's Road, and Angel had moved in with him.*

*At first, she'd intended to get another job, but as the weeks went by, the prospect seemed less and less inviting. Their evenings were a dizzying round of clubs and parties that lasted into the wee hours. Then there was bed to look forward to, sleeping intertwined until late in the mornings, when Karl got up to arrange the business meetings at which he liked her to play hostess. He was making a name for himself finding specialized antiques for well-off clients, and rather than expending capital on a shop, he conducted most of his transactions from the flat.*

To Angel it seemed a dream, so far removed was their life from her existence in the Colville Terrace flat. And if, in quiet moments, she missed her old friends, she pushed such thoughts away. She had made an effort, in those heady first weeks, to introduce Karl to Betty and Ronnie Thomas. She'd arranged for them to have tea in a Portobello café, but she could tell from the moment they sat down that the meeting was doomed. The café was the sort of place Karl particularly disliked, with rings on the table, cheap crockery, and the pervasive smell of chips frying in rancid oil.

Betty eyed Angel's new rabbit-fur coat and miniskirt with a mixture of dismay and envy. "My mum would die if she saw me in that," she whispered, and Angel could think of no reply that would not hurt Betty's feelings.

The tea, when it came, was coffee-colored and tasted like motor oil, and Karl didn't hide his distaste. Angel tried to carry the conversation, but Betty was shyly awkward, Ronnie hostile and condescending, and Karl obviously bored by the whole affair. When, after half an hour, he excused himself, pleading a business meeting, Angel was left staring at her friends across the table.

"Karl's awfully good-looking," Betty began hesitantly. "And older. Are you sure—"

"He's bad news, is what he is," interrupted Ronnie. "Have you any idea the sort of people he knows? Or what they do? It's nothing you've any business getting involved with—"

"I've met his friends," Angel retorted. "They're perfectly nice—"

"Nice! They do drugs, and worse. If you've any sense, you'll walk away from him before you get yourself in real trouble. I told you when you took that bedsit that no good would come of it—"

"That's enough, Ronnie," Angel spat at him. "You don't have any right to tell me what to do, and I'm not going to listen to you anymore." Trembling with fury, she stood with as much dignity as she could muster. Every head in the restaurant had turned towards them.

Betty's dark eyes had filled with tears. "Angel, don't. He didn't mean—"

"I'm sorry, but I have to go." Angel threw some money on the table and stormed out.

Huddling into her coat, she trudged up Portobello towards the tube stop. Yellow leaves rustled and whirled along the pavement, a harbinger of autumn, and she reminded herself how lucky she was not to be facing another winter with only a paraffin heater for comfort.

She hadn't told Betty and Ronnie that she'd moved in with Karl—God knew what Ronnie would have said then! But she had to look out for herself, move on with her life, even if it meant leaving Betty and Ronnie behind. Betty had her Colin, after all, and Ronnie... Why should she care what Ronnie thought?

What if she and Karl and their friends took a few pills? Everyone did; it was the latest rage. Blue, red, green, yellow, all the colors of the rainbow, the little capsules and tablets helped you stay up at night, then helped you go to sleep when the buzz hadn't quite worn off. And everyone who was anyone smoked pot. No party was complete without a few joints.

She got out of the tube at Sloane Square and walked west down the King's Road. New boutiques—you had to be careful to say "boutique" rather than "shop"—were springing up everywhere, and as she absorbed the bustle and energy of the street, her anger began to translate itself into purpose.

*Stopping in front of a hairdresser's, she put her hands to the glass and peered in. Yes, it was just the sort of place she had in mind. There was no point in hanging on to the remnants of her former life any longer.*

*An hour later, she emerged from the salon, her hair now the color of silver gilt, cropped close above her ears. A new op-art dress from a nearby boutique and a pair of strappy high heels completed the picture. That night Karl was taking her to the Speakeasy. It was one of the most popular clubs in town—she'd heard Cilla Black would be there that night—and she intended for every head to turn when she walked in the door.*

*She had shed that dumpy little Polish girl from Portobello, like a snake shed its skin, and she meant never to look back.*

# CHAPTER TWELVE

From the earliest days, pubs in Portobello Road were important meeting places. Shop keepers, carpenters, upholsterers, gardeners, clerks, stallholders, indeed anyone who lived or worked in the street, could find entertainment and companionship in them. The oldest surviving public house, the Sun in Splendour, near Notting Hill Gate, was built in 1850 and advertised itself with a great rising sun with golden rays.

—Whetlor and Bartlett,
from *Portobello*

ON CHRISTMAS EVE morning, ten days after Dawn Arrowood's murder, Gemma waited outside the veterinary surgery on All Saints Road for Bryony to arrive. It was miserably cold, the weather as bleak as it had been the previous day, and the air smelled more strongly of snow. Seeking protection from the wind's probing fingers, Gemma squeezed into the slight recess in the surgery's doorway.

She breathed a sigh of relief when she saw Bryony crossing towards her, her long stride rapidly closing the distance between them.

"Gemma! What are you doing here? Is Geordie okay?" Bryony wore a long striped scarf and matching stocking cap in yellows and purples, and managed somehow to carry it off.

"He's fine. He seems to be settling in remarkably

well, in fact." Although Tess had followed the boys to bed as usual, Geordie had stayed with Gemma and Duncan, curling up on the foot of their bed as if he had always slept there.

"Are we going to have a no-furniture rule?" Kincaid had asked, bemused.

"Tess sleeps with Kit."

"True. And our dogs always slept on our beds when we were kids. I'm not objecting—it's just that you need to start as you mean to go on."

Gemma found she hadn't the heart to make the dog move. "No, let him stay. He doesn't take up that much room, and he'll keep my feet warm."

"Right." Kincaid had grinned at her. "I can see I've already been displaced in your affections." But he didn't seem to mind, really.

"I hope you didn't mind my sending Marc yesterday," Bryony was saying as she unlocked the surgery door. "But Geordie's owner—former owner—left him at the soup kitchen, and I hated to expose him to the other dogs in case some of them had contagious illnesses. And I couldn't ask the owner to take him away until I'd finished—she was barely holding herself together as it was."

"No, it was fine, and Duncan and the boys were so surprised. You'll tell Geordie's owner he's all right?" She saw that Geordie's photo was still taped to the side of the monitor. Feeling proprietary, she asked, "Do you mind if I take this?" and at Bryony's nod she peeled it off and put it in her handbag. "Your clinic went well?"

"Beyond all expectation," Bryony said, switching on the computer and readying files. "But if you didn't come about Geordie—"

"It's Mr. Farley," said Gemma. "Can you tell me what time he left on the Friday Dawn was killed?"

Bryony froze, mid-motion. "Why?"

"Just routine, really. But he did have that little disagreement with Dawn. I'm just ruling out options."

Color stained Bryony's cheeks. "I should never have said anything. I never meant for you to take it seriously, and now I feel an absolute fool."

"Why? If Mr. Farley had something to do with Dawn's death, would you protect him?"

"Of course not. But I'm sure Gavin couldn't have done something like that, and having the police poke into his business is not going to make him happy." Bryony looked away from Gemma's gaze. "It's just that he's rather cross with me already . . . over my holding the free clinic."

"Why does he object to it?"

"I'm not sure if it's the money or the principle that aggravates him most. I think he sees it as a useless exercise, and since those supplies went missing, he's been like an old maid over expenses. It's odd, too, as the loss didn't really amount to more than a few pounds."

"He sees helping homeless people's animals as a useless exercise?"

"You can always trust Gavin not to be politically correct. But he's right, in a way," Bryony added with a sigh. "As much as I hate to admit it. There's so much I *can't* do. I'm not giving up, though. And Marc's been so good . . ."

"He *is* nice, isn't he? You're a lucky woman, I should think."

"Oh, no! I don't—We don't—We're friends, that's all."

"But I thought—I'm sorry. It's just that you seem so well suited."

"It's not that I'd mind," the other woman admitted. "But Marc's very focused on his work. You know how it is . . ."

"Unlike Mr. Farley, I take it." Gemma glanced at her watch. "Is he coming in at all?"

"No. He's given himself a long holiday. Boss's privilege." Bryony seemed to come to a decision. "Look, I don't see any harm in telling you that he left early that Friday, before five. But I think you should ask him yourself."

"That's just what I intend to do."

*"White girl, ain't got no sense," Betty muttered, kicking angrily at a tin can in the gutter and scuffing the toe of her saddle shoe. Then she felt ashamed of herself for speaking of Angel in that jeering way, even if there was no one else to hear, for she felt sure Angel never thought of her as a "black girl." Why, one day their last year in school, Mozelle Meekum, a pasty-faced bully with arms like hams, had called her a nigger, and Angel had gone and slapped that girl right up the side of the head. Got in trouble for it, too, detention after school. And never complained.*

*So why had Angel, who knew the difference between what was right and what wasn't, gone off with this man who was no better than he should be, good looks be damned? There was something wrong in that young man, Betty could feel it, a cold place inside him. But Angel wouldn't believe her, not now, not as long as she was blinded by lust, and any fool could see that she was.*

*And poor Ronnie, furious with Angel, furious with himself. Betty saw the way he looked at Angel when Angel wasn't looking, knew what he was suffering, knew that even if she could shake the stubbornness out of him and make him speak to Angel, it was too late. He had lost her.*

*There was no bloody help for any of it, as far as she could see. And she had her Colin to think of now, and their future— He wouldn't like her getting mixed up in others' business. Still, if only there were something she could do. . . .*

*It came to her as she neared the church, and her heart lifted a bit. Not that Angel had much use for Catholic practices . . . But it couldn't do any harm to light a candle for her soul . . . and she need never know.*

Kincaid organized the notes on his desk and took another appreciative sip of coffee from a polystyrene cup. Someone had apparently upgraded the communal pot, as the coffee actually tasted more like coffee than battery acid. Perhaps the departmental secretary had received an abundance of coffee beans as a Christmas gift.

He'd just returned from an informative meeting with a mate in the drug squad. It seemed that they'd had an eye on Karl Arrowood for years—since long before Kincaid's friend's tenure on the force, in fact. But Arrowood was a clever and cautious man, and they had never been able to come up with anything concrete against him. Years ago, they'd thought to make a case, but he'd managed to slip through their fingers.

His phone rang, and he took another sip of his coffee before lifting the receiver.

"Duncan? It's Gemma." She sounded discouraged. "The report's come back on Arrowood's office computer."

"No joy, I take it?"

"Not a blinking thing. He's got himself a very good bookkeeper, but then what would you expect? There are a large number of cash transactions, but that's not illegal, and he has reason to keep cash reserves on hand. A lot of antique trading is cash only."

"How very convenient." He told her what he'd learned from the drug squad, then asked, "Did you see the vet?"

"I've just come from the surgery. He wasn't in, but I did have a word with Bryony. She says Farley left the clinic before five that Friday. He's at home today, so I thought I'd have a word with him there."

"Hang on for a few minutes. I've a meeting with the guv'nor, but let me send Cullen with you. He's come up with a few interesting tidbits on Farley. Suspected tax evasion for starters, followed by sexual harassment of a client."

"Not bad," Doug Cullen murmured as he looked round, whistling through his teeth. The houses here were semi-detached, the curved, hilly street lined with mature trees. Every door sported a wreath, and every driveway a Mercedes, a Lexus, or a BMW.

"Up-and-coming Willesden—although I'm still inclined to think of it as the place the buses go home to bed," Gemma agreed. "But considering the area's up-market status these days, I'm not surprised Mr. Farley cheats on his taxes. Here it is," she added, checking the house number against her notes.

Gavin Farley's house was pseudo-Tudor, with freshly painted trim and a well-kept garden. A new model

Mercedes sat beside a workaday Vauxhall Astra in the drive. "Maybe we're in luck and Farley's wife is at home, too. Should we split up, interview them separately?" suggested Cullen.

"Let's see how it goes. It's the Astra that he drives to work—I remember seeing it in front of the surgery." The car was maroon, with a distinctive crack in the left taillamp.

Taking advantage of the wait after ringing the bell, Cullen glanced at his companion. As he'd discovered on Saturday night, the redheaded, faintly freckled Gemma James was not as formidable as her reputation had led him to believe. Nearer his age than he'd expected, she'd been friendly, if slightly wary, and this morning she'd done him the favor of not mentioning Saturday night's dinner.

Mrs. Farley, a thin, worried-looking woman of middle age, was indeed at home, and greeted them warily.

"I'm Inspector James and this is Sergeant Cullen," Gemma told her. "Could we have a word with you?"

"But—" Mrs. Farley looked round uncertainly. "My husband's out in his shop. I'll just go—"

"No, that's all right, Mrs. Farley. We'd like to speak to you first. It won't take a moment."

With obvious reluctance, the woman took them into the front room, but a glance towards the rear of the house had shown Cullen two preadolescent children sprawled in front of a television in a den. The boy and girl, both slightly overweight and smug-looking, glanced up at them with disinterest before turning back to their program.

Mrs. Farley perched on the edge of a chair while he

and Gemma sat opposite on a sofa. Doug had learned enough from Stella to realize that the furniture and objects in the room were expensive, and also that they had been put together with a complete lack of grace and style.

"Mrs. Farley," said Gemma, "can you tell us what time your husband arrived home from his surgery on the Friday before last?"

"Friday before last? However should I remember that?" Mrs. Farley picked at the reindeer appliqué on the front of her Christmas pullover.

"You must have heard about the woman who was murdered that evening? Dawn Arrowood? That should help you place it."

"I don't have time to watch the news, what with the children's activities."

"But surely your husband must have told you about it. She was one of his clients."

The hand on the sweater grew still. "Oh, of course. Gavin was so shocked when he read it in the papers the next day. And I do recall now, about that Friday. I had to pick up Antony, our son, from a football match, and when we got back Gavin was home. That would have been half past six or so. He was already out in his workshop."

"So you can't be sure of the exact time?" asked Cullen.

"No. But I heard his shower running, so he must have been home a few minutes."

"His shower?"

"Gavin has a shower stall out in his shop. I won't let him come in the house covered in sawdust."

"What does Mr. Farley make?" Gemma's face reflected nothing but friendly interest.

"Jewelry boxes, CD holders, pen trays ... things that are useful *and* decorative, he likes to say. He gives them to his special clients."

Cullen saw Gemma's lip twitch and made an effort to control his own expression. "Do you know if he meant to give one of his ... creations ... to Dawn Arrowood?"

"I've no idea," Mrs. Farley replied stiffly. "What is this about? Gavin barely knew this woman. She'd been into his surgery once or twice with her cat."

"That's odd." Gemma frowned. "We were under the impression that Mrs. Arrowood was quite a regular client of the surgery, and that Mr. Farley always made an effort to see her himself."

Mrs. Farley stood, jerking her cheerful reindeer sweater down over her bony hips. "I don't know about that. You'll have to speak to my husband. And I've things to do—the Christmas dinner ... I'll just go and get Gavin."

"If you'll just point us in the right direction, Mrs. Farley, I'm sure we can find him ourselves."

"She knows he's up to something, but she's not sure how bad it is," Cullen murmured to Gemma as they made their way down a path made of concrete stepping stones. At the bottom of the garden, light seeped from the door of Farley's workshop.

"I suspect that woman has lived in fear of the sky falling every day of her married life," Gemma said pensively. "And I don't like this business about the shower."

The whine of a saw came from inside the building. Gemma waited for a pause, then pounded on the door. "Mr. Farley? It's Inspector James."

"If she knows he's a rotter," whispered Cullen, "would she still protect him?"

"With her life."

The shop door opened and a heavyset, dark-haired man stared out at them. He wore a leather apron, and had pushed safety goggles up on his forehead.

"Well, well, well," said Farley, as jolly as one of Father Christmas's elves. "To what do I owe the honor? I'd invite you to come in and make yourselves comfortable, but as you can see . . ." His gesture swept the small room.

The smell of resin caught at Cullen's throat. He looked round the room, making out several different saws of incomprehensible purpose, a good deal of raw wood and sawdust, and shelves full of Farley's "objects." Cullen found himself hoping not to be a recipient of Farley's generosity, and wondered why the veterinarian chose to make boxes rather than representations of the cats and dogs he knew so intimately. Perhaps Farley didn't really like animals all that much.

"We'll manage," said Gemma, easing her way into the room without touching anything. "It's about Dawn Arrowood, Mr. Farley. On the afternoon of the day she died, she told a friend that she'd had an unpleasant encounter with you that morning. An argument."

"That's nonsense. Why would I have had an argument with Mrs. Arrowood—although I did remind her again that she must keep her cat in the house, regardless of her husband's preference."

"That's not what she said. She told her friend that you came on to her, that you were sexually offensive, and that when she told you to stop, you were abusive."

"The woman must have been imagining things. I never did any such thing, and I'll thank you not to malign my professional reputation." Farley's protest seemed just a bit too polished, as if he'd been expecting the accusation.

"She can't very well argue with you now, can she?" Cullen pointed out, then added, "What about the client who brought sexual harassment charges against you two years ago, Mr. Farley?"

"Those charges were dropped! The whole thing was a complete fabrication, and I was exonerated!" Farley took a step back and pulled off his safety glasses. The rubber had left a red imprint like a brand against the pasty skin of his forehead. "She had a grudge against me. Her dog had died and she couldn't deal with it. The judge accepted that." Lowering his voice, he said confidentially, "Look, Dawn Arrowood *did* flirt with me, I'll admit that. She was one of those women who think every man on earth should fall at their feet. But I never crossed the line with her."

"Then you won't mind telling us where you were from the time you left the surgery that day until you arrived home," said Gemma.

"But I—" Farley glanced from Gemma to Cullen. "I went for a drink. At The Sun in Splendour. You must know it," he added, as if that somehow gave his story credibility.

Cullen had met friends there for a drink. It was a yuppie pub, frequented by well-dressed, well-off young men and women, like Dawn Arrowood. "So you left your surgery before five o'clock, checked out the action at the pub, then arrived home about, what, half past six? Then what did you do?"

"I—I'm not sure exactly what time it was. I worked out here for a while, until my wife called me for dinner."

"And do you always shower before you begin working in your shop, Mr. Farley?" asked Gemma.

"What? I don't understand."

"Shower." Gemma pointed at the cubicle, just visible at the back of the room. "Your wife said you were showering when she came in at half past six. That seemed a bit odd to me—I thought the idea was to shower when you'd finished your project."

The whites of Farley's eyes glinted. "It was my wife. She doesn't like me going to the pub, so I showered to get rid of the smell."

Had he washed away the smoke and perfume from the bar, wondered Cullen? Or Dawn Arrowood's blood? "You didn't tell your wife you'd been to the pub?"

"No. I—I said I had to work late. You're not going to tell her, are you?"

"Oh, I'm afraid you've worse problems than that, Mr. Farley," Gemma said with a sigh. "Such as explaining to your wife why the police are searching your workshop and your car."


"Another house-to-house inquiry, then?" Doug asked as they drove back to the station an hour later. They had waited for the forensics team to arrive, then cautioned Farley to keep himself available for further questioning.

"For a sighting of the Astra? Yes. And it won't be popular on Christmas Eve, I can tell you."

"Arrowood made the nine-nine-nine call at six twenty-two. Would Farley have had time to kill Dawn, then get home and into the shower by half past?"

"That's making two assumptions," said Gemma. "The first is that Farley's wife is telling the truth about the time. For all we know he's primed her and she's lying through her teeth."

"And the second?"

"The second is that Dawn had just died when Karl found her. She might have died five, ten, even fifteen minutes earlier. Her body was in a sheltered spot, which could have delayed cooling, and the pathologist certainly won't swear to an exact time on the stand."

"One thing you can say about Farley," Cullen mused. "He would certainly know how to wield a scalpel."

Gemma frowned. "I've just remembered. Bryony told me the surgery was burglarized recently. She said some supplies and instruments were missing. I wonder..."

"A scalpel?"

"It's possible," Gemma said. "I'll ask Bryony. And I'll have forensic pick up some of the surgery's scalpels for comparison, just in case we *do* turn up a murder weapon. It is the season of miracles, after all."

Cullen was silent, concentrating on his driving. Then he said, "How do you manage to keep your patience? Sometimes I think it will drive me bonkers, the waiting."

"Me? Patient?" Gemma gave a snort of derision. "Kincaid would fall over himself laughing if he heard that. He's the one never gets his feathers ruffled, while he's always on at me about staying calm. But..." Her smile faded. "It gets easier as you go along, somehow. There's a place you get to, if you can put your mind in neutral, where sometimes things click into place."

She gave a little shrug. "I know that sounds like rubbish. . . . And of course you have to have the right bits of information floating round in your head for it to happen. . . ."

"Trust the process, rather than forcing it? Is that what you're saying?"

"Yeah, I suppose so." She gave him a conspiratorial smile. "But in the meantime, I'm going Christmas shopping."

How had she ended up in the last-minute Christmas crush, just like any man? Gemma wondered, but she suspected that indecision had fueled her procrastination as much as busyness. She shoved and elbowed her way to the nearest department store, riding the escalator up to the toy department with a torrent of shoppers.

She saw the perfect gift for Toby immediately. It was a fireman's kit, complete with a little bunker coat and hat, and a set of bright red, two-way radios with a base station. Toby would love it, she knew, but then she'd never expected any difficulty finding something that catered to a four-year-old's interests.

Kit, however, was a different matter. Teetering on the edge of adolescence, too old for most toys, but not yet ready to graduate to the teenage realm of music, clothes, and cash. She wandered through the aisles, chewing on a fingernail as she deliberated, rejecting one item after another. At last something caught her eye—a boxed set of science questions. It contained hundreds of cards (hours of fun for home or car, the label promised her) and it was just the sort of thing Kit would find irresistible.

But was that enough, she wondered as she rode back down to the ground floor with her purchases. Then a thought occurred to her and she stopped at the bottom of the escalator, blocking the traffic behind her until someone gave her a not-so-gentle nudge. In one of the boxes Kit had brought from Grantchester, she'd glimpsed an unframed photo of his mother. The lens had caught Vic laughing into the camera, full of life and energy.

Would she be barging too forcefully into Kit's emotional territory if she took the photo and framed it for him? And was he ready for such an ever-present reminder of his loss?

Well, she'd never know unless she made the attempt. She would do it, she decided, and went straightaway to the stationery department before she could change her mind. Choosing a lovely silver frame in what she hoped was the correct size, she watched in satisfaction as the clerk wrapped it in tissue.

That left Duncan, she thought as she reached the street once more, and his gift was the most difficult of all. It must be something special, something that would symbolize this new stage of their life together—but what? She walked along the street, looking in shop window after shop window. A few items prompted her to go inside, but in the end everything seemed too ordinarily personal, too practical, or revoltingly sappy.

She'd almost given up when she saw it, in the window of a housewares and pottery boutique. A hand-painted ceramic plaque, with a border of dark green leaves in which nestled berries the same brilliant scarlet as their front door, and in its center, in bold black on a white ground, their house number. It was perfect.

When she came out of the shop minutes later, humming the Christmas song that had been playing over the loudspeaker, the 59 bus was just pulling in to the bus stop. The gods were definitely smiling.

On reaching Notting Hill again, she felt so full of seasonal cheer that she made another spur-of-the-moment decision. Getting off the bus, she went into the elegant bakery just round the corner from Elgin Crescent.

They had just the thing, Christmas cakes with thick and creamy icing and interiors dark and rich with spices. They were the sort of cakes one had when the edge had worn off Christmas dinner, to be consumed with cups of strong tea while listening to the Queen's speech.

When the bakery had boxed the cakes for her, she balanced her parcels carefully and set out for Marc Mitchell's soup kitchen on Portobello Road.

To her relief, the light was still on and the door unlocked. "Marc?" she called out.

"Back here!"

She followed the sound of his voice to the kitchen at the rear of the eating area.

"Sorry, I couldn't leave this," he apologized. He was stirring a large pot of something that smelled delicious on an industrial-size gas range. "Cranberry relish, for tomorrow's dinner."

"What's in it?" asked Gemma, sniffing. She set her parcels down in a clear spot on the table.

"Cranberries, obviously." He wiped the steam from his brow. "And honey, vinegar, cracked pepper, mustard seeds, and diced chili peppers. I always hated the jellied stuff from a tin, so this is my rebellion." Nodding at a dozen freshly washed glass jars drying on a cloth, he added, "I mean to put some up for gifts as well."

"I've brought a couple of cakes." Gemma indicated the box. "They're teacakes, really, but I thought—"

"That's the one thing I was missing. You're brilliant." Giving the pot a last stir, he turned off the flame. "There. When the cranberries pop, it's finished. Now we wait for it to cool a bit." Lifting the lid on the cake box, he whistled. "They're too gorgeous to eat. I've got some tinned puddings donated by one of the supermarkets, but they're nothing compared with this."

A little embarrassed, Gemma changed the subject. "What else have you got on your menu? Bryony said you'd been planning for weeks."

"Two turkeys. Brussels sprouts, of course. Potatoes. Oh, and a case of nonalcoholic champagne, donated as well. Can't serve the real stuff, even if I could afford it. And look—" he showed her a box containing several dozen cylinders wrapped in brightly colored foil. "I've made crackers. They won't pop, but they've got paper hats in and some sweets."

"It all sounds lovely. I suppose you've got lots of help."

"Bryony's coming. Between us we can manage, although it might get a bit wild. She's a tremendous help."

Seeing a chance to play the matchmaker, Gemma observed, "She thinks you're pretty terrific, too."

Marc gave her a look she couldn't interpret and went back to his relish, giving the pot a desultory stir. "I know she does. It's just that it's a bit . . . awkward."

"Awkward?" Gemma echoed.

Marc gestured round the room. "You see this place? I

used the last of my grandmother's savings to start this. So I have no money—I mean *none.* If I have a cup of coffee at Otto's, it's squeezed out of the kitchen funds. I can't even take Bryony to the cinema, for heaven's sake, much less out to dinner at a nice restaurant."

"But—"

"I have nothing to offer her, and my chance of someday getting a job that would earn a fraction of what she makes is slim to nonexistent. Bryony deserves better than—"

"Marc, she doesn't care. She admires you for what you do—"

"I sleep on a cot in the upstairs room. How fast do you think admiration would turn to resentment if she had to share those circumstances?"

"But why should she? She has her own job, her own career, a flat. You could..." Gemma hesitated, certain she was getting in over her head.

"Stay in her flat? Let her buy groceries? Let her pay for her own Christmas gift?" He shook his head adamantly. "That's not right."

"Isn't that a little old-fashioned?"

"I suppose it is. I've spent most of my adult life looking after my grandmother—she was bedridden the last few years and had to have twenty-four-hour care—so I missed out on a good bit of the sexual revolution. But it's more than that... You see, I can't do what I do and live any other way. It's partly focus—"

"You can't afford to be distracted by a relationship? Sort of like a monk?"

He gave a snort of laughter. "Well, I suppose you could say that, although my grandmother would turn in her grave. She was nonconformist to the core. But the main thing is, I can't spend my days with these people who have nothing, and live at a different level. Mortgages, furniture, cars, clothing—all these things we take so much for granted mean nothing to them. And if I go there, if I live on that plane, I can't connect with them." He lifted his hands, palms up.

"I see," said Gemma, and she did. She could think of no argument to convince him his position was unreasonable, nor, she found, did she really want to. As Bryony had said, he had a unique ability to reach out to the homeless people he served. Who was she to question the source of that gift, or its importance?

Bryony locked the surgery door and closed the blinds, then washed down the two examining rooms. She'd run later than expected, of course, because of emergencies. A holiday always seemed to bring on a rush of last-minute calls, and any holiday involving candy more so, due to people's apparent inability to restrict their pets' access to it.

Not to mention the fact that Gavin had rung during the busiest stint, incoherent with fury, shouting something about the police turning his house and his car upside down because Dawn Arrowood had told some friend he'd had a row with her the morning she died.

At least Gemma had protected her, thought Bryony, but surely the police didn't actually think Gavin had anything to do with Dawn's murder?

*As if I would argue with a client,* Gavin had raged heatedly in her ear. Bryony had soothed him as best she could before rushing back to her patients.

Had she done the right thing in telling Gemma

about what she'd heard? And what about the thefts at the surgery? Gavin hadn't mentioned that, and if Gemma had questioned him about the incident, he would certainly guess that Bryony had told her.

She put up the mop bucket with a thump of irritation. This was not the day for worrying about things it was too late to change. She still had her bit of holiday shopping to do, but first she had to update her charts. Determined to concentrate, she sat down at Gavin's desk to work.

When her pen ran dry halfway through her task, she absently opened the desk drawer and rummaged for a new one. As her fingers closed round a pen, she looked down, catching a glimpse of what looked like the edge of a photograph in the very back compartment. Aware that she was snooping, Bryony started to close the drawer. Then curiosity overcame her scruples and she pulled the drawer out to its fullest extent, freeing the photograph.

She gazed at the glossy square in her hand and her stomach plummeted. The camera had captured Dawn Arrowood in an achingly unguarded moment, her expression rapt, her head tilted towards Alex as he spoke in her ear.

Setting the photo on the desktop, Bryony jerked hard at the drawer and scrabbled at the back. Her fingers closed on more slick squares: *Alex with his arm thrown protectively round Dawn's shoulders as she stepped in the door of his flat... Alex and Dawn in his stall at the market, his fingers brushing her cheek...*

There were other images, and while none of them were actually sexually compromising, they left no doubt as to the relationship between the couple, and they had all obviously been snapped without their knowledge.

Had Gavin taken these? She thought suddenly of the camera she'd seen recently in the backseat of his car, and felt another lurch of nausea.

Why would Gavin have followed Alex and Dawn, spying on them? And why had he kept these photos? If Dawn's husband had seen them . . . She thought of the raised voices she'd heard in the examining room that day, and could not escape the obvious conclusion. Gavin had been blackmailing Dawn.

Fern knocked at Bryony's door three times, with no answer but the chorus of Duchess's barking. Now, convinced of Bryony's absence, she paced up and down the west side of Powis Square, determined to keep the building in sight until Bryony returned.

She'd thought of trying the surgery, but surely Bryony wouldn't be working so late on the afternoon of Christmas Eve, and even if she were, she'd have to walk home this way.

Fern stopped at the bottom of the square, gazing across the street at the welcoming gates of the Tabernacle. The redbrick Victorian building housed the community center, and offered everything from dance and aerobics classes to coffeehouse to concert venue. And it provided a safe haven for many teens. Certainly it had done so for Fern.

But there was no help there now, and Fern turned away. She walked up to the top of the square again, keeping her eyes focused on Bryony's lavender door. Just exactly how Bryony could help her, she hadn't worked out—she knew only that she must talk to someone or go mad with worry.

After her row with Alex on Saturday night, and her discovery of the missing paper knife, she'd tried repeatedly to reach him. But he'd refused to answer door or telephone, although his car was still parked in the mews. She'd even gone so far as to appeal to Alex's odious landlord to let her into the flat with his key, but the man had refused, hinting that he might reconsider if she made it worth his while.

On Sunday, still doubting her own judgment over the paper knife, Fern had tracked down the owner of the antiques arcade and borrowed his key, claiming she'd accidentally left behind something she must have for a sale.

But ransacking her stall had not turned up the missing paper knife, leaving her two possibilities—that some passing customer had lifted it while her attention was distracted, or that Alex had stolen it. While she would have preferred the shoplifting hypothesis, her eye was sharp and her reflexes fast—she'd foiled every attempt at theft since she'd been in the trade.

That left Alex, and the question that had kept her from sleep for two days. If he *had* stolen the knife, whom did he mean to hurt—himself? Or someone else?

Fern stamped her feet against the cold and her own frustration. Where the hell was Bryony? And if Bryony didn't come home, who else could she talk to? Otto had taken his girls to their grandparents for Christmas Eve dinner, and Wesley had gone to his family as well. Her own dad was useless, poor sod couldn't help himself, much less anyone else. She'd tried the soup kitchen on her way here, thinking to find Bryony there, or at least Marc, but the place had been dark and locked up tight as a drum.

That left the holier-than-thou policewoman who had come to her flat—what was her name? Inspector James? No, she'd make a fool of herself if she did that, and of Alex, and he would never speak to her again. There must be some other way.

The street lamps came on, casting their sickly yellow glow on the pavement. Fern shoved her hands deep into her pockets, suppressing a shiver. Something damp touched her forehead, then the tip of her nose, like a caress from icy, invisible fingers. It was snowing.

# CHAPTER THIRTEEN

Notting Hill is sanitized now. It's yuppified. When you
look at it for its proximity to town you could take a stroll
down Bayswater Road and you're in Marble Arch.
——Charlie Phillips and Mike Phillips,
from *Notting Hill in the Sixties*

*IF SWINGING LONDON had begun to fade by the summer of
1966, the unexpected, gloriously hot weather brought it back
into full flower once more. Hair grew longer, skirts shorter, and
the heady haze of cannabis and incense seemed to drift into
every nook and alleyway.*

*But for Angel, the glamour of the London scene had begun
to dim. More and more often lately, Karl's "business meetings"
took place without her. He'd opened a small shop in a Kensington byway, but her offer to come and help out had been instantly rejected. Instead, he'd hired a girl to work the register, a
skinny brunette with hair that tickled her waist, and Angel suspected that his interest in the girl was more than professional.*

*Furious with him, she'd flirted openly in front of Karl on
one of their evenings out. Karl had responded, taking her home
early, making love to her with a ferocity that had left her
bruised and shaken.*

*It was a few weeks later when she learned the boy she'd
teased in the club had suffered a serious mishap that same evening. Set upon by muggers, he lay in hospital with fractured
legs and jaw.*

*Appalled at her own suspicions, she'd told herself not to be silly.* Then two months later, it had happened again. A different club, a different young man who had chatted her up while Karl was huddled in a corner with some of his mates.

This time, the young man had been beaten and left in an alleyway, and Angel heard the news the next day. Shaking with rage and shock, she'd confronted Karl.

"Whatever gave you such an absurd idea?" He sounded amused, but his smile didn't reach his eyes. "Do I look as though I'd been having a punch-up among the dustbins?" His handsome face was unmarked, his hands smooth and neatly manicured.

She remembered the men she'd seen him talking to in the club, big and heavily muscled. "Maybe you got your mates to do it. Or hired someone."

This time Karl laughed aloud. "Oh, really, Angel. You flatter yourself. How could you think such a thing?" He studied her, his gray eyes narrowing. "Still, you might do well to remember that I look after my possessions."

"I'm not one of your antiques, and I don't need looking after," she'd told him defiantly, but it didn't ease the clutch of fear in her heart.

As the months crept by towards Christmas, she spent more and more time on her own, listening to the plaintive lyric of "Eleanor Rigby," imagining herself growing old, alone. She had no family now, no friends that weren't Karl's friends. Sometimes she thought about leaving him, leaving London, finding a job as a shop clerk in some provincial town, but she had lived that life and was not yet desperate enough to go back to it. But there was more to her reluctance than that—bad things had happened to people because of her. What would Karl do if she made him really angry?

The pills brought her some ease, dulling her fears to a faint,

AND JUSTICE THERE IS NONE 271

*nagging discomfort. When she'd used up her mother's supply, Karl had got her more.*

*It seemed that everyone they knew was taking LSD, but after the first few times, Angel had made excuses to pass it by. The sharp, jangly feeling and disjointed images the drug produced frightened her—in fact, the last time she'd tried it, she'd spent the evening curled up in a fetal ball on the floor, terrified that the moving walls were going to crush her. Karl had laughed at her, but not even his disdain could convince her to go through that experience again. She would stay with the warmth and drifting ease of the morphine, and confine her nightmares to sleep.*

*Then, just before Christmas, her tablets ran out. When she told Karl, he shrugged and said his source had vanished.*

*She had no rest in the days that followed. Karl watched her growing misery with an interest that seemed calculated, rather than sympathetic. By Christmas Eve she was tossing in their bed, restless and sweating.*

*Karl came and sat beside her, smoothing the damp hair from her forehead. "I can help you if you want," he said gently, holding up a small bag of white powder.*

*She knew what it was. He kept a small supply for friends and clients, although he never touched the stuff himself. "No," she whispered, "I shouldn't." She heard the longing in her voice, and knew he had heard it, too.*

*"It will be all right," he murmured. "It will help you sleep, that's all."*

*"But I—It's—"*

*"Let me take care of you, Angel. Haven't I always taken care of you?"*

*She felt him sponge her arm with something cold, then a prick. The relief came instantly, coursing through her body in*

*a tingling wave. The room shifted, blurred, Karl's face soften-*
*ing like candle wax. The bed moved as he lay down and wrapped*
*her in his arms.*

*"It will be all right," he whispered, his lips warm against*
*her ear. "Everything will be all right. I promise."*

During the daylight hours, Alex sat in the dimness, the
heavy drapes pulled across the garden doors, the only
light from the display cabinet that held his Clarice Cliff
pottery. He'd unplugged the phone, and when he heard
Fern knocking, he held his breath as if his very stillness
would will her to go away. Eventually, she did.

He went back to the mental discipline he had set
himself, absently running his fingers over the handle of
the paper knife he'd stolen from Fern's stall.

It had taken him several days to realize he had no
photo of Dawn. She had never wanted him to take one,
had even refused to give him a copy of the bland studio
shot she'd had made as a gift to her parents. She insisted
he didn't need a reminder of her, that it would lessen
the impact when he saw her—but he thought now that
her reluctance had been merely another manifestation of
her growing fear of Karl.

So he sat in the dark and tried obsessively, memory
by memory, image by image, to put her together again
in his mind. If he could paint the perfect picture of her,
then he might, by some enormous act of will and concentration, imprint it forever in his brain.

He tried desperately to remember every time they
had been together, what they had said or felt or done.
But he found himself thinking instead of other girls,

charting the arcs of those relationships as if they might provide him a map of the one that mattered most.

What he found was that he had never felt a true emotional bond with anyone but Dawn. And the fact that the connection had been half lies on her part, half fantasy on his, left him a husk—having finally learned to value something that didn't exist.

Karl Arrowood had not only taken Dawn from him, he had taken his perception of himself and his way of relating to the world. No longer would he see himself as independent, self-sufficient, in control of his life.

When it grew dark, he slipped the paper knife in his pocket and silently let himself out of the flat, ducking low until he had passed Mr. Canfield's window. It took him a moment to realize snow was falling lightly, touching his face with icy fingers.

Reaching Portobello, he turned to the north, then right onto Chepstow Villas. The scent of food cooking drifted from a nearby flat, reminding him that he hadn't eaten for some time—a day, or was it two? But he pushed the thought aside and went on, set on his course.

From Kensington Park Gardens, he fixed on the spire of St. John's Church like a lodestone. A jogger brushed past, startling him—a tall, slender, hooded figure. Alex felt a shock of familiarity, but when he turned, the man had vanished.

By the time he reached the churchyard, the snow was coming down heavily, obscuring his view of the pale house across the street. But the car was in the drive, and he knew if he waited long enough, Karl was bound to come out.

Then he would know what to do.

Karl tightened the knot in his tie and shot his cuffs without taking his gaze from his face in the mirror. He had accepted the invitation to Christmas Eve dinner at the last moment, reluctantly, only because he'd realized he could not bear to stay in the house alone.

Why did it not show? he wondered as he examined his reflection. How could one go on looking so ordinary, muscle, bone and flesh forming an impervious shell over the devastation within? Nothing had prepared him for this—not even Angel.

It had been years since he'd thought of her, the loss put away along with the family and childhood he no longer acknowledged. Would she have laughed to see him now? Nothing he had thought of value mattered any longer, and too late he had realized the worth of those things held too lightly.

Death had taken Dawn's physical presence from him—Her betrayal had stolen his memories of her. And it was not only her he had lost, but his dream of continuance, of sharing himself with kindred blood and spirit, of leaving a legacy for the future. She had taken his hopes for Alex from him as well.

He switched out the lights and went slowly down the stairs, out into the cold air that pierced his lungs like grief.

"Look. It's snowing." Kincaid had come in from letting Geordie out into the garden one last time. They had sent the boys to bed, with much protest on Kit's part, and Tess had scrambled up with them.

Gemma came to stand beside him and he slipped an arm round her waist. A white veil of swirling flakes now obscured the garden. "I can't believe it," she murmured, her head against his shoulder. "I don't ever remember it snowing on Christmas Eve. It's like the poem you read earlier."

"Lovely, isn't it?" Kincaid had read *"A Child's Christmas in Wales"* aloud to them all after dinner, and he still felt the pleasure of the words on his tongue.

"Do you know it all by heart?"

"Only bits and pieces, now. I had it memorized when I was younger." His family had read not only Dylan Thomas every Christmas Eve, but the American poet Clement Moore's "The Night Before Christmas," from his father's treasured volume, illustrated by Arthur Rackam. For *A Christmas Carol,* they had each taken several parts, so that it became more like a play. Then they had read the nativity story from Luke; the familiar wording still gave him chills. And they had sung carols, accompanied by his dad on piano.

All in all, an ideal picture, if selective memory removed his and Juliet's incessant squabbling over who was to read what; the pinching during the carols; the year he foolishly attempted a solo of "Silent Night" just as his voice had begun to change.

As they grew older, of course, he and his sister had begun to beg off, planning engagements with their friends on Christmas Eve, until by their late teens all that remained of the family traditions had been attendance at midnight mass.

Not until recently had he realized how much the ritual and the structure of those childhood Christmases had mattered to him. He wanted to create something similar for their children, but he suspected that Gemma had been more enchanted by his attempt than the boys. Feeling her shiver against him, he said softly, "Let's go back to the fire. This is a night to be in, not out. I'm glad we decided not to go to church."

"I wanted to be here, in our home," said Gemma, curling up in the corner of the sofa. Geordie jumped up beside her and rested his head on her knee with a contented groan, making them both laugh.

Geordie had made it abundantly clear that he was Gemma's dog. He was friendly and affectionate with everyone else—he'd even made inroads with Sid—but Gemma he followed from room to room, watching her with alert adoration.

"Does that mean that you're happy?"

"Utterly contented. Well, almost..." He saw the flash of her smile in the firelight. "I was looking at the nursery, after I put Toby to bed, and thinking about cots."

"Cots?"

"Toby never had a proper cot, just a bassinet, then one of those portable cots you use for traveling. I want a real nursery for this baby, with all the trimmings."

"A boy nursery or a girl nursery?"

"Don't be sly. I'm not going to admit a preference."

"There's nothing wrong with having a wish, you know. It won't jinx you. Or make you love the baby any less if it turns out to be the opposite."

"It makes me feel disloyal, somehow. But if you really want to know, I'd like a girl. I dream of little girls. I stop and look at little girls' clothes in the shops."

"I suspected as much."

"What about you, then?"

"A girl, of course, if only to balance out the household a bit. Shall we talk about names?"

Gemma's hand went to her belly in the protective gesture that tugged at his heart. "No . . . It's too soon. I—"

The phone rang, shattering their peace like glass breaking.

"Damn." A glance at his watch told him it was almost eleven, and his heart sank. There was never a good reason for the phone to ring this time of night.

It was worse than he feared. He came back into the firelit room, knowing Gemma's face would be tense with waiting, hating to be the one to tell her.

"It's Karl Arrowood. He's been murdered."

# CHAPTER FOURTEEN

A lot of laws came in the mid-sixties the police got very
wise. The authorities started to try and tidy up the streets.
But like everything else, the war was over and they had to
take cognizance of the environment. They had to clean up
the act, bring it back to its imperial grandeur. We already
knew what it was all about.

—Charlie Phillips and Mike Phillips,
from *Notting Hill in the Sixties*

Murdered? Where?"

"In his drive."

"Oh, God." Gemma stood, and Geordie jumped
down from the sofa, his cocker spaniel brow furrowed at
her tone. "Surely not the same way?"

"It looks like it," Kincaid told her. "They're waiting
for us."

"I'll change. You wake Kit and tell him what's happening. Will he be all right on his own with Toby?"

"I don't know that we've much choice, have we?"

Kit sat up in bed, his fair hair sticking up like sprouts.
"Of course I'll be okay," he said, indignant. "But do you
really have to go, on Christmas?"

"Yes. I'm sorry. But Father Christmas has been and
left your stockings on the hearth. They were too heavy
for him to lug all the way up the stairs."

Kit rolled his eyes at the fiction, and Kincaid winked. "If we're not back when Toby wakes up, you can take him downstairs. In the meantime, we'll both have our mobiles if you need anything." He tousled Kit's hair. Much to his surprise, the boy reached out and pressed his hand for a moment before letting it go.

Kincaid, deeply moved, was tempted to say, "I love you," but resisted the impulse. He didn't dare jeopardize the delicate emotional balance they had achieved.

Instead, he took Kit's hand and pulled him out of bed. "Come and look, son, before you go back to sleep. It's going to be a white Christmas."

The crime scene looked much as it had ten days earlier, except for the white frosting of snow. Gemma stamped against the cold as Gerry Franks came up to them.

"Bloody snow," Franks groused. "Ruins the bloody crime scene. It's hopeless." He was obviously no happier at being dragged out on Christmas Eve than they were, and he gave them a scathing look that included them in his displeasure.

The corpse itself had been protected with a makeshift shelter, but a fine sifting of powder lay beneath the covered area. Emergency lighting had been set up round the perimeter of the scene. "Any idea how long he's been here?" Gemma asked.

"My guess, from the state of the ground and the look of the blood, is two to three hours. Pathologist's on her way."

"Who found him?"

"The next-door neighbor, Mrs. Du Ray. She wants to talk to you—won't give her statement to anyone else."

This bit of information seemed to sour Franks's disposition even further.

"All right," said Gemma. "But first we need a look at the body."

Once suited up, she and Kincaid made their way round the parked Mercedes. Gemma's sense of déjà vu intensified. There was only one car in the drive. Had Karl Arrowood already disposed of his murdered wife's?

The body lay a few feet in front of the car, half on its side. There were smudges in the snow near his hands and feet, as if he'd attempted to crawl towards the house. Kneeling, Gemma could see that the blood from his wounds had congealed into dark and syrupy clots, and she couldn't help but remember that Arrowood had been terrified at the sight of blood.

He had not been wearing an overcoat, in spite of the cold, but the dark jacket of his suit had been torn away at the front. His tie had been slashed loose; his once-white shirt was missing its top buttons where it had apparently been ripped open from the collar.

"He fought," she said to Kincaid, who knelt beside her.

"Multiple wounds in the throat, rather than a single clean cut," Kincaid agreed. He reached out with a gloved finger and moved aside the fabric of the shirt. "It's hard to tell with so much blood, but it looks as though there might have been an attempt at mutilating the chest."

"Why slash a man's chest? And if that was the killer's intent, why didn't he finish the job?"

"Perhaps he was interrupted," Kincaid mused. "Or

perhaps he was afraid that the struggle had attracted attention. I can tell you one thing, though—if whoever did this managed to get home without notice, he had to have some way to dispose of his bloody clothes and clean himself up before he was seen by anyone. So he either lives alone—"

"Or has an unusual amount of privacy. As in Gavin Farley's workshop and shower. I think we should get a car on the way to Willesden even before we see Mrs. Du Ray."

"I blew it," Gemma raged to Kincaid as they stripped off their coveralls. "I should have prevented this." She had not liked Karl Arrowood, but to see such strength and force extinguished had shaken her badly.

"How? What could you have done differently?"

"If I knew that, I would have done it, wouldn't I? At least we can rule out Arrowood as the murderer—"

"Can we? What if someone learned he'd committed the first two murders and decided to take retribution into their own hands?"

"I suppose that's possible. But Karl Arrowood was a powerful man, quite a different proposition for the killer than two unsuspecting women—"

"Accounting for the lack of finesse. Dr. Ling may be able to tell us if the murders were committed by the same person. But if that's the case, it's quite a departure from the usual serial killer pattern."

Fully dressed again, they followed the walk to Mrs. Du Ray's porch, their footprints leaving dark gashes in the fresh snow. "Bloody hell, your sergeant's right about the crime scene," Kincaid muttered as he rang the bell. "Might as well wash everything down with a fire hose."

Mrs. Du Ray greeted Gemma with a whispered, "Oh, my dear." Her skin appeared paper-thin, the lines round mouth and eyes much more pronounced than a week earlier.

"I'm so sorry you had to deal with this, Mrs. Du Ray," she said. "It must have been a terrible shock."

"Yes." Mrs. Du Ray gave a small negative shake of her head, as if further words escaped her.

When they were seated in the warm kitchen, Gemma said, "Why don't you start from the beginning."

"After my supper, I did the washing up, then went upstairs to get ready for bed. Sometimes I put on my dressing gown and come back downstairs to watch a little television. When I glanced out the window, I noticed Karl's car standing in the drive. There was a faint light coming from the interior, as if perhaps one of the doors hadn't quite closed." Mrs. Du Ray spoke clearly and precisely, as if giving a report, but the blue veins stood out on her hands, clasped in her lap. "I thought I saw something dark in front of the car, but it had begun to snow, and I decided my eyes were deceiving me."

"What time was this?" asked Gemma, her notebook ready.

"Before nine o'clock. I'm sure of it because there was a program on at nine I wanted to see. I came downstairs again and made some cocoa, but I couldn't settle. I kept wondering if I had really seen something, or if my imagination had run wild. So I went back up and looked again, and this time there *was* a dark shape in the drive—I was sure of it—and I saw someone crossing the street from the churchyard.

"It was a young man, or at least that was my impression. He was bareheaded, with that floppy sort of Edwardian hairstyle you see young men wearing these days. He came into the drive, almost tiptoeing, and walked round the car. Then he froze, and went closer. I saw him bend over and reach out, then he turned and ran as if the hounds of hell were after him."

"What else did you notice about the young man?"

"He was tall, and on the slender side, I think. It's hard to tell with a coat, and the snow..."

"Did you see his face well enough that you'd recognize him again?"

"I don't know." Mrs. Du Ray seemed distressed. "I'd not want to accuse someone unfairly."

"I wouldn't worry about that at the moment," Kincaid assured her. "It sounds very much as if Mr. Arrowood was already dead. It was after this that you rang the police?"

"Well, no. I had to be sure, you see. I dressed and went out to look for myself... Poor Karl... There was so much blood." She looked up at them in appeal. "Why would someone do such a terrible thing?"

Kit lay awake for a long time after Duncan and Gemma left, listening to the rhythm of Toby's breathing. Tess was curled up at his feet, and after a few minutes, Geordie padded upstairs and jumped up on the bed, stretching out against his thigh. Resting his hand on the dog's head, Kit snuggled further down into the bedclothes and told himself he should be content. It was Christmas, after all.... It was snowing.... He was part of a family again....

But he had dreamed of his mother, and as hard as he tried during the day not to think of her, now his mind refused to let her go.

Had she known the poem Duncan had read tonight? It was the sort of thing she would have liked, of that he was sure, with the sound of the words making pictures that went along with the meaning.

Had his mum and Duncan celebrated Christmases together? He'd never thought much about the time they'd spent together before he was born—it made him feel decidedly odd—but now he worried at it. They *had* loved one another, he supposed. They had been married, had meant to be a family, but something had gone wrong. If his mum and Duncan had stayed together, would she still be alive?

He didn't want to think about that. Then Duncan wouldn't be with Gemma, and Kit genuinely loved Gemma, although even admitting that to himself made him feel disloyal to his mother.

Stroking Geordie's silky muzzle, he squeezed his eyes shut and tried to picture the snow swirling outside, but instead remembered the last time it had snowed in Grantchester. Near their house, a gentle hill sloped down to the towpath beside the river. He and his mum had sledded down on baking pans, shouting and tumbling off together at the bottom. Her face had glowed pink with cold and happiness, and he remembered how her laughter had rung out in the clear air.

But what he recalled most was the moment they had stood at the top of the hill, holding their baking pans, looking down at the white blanket enveloping the familiar folds and hollows. The pristine expanse was undisturbed, except for the tiny, three-toed track of a bird, as sharp and crisp as a hieroglyphic, and the tidy paw prints of a cat, or fox, near the hedgerow.

Kit had stood, transfixed, and it seemed to him that to make a mark upon such beauty was more than he could bear. Then his mother had called out for him to join her.

He'd put aside his hesitation and plunged out into the snow, and it had been a good time, one of the best. With that thought, he fell asleep.


According to Dr. Ling, Arrowood had been dead several hours, but she would have to use calculations involving air temperature and environmental factors to be more precise. Nor could she give them any immediate guess as to the nature of the weapon until she had cleaned up the corpse—the wounds were simply too much of a mess.

She did speculate, however, that unlike his wife, Arrowood might have lived for some time after the attack, too weak from loss of blood to do more than make a futile attempt at getting help.

None of this came as any surprise to Kincaid and Gemma. Adding to their frustration, the crime-scene officers reported no evidence of disturbance inside the house. The front door had been locked, and Arrowood's keys had been found in the drive a few feet from his body, as if he'd dropped them in the struggle.

When the responding officers arrived, they had indeed found the driver's door of the Mercedes ever so slightly ajar, and the dome lamp burning.

"He must have been jumped just as he opened the door," Kincaid said as they shed their coats in the warmth of Gemma's office.

"If that door had been closed properly, he might have lain there, covered in snow, until someone missed him."

"Apparently, since it looks as though Mrs. Du Ray's creeping figure didn't feel inclined to call for help."

"It must have been Alex Dunn," said Gemma. "The description fits him to a tee. And it means he can't have murdered Karl, if he found him already dead——"

"What if he fought with him, then came back to see if he'd been successful?"

"Then why run away, as if he were frightened by what he'd found?" argued Gemma.

"I don't see that we can get much further until we've had a word with Dunn. Why don't we send a car to bring him in, and get a forensics team started on his flat?"


"I demand my solicitor," Gavin Farley snarled as they entered the Spartan confines of the interview room, with its metal-and-laminate table and molded plastic chairs. "I'm not saying anything without my solicitor here." His hair was uncombed, and although he'd pulled on jacket and trousers, he still wore a purple satin pajama shirt, which detracted considerably from his authority.

"Surely there's no need for that," rejoined Gemma mildly. "We only want to ask you a few routine questions."

"And for that you drag me out of bed with my wife, in the middle of the night, and you frighten my children half to death? I'm telling you I won't have it. I want my solicitor." Farley folded his arms across his purple satin chest and glared.

Gemma sighed and summoned a constable. "Please take Mr. Farley to phone his solicitor, then bring him back here."

As soon as the door closed, Kincaid said, "Can't say I blame the chap. I've seldom had less reason to rouse a man from his bed on Christmas Eve."

"And what about the shower in his shop, and his lying about his row with Dawn?" countered Gemma. "Besides, I think he's cleverer than he'd like us to believe."

Escorted by the constable, Farley came back in, a smug look on his face. "My solicitor's on his way. You'll have to wait until he gets here."

"Fine." Kincaid smiled at him and relaxed into his chair. "Can we get you anything? A coffee?" When Farley shook his head, Kincaid continued, "There's no reason we can't get acquainted while we wait, is there, Mr. Farley? I hear you're quite an expert in woodworking. Is this a longtime passion of yours?"

The struggle between caution and pride was evident in Farley's expression, with pride the winner. "Since I was a boy. My father had a little shop. My own son, unfortunately, only seems to be interested in videos and computer games. No respect for the handicrafts these days."

"Is it animals you carve? With such firsthand experience—"

"No, no. I need a complete break from work; otherwise, the stress..." He shrugged, as if Kincaid would understand his predicament. Just out of Farley's line of sight, Gemma rolled her eyes.

"I've never quite managed a hobby, myself," Kincaid admitted. "But it must be very nice to get away from it all, have one's own space."

"No way." The veterinarian pinched his lips together and set his jaw in a stubborn line. "I see what you're doing, and I'm not going to talk about my shop."

"Then what about the thefts from your surgery, Mr. Farley?" Kincaid inquired, all innocence. "Surely you want the help of the police with that? I understand you have some supplies and medications missing?"

"How did you—That's a purely internal matter."

"You're not accusing Miss Poole, are you?" asked Gemma sharply.

"I—No! She was merely negligent, but I don't see why it's any of your business."

"If some unauthorized person came into your clinic and stole your property, Mr. Farley, it should have been reported to the police," said Kincaid. "Was there by any chance a scalpel among the items missing?"

Gavin Farley's mouth dropped open. "Yes, but—I— You can't think—" He gaped at them, fishlike, his pupils dilating into black orbs.

At that moment there was a knock on the door, and a constable brought in a man in a neat pinstriped suit.

"Miles!" Farley exclaimed, shooting from his chair and clasping the man's hand fervently.

"Hullo, Gavin." The solicitor disengaged his hand and turned to the two detectives. "I'm Miles Kelly, Mr. Farley's solicitor." He was in his mid-thirties, Kincaid guessed, dark-haired, with a strong face. In spite of his suit and crisp white shirt—the obligatory solicitor's badge—the dark blue shadow on his chin revealed that he hadn't taken the time to shave. "What seems to be the problem here?"

"I take it Mr. Farley has made you aware of our investigations," Gemma answered, "and of his involvement with the woman who was murdered just over a week ago—"

"She was my client, for God's sake!" Farley interrupted. "I keep telling you—"

"Gavin, calm down." Kelly turned back to Gemma. "Inspector, he rang me yesterday to say you were having his house searched. As all the documents were in order, I told him that cooperation was the only appropriate response."

"Very wise of you, Mr. Kelly," Kincaid said. "And he followed your instructions. The problem is that there was another murder, hours ago, and we'd like to ascertain Mr. Farley's whereabouts during the time in question."

"Another murder?" Farley's voice seeped out in a whisper. "Where—Who—"

"Karl Arrowood," Gemma informed him tersely. "Are you sure you never met Dawn's husband, Mr. Farley?"

"No. Never. I wouldn't have known the man if I'd passed him in the street."

"Then why should you mind telling us where you were last evening?"

"I—It's a violation of my privacy. Why should I tell you, if I had nothing to do with this? You can't just go about—"

"Gavin," interrupted Miles Kelly, "don't be difficult.

Tell them what they want to know, and then we can all go home."

Farley stared at his solicitor as if he might protest, then gave a shrug of acquiescence. "I was at home. All evening. With my wife, and my mother- and father-in-law. Our next-door neighbors stopped in for a drink as well."

"What time did your in-laws arrive?" asked Gemma.

"Around half-past six. My wife always has them for Christmas Eve dinner, then on Christmas day we go to my parents' in Henley."

"And they left when?"

"About half-past nine, I believe. I didn't know there was any reason to make note of the time."

Gemma ignored his sarcasm. "And you didn't leave your house at all in the interim? Not even to go to your shop?"

"No."

"Mr. Farley, if this is the truth, you could have saved us all a good deal of time and trouble by telling us so in the first place. And you could have let your solicitor stay in his bed on Christmas Day."

"We've got confirmation from the wife," Gemma told Kincaid, looking at the report Gerry Franks had just sent up. "For whatever that's worth. Sergeant Franks has a team lined up to question the in-laws and the neighbors as soon as it's a civilized hour."

"Daybreak?" That would not be long in coming—it was almost five now.

"Right. The initial search of the house and shop, and of Farley's car, haven't revealed anything obvious. Of course, we won't know for certain until forensics has had a chance to go over things again."

They were holding Farley temporarily, pending confirmation of his alibi, but they wouldn't be able to keep him for long without something concrete.

"What about Alex Dunn?" asked Kincaid.

"Downstairs, in another interview room. They roused him out of an apparently sound sleep, and there was no visible evidence in his house or his car. They did find a silver-handled paper knife," she added, "in his coat pocket. It's apparently quite sharp, but there was no sign of its having been used. It's gone to forensics." Standing, she gathered her notebook.

"Gemma, before we go downstairs . . . Why don't you let me take the postmortem? You look exhausted. And it's a good division of labor."

"You just want some time alone with Kate Ling," she retorted, only half teasing. But she was too tired to feel really jealous, and besides—there was no point in their both going to the morgue, and she could be more useful directing things here. "Okay," she agreed. "That's at what—eight? I'm going to stop at the loo before we begin with Alex."

Duncan was right again, she thought as she examined herself in the mirror of the ladies' toilet. She did look exhausted, and she wasn't sure how long her reserves would hold out. This pregnancy was sapping more energy than she'd bargained for, even into the second trimester.

Turning sideways, she saw that, even in jeans and sweater, the bulge was becoming obvious. And only then did she realize that in daydreaming about the nursery the previous evening, she'd finally, truly, accepted this baby on a personal level—now she must do it on a professional one.

When Superintendent Lamb came back on Boxing Day, she would tell him first thing. As if the child had somehow sensed her resolution, she felt the faintest flutter of movement in her abdomen.

'I did go to the churchyard," Alex said immediately. He looked ghastly—pale, with dark hollows under his eyes, and his once-glossy hair unwashed. "I don't know what I was thinking—I suppose I wasn't thinking, really."

"There was a silver knife in your coat," Gemma told him. "Did you take it with you deliberately?"

"I—Yes. It's Fern's. I took it from her stall on Saturday. I should say that I stole it, shouldn't I? Except that I meant to return it."

"Why did you take the knife?"

"I thought I might kill Arrowood with it."

Gemma and Kincaid stared at him as the tape recorder whirred in the sudden silence. "And did you?" asked Gemma, recovering. "Did you kill Karl Arrowood with it?"

"No." Alex met their eyes, looked away. "I—I didn't have the nerve, in the end. I watched the house for two nights, waiting for him to come out. I felt I had to confront him, tell him who I was, what she'd meant to me. And then ... then I was going to put it in the lap of the gods. That sounds absurd now, but it seemed to make sense at the time. I hadn't really imagined myself ... hurting him, you know? I mean, I never even got into a fight at school, so what did I think I was going to do?"

"What happened last night?" Gemma prompted.

"I got to the house a little after eight. His Mercedes was in the drive, so I hid in the trees by the church and waited. I hadn't counted on the cold, and the snow. After a while, my hands and feet went numb, and my vision started doing funny things. I'd think the light was on inside the car, and then I'd think I'd imagined it.

"But he didn't come out of the house, and finally I crossed the street to see if I was right about the light. I can't tell you why it seemed so important to me at the time, to see if I was imagining things. And then when I reached the car and saw that the dome lamp really was on, I thought I saw something on the pavement in front of the car—" Alex rubbed the back of his hand against his brow and took a ragged breath.

"Was he dead?" asked Gemma.

"He was . . . cold. I don't know how I could have thought I could—His throat looked like mince. I ran. I don't mean that I decided to run—I just found myself running. And then I was sick.

"I know I should have called the police straightaway, but I wasn't . . . And afterwards . . . afterwards, I didn't know how I would explain what I'd done, or why I'd been there in the first place."

"What did you do then?"

"I went back to my flat. I had a few drinks. I suppose I must have gone to sleep." Alex met Gemma's gaze bleakly. "This means he didn't kill her, doesn't it? That all this time, I've been hating him, and hating myself because I felt responsible for what I thought he'd done . . . and all this time it was someone else."

"Alex, did you see anything last night?" she urged.

"Anything odd or suspicious around Arrowood's house, or the church?"

"No." He looked devastated by his failure. "I didn't see anything at all."

"Nice musculature," commented Kate Ling. The corners of her eyes crinkled in a slight smile as she glanced at Kincaid. She was masked and gowned, and had Karl Arrowood's naked body laid out on her table, his mutilated throat exposed to her lamp.

"If you're trying to shock me with pathologist's humor, you won't succeed," Kincaid replied, grinning.

"Well, I am entitled to notice that he was a nice-looking man—I mean that in a professional way, of course. And it's obvious he took pride in himself. I'd say he worked out at a gym several times a week. He had regular manicures, too, which make the defense wounds on his right hand all the more obvious. See the cuts in his fingertips, and across his palm?"

"So he fought hard?"

"Very. See these blood smears in his hair? My guess is that's how the killer finally overpowered him, by getting a grip on this nice, thick hair and forcing his head back."

"What about the wounds themselves? Can you tell if they were made by the same weapon as his wife's, or by the same perpetrator?"

"The instrument was sharp and clean-edged, that I can tell you. The killer just never managed to get really good purchase. This man died from blood loss from multiple wounds, not from a complete severing of a main artery. And I'd guess that your killer was male, and of good height, and right-handed."

"Well, that rules out a certain percentage of the population, anyway. What about the chest wound? Did the killer intend the sort of mutilation performed on Dawn Arrowood?"

"You're thinking he was interrupted? That's possible. Although the psychology of inflicting that sort of injury on both women *and* men is beyond my scope."

"Time of death?"

"That old chestnut?"

Again he heard the suggestion of a smile in her voice. "I'm afraid so."

Ling reached up and turned off the tape recorder. "Off the record? I'd say somewhere in the vicinity of eight P.M. Officially, I'll have to be boringly vague, say, somewhere between seven and ten. Once I've done the stomach contents, you may be able to pin it down a bit more accurately."

"Thanks," he said with genuine feeling.

"Let's go outside for a minute," the pathologist suggested. "There's no need for you to stay for the icky part, organs and so forth. I'll send you a report." When they reached the hallway, she pulled off her mask and her cap, letting her glossy black hair swing loose, and stripped off her gloves. "That reminds me. I said the same thing not long ago to Gemma. I thought she might faint on me for a moment—That's not like her, is it?"

"No." He replied noncommittally, wondering where this was going. "She must have been having a particularly bad day."

Kate Ling frowned at him. "Duncan, I've always wondered... I know it's none of my business, but are you two an item?"

"We've just moved into a house together," he answered, seeing no reason to dissemble. "Now that she doesn't work with me directly, it's a bit more politically correct."

"Oh, well," Kate said, then shrugged and flashed him a smile whose meaning he couldn't mistake. He found himself utterly and unexpectedly tongue-tied, but she rescued him. "I hope things work out for you. She *is* pregnant, isn't she?"

"Yes. The baby's due in May."

"Is she feeling all right? She looked a bit peaky when I saw her that day."

"She *has* had a problem with her placenta. Some bleeding. But she seems to be fine now."

"Good." Kate gave him a reassuring smile, but not before he'd glimpsed the flash of concern in her eyes.


Gemma stepped out into the late-morning daylight outside the station, blinking as if emerging from a long, if unwelcome, hibernation. It had stopped snowing during the night, but gray clouds still hovered over the rooftops, and dirty slush filled gutters and pavement.

Shivering as she waited for Kincaid to fetch the car, she thought of the morning's progress, and her spirits sank even lower.

They had kept Alex Dunn at the station until Mrs. Du Ray had been able to come in and make a positive identification, but once that formality was completed, they'd had to send him home with a caution.

The same was true of Gavin Farley, which galled Gemma considerably more. Both his in-laws and his neighbors, the Simmonses, had confirmed his alibi, insisting that Farley had not left their sight for more than five minutes during the time period in which the pathologist estimated Arrowood had been murdered. The Simmonses had also made it clear they didn't care for Farley, so it seemed unlikely that they would be inclined to protect him. Nor had the search team found anything, although with the Christmas slowdown there was no telling how long it would take to get the trace evidence results back from the Home Office lab.

Then, it had fallen to Gemma to inform Karl Arrowood's sons and his ex-wife of his murder. Sean, the younger son, had answered the door at his mother's residence.

"Inspector James!" Wariness replaced his first cheerful response. "Do come in."

"I'm afraid I have some very bad news. Your father was killed last night."

He gaped at her, shock draining the color from his face.

"Sean, do you want to sit down?"

He ignored the suggestion. "My father *can't* be dead. There must be some mistake. We're having lunch today, a make-up-with-Richard occasion. Dad actually rang us."

"I'm sorry. There's no mistake. He was found in his drive by a neighbor."

"You mean . . . he was killed . . . like her?"

"The circumstances are quite similar, yes. Would you like me to speak to your mother? Is she here?"

"No. She and Richard have gone out for a bit." More

firmly, he added, "I'll tell Mum. And Richard." His face had aged decades in five minutes.

"Is there anyone else we should inform?"

"Not that I know of. Dad's parents have been dead for years. I suppose I can ring his staff. And his business associates."

"We'll let you know when you can make funeral arrangements. Sean...there is one other thing." She hesitated, in the face of his obvious grief and shock, but knew she must ask. "Where were you and Richard yesterday evening?"

"Here," he answered without rancor. "Mother gives a monster party every Christmas Eve—a gala, she calls it. Rich and I are expected to dance attendance on all the old dears, without fail. Our mother's wrath is not something to be trifled with. Oh, God," he groaned, as if it had finally sunk in, "she's not going to want to hear this."

"I'm sorry." Gemma felt as helpless as she always did when faced with the response to sudden death. "We will be in touch, possibly with a few more questions. But we'll try to intrude as little as possible. And you can ring me if you like." She left, not envying him the task he faced.

It was still possible, of course, that one or both of the brothers had hired a professional to commit all three murders, but Doug Cullen's investigation had not turned up a shred of corroborating evidence—and she'd never really thought the idea likely. The nature of the crimes was too personal—too intimate, she was certain—to be the work of a hired killer.

Still, she'd have to send someone to get a guest list

from Sylvia Arrowood tomorrow, so that they could check the boys' alibis.

When Kincaid picked her up a moment later for the drive home, she noticed that he avoided passing by St. John's Church. It was thoughtful of him: Even the idea of the bloodstained snow in Karl Arrowood's drive made her feel queasy.

It occurred to her that she hadn't eaten, except for a bite of a muffin brought to her unexpectedly by Gerry Franks, and that might account for her light-headedness.

But the very worst thing about the day became painfully clear to her as they pulled up in front of their house. She hadn't realized how fiercely she'd looked forward to spending this morning with the boys until she'd missed it, an opportunity gone forever.

Kincaid had at least checked in with Kit several times on his mobile, but she hadn't even had the chance to wish Toby a happy Christmas.

"Mummy! Kit's made French toast for breakfast, with sausages, and he's put some in the warming oven for you!" Toby looked like a little elf in his footed red flannelette pajamas, and he was jiggling up and down with excitement. "Wait till you see—"

"I've got tea in the pot, as well," Kit interrupted, giving Toby a warning glance. "Come in the kitchen." As he took her arm, she noticed absently that the dining room doors were closed, but she thought no more about it.

Kit sat her down at the table and served her with a flourish, while Kincaid looked on affectionately, saying he'd had something earlier. Only halfway through her breakfast did she remember they were supposed to go to Hazel's for Christmas dinner. A wave of exhaustion washed over her; she put down her suddenly leaden fork.

"You'll have to go to Hazel's without me," she said, near tears. "I don't think I can manage it."

"Don't worry," Kit told her. "I've arranged everything. They're coming here—Hazel and Tim and Holly—and you don't have to do a thing but sit down and eat. Toby and I have even set the table. I'll show you when you're finished."

Gemma's throat tightened. "Kit, I don't know what to say. You are so thoughtful, and so grown-up. I don't know how I ever got along without you."

The boy flushed with pride, then urged her to finish her breakfast with proprietary zeal. "Are you ready, then?" he asked, with barely contained excitement. "You can bring your tea."

As they reached the dining room, a look passed between Kit and Kincaid, who said casually as he swung open the doors, "Oh, by the way, Father Christmas has been here as well."

She had a brief impression of the table, splendidly set with assorted dishes and glassware, a shining Christmas cracker at each place.

Then the piano filled her vision. A baby grand, its polished ebony surface reflecting every sparkle and gleam from the room. They'd moved the dining table to one side to accommodate the instrument, which had been placed facing the garden doors. "So that you can look outside when you play," Kit explained gravely.

"But what—How did you—and on Christmas—"

"Kit was my partner in crime," Kincaid explained,

grinning. "And the piano company was delighted to cooperate in the surprise. Do you like it?"

"Like it? I—" Mesmerized, Gemma sank onto the padded bench. With one finger, she touched middle C, and the single pure tone resonated through the room.

She put her hands over her face and wept.

# CHAPTER FIFTEEN

Though most people still gave counties in England as their birthplace, the inhabitants of the road were becoming more diverse as people who had been born overseas came to live in the area. A sample from the same census shows one person originated from Russia, one from Poland, eight from Ireland, one from Belgium . . .

—Whetlor and Bartlett,
from *Portobello*

BY UNSPOKEN AGREEMENT, they had not discussed the case at home over Christmas. But as they drove to the police station the next morning, Kincaid said, as if continuing a recently interrupted conversation, "We can't rule out Alex Dunn altogether, you know. We can't be certain that he didn't attack Karl, then come back to see if he needed to finish the job."

"I think Mrs. Du Ray is a reliable witness," Gemma protested. "If she says he was frightened—"

"I'm not questioning her interpretation, just whether his fright absolves him of murder. You can kill someone in the heat of a struggle and still be horrified by the consequences."

"Yes, of course, but say he did kill Karl—and he's admitted intent and motive—he has an alibi for the time of Dawn's—Bryony!" she exclaimed as they entered the station. "What are you doing here?"

"Hullo, Gemma." Bryony rose from a seat in the

reception area. "I hoped I could have a word with you, if I'm not too early. I had to come before the surgery opened."

"No, that's fine. Bryony, this is Superintendent Kincaid, from Scotland Yard."

Bryony shook Kincaid's hand, and Gemma noticed that her right index finger was bandaged. "Is there somewhere we could talk?"

"We'll go in my office."

"How's Geordie?" Bryony asked as Gemma signed her in and led her through the security door.

"A little worn out from the excitement of Christmas, I think. We had two little ones who took it upon themselves to run him ragged in the snow."

In spite of Karl Arrowood's death, it had turned out to be a lovely Christmas. Hazel, in her marvelously organized way, had arrived with a car boot of food ready to reheat in the Aga. They had supped around Kit's festive table with much jollity, and if Gemma fell asleep during the Queen's speech, no one seemed to mind.

Then, before succumbing to bed, Gemma had at last managed a half hour alone with the piano. For that brief time, all that had mattered was the sound of the notes as they followed one another.

"—Boxing Day," Bryony was saying to Kincaid as they reached the conference room. "Do you know, when I was a child, I thought it had to do with fighting? What a fool I felt when I found out that was the day they gave out alms from the church boxes." She sat, twisting her plain, strong hands in her lap.

"What happened to you?" Gemma asked, nodding toward Bryony's injured finger.

"A Yorkshire terrier the owner assured me *never*

bites." Bryony glanced up at them with a crooked smile, which immediately disappeared. "I heard about Karl Arrowood. Have you any idea who did it?"

Obviously, she hadn't heard about their investigation of Gavin Farley—but then it wasn't likely he'd have broadcast his troubles. "We're pursuing some leads," Gemma replied noncommittally. "What is it, Bryony? Has something else happened?"

"I didn't know what I should do. It seems petty and disloyal to come tattling like a schoolgirl, but on the other hand . . ." She glanced uneasily at Kincaid.

"Go on," urged Gemma. "Superintendent Kincaid is working with me on these cases. Anything you can tell me, you can tell him."

Bryony took a breath, then nodded. "When I was finishing up in the surgery on Monday, I found some photos in Gavin's desk. They were all of Dawn and Alex."

"Dawn and Alex?"

"I'd no idea Gavin knew. Now I wonder if he overheard me mention their relationship to Marc . . . but even so—"

"Blackmail!" Kincaid exclaimed. "That would explain a good deal. If he was blackmailing her, and she refused to play along any further—"

"But then why kill her?" protested Gemma. "It's usually the victim who murders the blackmailer, not the other way round."

"Maybe she threatened to expose him, regardless of the consequences to herself—"

"Or to Alex?" Gemma asked dubiously. "You think Dawn would have sacrificed Alex to Karl's wrath, just to get Farley off her back?"

"Perhaps. If she meant to leave Karl for Alex, it would have to come out eventually. But I admit I'm getting ahead of the evidence. We need to see those photos."

"What did you do with them?" Gemma asked Bryony.

"I left them where they were."

"Okay. Good. Don't touch them. And don't say anything to Mr. Far—"

There was a knock at the door and Melody Talbot asked, "Could I see you outside a moment, boss? Superintendent?"

Excusing themselves, they followed Melody out into the corridor. "What's up, Constable?" asked Kincaid.

"The search team found a surgical scalpel in a rubbish bin about two blocks east of the Arrowood house. It's been wiped clean, but they've sent it to forensics with a rush request."

"Farley should be at work by now," Gemma said decisively. "Have him brought in again, alibi or no alibi. And then have a team search his surgery." She related Bryony's information.

"The surgery!" Melody exclaimed. "It's the perfect place to clean up. He could even have worn surgical scrubs, then tossed them in the laundry. Under the circumstances, no one would think anything of a bit of blood."

"True." Gemma looked up from the rough list she'd scribbled in her notebook. "Melody, once you've got things in motion, go and interview Farley's neighbors again. See if there's any way they'll budge on his whereabouts last night."

When Melody had gone, Kincaid said, "I don't like this business about Farley, Gemma. No matter how damning the circumstantial evidence, we can't charge him unless we can budge his alibi. Nor is there any connection between this man and Marianne Hoffman, and I'm absolutely certain that these three crimes are connected."

"Maybe he was practicing?" offered Gemma.

"Hoffman as a random victim? I don't buy it. But we might as well tackle him about the scalpel while we're waiting for confirmation on the other—"

His mobile phone rang.

As he took the call, Gemma thought about what he'd said. He was right: A good defense lawyer would make mincemeat of the prosecution's case for Farley as the murderer of either Dawn or Karl Arrowood. The scalpel could have come from any one of a thousand places; Farley might have photographed Dawn and Alex with no motive other than prurient curiosity; they had only Bryony's word that he'd had a disagreement with Dawn on the day she was murdered.

Nor, as she knew from last night's experience, would they even be able to talk to Farley until his lawyer got there.

"That was Marianne Hoffman's daughter in Bedford," Kincaid said as he returned to her. "She's found some things she wants me to see. Do you mind interviewing Farley on your own, if I drive up there?"

"No, but why not send someone else?"

"Apparently, she wants to talk to me specifically. Must be my pretty face."

"Right. Go on then. I'll ring you if we make any

progress." Gemma repressed a sigh as she watched him go. It was going to be a long morning.

"Thank you for coming," said Eliza Goddard as she led Kincaid into her kitchen. "I've sent the girls next door to play for a bit."

Kincaid followed her, curious about the difference in her reception of him compared to his last visit. They sat down at the table where Eliza's twins had squabbled over their coloring books, and he saw that she had placed a shoe box beside the stack of children's projects.

"You said there was something you wanted to talk to me about," he said, to give her an opening.

"Yes. I'm sorry about the other day. . . . It's just that I had to get through Christmas. It was so hard for the girls, but Greg came, and I think that helped."

"Greg Hoffman, your stepdad?"

Nodding, she said, "He made everything seem a little more normal, more ordinary, and for a day we could pretend that Mum had just gone away. But then last night, when everyone was asleep, I forced myself to go through the box again." She glanced at the shoe box but made no move to touch it. "I think I should tell you. . . . One of the reasons I didn't feel I could talk to you about my mother—or my father—was that she'd always cautioned me against it."

"I'm not sure I understand."

"Mum said that my safety depended on never talking about my background. Of course I didn't take it seriously—you know how children are—but then after she was killed I began to wonder . . ."

"Do you know anything about your father? Were they divorced?"

"I always assumed so. Mum wouldn't talk about him at all. But I was curious, and one day I looked through the things she kept in the special drawer in her bureau. She caught me at it—it was the one time I remember her truly losing her temper."

"Are these the things from her drawer?" Kincaid asked, indicating the box.

Without answering, Eliza pushed it towards him.

He lifted the lid and reached for the top document. It was a birth certificate, issued in the Borough of Kensington and Chelsea, in 1971. The child's name was given as Eliza Marie Thomas, the mother as Marianne Wolowski Thomas, and the father as Ronald Samuel Thomas. The address of record was Talbot Road, W. 11.

"You were born in Notting Hill," Kincaid said.

"Yes, but I don't remember the area. We must have moved away when I was a baby. That's me with my parents." She lifted a photograph and he took it by its edge.

The color had faded, but the young woman was instantly recognizable as the girl he'd seen in Edgar Vernon's photo. But here she looked older, the platinum hair darker, longer, with a fringe, and he thought he could see a new wariness in her eyes.

She stood beside a tall, dark-skinned man whose face looked vaguely familiar, and between them they held a laughing infant.

"It must have been hard for your mother," he commented. "An interracial marriage at that time."

"If it was, she never let on. Nor did it ever seem to occur to her that I should mind my skin being a different color than my schoolmates'." Eliza's voice held a trace of bitterness. "When I came home crying because I'd been taunted and teased, she'd tell me I should be proud, and that was the end of it. It was better after she married Greg."

"How old were you?"

"Eight. Greg would tell me that I was beautiful, that I was special, and that one day the other children would be sorry they weren't like me." She smiled, and Kincaid realized how right Greg Hoffman had been. Taking the photo back from him, she studied it. "I'm ashamed to admit this, but after Greg came to live with us, I used to tell people I was adopted. That way I didn't have to admit my mother had been married to a black man. Now I only wish that I had known my father."

There were other photos in the box of the chubby little girl who had been Marianne Wolowski, standing stiffly with parents who wore the formal-looking dress of the fifties, receiving a prize at school, blowing out candles on a birthday cake. In another, a bit older, she and a thin black girl in a pink dress smiled out at the camera together.

Stuck to the back of the photo was a folded piece of paper. When Kincaid uncreased it, he saw that it was a school report from Colville School, dated 1957. Not only had Marianne Wolowski lived in Notting Hill when she'd given birth to her child, she had grown up there.

"Do you mind if I take this?" He indicated the birth certificate. "I'll have it returned to you as soon as I've made a copy."

"Will any of this help you?" asked Eliza. "You know, at first the why of it didn't matter so much to me—I was too busy trying to accept the fact that she was gone. But now... What makes it really difficult is that it seems to me she had finally reached a good place in her life. I don't think she was happy when I was a child—I don't mean she wasn't a good mum, but I think there was more duty in it than joy. But with my twins...She loved them so unreservedly, and there was no worry in it."

"That's the blessing of being a grandparent—or so I've heard."

She gazed out the window a moment, then turned back to him. "There's something else. Now that Mum's gone, my father is all I have left. Do you think you could find him for me?"

By late afternoon, Gemma would have been happy to murder Gavin Farley herself. The veterinarian had obviously taken his solicitor's advice to keep his mouth shut, stating flatly that he knew nothing about Dawn Arrowood's affair with Alex Dunn, nor had he ever taken photos of either of them. Not even Sergeant Franks's natural belligerence in the interview room had goaded him into any further response.

She finished writing up another discouragingly noncommittal release for the press—though fat lot of good her discretion would do. The headline of the latest edition of the *Daily Star* glared at her from her desktop: *Slasher Strikes Again—Is There a New Ripper Abroad?*

The other papers had followed suit, if slightly more sedately, and the station switchboard had rung nonstop all morning with calls from citizens concerned about their personal safety.

Melody Talbot came into her office, collapsing into a chair with a groan.

"Any luck?" Gemma asked, although the expression on Melody's face told her it was a faint hope. "Did you find the photos?"

"Not a trace. All we turned up was a bit of ash floating in the toilet. We interviewed Farley on Christmas Eve—if he'd got the wind up, he could have come in anytime on Christmas Day to destroy the evidence."

"Bloody sodding hell!" snapped Gemma, unable to contain her frustration. "The bastard!"

"Now what, boss?"

"What about Christmas Eve, then?"

"It took me all afternoon to track down Farley's neighbors. But in the meantime, I had a good natter up and down the street."

"And?"

"The upshot is, you couldn't find more reliable witnesses. Simmons is a banker; Mrs. Simmons belongs to every parents' organization imaginable. The neighbor across the street told me that the only reason the Simmonses put up with the Farleys' social invitations is that Mrs. Simmons wants to stay on good terms with Mrs. Farley, because their kids share rides to school and sports. So that's pretty well that. What about your end?"

"Now I go and give the super a progress report. But I'm not giving up on this. Get the surgery's phone records. If Farley was blackmailing Dawn, he had to have communicated with her somehow."


Superintendent Lamb listened impassively while she recited the day's events.

"What about the area where the scalpel was found?"

he asked when she'd finished. "Have you had a forensics team in?"

"Yes, sir. They've gone over the rubbish bin and anything else he might have touched in the immediate vicinity. So far no prints have matched anyone involved in our inquiries. We've also had a team questioning anyone who lives nearby, and we've put out a notice asking for help from anyone who might have been passing."

"We've got to turn up something, Gemma." He nodded at the newspapers spread out on his desk. "Not to mention I've had the commissioner on the phone. Arrowood's friends have been complaining loudly about our failure to prevent his death—and I can't say I blame them."

"I know, sir." It took an effort of will, as well as clenched teeth, to stop Gemma venting her frustration. The super didn't care how hard they'd tried; he wanted results. She realized suddenly that this was the first time she'd had to assume responsibility for failure in a difficult case without Kincaid as a buffer.

"I'm not criticizing your work," Lamb added with uncomfortable proximity to her thoughts. "But perhaps you need to put the pieces back in the box, shake them up and dump them out again, to see if they settle a different way. Sometimes we get so attached to one idea that we can't see another under our nose."

"Superintendent Kincaid's following up something different, sir. Some information pertaining to the first victim, Marianne Hoffman."

"And you're still convinced these cases are related?"

"I don't discount coincidence, of course. But in this

instance, my gut feeling is that there *must* be a link, if only we could see it."

Lamb nodded. "Perhaps. Any more problems with Sergeant Franks, by the way?"

"Not at the moment." Although she'd had her reasons for asking Franks to lead this morning's interview with Gavin Farley, Franks seemed to have taken it as a personal commendation and had been almost solicitous to her for the remainder of the day. She knew she walked a fine line between gaining his cooperation and compromising her authority, but for the moment it was working.

"And your liaison with Scotland Yard?"

"Fine, sir," Gemma answered, feeling awkward. She was certain that Lamb was aware of her personal relationship with Kincaid, but he'd never said anything directly.

Lamb smiled, confirming her suspicions. "I hear congratulations of a sort are in order." She must have gaped at him, because he added, "On your move. Duncan and I are old friends. I wish you luck in putting up with him on a regular basis."

Swallowing, Gemma grabbed at her opportunity. "There is one other thing, sir. It's just that I'm pregnant. The baby's due in May, but I won't be taking more than minimum leave. And it will in no way—"

"Congratulations! That's wonderful news." Lamb looked genuinely delighted. "Although I hate to lose you for even a short while, you take as much time as you need, Gemma. Will I be getting an invitation?"

"An invitation?"

"To the wedding, of course."

Gemma felt the blood drain from her face, then rush back in like petrol set alight. This was the one response she hadn't expected, and she was utterly unprepared.

"Oh, I'm far too stubborn to make a good candidate for marriage," she heard herself saying lightly. *And besides,* she thought, *he hasn't asked me.*

When Gemma sat down in her office to change into her boots, she found that her hands were shaking. So much worry expended, so much dread over confessing her condition, and it had turned out to be no problem at all. Of course it remained to be seen how things at work would develop in the long term, but she had passed the first hurdle.

She felt suddenly exhilarated, and was glad that when Kincaid had rung asking if he should pick her up, she'd said she'd walk home. It wasn't far, and the cold air might clear her head of the giddy rush brought on by relief.

It was dark when she came out of the station, the remaining snow gleaming pale gold in the glow of the sodium lamps. In spots the slush was glazing over; she had better tread carefully.

She'd buttoned the top of her coat and started towards Ladbroke Grove when a voice called softly from the shadows. "Inspector."

Surprised, Gemma turned. A small figure wearing a peacoat stepped forward, and in the light she saw that it was Fern Adams. Fern wore a striped Peruvian cap over her spiky hair, and her face was unadorned by jewelry except for the sparkle of a tiny stud in her left nostril.

"Can I speak to you for a minute, Inspector? It's just that I thought..."

Glancing back at the station, Gemma immediately rejected it as intimidating, but it was too cold to stand about chatting on the pavement. She gestured towards the Ladbroke Arms across the street. "Let's go in the pub, shall we?"

The pub was busy, the noise level reflecting holiday hysteria, but they managed to find a table in the back. When Gemma offered to buy Fern a drink, the girl seconded her request for orange juice.

When Gemma came back from the bar, Fern said, "I don't drink much," as if she felt an apology were needed. "Personal reasons."

"Nor me," Gemma said, "at the moment. Did you want to see me about something in particular?"

"It's Alex. I heard about last night...about Karl Arrowood...and I—There's something I thought you should know. Alex told me about finding the body, and about watching the house beforehand. He told me about taking my knife. And he said that you knew all about it. But there's something he didn't tell you." Fern glanced up, and before her eyes flicked away Gemma saw that they were green. "He didn't go home last night after he found Karl, like he said. He came straight to my flat, a little after nine. He had a tiny bit of blood on his finger, where he'd reached out to touch the body, and he scrubbed and scrubbed at it in my sink."

"Why are you telling me this?"

"Because there was nothing else. Nothing! Because I *know* that Alex didn't kill Karl. He was so upset—he said he'd never seen anyone he knew dead before...and he said it made him think of Dawn."

"What time did he leave your flat?"

"After midnight. I made him tea—that's all I had—and eventually he calmed down."

Fern was leaving something out. "Then why didn't he tell us he came to you?"

"I don't know. That's why I wanted to talk to you. I think he has some crazy idea of protecting my honor or something. Today he kept muttering about not wanting me to be involved. Unless..." Fern straightened the stack of coasters, then pushed them away. "Unless he didn't want to admit he'd been with me because it would seem like he'd been disloyal to *her* memory."

"Dawn?"

"It was hard enough to measure up to her when she was alive—but now she can never be less than perfect, can she?" Fern asked her bitterly. "There's no way I can compete with a ghost."

"Okay." Kit shuffled a stack of small, oblong cards. "Are you ready for another one? What plant did the monk Gregor Mendel use for his experiments in genetics?"

"That's not fair," said Gemma from the sink, where she and Kincaid were doing the washing-up from dinner. "You haven't given us any choices for the answer."

"That makes it too easy," protested Kit. "Just guess."

Kincaid dried a saucepan with a flourish. "I don't have to guess. I know the answer. Sweet peas."

"Oh, majorly unfair," howled Kit. "I'm going to find a harder question."

"What? You want us to guess but you don't want us to get it right?" teased Kincaid. "Why don't you take

Toby upstairs for his bath while we finish up in the kitchen? That way we'll have more story time."

Toby was under the table, playing with a new tugboat and singing to himself, utterly oblivious to the history of biology going on over his head.

Gemma and Kincaid were taking turns reading to Toby before bed, a practice Gemma had acquired from Kincaid in the time they had known him. It was something her family had not done, so that she enjoyed old books as much as new, and often found herself wishing she'd had the comfort of such a bedtime ritual as a child. She found it touching that since they'd moved into the house, Kit, who of course was allowed to stay up a good deal later, seemed to find some reason to come upstairs just in time to curl up on his bed for the night's offering.

As the boys trooped upstairs after the expected grumbling, Gemma thought about the success of Kit's Christmas gifts. The science questions were an obvious hit; the lead soldiers were proudly arrayed on his desktop, where he could continually rearrange their formations; and although he hadn't said anything directly about the photo of his mother, Gemma noticed that he'd put it on his nightstand.

"I haven't had a chance to tell you what happened today," she told Kincaid as she hung up the dishcloth. "I came out to Superintendent Lamb."

He gave her a quizzical look. "Came out?"

She patted her stomach. "I am now officially pregnant. I can bulge as much as I like."

"That's terrific, love," he exclaimed, giving her a hug. "I take it he was politically correct?"

"More than." Remembering what else Lamb had said, her smile faded. She was not going to mention that! "Fern Adams came to see me just as I was leaving the station," she added, wanting to change the subject. "She wanted me to know that Alex came to her flat after he left the crime scene last night."

"Why tell you? It doesn't provide him an alibi."

"I'm not sure. She's a bit of an odd duck, and something of a loner. I had the feeling she wanted a chance to plead Alex's innocence . . . and that maybe she just wanted to talk to someone."

"You do tend to radiate empathy like the pied piper," said Kincaid.

Hearing an odd note in his voice, Gemma turned to look at him. "What?"

"I'm just wondering about Bryony Poole. Has it occurred to you that she's as tall as a man, and probably as fit? And that she might have made up the business about the photos of Dawn and Alex just to put suspicion on Farley?"

"You're not saying you think Bryony could be the killer? I don't believe it! And even if she were physically capable, what motive could she possibly have?"

"If we knew that, we'd be laughing, wouldn't we? Maybe she was in love with Karl—"

"That's ridiculous. She's crazy about Marc Mitchell, and besides that, it doesn't account for Marianne Hoffman."

"True. I just think the idea is worth considering. And can we afford to overlook anything at this point?"

There was no arguing with that, but Gemma didn't feel any happier with the idea of investigating someone she'd come to think of as a friend.

Not even half an hour of *The House at Pooh Corner* improved her temper, and she went to bed still cross with Kincaid. Glad enough to have Geordie's warm body as a barrier between them, she found herself wondering if combining home and work was really such a good idea.

# CHAPTER SIXTEEN

By the mid sixties Portobello Road was on the tourist map.
The antique stalls had attracted the attention of the picture
post in the fifties. By 1966, Reader's Digest was writing in
glowing terms of the bargains to be had in Portobello Road,
claiming there were '20,000 potential customers, antique
dealers and American store buyers' every Saturday.

—Whetlor and Bartlett,
from *Portobello*

BY THE SPRING of 1968, Angel had long since come to know
the girl Karl had hired to work in his shop as friend rather
than rival. Her name was Nina Byatt, and she was married,
with a small son. Nina's husband, Neil, a taciturn, bearded
man, now worked with Karl, taking selected items round to the
auction houses.

These days Karl kept the shop stocked with things Indian
and Oriental along with the more traditional antiques, catering to the new fascination with meditation and the exotic.

The shop flourished, as did everything Karl touched. He
moved them from the flat in Chelsea to a town house in Belgravia, in Chester Square, an exclusive address befitting his
growing status. But Angel found the severe, gray brick house
unwelcoming, the neighborhood cold and unfriendly compared
to their Chelsea mews. Nor did it suit the farmhouse furniture
she had begun to covet.

Not that it mattered what she thought—Karl was entertaining clients from abroad more and more often, and their tiny Chelsea flat had not been suitable for such affairs.

Usually these customers spoke German. Using his family's connections in Germany, Karl had found a source of Russian art objects "liberated" by the Germans during the war, particularly Russian icons. Karl arranged for them to be shipped into the country; Neil then sold the goods for him at auction, fetching a large profit.

On the few occasions when Angel saw these icons before they went to auction, she found them terribly moving. The sad faces of the saints and the jewellike colors reminded her of the paintings she'd seen in the Polish café as a child. Of course, she knew now that those paintings had been cheap reproductions, but at the time they'd invoked wonder. Wonder had been possible then, the world still a place where the good were rewarded and the wicked punished for their transgressions.

Karl had proved that homily false, if he had done nothing else.

With Angel now thoroughly dependent on heroin, Karl saw no reason to keep the rest of his business dealings from her. The little stash he kept in the house was only the tip of the iceberg. Nor did he buy it just for the occasional use of his friends—he bought it to sell, in large quantities, and at an enormous profit. That money in turn fueled the antiques business, giving him the inventory to make a success of it. Money begat money, and if a few poor souls fell by the wayside because of it, Karl considered it no business of his.

As for Angel, if she failed to please him, or stood up to him over something, he simply withheld her supply until she complied with his wishes. The longest she managed to hold out was two days, but in the end her will was no match against her craving for the drug.

*After that she managed her habit fiercely, refusing to increase her dose, but she'd finally learned the bitter lesson that she couldn't walk away—not from the drug, not from him. And she'd seen what happened to those without help or support, gaunt specters begging in doorways, or selling themselves on the street. Once, she walked in on two prostitutes shooting up in the public toilet in Hyde Park. She ran out and was promptly sick in the shrubbery, weak with horror over what lay in wait for her.*

*There were days, however, more bearable than others, particularly those that involved minding Nina and Neil's six-year-old son, Evan. On one such lovely day in May, she and Evan had the house to themselves. They had returned from a lunchtime picnic in the park, and now were lazing over a puzzle, listening to the new Donovan album she'd bought.*

*She'd taught Evan to sing along with an infectiously happy verse about a girl called "Marianne," and when the verse ended the usually solemn little boy laughed aloud with glee.*

*"That's your name," he crowed, fingering her silver locket.*

*"And it's our secret. No one can call me that but you, because you're special." No one had called her by that name since her father died, and she found the evocation of that little girl oddly comforting. She snapped open the locket, holding it out for Evan's inspection. "Look, I've put your picture here, so I can keep it close to me."*

*"Where did you get the locket?" Evan touched the shiny heart.*

*"It was my father's."*

*"Marianne," Evan whispered, cuddling closer. "That's a pretty name. But I think I like Angel better."*

*As the afternoon grew warmer, Evan fell asleep in her lap, his long eyelashes casting shadows on his cheeks. Angel gazed out the open window at the fresh green of the treetops and the*

*spire of the church in the square. The album liner notes lay
open beside her. In a personal appeal, Donovan admonished his
listeners to give up drugs, as if it were something that one could
do as easily as deciding to cut one's hair, or stop eating meat. If
only it were that simple.*

*What lay before her? Karl would never willingly give her
a child, of that she was sure. She stroked Evan's hair from his
forehead, feeling the reassuringly solid weight of his relaxed
body against her own. Would she ever have a chance to love a
child of her own?*

Kincaid called Doug Cullen into his office at the Yard
first thing on Thursday morning, three days after Karl
Arrowood's murder. "See what you can find out about a
Bryony Poole," Kincaid asked. "She's a veterinarian, and
Gavin Farley's assistant."

As Cullen raised his eyebrows his spectacles rode
down his nose, giving him the look of a surprised owl.
"A woman? You think that's a serious possibility?"

"She's as tall as a man, and strong," answered Kincaid.
"We can't afford to overlook it. But there is a slight
problem with this...um, inquiry. Bryony and Gemma
have a connection—Gemma adopted a dog through
her—so I think it will be better if we handle this one on
our own."

"That's awkward," Cullen said with obvious sympathy.

"Yes." Kincaid thought of the cold back Gemma had
presented to him in bed the previous night. How wise
had it been to encourage her to live in her own patch? It
was always risky, because one couldn't help forming
friendships and alliances as Gemma had done, but he

hadn't expected a situation this difficult, or this soon. This case was nightmare enough without adding personal complications.

"There's something else I want you to look into while you're digging." He slid a copy of Eliza Goddard's birth certificate across his desk. "Ronald Thomas, Marianne Hoffman's first husband. If there's something in Hoffman's past that has a bearing on this case, maybe he can tell us what it is."

Kincaid did not mention Eliza Goddard's request that he find her father—Scotland Yard was not, after all, in the business of private investigations.


At Notting Hill Station, Gemma waded through her own accumulated paperwork with less than her usual alertness. She'd tossed and turned throughout the night, worrying about Bryony Poole.

Knowing that Kincaid was justified in making inquiries and dealing with the consequences were two different things, she'd discovered. She couldn't say anything to Bryony beforehand—that would be highly unprofessional. And yet if Kincaid went to Bryony on his own, as Gemma was certain he would, it must surely seem to Bryony as if Gemma had betrayed their friendship.

A knock on her door provided a welcome interruption to her thoughts. Gerry Franks came in with a sheaf of papers. "The lab boffins must have given up their Christmas dinners to get this done, guv."

Gemma indicated a chair. "Let's hear it, then."

"The paper knife was clean as a whistle. It could have been scrubbed, of course, but the blade edge showed no signs of nicks from a scuffle, and it's doubtful whether Dunn would have had a chance to get it sharpened.

"And the paper knife is a no-show, anyway," Franks continued, "because the scalpel we lifted from the rubbish bin *did* show traces of Karl Arrowood's blood in the groove between the blade and the handle."

Gemma's hopes rose. "What about prints?"

"No prints. No fibers. No other blood." Franks looked more pained than usual. "The scalpel is of the same type Farley uses, but that doesn't get us far. Every medical supply carries them."

"What about the surgery itself?"

"Nothing there, either. Nor in Farley's workshop shower. And the bits of ash found in the surgery toilet were too far gone to be identified as photographs."

"Any response from the media release?" Gemma had placed her hopes on the request for information from anyone passing in the vicinity of the rubbish bin where the scalpel had been found, as the last appeal had brought them the report of the dark-suited jogger. But that, she reminded herself, had turned out to be just a tantalizing glimpse of a lead that had never materialized.

"Not unless you count one sighting of a space-suited alien and another of Santa Claus," Franks replied with deadpan delivery.

Not sure if he meant to be funny, Gemma said merely, "Figures. Thanks, Gerry. We'll just have to come up with something else."

Standing, Franks clasped his hands in parade-rest fashion and looked determinedly at a point just past Gemma's head. "Um, I understand congratulations are in order, guv."

"Oh. Yes. Thanks. That's very kind of you, Sergeant."

Franks nodded with the relief of one whose duty has been performed. Gemma had told Melody her news first thing that morning, and it had required no great sacrifice on the constable's part when Gemma had asked her to do a bit of discreet gossiping. The dissemination technique had saved Gemma the awkward task of making an announcement to everyone she met.

By early afternoon, Gemma had pored over the fine details of the forensics reports until her eyes ached. Looking up, she saw that the sun, visible for the first time in days, was making a pallid attempt to illuminate the grime on her office window. Perhaps she would go out and fetch coffee for Melody for a change, give her head a chance to clear.

Ten minutes walking brought her to Pembridge Road, but instead of crossing over to the Starbucks, as she had meant to do, a sudden thought made her turn to the left, following Kensington Park Road. A few blocks down the hill, she stopped in front of Arrowood Antiques, gazing at the "Closed" sign hanging from the door. What would happen to the little empire of beautiful things Karl Arrowood had created?

With decision, she pulled out her phone and rang the station. "Is there still no word from Arrowood's solicitor on the terms of his will?" she asked Melody. The senior partner in the firm representing Arrowood was away for the holiday, and no one else in the office knew of a document with a date more recent than that of Karl's marriage to Dawn.

"No, boss. They say they've left word for the senior partner, but he hasn't rung back."

"Then have the house searched again. If Arrowood left a copy there, we might have missed it the first time round." And if he had, she wondered as she rang off, had his wife seen it? What had prompted Dawn to contact Sean Arrowood?

Thoughtfully, she continued down the hill to Elgin Crescent. Otto's Café appeared empty. There were, however, still lunch dishes on a few of the tables, and a lovely, garlicky smell emanated from the kitchen.

Before Gemma could call out, Otto appeared from the back, wiping his hands on his apron. "Inspector! This is an unexpected pleasure."

"Hullo, Otto," replied Gemma, inordinately pleased at her reception.

"Can I get you something? It was quiet today— the customers are either on holiday or still recovering from their Christmas dinners—and I have made a nice borscht."

"Thank you, no. I had something at the office. Is Wesley not here?" she asked, only then realizing how much she'd been looking forward to seeing the young man.

"No. He takes a few days at Christmas, as the business is slow, and he has family visiting."

"It's just that I wanted to thank him again for bringing our Christmas tree—and you, Otto, for contributing your van."

"It was successful, then? Wesley was very pleased with himself as Father Christmas."

"Otto, there is another reason I'm here. I wanted to talk to you about Karl Arrowood, if you don't mind." She'd had an officer check Otto's whereabouts at the time of Karl's murder: He had taken his daughters to their grandparents' for Christmas Eve festivites.

"I have heard the news," Otto replied somberly. He pulled out a chair for her and took another himself. "You know, I had thought for a long time that nothing would please me more than that man's death, but now I find it is not so. Whether this is a good thing or a bad one, I cannot tell. It also means I was wrong in accusing him of murdering his young wife, and for that I'm sorry."

"You knew Karl for a long time. Everyone talks about his successes, but no one ever mentions where he came from, or how he got started in his business. Did he grow up here in Notting Hill?"

"He never talked about these things himself, even when I worked with him. But I know a little from the neighborhood gossip, and from my mother and her circle of friends. It was their way of making themselves at home in a strange country, to learn everything they could about everyone," Otto added with a smile. "Karl's family was German. They came here as refugees right after the war, so that Karl was born here, in Notting Hill. I don't think he ever considered himself to be anything other than English."

"They were Jewish?"

"Yes. His father was a grocer, if my memory serves me. They would have had little, and Karl certainly had no exposure to fine things through his upbringing. But the antiques market was growing rapidly in those days, and I always assumed he had worked for a stallholder or a dealer as a boy." He gave a shrug of regret. "I'm sorry I can't tell you more."

It occurred to Gemma that she knew someone else

in the neighborhood who had come to England as a German refugee just after the war. And it was, as Otto had said, a close-knit community. Was it stretching probability too much to think more information might be forthcoming from a different quarter?

# CHAPTER SEVENTEEN

Portobello Road, with its shoppers, tourists and those
merely hanging out, offered stimulating subject-matter for
photographers and artists. The flea market attracted Peter
Blake, a pop artist who decorated his paintings with
badges, labels, bits of signs, medals and paraphernalia. He
is best known for designing the record sleeve of the Beatles'
album 'Sergeant Pepper's Lonely Hearts Club Band.'

—Whetlor and Bartlett,
from *Portobello*

IT BEGAN AS a dream. He was alone in the dark, cold
and frightened, his stomach cramping with hunger. He
lay in a bed that was damp and stank, and he desperately wanted his mother.

The dream moved on in interminable dreamtime...
hours...days, he couldn't tell. Then suddenly his
mother was there in the room with him, but she didn't
answer when he called out to her. The room spun and he
saw her clearly, sprawled on the floor beside the other
bed, her red dress hiked up, one delicate sandaled foot
hung in a fold of the counterpane.

Now he was out of his bed, creeping across the room
on his hands and knees. He touched her. Her skin was
cold; her breath came in labored snorts. She smelled of
the stuff that came in bottles, and of the other...the
sweet, sickly smell that made his throat close with
dread. Tonight he would not be able to wake her.

It was only when he reached his bed again that he acknowledged the smell and the dampness were his fault. His mother would kill him when she woke, she had told him so, and he had no doubt that she meant it. Terror washed over him and he scrabbled at the wet bedclothes, willing himself desperately to disappear—

Alex woke sitting bolt upright in bed, gasping.

Where the hell had that dream come from? He couldn't remember having it before, but it was all horribly, intimately familiar to him in a way he didn't understand.

He'd had dreams occasionally where he had inhabited another person, another body, like an actor in a film. But he had *been* the little boy in the dream, or the little boy had been him.

Shivering now, he wrapped the duvet round his shoulders and stumbled into the kitchen. Taking a mug of hot, sweet tea into the sitting room, he sat on the floor, swathed in the comforter, watching wretchedly for the first intimation of dawn at his garden window.

Then the dream began again, and this time he knew he was awake. There was a man in the bedroom; he could smell the tobacco and the rank sweat. The man and his mother were together in her bed, making the sounds he couldn't bear to hear. He stuffed his fingers in his ears to shut out the noise, digging until he loosened the scabs from the last time.

There was blood, he was drowning in it, and through the haze he saw the blue swell of his mother's vein and the springing drop of scarlet as the needle went in.

After that she went away from him, her eyes skittering across his face as if it were a strange landscape. Nothing he said or did could reach her, and he knew that she went away because she did not love him.

As the memory faded into the pearly mauve of daybreak at his window, Alex saw that the dream-child's
logic was flawed—but he also knew that logic mattered
not at all.

All Saints Road was not a particularly cheerful place
early on a Friday morning, Kincaid decided as he and
Doug Cullen got out of the car in front of Gavin Farley's
surgery. Most of the shops and businesses were closed,
their windows covered by the rolling metal gratings
that marked London as a cosmopolitan city. Nor did the
rutted, mottled mixture of snow and slush lining the
gutters help matters.

"That's Farley's car." Cullen indicated a maroon
Astra parked at least a foot from the curb.

"I hope his veterinary skills are an improvement on
his driving."

"Maybe that's why he leaves the Mercedes to his
wife," Cullen replied with a grin as he swung open the
surgery door.

Bryony Poole stood at the reception desk, a chart in
her hand. She looked up at Kincaid with an instant
smile of recognition that made him wish with a pang of
guilt that he'd never thought of her as a suspect, but the
information Cullen had dredged up about her relationship with a former lover had given him no choice but to
see the interview through.

"Superintendent, isn't it?" Bryony said. "Can I help
you? Gavin—Mr. Farley—is with a client at the moment, but I can tell him you're here."

"It's you we wanted a word with, actually, Miss Poole.

Is there somewhere we could talk? This is Sergeant Cullen, by the way."

She nodded at Cullen, her expression more wary now. "I'm rather busy this morning, I'm afraid. And I really don't know what else I can tell you." Glancing towards the exam room that presumably held her boss, she added, "This has been awkward enough for me as it is..."

"It's not Farley we're interested in at the moment," said Cullen, stepping into the breach with enthusiasm. "Would you mind telling us where you were on Christmas Eve, Miss Poole?"

Bryony's half-smile froze on her face. "You're not serious?"

"We have to speak to anyone with access to a certain type of instrument—"

"A scalpel. Karl was killed with a scalpel, wasn't he?"

"It was in fact the same brand you use, Miss Poole," said Cullen. "The same type of scalpel that was stolen from this surgery."

"And since you haven't been able to pin anything on Gavin, you thought you'd try me! That's simply beastly! I wish I'd never told Gemma about the thefts— or about Gavin's row with Dawn."

"Or the photos?" Cullen interjected stubbornly.

"Oh, yes. I made a right fool of myself over that, didn't I? Well, I don't care what you think. I saw those photos. I know Gavin was spying on Dawn and Alex, and I'm not crazy. What I don't understand is why you think I'd have told you any of those things if I were guilty? And why on earth would I have wanted to hurt either Dawn or Karl Arrowood?"

"You might have told us because you thought it would throw suspicion on Mr. Farley, as it did. And as for motive, you do have a bit of temper, Miss Poole," Cullen told her. "There was a matter of a former boyfriend, I believe, who charged you with assault after you pushed him down the stairs—"

"And do you know that he dropped the charges because no judge would touch the case? I came home after taking my final exams at veterinary college—I had literally studied night and day for months—to find my so-called fiancé in *my* bed, in *my* flat, with a prostitute. I threw them *both* down the stairs, and their clothes after them." Bryony folded her arms tightly across her chest and glared at them, but her eyes had filled with furious tears.

"I think I might have done the same," Kincaid said, remembering the fury he'd felt when he'd learned of Vic's affair with Ian McClellan—and he had not been unfortunate enough to catch them in the act.

"It was not a good time in my life, but I didn't go around murdering anyone, and I certainly haven't done so now." Bryony scribbled something on a pad, tore the page loose and thrust it at Kincaid, ignoring Cullen's outstretched hand. "This is my parents' address and phone number in Wimbledon. I arrived there late in the afternoon on Christmas Eve and stayed until midmorning on Christmas. I'm sure my parents and my assorted relatives will be able to vouch for me. Now, if you don't mind, I have a surgery scheduled this morning, and I'd like to get to work."

"You've been very cooperative, Miss Poole," said Kincaid, "and we appreciate that, as well as your previous help."

"Obviously," Bryony spat back. "Do give Gemma my

best, won't you?" Her sarcasm was scathing. "I'm sure you can see yourselves out."

"How would you like to go to Wimbledon this afternoon, Doug?" Kincaid asked as they reached the car.

"But it's bound to be a wild-goose chase, isn't it? If she was really with her family in Wimbledon, she couldn't very well have just popped out for a quick murder," Cullen protested.

"We still have to follow through on it, but rather you than me. And I have other things on my agenda."

One of which was his commitment to take Kit to meet his grandparents for tea—an outing neither of them was anticipating with any enthusiasm; the other was to try to salvage things with Gemma over the matter of Bryony Poole.

When she pulled up to the curb outside Alex Dunn's mews flat, Gemma saw that the boot of his Volkswagen stood open. Before she could ring the bell he came out, carrying a duffel bag.

"Inspector James!"

"Hello, Alex. Do you have a minute?" She looked from the bag in his hand to the car. "Are you going somewhere?"

"Just down to see my aunt in Sussex for a day or two. Is that a problem?"

"No. Not as long as we can get in touch with you if we should need to. You won't leave the country, will you?" she asked with a half-smile.

"You can have my passport, if you like."

She shook her head. "That's not necessary. But a phone number would be helpful."

"Would you like to come in? Have a coffee or something?" Beneath his unfailing politeness, she sensed impatience.

"No, that's all right, thanks." She held out the small, brown paper package she'd brought with her. "This is Fern's knife. I thought you might want to return it to her yourself."

"Oh, right." Taking the package from her, he looked around vaguely before stuffing it in the pocket of his bag.

"Is there some particular reason you're going to visit your aunt? She's not ill, is she?"

"Jane? No, of course not. It's just that it's where I grew up. My aunt Jane raised me." He seemed to focus on her a little more clearly. "Um, I take it the knife got a clean bill of health?"

"Yes."

"Right. I'll just give you that address." He wrote it for her on the back of one of his business cards.

As she said good-bye and returned to the office, she realized something odd: Alex Dunn seemed suddenly to have lost all interest in his lover's murder.

It was almost noon before Gemma managed to get away from the station again for the little outing she'd planned. First, she bought the best bottle of sherry the corner store possessed and had it wrapped in a decorative gift bag.

She knew from previous visits that her friend Erika Rosenthal liked sherry. Gemma had discovered quite by chance, while investigating a burglary a few months previously, that the elderly victim was Dr. Rosenthal, a noted historian. Erika was also a German Jew who had come to Notting Hill shortly after the war, and as far as Gemma knew had been there ever since. She lived in a pale gray brick town house in Arundel Gardens, not terribly far from Otto's Café.

"Gemma James! How lovely."

"I've brought you a little gift," said Gemma, smiling at the sight of her friend's beaming, wizened-apple face.

"Sherry! Even more lovely. Come in by the sitting room fire and we'll pour a glass."

"Just the tiniest bit for me, please." The room was just as she remembered it, filled with books and paintings, fresh flowers, and, of course, the piano.

Handing her a half-inch of amber liquid in a crystal glass, Dr. Rosenthal examined her with bright, shoe-button eyes. "You're pregnant, aren't you, my dear? I thought as much the last time I saw you, but it was too soon to be sure."

"I suppose I *am* beginning to show! The baby's due in May." One of Dr. Rosenthal's specialties was the history of Celtic goddess cults, and Gemma couldn't help wondering if the woman had absorbed more than facts in her study.

"It's more that certain glow, actually," Dr. Rosenthal said. "And then there's the sherry. I won't mind if you don't drink it, although in my experience a sip or two of sherry never did anyone any harm."

"It certainly hasn't done you any damage," observed Gemma, laughing. "I do have some other news, if you haven't worked it out just by looking at me."

"I confess I am utterly baffled."

"I've moved house. It's just a few blocks from here. Or I should say, we've moved house—my son and I,

my . . . friend, and his son, along with two dogs and a
cat."

"You're taking on the settled life, I see. That's quite a
challenge, with your job, and another child on the way.
Congratulations. But I find it hard to believe that with
all that, you've found time to make a purely social call,"
Dr. Rosenthal added with a twinkle. "Go on, ask away. I
don't mind. In fact, it's rather gratifying to be considered useful."

"There is something I thought you might be able to
help me with. A family called Arrowood came to this area,
just after the war. They were German immigrants—"

"But they weren't named Arrowood at all. It was
Pheilholz. Their only son Anglicized the name, and I
think it broke his parents' hearts to see their heritage
tossed away."

"You knew them?"

"Oh, we weren't close friends, but I met them often
enough in those days, at the German cafés and the social
clubs. They were a nice couple, hardworking, very firm
in their values. They owned a small grocery in Portobello Road."

"And the son, Karl? Did you know him?"

"This is *your* case, the murder of Karl Arrowood? I
thought of you when I saw it in the news."

"I've been investigating Karl's death, as well as his
wife's," Gemma admitted. "But we seem to be making
very little progress."

"So you thought you would go back and start at the
beginning. Very wise. Karl was a beautiful child, and I
think he was much loved by his parents, but that's not
always a guarantee that the child will grow up as the

parents wish. He jeered at their stodginess, their lack of ambition. It was fine things Karl wanted, and he seemed willing to go to any lengths to get them. The boy was involved in scrape after scrape, each a little more serious than the last, until his father told him he was no longer welcome in their house. I don't believe they were ever reconciled."

"There were rumors of Karl's involvement in the drug trade when he was quite young, but nothing was ever proved."

"Ah . . ." Dr. Rosenthal sighed. "Here I have to admit my memory fails me. There *was* something about drugs, and prison, but it wasn't Karl who went to prison . . . and there was a girl in it somewhere . . . There always is, isn't there?" Lifting her shoulders in a shrug, she continued, "He disappeared from the neighborhood altogether for a time, and it was a good many years—not until after his parents were both gone, as a matter of fact—before he came back."

"But he did come back in the end, didn't he?" pressed Gemma. "He could have opened that shop any-where in London . . . say, Kensington, or Mayfair . . . Do you suppose it was pride, wanting to show anyone who remembered him as a child what a success he'd become? Or was there something else that drew him back to Notting Hill?"

If one had to choose somewhere to sit and wait for an hour, thought Kincaid, Brown's Hotel was not a bad place to be on a Friday afternoon.

At the stroke of three, he had delivered an unsmiling

and abnormally brushed and polished Kit for his meeting with his grandparents. Robert Potts, Kincaid's former father-in-law, had greeted Kincaid with his usual strained courtesy; his wife had merely nodded an acknowledgment of his presence, not disguising her loathing. They had not invited Kincaid to join them for tea—not that he had expected them to do so.

It must present Eugenia quite a challenge, deciding whom she hated more, him or Ian McClellan, but Kincaid did not find the thought amusing. This monthly meeting with Kit had been Ian's method of forestalling her suing for the legal right to have her grandson for regular visitations, but Kincaid had no confidence that the arrangement would satisfy her indefinitely. One would think the court would take into account the fact that the woman was obviously mentally unbalanced, and that Kit despised her, but it wasn't a chance Kincaid was willing to take.

He found a comfortable chair and immersed himself in the book he'd brought with him, determined not to borrow trouble unnecessarily. Still, the minutes crawled, until at last Kit appeared from the lounge. In his navy school blazer and tie, with his hair neatly combed, Kit looked unexpectedly grown-up. But as he drew near, Kincaid saw that the boy's lip was trembling and his eyes were red with unspilled tears.

Kincaid jumped up. "Kit! What's wrong?"

Kit shook his head mutely.

"Where are your grandparents?"

"They left. She didn't want to see you. She—" He shook his head again, unable to go on.

Kincaid put an arm round his shoulders. "Let's go, shall we?" He helped Kit into the anorak he had held for him, then shepherded him out into the frosty air. What on earth had Eugenia done to upset his usually stoic son so badly? "Why don't we walk down to Piccadilly," he suggested. "We could get the bus from there, rather than the tube."

After a few minutes, when Kit seemed calmer, Kincaid said, "Now. Tell me what this is all about."

"She—she said I couldn't live with you, that you had no right to keep me. She said that she was going to get a lawyer, and that the court would have to grant her custody since I had no responsible parent."

"She's threatened lawyers before. I wouldn't pay it too much attention," Kincaid said soothingly. But the boy's jaw was still tightly clenched, and he wouldn't meet Kincaid's eyes. "That's not all, is it? What else did she say?"

"She said that if I'd been a proper son, I'd have taken better care of my mother, and she wouldn't have died."

A sudden rush of fury left Kincaid shaking. He took a breath to calm himself. "Kit. That is absolute nonsense. Do you hear me? I know how well you looked after your mum, because she told me. And I know that you could *not* have saved her, no matter what you did. Are we clear on that?"

Kit nodded, but Kincaid was unconvinced. What he did know was that he had to put a stop to Eugenia Potts's poison, and that meant he had to keep her from seeing Kit, full stop. But Eugenia was correct in one thing—he had no legal rights over Kit. There was only one way to remedy the situation—he would have to prove his paternity.

.    .    .

"I want you to tell me about my mother." Alex Dunn sat in Jane's sitting room, in front of the unlit Christmas tree. He'd had to stop once on the way down, so buffeted by memories he'd been unable to drive. Then he'd found the cottage empty, and had waited impatiently for Jane to return.

"Your mother?" Jane repeated blankly.

"Is she really dead?"

"I expect so. Why, Alex?"

"When I was little, you said she couldn't take care of me because she was ill. That wasn't true, was it? She was a drug addict."

"Alex—What—How do you—"

"Why do you always lie to me? All my life I've carried around this rosy, consumptive image of my sainted mother handing me over to you with her blessing, and it was all a lie. She didn't give a damn what happened to me."

"Alex, that's not true. She did care. That's why she brought you to me. And for God's sake, you can't tell a five-year-old that his mother's an addict!"

"You could have told me later, when I was older."

"When you were what? Twelve? Sixteen? Twenty? How would I have decided when to shatter your life? And besides," she added more calmly, "stories have a way of generating their own reality. After a while, I almost came to believe it myself. Who's told you this, Alex?"

"No one. I dreamed it. And then I started to remember."

Jane's face went ashen. "Oh, God. I'm sorry, Alex. You used to have nightmares when you were little. I thought they'd stopped years ago."

"Did she really bring me here, to the cottage? Or was that a lie, too?"

"She did. It was the last time I saw her. I tried to find her for years after that, but she'd vanished without a trace."

"Then what about my father? Was he just another junkie, a one-night stand?"

"I honestly don't know, Alex. But there was a man . . . She came down here with him once, when she was pregnant with you. It was after Mum and Dad had died. She hadn't even known." Jane shook her head, as if remembering her own amazement. "But I think she was clean then, at least for a while. She looked good, and she seemed happy."

"Who was he? What was his name?"

"I don't know. He waited for her in the car. I never met him. All I can tell you is that his car was expensive, and I thought that perhaps he would take care of her."

Alex felt unable to contain the sudden and inexplicable dread that had lodged in his gut. "This man—What did he look like?"

# CHAPTER EIGHTEEN

In the 1950's, into an already pressurized situation, came
newcomers from the West Indies. Their easily indentifiable
presence in an already overcrowded area served as an irritant
to some of the white community who resented the competition for homes and jobs.

—Whetlor and Bartlett,
from *Portobello*

ALEX DROVE DOWN the lane until it came to an end.
After that, he left the car and walked, finding his
way blindly through the marsh. But the smell of salt
drove him on, until at last he sank down into a tangled
clump of grass, looking out over the dark expanse of the
sea.

It couldn't be true, could it, what he had imagined?
He must be raving, delirious; it was an absurd fantasy.
There had to have been hundreds—thousands—of young
men that age in London at that time who were blond
and handsome, and who had the means to wear nice
clothes and drive an expensive car.

It didn't mean the money had come from the sale of
the drug that had destroyed his mother—nor did it
mean that the particular young man Jane had described
had been Karl Arrowood.

But what difference *did* it make, if it were true? Alex
wondered. It was an accident of genetics, that was all. It
was nothing to do with him, or who he had become.

He could find out the truth, perhaps, simply by showing Jane a photograph of Karl Arrowood. But did he really want to know?

All his certainties had been torn from him, beginning with Dawn's death, and he had begun to see that if he were to survive, he must put himself back together, piece by piece. He must decide what mattered, and what did not. Was his mother important, if it came to that? Wasn't it his life with Jane that was real, those years of her care and concern that had shaped him?

He loved this place, that he knew. He loved Jane. He loved Fern, he realized, who had been such a staunch friend.

And he loved the porcelain that had spoken to him since he was a child. He thought of the blue-and-white delft bowl, now tucked into the display cabinet in his flat, and of the lives through which it had passed. All suffering faded, given time, as did all joys, but they left their imprint upon such objects, providing comfort for those who came after.

It gradually occurred to Alex that he was cold, and terribly hungry. The wind blowing off the bay tugged at his clothes, finding every tiny gap, reminding him that his flesh was subject to its whims.

It was then he realized that such things mattered desperately to him; that he wanted food and warmth and companionship. That, surely, was a good thing; a beginning. He would deal with the nightmares and the memories of Dawn and his mother as he must, but in the meantime, life would go on. He would go on.

He brushed himself off and went home to Jane.

·  ·  ·

*Angel had just sent Evan home on the afternoon that Neil and Nina Byatt were arrested by Scotland Yard. It seemed that the Yard had got wind of the fact that the Russian icons Neil was selling at auction had been carefully packed with top-grade heroin. Some of the icons had gone to private buyers as well—all in all, the price of Russian art objects had sky-rocketed.*

*After the first shock, Angel felt a rush of relief that it hadn't been Karl—and then she began to wonder* why *it hadn't been Karl. Neil and Nina worked for him; the artifacts came into the country through his connections. Why didn't Karl seem worried that the police might spring on him next?*

*After a few days, she managed to get in to see Nina during the prison's visiting hour. As Angel came in, Evan and his grandmother were leaving. The woman smelled of stale sweat and must, and very faintly, of illness—a combination of odors that Angel would forever after associate with righteousness. "God will see you in hell for this," the woman hissed at her. Evan reached out towards her, his small face pinched with misery, but his grandmother snatched him away.*

*Shaken, Angel sat down at the visitor's table, but Nina looked no happier to see her than had her mother. Nor did she look well. Her face was pale and drawn, her long, lustrous hair dank and flat, as if the life had drained from it.*

*"You have a lot of nerve, coming here," spat Nina. "More than I gave you credit for."*

*"But I wanted to see you. You're my friend—"*

*"Friend? As long as you have anything to do with Karl Arrowood, you have no friends."*

*"But surely we could do something to help—I could take care of Evan—"*

*"Don't you touch my son! You just don't see it, do you, Angel? You really don't know what's happened?"*

"Nina! What are you talking about?"

"Your bloody Karl shopped us, that's what. The police must have found out about the business. They couldn't quite pin it on him because he never actually touched the stuff—He just planned everything. But they were making his life a misery, interfering with his transactions. So he made them a deal."

"A deal?" whispered Angel.

"Yeah. Neil and me, red-handed. So now they leave Karl alone, and my son will be grown before I can be with him again."

"I don't— He wouldn't—" Angel protested, but faintly. Things were adding up too fast. That's why Karl hadn't been worried: He'd known already that he had no cause for concern.

"There's got to be something I can do, Nina. I want to help you."

Nina glared at her with contempt. "It's too late for that. And it's too late for you, too, Angel."

She went straight to the shop, finding Karl alone for once. "You've got to help the Byatts," she told him. "I know what you did to them, and you've got to do something to make it right."

He looked amused. "And what exactly do you suggest?"

"Tell the police the stuff isn't theirs—"

"You're not suggesting I lay claim to several kilos of uncut heroin myself, are you? And why do you think the police would believe me, Angel? They have hard evidence in their hands connecting the Byatts to the drug sale—They're not going to give that up for some pie-in-the-sky story."

"Nina says you set them up."

"Well, she would, wouldn't she? She and Neil refuse to take responsibility for their own carelessness."

*She stared at him, furious, unconvinced. "What if I tell the police what you've done?"*

*"Assuming they were stupid enough to arrest me on hearsay, it still wouldn't help the Byatts." His finger touched her under the chin. "But if they did arrest me, then where would you be? Have you thought about that, Angel?"*

*In that instant she knew that all her protest had been a sham—she could do nothing for her friends. She hated Karl, but she hated herself even more.*

*"What about their little boy?" she demanded. "What will happen to Evan?"*

*Karl shook his head, as if disappointed in her lack of understanding. "I really don't think that's any of my concern, do you?"*

Bryony rolled over and squinted at the red glow of the clock once more, then turned on her back with a sigh. Monday morning, and New Year's Eve to boot. But there was no point getting up until the central heating switched itself on at six, and she had a half-hour to go.

Beside her, Duchess lay on her back as well, her paws twitching as she ran in some tantalizing doggy dream.

What had she come to, Bryony wondered, a woman approaching thirty whose only bed companion was a large and hairy dog?

That thought, however, led her to Marc, and that was a subject too distressing for the predawn hours. Much better to think about her brief career as a murder suspect, she told herself with an attempt at humor. Superintendent Kincaid's smarmy, schoolboy sergeant had made her sound like a harpy as well as a killer—and what was even worse, she had felt inexplicably guilty. Now, even though her family had, of course, confirmed her story, she had to live with the memory of her furious, stammering humiliation as the policeman questioned her.

She knew Gavin had burned those sodding photos in the toilet, the bastard. Nor, she found, did she have any trouble believing that Gavin had been blackmailing—or attempting to blackmail—Dawn. But she could not bring herself to imagine that Gavin had killed Dawn—She couldn't go on getting up and going in to work with him, if she did.

The hot water from the boiler grumbled and clanked its way into the radiator; a moment later she heard the coffeemaker click on. No, of course Gavin hadn't killed Dawn, she thought as she threw back the covers. There simply must be some other explanation.

An hour later, somewhat fortified by a hot shower and coffee, she reached in her coat pocket for her keys and found nothing. After digging deeper with no success, she turned her coat upside down and shook it. She hadn't locked the flat this morning when she'd taken Duchess out, but she had certainly let herself in with her keys last night—had she just put them somewhere else?

Her panic mounted as she tried every likely spot in the flat. It wasn't so much her inability to lock the flat that worried her. Duchess had a big bark, and if anyone was brave enough to ignore the dog, there wasn't much to steal.

But without her keys, she wouldn't be able to get into the surgery, and that was essential. The thought of having to ring Gavin and ask him to drive over from

Willesden with his own set gave her renewed energy for her search.

It was only when she been through the flat a third time that she remembered the spare keys in her kitchen drawer. A thorough turning out of the drawer, however, revealed no keys. Bryony sat down, completely baffled, and it was from that angle she saw a metallic gleam under the edge of Duchess's dog bed. Duchess watched her as she retrieved the keys, her tail innocently wagging.

"You haven't turned into a magpie, have you, girl?" Bryony said, hugging the dog in relief. The keys must have fallen from her pocket and got kicked or batted across the floor. Duchess had been known to play football occasionally with small objects.

But what had happened to the keys from the kitchen drawer? She could think of no explanation for their disappearance at all.

She knew her day was not improving when she arrived at the surgery and found Gemma James waiting for her, with Geordie. Gemma was the last person she wanted to see at the moment.

"Bryony, I'm sorry to show up so early without an appointment, but there's something wrong with Geordie's eye."

The dog cocked his head at Bryony, wagging his tail, and she could see that his left eye was indeed inflamed. "Well, let's get him inside, shall we?" she said, unlocking the door and switching on the lights. "Take him in Room One. I'll be there as soon as I find his chart."

"I feel like a mum with a new baby," Gemma said as

Bryony came into the exam room. "I'd no idea whether or not it was serious, or what I should do, and I have to go to work this morning."

Bryony softened a little. "Don't worry. It's usually better to panic than ignore—just like with kids."

"Bryony..." Gemma fidgeted with the dog's lead, and Bryony saw that she looked tired and strained. "Geordie's not the only reason I came. I owe you an apology for what—"

"You were just doing your job. I understand."

"No. It wasn't my call, even though I understood Superintendent Kincaid's point. But I never doubted anything you told me."

"Not even the photos?"

"Especially not the photos. And the fact that Mr. Farley must have destroyed them when he knew we might search the surgery makes me very uneasy."

"Yeah, me, too," Bryony admitted. "But he's not coming in today, so that's something. After the morning I've had, I don't think I could deal with Gavin's sulking and bullying—or gloating because he thinks he's put something over on the police. That's the worst."

"What happened to you this morning? I noticed you were late."

"I lost my keys and had a major panic," Bryony explained as she lifted Geordie up on the table. "I found them again, but after the burglary here, having my keys turn up missing gave me a fright. What if I'd left them in the surgery door, or dropped them on the pavement for anyone to find?" To her horror, she felt her eyes smart with tears.

"Let's get your temperature, Geordie," she said

briskly, turning away and reaching for the thermometer. "Has he shown any unusual symptoms, besides the eye? He's eating and drinking normally?"

"Yes, but now that you mention it, he did seem a bit dozy yesterday."

"His temperature is a little elevated. That would account for it. Now, let's see that eye."

After a thorough examination of the dog's eyes, ears and mouth, Bryony said, "He's got a slight infection, but it's only the one eye. Cockers are prone to this sort of thing, because their eyes are large and exposed. If they get a bit of foreign matter lodged under the lid, the eye gets irritated and bacteria can get a start.

"I'm going to give you some ointment and some tablets you can begin as soon as you get him home. Bring him back on Wednesday if the eye hasn't improved."

As Gemma collected her medications, she said, "How's Marc, by the way?"

"Fine, I suppose..." Bryony felt an unexpected urge to share what had been eating at her the past few days. "I haven't heard a word from him since Christmas."

"Well, sometimes the holidays take people that way. I wouldn't worry too much. Bryony...I know it's none of my business, but didn't you say that Gavin is always complaining about the surgery's profitability? I think you might want to visit him at home sometime."

Bryony groaned. "Are you saying that Gavin is cheating me?"

"I'm just saying he's living quite comfortably. And, um...you might want to check over the books. It seems he's had a bit of trouble in the past with the Inland Revenue."

• • •

At first Angel was determined that she would go to Nina's trial, to defy Karl even if Nina didn't want her support. But as the time drew near, she found she hadn't the strength to face Nina's hatred again.

And Karl had been more difficult lately, always watching her, checking up on her. He'd removed the ready supply of heroin from the flat, insisting that it was a precautionary measure against being searched by the police, and instead brought her just enough for each day. What he gave her was stronger than what she'd been using, and she suspected it grew a little more so as the weeks went by. If she kept this up, would she some day lose consciousness; perhaps die from an overdose? How very convenient for him—an easy solution to the problem of the girl who knew too much.

Once, as the summer faded into autumn, she tried to visit Evan. She found him playing alone in his grandmother's front garden, but when she knelt to hug him, the boy stiffened and pulled away from her. "You took my mother away!" he shouted at her. "It's all your fault! My granny says so."

She gasped. "Evan, no! I would never hurt you like that. I love you. Look"—she opened her locket—"I still have your picture."

For a moment, she thought she had reached him. Then he spat in her face.

The trials took place in October of 1969. The court showed no leniency; Nina went to one prison, Neil to another.

At first, Angel sent Nina a card every few weeks, but each card came back, unopened. In January, she heard from a mutual friend that Nina had been ill with a bad cold and cough.

*Then, a few weeks later, the friend rang to tell her that Nina had died. She'd had pneumonia, but the prison doctors hadn't diagnosed it until too late.*

*Angel was still grappling with Nina's death when, a week later, she heard that Neil Byatt had found a way to hang himself in his cell. Poor, melancholy Neil, who had doted on his wife to the exclusion of all else, even his son, had not been able to go on without her.*

*It was then Angel realized she had two choices. She could follow Neil's example—or she could leave Karl, regardless of the consequences.*

*The first was beyond her courage. If she chose the second, she would have to do it now, or she would lose her resolution. She stuffed a few things in a bag, including the few bits of her father's jewelry she'd saved over the years, then walked round the flat, thinking how little imprint she'd made upon it. It was Karl's—the decor, the furniture, the art—in the end none of her contributions had mattered. She was insignificant.*

*Then Karl walked in, home hours earlier than expected.*

*Her heart plummeted. "What are you doing here?"*

*"I felt like closing the shop. And I might ask you what you're doing?" His tone held the faint amusement that had come to characterize his conversations with her, as if it were unthinkable to take her seriously.*

*She was suddenly furious. "I'm leaving, that's what I'm doing. Did you know that Nina and Neil are both dead?"*

*"Of course. Are these two things somehow connected?"*

*"You bloody well know they are. You sacrificed them deliberately, to save yourself, and I can't live with that—or with you—any longer."*

*"You won't leave," he said, still with a trace of a smile.*

*"I will. Are you going to try to stop me?"*

*"No. But if you go, I promise you you'll regret it. You have*

*nothing, and no one, and you can't go a day without a fix.
And I have friends, connections, everywhere. I'll know where
you are."*

It was as open a threat as he ever made, and Angel felt the
fear sucking at her like quicksand. *"What happened to you,
Karl? There was good in you, once. And you loved me—I
know you did."*

His gaze softened, as if memory touched him. Then he
pinched his lips together and shook his head. *"You can't allow
sentiment if you're going to get on, Angel. You know that.
There's no room for weakness."*

*"Isn't there?"* A small spasm of pity stirred within her, but
it was too late for that. If she didn't act now, she would be lost.
She picked up her bag and walked out the door.

Having stopped at the house to leave Geordie in Kit's
care, Gemma pulled the car up at the station, but hesitated before getting out. She had turned Ronald Thomas's
name over to Sergeant Franks with a request to search
the Notting Hill database—There was nothing more
she could do on that front.

But while Melody's team had gone through the
Arrowoods' house looking for Karl's will with no success, and Karl's solicitor reported having only the version Karl had given him on his marriage to Dawn,
dividing his estate between his wife and his children,
Gemma couldn't quite silence a nagging worry over the
matter. Had it been merely some remark of Karl's that
had made Dawn ring up Sean Arrowood, or had she actually seen evidence that Karl meant to cut his sons
from his will?

Coming to a sudden decision, she dashed into the

station and picked up the Arrowoods' keys. She would not be content until she had searched the house herself.

She began in the obvious places, those she knew Melody's team had already searched: the desk and bookshelves in Karl's study, the shelves and cubbies in his wardrobe. An hour later, tired and disheveled, she sat back on her heels in front of the wardrobe. She should give it up, finish her paperwork at the station, go home early to begin preparing the quiet New Year's Eve supper she and Duncan had planned with the boys.

The house echoed around her in the unique way of empty dwellings, every creak and shift magnified. For a moment, it almost seemed as if the house were speaking to her, then she shook her head at such an absurd fancy. Unbridled imagination, that was all it was. Still… Getting up, she moved to Dawn's closet and pulled open the doors. The clothes rustled with the draft, as if drawing breath, and the scent of Dawn's perfume drifted out, elusive and evocative.

On hands and knees, Gemma squeezed into the narrow space and pulled the storage box from beneath the bottom shelf. This time she took it out into the bedroom and removed each item, one by one. She found the paper, folded neatly into a small square, in the very bottom book, an illustrated copy of Arthur Ransome's *Swallows and Amazons.* It was a will, all right, signed by Karl Arrowood and duly witnessed. In it, he left his personal property to his wife, Dawn Smith Arrowood, with small provisions for his sons, Sean and Richard Arrowood. Arrowood Antiques and all its assets he gave to his son, Alexander Julian Dunn.

Gemma read the line again. Alex? Alex was Karl's son? *Bloody hell!*

She drew a breath, trying to piece together the sequence of events leading to Dawn's death. Had Dawn come across the will by accident? Or had she searched for it after Karl's row with Richard, trying to ascertain if he really meant to do what he'd said? Or had the row prompted her phone call to Sean, and that meeting had then led to her search for the will?

In all likelihood, she would never learn the answers to those questions. What she did know, without a doubt, was that Dawn had learned Alex was Karl's son. And then she had found that she was pregnant with Alex's child.

"Dawn knew?" As if his knees had suddenly dissolved, Alex collapsed onto his sofa.

"She didn't tell you?" Gemma asked.

"No! How long did she—had she—I mean—"

"You don't seem surprised to learn that Karl was your father."

"When I saw my aunt Jane, she described the man my mother was seeing when she was pregnant with me. I wasn't absolutely sure, but now ... Oh, my God ..." He stood and began to pace, running his fingers through his thick hair until it stood up in hedgehog prickles. "Poor Dawn. She must have been terrified, devastated. She'd chosen the worst person imaginable to fall in love with, the one person Karl could never forgive—and then she found she was carrying Karl's grandchild."

"It's possible she was drawn to you because of some resemblance, some similarity. Karl saw something of himself in you, obviously, that he didn't find in his acknowledged sons."

"It was the love of antiques. He told me once that he felt a kinship with me, because I recognized the value of beautiful things. He wanted to teach me; every time I came into the shop, he would have something new to show me." Alex frowned. "But if he knew I was his son, why didn't he come forward years ago?"

"Perhaps he lost track of you as a child, and it was only meeting you that triggered some spark of familiarity. He certainly had the resources to go on from there. Or it might have been his disappointment with Sean and Richard that made him search for you, and lo and behold, you were right on his doorstep."

"But if he knew about me—and he must have, if he took my mum to see Jane while she was pregnant with me—why did he let such terrible things happen to my mum? And me, until Jane took me in."

"I don't suppose there's any way you can know that, now," Gemma said softly. "But perhaps he meant to make amends. He left his business to you. I've just found the will. Dawn had hidden it among her things."

"His business? Arrowood Antiques? You're not serious!"

"Absolutely. The document was dated in mid-October, which I believe is about the time he had a huge row with Richard."

"But if he knew about Dawn and me, he'd have changed it, surely. Maybe he never—"

"I told him. The day of Dawn's funeral." Seeing Alex's appalled expression, she added hastily, "We had no choice. We still considered him a major suspect at that point."

"And he—was he terribly angry?"

Thinking back over their graveside interview with

Karl, Gemma felt an acute sense of loss, as well as renewed guilt over her failure to prevent Karl's death. "He seemed more shocked than angry," she told Alex. "I remember noticing that he said, 'Oh no, not Alex— It couldn't be Alex,' rather than, 'Not Dawn,' and I thought at the time it was odd."

"He was kind to me . . . in spite of whatever else he may have done. I wish . . ."

"If the will is valid, you'll have the legacy he meant for you—"

"A business built on drugs? An inheritance he *must* have intended to change when he learned about Dawn and me?" Alex sounded aghast.

"Karl had a week between the time he learned about you and Dawn, and his death. And if he made another will, we didn't find it."

A shudder ran through Alex's lanky body. "Do you really think I could bear to profit by their deaths? And in spite of my dishonesty—and Dawn's? No." He shook his head vehemently. "I don't want any part of it."

*She spent the first night in a shabby room in Earl's Court, far from Karl's usual haunts. Her money would scarcely stretch to cover a meal or two and a few more nights in similar accommodations, but by the second day that was the least of her worries.*

*Her body ached as if she had a bad case of flu; she was chilled and burning by turns, shaking and sick—and it was growing worse by the hour. Nothing would help her but a fix. But even if she'd had enough money to make a buy, her only connections were friends of Karl's, and contacting anyone associated with him was a risk she could not take.*

*She lay on the bed, shivering, as the shadows of the early winter dusk filled the room. The chills grew harder. Drawing her knees up into a fetal curl, she pulled the pillow over her head, but nothing offered relief.*

*At last, when it was fully dark, she gathered her few things and left the hotel. Too unsteady to walk, too nauseated to risk tube or bus, she hailed a taxi, regardless of the cost.*

*By the time she reached Notting Hill, it was all she could do to fumble the coins into the driver's hand and climb out onto the pavement. The street looked just as she remembered it—crumbling stucco, peeling paint, uncollected rubbish piled on the stoops—but her heart clenched in a faint spasm of hope. This place held no connection with Karl, no memories of him. And as he'd never known this part of her life, he would have no reason to look for her here.*

*She climbed the stairs, clinging to the railing and breathing a silent prayer that they would still be here. Where else could she turn?*

*It was Ronnie who answered her tentative knock. "Angel? What you doing here?"*

*As he gazed at her in surprise, she took in the changes in him, visible in the lines of his face and the way he held himself. Boyish brashness had matured into a quiet assurance.*

*"Are you all right?" he asked, his shock turning quickly to concern. "You're trembling—"*

*"I—I need—I can't—" Words failed her. How could she tell him what she had become?*

*But he had seen it often enough to know the signs. Gently, he took her hand and pushed up the sleeve of her sweater. "Oh, Jesus Christ." He looked up at her, dark eyes meeting hers. "I should never have let you go, Angel. Did he do this to you?" When she didn't answer, he said, "Never mind that now. I'm going to help you, don't you worry. You just trust me. Everything is going to be all right."*

· · ·

Gemma found Sergeant Franks waiting in her office when she returned from Alex's flat, his blunt face reflecting an odd combination of triumph and hesitation.

"What is it, Sergeant?" she asked, motioning him to a seat.

"Those phone records you were wanting, guv—I've got them. And you were right, Farley did make a number of calls to Dawn Arrowood, and the calls grew more frequent over the last few weeks before her death." Franks shifted in his chair, straightening his back as if it hurt him. "With that in hand, and you being out of the station this morning, I took the liberty of having Mr. Farley brought in, along with his shadow."

"Mr. Kelly?"

Franks nodded. "I told Mr. Farley we had records of his calls to Mrs. Arrowood, and I'm sorry to say his answer to that was as obstructive as ever. So . . . I practiced a bit of a deception on the man."

Gemma raised a noncommittal eyebrow, and after a moment, Franks went on. "I told him that Mrs. Arrowood had been no fool, and that she had recorded all their conversations, including the one the day before she died, in which he demanded that she say her cat was ill and that she bring it to the surgery."

"But if she didn't really record the calls, how did you know—"

"A good guess, guv. He *did* ring her that day, I had proof of that. The cat being ill the very next morning seemed a bit too convenient, if you know what I mean."

"So did he deny it?"

"No, funny enough. I suggested that he'd told her to

bring money to the surgery, then when she didn't, he arranged to meet her again that evening. That knocked him for a loop. Mr. Kelly couldn't shut him up after that."

"You must have guessed right about the call. I can't imagine anything else putting the fear of God into him."

Franks allowed himself a small smile. "He said two thousand pounds was nothing to her, pin money, and he needed it to pay some debts. But she came to the surgery empty-handed, stalling him. Then when he got angry with her, she told him to go to hell, she'd tell her husband herself and he could do whatever he liked with his photos."

"Did he admit he met her again?"

"No. He says he went for a drink after work, trying to work out what to do, but he decided he'd no choice but to hope she was bluffing. When he heard she'd been killed, he thought she really *had* told Karl, and that Karl had killed her."

"But she didn't tell him, and he didn't kill her. So we're right back where we started."

"Afraid so, guv." Franks actually sounded as if he was sorry to disappoint her. "There is one other thing, though. You remember the name you asked me to run through our database?"

"Ronald Thomas?"

"That's the one. Well, it rang a bell somehow, and the more I thought about it, the more I thought I remembered the case. When I found the record, I was sure." Here Franks hesitated, looking uncomfortable.

"What is it, Gerry?"

He cleared his throat. "I was new on the beat then. It

was the winter of seventy-one, a miserable wet night, visibility like the inside of a waterfall. There was a hit-and-run, at the bottom of Kensington Park Road."

"Oh, no," Gemma breathed with dawning comprehension. "Ronald Thomas?"

Franks nodded. "Torn up bad, he was. My first fatality accident. There were no witnesses, and we never found the responsible party."

"But you were sure it was an accident?"

"We had no reason to think otherwise. I was given charge of the death notification, and of interviewing the next of kin. But the widow—"

"That would have been Marianne Thomas?"

"I remember I was surprised at first," Franks said, coloring slightly, "to find she was white, I mean. In those days it wasn't so common. But she was so distraught I couldn't get a word of sense out of her, had to talk to the sister instead. She—Marianne Thomas—kept saying it was her fault, that she should never have come back, that she should have known *he'd* find her."

"He?"

"That's what I asked her. But then she stopped crying and went silent as death. After that she just rocked her baby and shook her head, over and over."

"And you didn't follow up?"

"Nothing to follow up," Franks said defensively. "She wasn't the one hurt, after all, and we had nothing else to go on, without her giving us a name, or some reason why someone would have wanted to hurt her husband."

"You said you talked to the sister—you mean Ron Thomas's sister? Do you remember her name?"

"I've printed you a copy of the file." Franks gestured

to the manila folder on her desk. "It was Betty Howard, and the address was in Westbourne Park Road, here in Notting Hill."


Gemma met Kincaid in front of the rather shabby terrace in Westbourne Park Road, just a few yards from the veterinary surgery on All Saint's Road. She had told him about Ronald Thomas's death, and about finding Karl's will.

"So if Dawn told Alex about the will, he had the perfect motive for killing Karl," Kincaid mused. "And for killing Dawn, for that matter, because she knew that he knew. Perhaps the paper knife was a blind," he added, warming to his theme, "and he intended all along to use a scalpel. Alex is Bryony's friend—he could easily have taken a scalpel from the surgery—"

"But we know he can't have murdered Dawn," Gemma protested. "Because of Otto's and Mr. Canfield's evidence. And I'd swear he didn't know about the will. Not to mention the fact that Alex has no connection with Marianne Hoffman." She looked up at the terraced house before them, its once ornate plasterwork now worn and chipped at the edges. "It's flat C we want."

In contrast to the building's deteriorating plaster and stained stucco, the green paint on the front door was fresh, and as they entered the foyer they were met by the aroma of exotic spices. It became clear as they climbed that the scents emanated from the top floor, and Gemma's mouth watered involuntarily.

The occupant of flat C was middle-aged and pleasantly stocky, with abundant graying hair tied up in a bright Caribbean scarf.

"Mrs. Howard?" asked Kincaid. When she nodded in the affirmative, he introduced himself and Gemma, explaining that they wanted to talk to her about her brother.

"Ronnie? After all this time?" She shook her head in consternation, but guided them into her sitting room, gesturing at them to sit as she sank into a large armchair. "You'll have to excuse me if I don't leave my kitchen for long. I'm cooking a stew—two of my daughters are here visiting."

As they sat down, footsteps came from the rear of the flat. "That should be my son," said Mrs. Howard. "He can look after—"

Wesley came into the room and stopped dead, staring in astonishment at Gemma.

"Wesley," said his mother, "these people are from the police. Can you see to the lunch while I talk to them? Your sisters will be back from the shops soon."

"Mama, this is the lady I told you about, the one—"

"You made my angels!" exclaimed Gemma. "It was so kind of you, Mrs. Howard. They're lovely." At first she had registered merely a jumble of color and shapes in the flat—now she saw that there was a sewing machine and many scraps and bolts of colorful fabrics.

"You didn't know this was my mother?" asked Wesley, looking utterly baffled. "You didn't come to see me?"

"No, it's something else entirely," said Gemma. "We wanted to talk to your mother about your uncle, Ronald Thomas."

"The stew can wait, Mama." Wesley moved a bolt of red beaded satin from a chair and sat down. "I want to hear this, too."

"Didn't you tell me you had an uncle that was a photographer?" asked Gemma. "Was it by any chance this uncle?"

"Yeah. He was brilliant, my uncle Ronnie. But what you want to know about him for?"

"It's his wife, actually," Kincaid explained. "We thought your mother might be able to tell us something about her background."

"Angel?" whispered Mrs. Howard. When they looked at her in surprise, she said, "That's what we called her. It was me started it, when we were kids, and I've wondered since if I cursed her somehow. I never knew anyone whose life was less blessed."

Gemma glanced at Kincaid, who gave her a barely perceptible nod of encouragement. "Mrs. Howard, were you aware that your sister-in-law is dead?"

"Oh, no." Mrs. Howard clutched a hand to her breast. "Not Angel, too?"

"How did it happen?" asked Wesley. "Was she ill?"

"She was murdered, two months before Dawn Arrowood," Gemma replied gently. "And in the same way. Since Dawn's death, we've been trying to find a connection between the two victims."

Mrs. Howard stood abruptly. "You'll excuse me. I have to see to my stew." She disappeared into the kitchen, and after a moment they heard her sobbing.

Frowning, Wesley told them, "You have to understand. They were, like, best friends. Sisters, almost. She's said for years that one day Angel would come back."

"I'm sorry to be the one to tell her about her friend's death. I suppose if they had lost contact, there's no way your mother could have known."

"I'd better see to her."

As Wesley joined his mother, Gemma took the opportunity to look round the room, curious as to its use. On closer inspection, she saw that there were rolls of wire framing interspersed among the bolts of fabric.

"She'll be all right," Wesley said softly as he returned from the kitchen. "It's just the shock. She's making us some coffee." Apparently having noticed Gemma's interest in his mother's materials, he added, "My mother makes costumes for Carnival, did I tell you that? She started back in the seventies when Carnival was a steel band going round the streets with a few kiddies following behind. Now it's big business—she works on the costumes all year."

Mrs. Howard returned with a tray holding mugs of milky coffee, her eyes red but dry. "I just can't believe it," she said as she handed round their drinks. "I thought I would have felt it if something happened to her—especially something so terrible."

"Wesley said you were best friends," prompted Gemma.

"Next-door neighbors. We moved into this building in 1959, straight off the boat from Trinidad. It was mostly Polish around here then and we weren't welcomed, except by Angel. Her parents were furious with her, but after a while they got used to us, and so did everyone else. She made a difference—There were other black families, immigrants like us, who had bottles thrown at their doors, and worse. But Angel told off the crowd that very first day, and after that we never had any serious trouble.

"Then when school began that autumn, we were in the same class, and after that we were like twins. . . ."

"Why did you say she was cursed?" asked Kincaid.

Mrs. Howard shook her head. "So much death, no one should have to bear, both her parents gone by the time she was seventeen. She nursed her mother through a terrible cancer, right to the end. After Mrs. Wolowski passed, I remember Angel asking my mother if she could live with us. But my mother said no, Angel had to look after her father.

"When her father died a year later, Mama tried to take her in, but Angel refused. She was so stubborn, and her pride had been hurt. And there was Ronnie, criticizing her one minute and paying her no attention the next. I can't say I blame her for turning down my mother's offer, but she had no one else, and not a penny to her name. She took a job in a grocer's and moved into a flea-bitten bedsit. Ronnie was so furious when he saw the place that he wouldn't speak to her for weeks.

"Oh, he was cruel to her in those days. It was only later I understood it was because he loved her and he didn't dare admit it to himself, much less anyone else. Angel was only seventeen, and Ron was twenty—a great gap at that age. And she was white."

Intrigued by the story, Gemma asked, "How did they end up married, then?"

"Ah, that was a good few years later, after Angel had left us...or I should say, we let her go. She met a man—a boy, really, but to us at that age he seemed terribly sophisticated. What was his name? Hans...Kurt? Something like that. We only met him the once, but Ronnie despised him—"

"Karl? Was it Karl?" said Wesley, beating Gemma to it.

"You know, I think it was. But she would never talk

about him, even after. That's not the man you were telling me was killed, Wesley?"

"We don't know," Gemma told her. "Please go on, Mrs. Howard."

"Well, as I said, she disappeared with this Karl, and we thought we would never see her again. Then one day five or six years later, she turns up at our door. She was in a bad way, so sick. I'd never seen anybody that sick. She'd left him, and she had nothing, nowhere to go, no one to help her."

"What was wrong with her?"

Mrs. Howard looked away as if she was ashamed. "It was the drug. He got her started on it."

"Heroin?" Wesley sounded as if the idea of anyone his parents' age using heroin astonished him.

"She was so desperate. We took her in—or Ronnie did. I was married to my Colin by then, but we were living here with my parents while we saved up for a flat. But Ronnie had a little place of his own, so he took her there." Mrs. Howard sat quietly for a moment, her eyes wet with tears. "I had never seen my brother like that. He was so strong with her, but gentle, even when she fought him. The first few days were terrible. We thought she might die, but she begged us not to call anyone.

"Ronnie never lost patience with her. I think at first he helped her because he felt responsible for what had happened to her, but as she got better he realized how much he loved her. They were married within six months, and little Eliza was born the next year. I think that they were truly happy . . . but sometimes I would see Angel watching Ronnie and the baby with the strangest look, as if she was afraid someone might snatch them away."

"And then Ronnie was killed," Gemma said softly.

"It was December of that year, a miserable night with a cold, blowing rain. He'd worked a wedding, over in Notting Dale, and was on his way home." Mrs. Howard stopped, folding her hands in her lap.

"It was a hit-and-run," supplied Wesley, who Gemma was sure knew the story by heart. "He was wearing a dark overcoat, and the police said the driver must not have seen him. They never found the driver."

"No. And Angel left us," continued his mother, "and took that poor baby with her. She said— Oh, it's all mixed up in my mind now, it's been so long—but there was something about friends who had died in prison— their name was Byatt, I do remember that, oddly enough, because we'd had a friend at school called Byatt—and Angel feeling it was her fault, that she had let it happen when she might have prevented it. They'd had a son, and she felt responsible for him. Then she said that she was terrified for us, that no one was safe around her, and that we must never try to find her."

# CHAPTER NINETEEN

In North Kensington in the nineteenth century, it was left
to the Church and charities to help those who fell on hard
times and needed more assistance than family or neighbors
could provide. As the population grew, a number of reli-
gious and philanthropic bodies became established around
Portobello Road. Their aim was to help those who were
sick, old or suffering the effects of poverty.

—Whetlor and Bartlett,
from *Portobello*

"NOW WE HAVE a connection between the victims,"
Kincaid said.

"Karl Arrowood," agreed Gemma. "I don't think
there can be any doubt. But that still doesn't tell us why
three murders were committed, or by whom."

"If Karl were still alive, we could assume he was after
any woman who'd ever crossed him, and put a guard on
his ex-wife."

"And what about Ronnie Thomas?" asked Gemma,
ignoring the quip. She looked down at the album she
held in her hands, pressed on her by Wesley as they left
the flat. Ronnie's nephew had carefully mounted and
preserved all his photographs. "Did Marianne think
that Karl had him killed? Was that why she was so
afraid?"

Kincaid watched as a motorcyclist roared by them, his
face rendered blank and anonymous by his helmet. "You

know how hard those sort of cases are to solve. They would naturally assume it was manslaughter rather than homicide, given no other evidence. Gemma, are you all right?"

The cramp had caught her by surprise, but she kept her voice even as she replied, "Fine. I just need to get off my feet for a few minutes. And I've got to get back to the station, anyway. I've a meeting with the super, though I've no idea what I should tell him at this point."

"Let me go back to the Yard and see what I can find out about the couple who went to prison. We've got a name, we can assume that the offense was drug-related, and we have an approximate date—sixty-nine or there-abouts. I'll put Cullen on it. His research skills almost make up for his lack of bedside manner."

"Ring me?" she asked, suddenly loath to see him go.

"Of course." He kissed her briefly, a touch of warm lips against her cold cheek, then they went their separate ways.

When Wesley's sisters came in with their children, he made an excuse to leave the flat. While his mum seemed to find the bedlam comforting, he felt an urgent need to sort out his thoughts.

He walked quickly down to Portobello Road, then his feet turned him automatically to the left, towards Elgin Crescent and the café.

They were all there: Alex, looking subdued, with new hollows under his cheekbones; Fern, hair sparkling with glitter, green eyes inscrutable; Marc, who sat back, observing, as he usually did; Bryony, animated for Marc's benefit; and even Otto, who appeared to have joined them over the remains of their sandwiches and a pot of coffee.

"Wesley!" called out Otto. "You see, you cannot stay away, even when you have the day off. Is this a good thing?"

"Sit down, Wes," urged Bryony. "You look as if you've seen a ghost."

They were all gazing at him expectantly.

"It's the oddest thing," he said reluctantly, then proceeded to tell them about his aunt and uncle, and how he had learned of their unexpected connection with Karl Arrowood.

Kit and Toby had just come back from taking the dogs for a walk down the street. The sun had come out, briefly, and Kit had taken advantage of the warmest part of the day. Once the sun passed its zenith, the afternoon would cool quickly.

The boys had developed a routine for their days together, and Kit had just begun to realize how much he would miss it when his school term started the following week.

After Duncan and Gemma left for work, he made Toby eggs for breakfast, then they took the dogs for a run in the big garden. Before lunch they played indoor games, then after their cheese-and-pickle sandwiches (Toby's without the pickle) they had quiet time. Toby, of course, insisted that he was too old for naps, but Kit had found that if they read books together, Toby would usually drift off to sleep for an hour or so and be much better tempered for the remainder of the afternoon.

Now, he would make them something for tea, and they could watch *Blue Peter* on the telly.

There was still a drift of snow under the eave of the house, and Kit paused to pick up a leaf that had lodged in its surface. It was golden, and completely encased in a clear coating of ice, a momentary jewel. As he turned to show his find to Toby, Tess barked suddenly. Startled, Kit dropped the leaf and looked up. A man walking along the pavement had stopped and stood watching them. Geordie gave a few halfhearted woofs, but his tail was wagging, and Kit recognized Marc, the man who'd brought Geordie to them.

"Hullo, Kit," Marc called out. "Hullo, Toby. Is your mum at home, by any chance?"

"No, she's still at work."

"Oh, well, tell her I said hello," he said, with an odd sort of smile. "Happy New Year to you, then," he added, and walked on.

Kit stared after him. There was something in the line of Marc's body, the length of his stride, that triggered a memory. He had seen the man a few days ago, just up the street, but had only glimpsed him from the back.

Oh, well, he thought, shrugging, perhaps Marc lived in the neighborhood, and liked to take walks. People did take walks without dogs, although Kit now found that hard to imagine.

His own charges were tugging at their leads, claiming his attention, and Toby had managed to find a muddy patch beneath the tree. Pulling in the dogs, Kit gathered up Toby and shepherded his brood into the house, the walking man already forgotten.

·    ·    ·

Oh, God, it was all such a muddle, Gemma thought, running her hands through her already disheveled hair. The files and reports on all three murder cases lay strewn across her desk as if a whirlwind had picked them up and dropped them again, a jumble of utterly useless facts. She stood abruptly, feeling that if she didn't get some air, her head would burst with frustration. Patting her jacket pocket to make sure she had her phone, she slammed out of her office. "I'm going out for a bit," she called out to Melody as she passed the staff room, but she didn't stop to explain.

She walked without thinking for the first few minutes, concentrating on nothing but the regular jab of the frigid air filling her lungs and the crisp step of her booted feet on the pavement.

Then, as she relaxed, bits of the reports began to shift and jostle in her mind like pieces in a child's puzzle square. She sorted them as if it were an exercise, running through each possible suspect, each discarded avenue of investigation. It was only when she reached Alex Dunn that something began to niggle at her. Her steps slowed.

*Alex was Bryony's friend,* Kincaid had said. *He could have taken the scalpel from the surgery* . . . On the pretext of a visit, perhaps, Gemma added to herself, as could any of Bryony's friends. But the scalpel had disappeared at night, in an obvious theft. . . .

A fragment of that morning's conversation with Bryony floated back to her, only half heard in her worry over Geordie. Bryony had panicked because she'd misplaced her keys, fearing she might have compromised the surgery's security. All had been well in this morning's case . . . but what if it had happened before? Gavin had accused Bryony of absentmindedly leaving the surgery unlocked, but what if someone Bryony knew—and trusted—had taken her keys without her knowledge? Only a few minutes would have been needed to make a copy of the key to the surgery door, then the keys would have been returned, no one the wiser.

But which of them had it been? Alex and Otto had alibis for the time of Dawn's death, as did Otto for Karl's, and Alex's involvement in Karl's death seemed unlikely. Fern they had never considered seriously, simply because she did not possess the physical size and strength to wield the knife.

That left Marc.

Gemma's blood ran cold. If anyone had access to Bryony's keys, as well as knowledge of the surgery, it was Marc. He was fit and strong; she had seen him lift their Christmas tree as if it were a twig.

And he lived alone. As far as Gemma knew, his movements on the nights of Dawn's and Karl's murders had never been checked. But why would Marc commit such crimes?

No, it just wasn't possible! The whole idea was a fabrication of her overstressed imagination—

And yet . . . Looking up, she realized she had come to the intersection of Kensington Park and Elgin Crescent. She was near enough. It couldn't hurt to have a friendly word with Marc, ask in a roundabout way what he'd been doing on those nights, just to set her mind at rest.

She glanced in Otto's window as she passed the café, seeing Wesley wiping down a table, his head bobbing to unheard music. Then she turned into Portobello Road and started down the hill.

·        ·        ·

Shortly after Kincaid's return to Scotland Yard, Cullen appeared in his office.

"I found the case—or cases, I should say, as they were tried separately," he reported. "Neil and Nina Byatt. Both were convicted of selling heroin, which had apparently been smuggled into the country in art objects that were shipped to Karl Arrowood, their employer."

"And Arrowood was never charged?"

"According to the report, the investigating officers found no proof of his involvement."

Kincaid frowned. "I smell a deal, Sergeant, and a nasty one. No wonder Marianne Hoffman felt responsible for what happened to her two friends, but I doubt she had much influence over Karl. Were you able to locate the Byatts' son?"

"I rang a friend at Somerset House, who was able to turn up the record for me. Neil Wayne Byatt and Nina Judith Mitchell Byatt had a son in 1961. They named him Evan Marcus Byatt."

"I wonder what happened to the boy when his parents died?"

"He was legally adopted by his maternal grandparents."

"Good God, you're amazing, Cullen."

"It's all in knowing what to access."

"Mitchell?" Kincaid mused. "I wonder if he took his grandparents' name. . . . He'd be near forty now, wouldn't he? And hasn't Gemma mentioned someone named Mitchell?"

He reached for the phone, unable to quell a sudden uneasiness.

.    .    .

Although the lights were out in the dining area of the soup kitchen, Gemma heard a murmur of voices from the back. "Anyone at home?" she called out.

"In here," Marc answered, and as she reached the kitchen she saw that it was Bryony with him. He stood at the long, stainless steel worktable, preparing the ingredients for what looked like a chicken soup or stew. Bryony sat on a stool nearby, tearing herbs into a bowl.

"Bryony! I thought I might find you here," Gemma improvised, seeing how she might proceed.

"Is it Geordie? He's not worse, is he?" Bryony slid from her stool, but Gemma hurriedly waved her back.

"No, no, he's fine. I just wanted to ask you something. Hullo, Marc," she added, and he nodded at her without breaking the rhythm of his work, dismembering chicken carcasses with swift precision. Turning back to Bryony, Gemma said, "It's about your keys. Do you remember misplacing them, even briefly, before the theft in the surgery?"

"No..." Bryony frowned, her hand poised over the bowl, and Gemma caught the strong scents of thyme and rosemary. "It's odd, though, now you mention it. When I was searching for my keys this morning, I discovered my spare set was missing from my kitchen drawer. I can't imagine what could have happened to them."

Who had had access to Bryony's kitchen, other than Marc? Gemma felt her pulse quicken—perhaps her suspicions had not been so far-fetched, after all. "Have you any idea how long the keys have been missing?" she asked Bryony.

"Absolutely none. I haven't used them in ages, and

it's not the sort of thing you think to check on a regular basis, is it?"

"No," Gemma agreed, glancing at Marc, who still seemed to be concentrating on his chopping. "Is that a New Year's Day feast you're preparing?" she asked, with studied casualness. "For your clients?"

He looked up at her and she thought she saw a flicker of wariness in his eyes—or had it been amusement? "It is. Not that many of them have much to celebrate, other than having endured another twelve months. Unlike some, who don't know the meaning of lack." There was a bite to his voice she hadn't heard before.

"What about you, though? Surely you must take some time for yourself? I know you fed the homeless on Christmas Day—did you at least treat yourself on Christmas Eve?"

Bryony looked from Gemma to Marc with a puzzled frown—perhaps she had wondered how Marc had spent Christmas Eve, as well. The blue light from the fluorescent fixtures bleached the red from her auburn hair and gave a faint gray cast to her skin.

"And I was beginning to feel a bit neglected," said Marc. "I thought I was the only one you hadn't questioned about Christmas Eve, and about the night Dawn Arrowood was killed. I was here, alone, on both occasions."

Bryony gave a startled laugh. "I'm sure that's not what Gemma meant."

Using the flat of his knife, Marc scraped the chicken pieces and chopped vegetables from the steel table into an enormous pot. "Isn't it?" he asked lightly.

"But Gemma, you can't seriously be suggesting that Marc had something to do with the Arrowoods' deaths? That's—"

Gemma held up her hand to silence Bryony's protest.
The last piece of the puzzle had fallen into place. How
had she not seen it before? "Marc. You said your grandmother raised you. How did you lose your parents?"

He met her eyes. "Oh, I think you know. So does
Bryony, in fact, because Wesley just told everyone the
whole story half an hour ago. Bryony, bring me your
herbs," he added, with a nod towards the pot.

Before Gemma could call out an instinctive warning,
Bryony had slipped from her stool and gone to him.
Marc's arm snaked round her; with the other he held the
knife to her long, slender throat. The bowl of herbs slid
from Bryony's grasp and shattered on the floor.

"Marc. Don't—" Gemma jerked as her phone began
to ring. She reached automatically towards her pocket,
then froze when Marc shook his head.

"I wouldn't do that, Gemma." His grip tightened on
Bryony until she whimpered. "You wouldn't want me
to cut her, would you? Switch the phone off."

Gemma took the phone from her pocket. The insistent ringing stopped as she turned it off, and she let
it fall back into her pocket. Praying that he wouldn't
take the phone from her, she tried to keep her voice
calm. "I'll do whatever you say, Marc. Just don't hurt
her." Visions of Dawn and Karl Arrowoods' mutilated
bodies swam before her eyes, and she heard the pulse
pound in her ears. He was insane, she had been unforgiv-
ably stupid, and now he held Bryony's life in his hands.

Otto's café was empty except for an older woman drinking a cup of tea, her greyhound stretched out beside her
chair.

"Anyone here?" Kincaid called, and Otto emerged from the kitchen.

"What can I do for you gentlemen? It's Super-intendent Kincaid, is it not?"

"Otto, is there anyone called Mitchell that comes in here? You know, one of the regular group?"

"You must be thinking of Marc Mitchell. They were all in earlier this afternoon, Marc, Bryony, Alex and Fern. Wesley was telling everyone the latest developments."

"Marc, the chap who runs the soup kitchen? Jesus." Kincaid had met the man when he'd come to their house, but if he'd been told his last name, it hadn't registered. "Where is his place?"

"Just down Portobello Road, before you get to the flyover. Next to the old Portobello School entrance."

"It's the perfect situation," Cullen said, excitement tightening his voice. "He lives alone, has facilities for washing things, and a kitchen where a trace of blood wouldn't be amiss. And if Wesley told him we'd learned about his parents, he'd know it was only a matter of time until we made the connection—"

"Whose parents?" asked Otto, bewildered. "What are you talking about?"

But Kincaid had taken out his phone and was dialing Gemma again. This time the call went directly to voice mail. "Why in bloody hell would she have switched her phone off?" he muttered as he hung up. He dialed again, this time Notting Hill Station. When he had Melody Talbot on the line, he asked without preamble, "Where's Gemma? Is she there?"

"No." Melody sounded surprised, and a little worried. "She went out about an hour ago. She didn't say where she was going. Have *you* any idea where she is?"

Kincaid told himself Gemma could have gone anywhere—to run an errand, check on the children, to buy herself a coffee—but none of his logical suppositions lessened the dread that gripped him.

"I'm not mad, you know," Marc said as if he'd read her thoughts.

"Then let us go. The Yard is on the way," she bluffed. "You know they've traced your history. I only came along first because I thought we were friends. Talk to me, Marc. Let me help you."

"We'll talk," Marc agreed pleasantly. "But first let's make Bryony a bit more comfortable. Come over here." He gestured towards a ball of brown kitchen twine on the table. "Tie her up, hands behind her back." In a mockery of a lover's embrace, he turned Bryony towards him so that Gemma could reach her hands.

With a wary eye on the knife, Gemma did as he asked. Gemma could feel Bryony trembling.

"Now her feet," Marc commanded, and when Gemma had finished he pushed Bryony up against the wall next to the cooker. Released from his grip, Bryony slid limply down into a sitting position, knees drawn up to her chin, eyes dark with terror.

Marc stood between them, still holding the knife firmly. "You make one wrong move," he told Gemma, "and I can reach her in an instant."

"Why are you doing this?" Gemma asked softly. "I know you don't want to hurt Bryony, or me."

"Then you can listen to the truth. Someone needs to know what Karl Arrowood did. He took my parents away from me—he murdered them. And *she* let him do it. That's not right, is it?"

"She? Who do you mean, Marc?"

"Angel, of course. Or Marianne, if you prefer. She said that was our secret, her name, because I was special to her. She said she loved me—and I loved her, until my grandmother told me what she'd done."

"Angel couldn't have prevented Karl doing what he did. She was just as much his victim as your parents, and she suffered, too—"

"Not enough. All the time I was growing up, my grandmother told me that God would punish them, Angel and Karl. I waited and waited, but nothing happened. My grandmother died without seeing retribution."

"But surely she didn't mean for you—"

"You know what the irony of it was?" His lips curled in a smile that didn't reach his eyes. "Two days after I buried her, I saw Karl on the telly. Getting an award for his humanitarian efforts. He and some political bigwig friends had raised money to benefit the homeless. 'The less fortunate,' he called them." He shook his head. "Do you know that it took my grandmother fifteen years to pay off my parents' legal fees? There were months we lived on porridge, months when she couldn't pay the electricity. Do you think Karl would have considered *us* less fortunate?"

"But Angel—Marianne—Why—"

"I had to sell my grandmother's bits and pieces to pay off the last of the debts, so I took her jewelry to the little shop in Camden Passage, near our flat. When I saw her, I knew God had spoken to me directly."

"You recognized Angel?"

"I thought she seemed familiar at first. Then she bent over, and I saw her locket." He touched his chest, and Gemma saw he wore a silver chain that vanished beneath his shirt. "She always wore a heart-shaped silver locket. She put my picture in it. It was still there." There was a note of wonder in his voice. "But then, I didn't know that until after I'd killed her."

*He is utterly mad.* Gemma put a hand on the worktop to steady herself, trying frantically to think of something within reach she could use for a weapon. If she could only distract him long enough to switch on her phone and dial 999, the open connection would lead the police to her. But how could she do so without him hurting Bryony, or her?

"Are you telling me God chose you as his means of retribution?" She willed him to keep talking. "Did you kill Marianne to punish her?"

"And Karl. He must have cared about her, once. But I had no way of making sure that he knew, and understood, what had happened. So then I thought of his wife. I saw her on the telly with him—so young, so blond, and I knew he must love her, if he were capable of loving anyone."

"But Dawn Arrowood had never hurt anyone! How could you take such an innocent life?"

"I *was* sorry about that." Marc spoke with chilling sincerity. "She was so beautiful—a little like my mother. But then my mother died gasping for breath, her lungs filled with fluid. Dawn was a lamb, a necessary sacrifice. I'm sure she would have understood."

"That's why you pierced the victims' lungs—because of your mother?" A horrid fascination gripped Gemma.

"And their throats—"

"My father hanged himself."

"And Karl? You had to make Karl suffer first."

Marc smiled at her, as if pleased with a bright pupil. "I sensed you were perceptive."

"Did he know who you were, when you killed him?"

"I told him. He had to know. Then he fought me, but it didn't matter in the end."

Bryony moaned, as if the flat assurance of Marc's words had pushed her past the bounds of endurance.

As Marc's eyes flicked towards Bryony, Gemma lunged at him. If she had any conscious thought, it was that she might knock him down, giving her a chance to use the phone before he could recover.

But in a flash of movement, his hands grabbed her, swinging her round. Her hip hit the steel table, hard, and the impact loosened his grip. As she fell to the floor she felt a tearing pain.

Had the knife caught her? Pushing herself up, she grabbed for Marc's ankles, but the pain bit again, fierce and insistent. She cried out, and Bryony scooted towards her along the floor.

"Gemma! What is it? Are you okay?"

"Get back," Marc hissed at Bryony.

Bryony stopped, her face very white. "Gemma, you're bleeding."

Gemma felt a wet, spreading warmth. When she touched the floor beneath her, her hand came away red and sticky.

"Marc," she whispered. He had knelt beside her, looking suddenly as bewildered as a child. "Something's wrong. You have to get someone—an ambulance—"

"I didn't mean—I never wanted to hurt *you*, Gemma," he whispered. "Let me help you. I can make it better."

He lifted her shoulders, cradling her in his arms, and gently began to rock her.

The tires screeched as Cullen pulled into the curb, and Kincaid leapt out before the car had stopped rolling. Kincaid had ordered Melody to dispatch officers to the address on Portobello Road, but he and Cullen arrived first. The lights were out in the front of the soup kitchen, but the door swung open to his touch.

"Gemma!" he called out. There was no point in stealth—Mitchell would have heard the car, and the door.

"Here! Back here!" came an answering voice, high with panic. Not Gemma—but it struck a faint chord of recognition. Bryony.

He ran for the back.

The scene that met his eyes seemed drawn from hell. Gemma lay on the floor, cradled tenderly in Marc Mitchell's arms. A few feet away, Bryony, bound hand and foot, tried to push herself upright. The harsh light gleamed from the blade of an abandoned knife near Mitchell's side.

For an instant, Kincaid thought Mitchell held Gemma by force, then the hot-iron stench of blood reached his nostrils. *She's hurt, dear God. How badly?* Her face was paper-white; her eyelids fluttered as she tried to focus on his face. "Duncan," she whispered. "I can't . . ."

*He's stabbed her,* he thought. *The bastard's stabbed her.* Then, where her coat had fallen open, he saw the bright stain of fresh blood soaking through her trousers. With a cold and terrifying certainty, he knew what was happening. Gemma was hemorrhaging.

# CHAPTER TWENTY

> Notting Hill has changed further and faster than almost
> anywhere else you can name in London. The impetus for
> that change came from the Caribbean immigrants in the
> sixties and by the richest of ironies, the same changes made
> it impossible for them to hold on to the ground which had
> been gained at such cost. On the other hand, change is fun-
> damental to the nature of city life. People ebb and flow like
> the tides, buildings decay, are rebuilt and renovated, turned
> to other uses. The big wheel turns.
>
> —Charlie Phillips and Mike Phillips,
> from *Notting Hill in the Sixties*

LATER, GEMMA WOULD remember the events of that
night only in snatches. Kincaid's voice, jerking her back
into consciousness. Opening her eyes, feeling Marc's muscles tense beneath her...A flash of light from the blade of
the knife as Kincaid scooped it up from the floor...His
voice again, steady and confident. "Ease her down, Marc.
Good man. Gently, gently..." Then the warmth of
Marc's body slipping away from her. Cold...She was so
cold....The dimness began to steal over her again, but
she forced her eyes open once more.

Marc stood in the doorway, Cullen on one side, a uni-
formed officer on the other. Resisting them, he turned
back to look at her, and the yearning despair she saw on
his face would stay etched in her memory forever.

．　　　．　　　．

After that came a darkness filled with pain and jostling, punctuated with a loud wailing her fogged brain only gradually identified as sirens. Then words jumped out at her from a blur of bright lights and gurneys... Placental abruption... Fetal distress... Internal bleeding... Cesarean...

"No, please," she had tried to protest. "It's too soon." But her body would not respond, and she knew now that her plea would not have mattered.

After the delivery, they held their tiny son in their arms as his respiration failed.

A priest came and said kind and comforting words. None of them penetrated Gemma's anguish. Then they took her child away.

After the first two days of Gemma's stay in hospital, Kincaid sent Toby to Hazel's, hoping that the familiar environment and Holly's company would ease the child's distress. Toby missed his mother terribly, and neither Kincaid nor Kit seemed to be able to comfort him.

The house seemed echoingly empty without her presence, a constant reminder to Kincaid that he had almost lost her. And now, although she seemed to be recovering well enough physically, she had refused to talk about the baby at all.

Hazel, when consulted, had told him, "You can't rush her. You're going to have to let her do this in her own way, in her own time. There's more than grief over the baby's death here—she's blaming herself for what happened, and no one else can absolve her of that burden."

He knew Hazel was right, yet he also knew that he must be ready to support Gemma in any way he could—and that he must put aside his own grief for the moment. Later, he would think about his son, so perfect, so still . . . and of what might have been.

But now he must concentrate on Toby, and Kit, and on providing the foundation that would hold their family together.

Wanting to spend as much time with Gemma and the children as possible, he rearranged his schedule, going into the Yard only to finish up the most essential paperwork on the Arrowood case. So it was that he was at home with Kit on an afternoon later in the week when Wesley Howard came to see them.

"I hope you don't mind me coming round," Wesley said hesitantly. "I wanted to ask about Gemma . . . and to say how sorry I was."

Kincaid invited him into the kitchen, where Kit made them all coffee. "It's just that I feel responsible," Wesley continued, gazing morosely into his cup. "If I hadn't told Marc what I'd learned, none of this would have happened."

"It's not your fault, Wes," said Kit. "I should have told someone I'd seen Marc hanging about—"

"Stop right there, Kit," interrupted Kincaid. "We'd have thought nothing of it if you had. The doctors say it's likely Gemma would have lost the baby anyway. And as for what happened in the soup kitchen—that's no one's fault but Marc Mitchell's."

But how true was that, Kincaid wondered?

How much blame lay with the parents who had let themselves become involved in something illegal and dangerous, how much with the grandmother who had poisoned an already damaged child, and how much with Karl Arrowood, whose ruthless ambition and disregard for others had begun the tragic chain of events?

According to the police psychologist, Mitchell's already unstable personality had begun to disintegrate on his grandmother's death. Then, his mission accomplished with Karl Arrowood's murder, he had been desperate for some purpose in his life, as well as some sense of justification for the things he'd done. It seemed likely that he'd have sought out Gemma as a confidant, had she not gone to him.

"What I don't understand," said Wesley, "is how Marc could have done such terrible things. I saw him help people all the time and he seemed to genuinely care for them. I can't believe that his charity was simply a sham, a blind for tracking down his victims."

"No. Perhaps he saw the homeless as fellow lost souls. I don't know." Had the grief that twisted Marc's psyche left some small portion undamaged? And if so, was it that kernel of wholeness that had led him to reach out to Gemma? Kincaid found the irony too painful to contemplate.

"There is at least one good thing that's come of all this," he said aloud. "Wes, I've spoken to your cousin Eliza in Bedford. She's asked me to give you her phone number. It would mean a good deal to her to get to know her family."

•   •   •

Flowers filled every spare inch of space in Gemma's hospital room, and when she returned to it after her enforced walks in the corridor, the hothouse scent seemed overpowering.

She had a stream of visitors as well, including Hazel and Kate Ling, Doug Cullen, and an unexpected and gruff Gerry Franks. She managed to nod when they extended their condolences, and then to carry on ordinary conversations as if the content mattered to her.

But when her parents came, she found she could not talk to them at all, and simply turned her face away while her mother sat beside her and patted her hand.

Bryony hesitated outside the door of the hospital room, not at all sure she could bring herself to go in. She thought of Gemma as she'd seen her last, and felt a wave of terror so intense she clutched at the wall for support. Breathing deeply, she let the familiar, faintly antiseptic hospital odors soothe her.

She realized her fear was mixed with shame—shame for not having done more to help her friend, shame that she had been so blindly deceived by Marc—and shame that within those emotions lay a small knot of resentment. Why had it been Gemma Marc confessed to, and not her?

Furious with herself for even entertaining such a thought, Bryony squared her shoulders and entered the room.

"Bryony!" Gemma looked pale and oddly defenseless, with her coppery hair spread out against the pillow like a fan, but her smile was warm and welcoming.

"I'm so glad you're all right," Bryony told her. She pulled up a chair beside the bed. "And I'm sorry about—"

"Thanks. And what about you?" Gemma asked quickly, forestalling any further conversation about the baby. "Are you okay?"

"I quit the surgery. Somehow I couldn't see going in to work with Gavin every day, wondering what he was up to..."

"I can't say that I blame you. But what will you do?"

"At first I thought I'd pack it in, leave London altogether. I even looked at job adverts up north. But then Alex and Fern and Wesley came to see me. They said I should keep on with what I'd started, that they'd help me find funding for the clinic. And I realized..." She rubbed at the healing dog bite on her finger. "...I realized that I didn't want to leave my home, my neighborhood, my friends. I won't let *him* take those things away from me!"

"How are you...about Marc, I mean?" Gemma asked, her hand clenching on the coverlet. "Will you go to see him?"

Bryony stood and went to the window, looking out over the grimy spires of the hospital rooftops. "I—" She swallowed convulsively, tried again. "No. I don't think I could bear that." Turning back to Gemma, she asked, "Do you think he started the soup kitchen just because Karl got that award for helping the homeless? A sort of sick one-upmanship?"

Gemma frowned, then answered slowly, "No...I think he had an honest desire to help. And a genuine connection with those in need, however convoluted its inception—"

"And what about me? Was I ever anything more than a convenience to him? A means of access to . . . things he needed?" Bryony heard the bitterness flood her voice, and despised herself for it.

"I'm sure he cared for you," Gemma answered, just a little too quickly.

Bryony smiled and came back to the bedside. "It doesn't matter. But I'll never be quite certain, will I?"

One day, as Gemma's hospital stay drew to an end, Alex Dunn came to see her. He carried a gift bag, which he handed to her.

"I've brought you a little something."

Reaching into the nested tissue, Gemma felt a cold, hard object, which she gently lifted out. It was the Clarice Cliff teapot she had so admired in his flat.

"Alex! You can't—I can't accept this. It's worth a fortune, and besides . . ."

"I want you to have it. It suits you. I've decided I don't need a daily reminder of what might have been—or of what I imagined might have been, to put it more accurately."

Gemma glanced again at the vibrant red-roofed houses dancing across the pot. "But Alex—I hardly—"

"You can begin your own collection. And there's another reason I want you to have it. It's a reminder, from me to you, that we have choices in how we deal with things . . . and that we're capable of more than we think." He smiled at her and changed the subject, forestalling any more argument on her part. "Fern says hello, by the way."

"How is she? Did she— Have you—"

"We're working on being friends. For the moment, that's enough."

*She took the baby and fled north. It was only a name on the railway schedule, and a half-remembered comment by one of the father's friends, that made her decide to stop in York. "A good place for antiques," she had heard, "full of tourists with money to spend." But what mattered most to her was that it was far away from Karl.*

*With the money Ronnie had saved for his own business, she rented a tiny shop near the city wall and stocked it with whatever antiques and bits of jewelry she could find at a decent price. She went back to using her maiden name, and her father's things took pride of place in the display case.*

*The shop had living quarters upstairs, a blessing, as she had no money left for a flat. The single room was small and shabby, but sufficient for her and the baby.*

*She tried not to think of Ronnie, or of the life she had left behind. Still, there were days when grief and loneliness threatened to overwhelm her, when she thought she couldn't possibly go on. Then she would cuddle Eliza to her breast, stroking the baby's soft cheek, twining her finger in the dark, curling hair.*

*It was enough. It would have to be enough. They would be all right.*

A week after Gemma came home from the hospital, she went back to work at Notting Hill Station. At first, everyone was a bit too kind, a little oversolicitous. Although she appreciated her colleagues' concern, it made her feel awkward, and she was much relieved when after a day or two things seemed to return to normal.

She could not say the same for life at home, where it was required that one do more than show up and go through the motions—because going through the motions seemed all she was able to do. Although she was there in body, nothing seemed really to touch her.

Kit grew silent, and Toby fretful, waking often in the night with bad dreams. And although she knew that Kincaid was grieving over the baby as well, she found herself paralyzed, unable to reach out to him.

He came to her one day as she stood on the threshold of the second bedroom, looking in.

"We should move Kit into this room," she told him. "There's no need now for him to share with Toby."

"Gemma." Kincaid put his hands on her shoulders. "Let's leave it for now. It's too soon to be making any changes."

She let him pull her to him, and although she relaxed against him, there was a small hard core within her that would not soften, would not dissolve, even under his touch.

One afternoon, as the month drew to an end, she left work early to pay a call that had been weighing on her.

Erika Rosenthal was at home, and her glance took in Gemma's now slender figure. "Something has happened," she said when she'd led Gemma into the sitting room. "I read in the papers about the man arrested for the murders, but I didn't know about your child . . ."

"I lost my baby," Gemma confirmed bluntly. "I thought you would want to know."

"I am so sorry, my dear. Why don't you tell me everything?"

As Gemma related the story of Karl Arrowood and Marianne Wolowski, of little orphaned Evan Byatt, who had become Marc Mitchell, the elements joined together in her own mind in a way they had not until that moment. "It all seems such a terrible waste," she said wearily. "And there are so many questions that will never be answered now. So many 'what ifs,' so many little choices that might have changed everything, might have prevented..."

"You're thinking you could have prevented the loss of your child?"

"If I hadn't worked so hard," Gemma cried, the words tumbling out. "If I had never adopted the dog from Bryony. If I had never talked to Marc...If I had never doubted whether or not I should have the baby... That's the worst of all..."

"You cannot torture yourself with 'what ifs.' What happened to your child is no one's fault—not yours, not that poor, twisted man-child's, not God's. Some children die, some children live. As will you, my dear..."

Gemma walked home from Arundel Gardens. It had grown dark, and the glow of the street lamps etched the bare branches of the trees as sharply as an image in Ronnie Thomas's photographs.

She thought of Marianne—Angel—of Bryony, of Alex. All had faced loss and gone on. Angel had built a life for herself and her daughter, Eliza; Bryony had consciously focused on her friends and her work. And Alex had indeed turned down Karl's inheritance, Gemma had learned, choosing to live a life of his own making. How had they found the strength?

When she reached the house, it was silent. Kit had

gone to a new friend's; Kincaid would be fetching Toby from his after-school care.

She let the dogs out and put on the kettle. Then, on an impulse, she reached for the bold yellow-and-red teapot that sat in the place of honor above the Aga. It was daft to actually use such an expensive object, but it seemed to her that in a way it was sacrilege *not* to use it, and that Alex had understood. This pot had been lovingly designed and crafted for hands to grasp, for ordinary teas, for everyday lives—and those moments were all one had.

Suddenly the things around her seemed intensely beautiful; the scuff marks inflicted on the chair legs by the boys' shoes, the dishcloth, a crayoned drawing hanging haphazardly from the refrigerator door.

Names formed in her mind... *Angel, Marc, Dawn, Alex, Bryony, Ronnie*... A chain of lives damaged or destroyed by Karl Arrowood's actions... ending with her own child. And yet... Of all those affected, only she had kept what was most precious to her.

The water boiled, the steam rose from the pot, and Gemma sat down to wait for her family.

# ABOUT THE AUTHOR

Deborah Crombie lives with her family in a small town in North Texas. Visit the author's website at www.deborahcrombie.com.

### *And then she pointed. "Look! A shooting star."*

It was visible for only a few seconds, but he saw it streaking across the sky, a trail of silver and turquoise like a lone and silent firework. "They're meant to be lucky. And you're supposed to make a wish when you see one," he said.

"A wish." She looked wistful.

Whatever she was wishing for, he'd make it come true. If she'd tell him what she wanted.

He knew what he wished for.

He wanted her to kiss him.

She looked up at him, and he felt his heart stop for a moment.

And then, at last, her mouth was touching the corner of his. Every nerve ending zinged with awareness of her.

"Sophie," he said softly and rubbed the pad of his thumb against her lower lip. "Sophie."

Those beautiful blue eyes were huge in the starlight.

And he couldn't resist her anymore.

He dipped his head and brushed his mouth against hers. Once, twice. The lightest touch, but it made his whole body ache with need.

And at last she was kissing him back, her arms wrapped around his neck and his wrapped around her waist.

Dear Reader,

I thought I'd set myself a challenge with this one. Like my heroine, I am not a fan of snow. So what would make someone who hates snow and is terrified of even the idea of skiing go to work in a ski resort? And why would a world-skiing champ stay incognito in said quiet little resort? (I did have the setting, though. The Dolomites—particularly in the middle of the summer, when I visited—are stunning.)

When Sophie's and Josh's paths first cross, it's dislike at first sight. And awkwardness. They're the least likely people to get together, particularly as they both have trust issues. Yet the romance of Christmas and snowflakes and a cottage in the middle of nowhere make them lower their barriers and fall in love—until his past returns to tear them apart...

Can they find their happy ending as the snow falls? You'll have to read on to find out!

With love,

*Kate Hardy*

# Snowbound with the Brooding Billionaire

## Kate Hardy

—

Recycling programs for this product may not exist in your area.

ISBN-13: 978-1-335-40690-3

Snowbound with the Brooding Billionaire

Copyright © 2021 by Pamela Brooks

This edition published by arrangement with Harlequin Books S.A.

For questions and comments about the quality of this book, please contact us at CustomerService@Harlequin.com.

Harlequin Enterprises ULC
22 Adelaide St. West, 40th Floor
Toronto, Ontario M5H 4E3, Canada
www.Harlequin.com

**Printed in U.S.A.**

**Kate Hardy** has been a bookworm since she was a toddler. When she isn't writing, Kate enjoys reading, theater, live music, ballet and the gym. She lives with her husband, student children and their spaniel in Norwich, England. You can contact her via her website: katehardy.com.

### Books by Kate Hardy

### Harlequin Romance

#### *A Crown by Christmas*

*Soldier Prince's Secret Baby Gift*

#### *Summer at Villa Rosa*

*The Runaway Bride and the Billionaire*

*His Shy Cinderella*
*Christmas Bride for the Boss*
*Reunited at the Altar*
*A Diamond in the Snow*
*Finding Mr. Right in Florence*
*One Night to Remember*
*A Will, a Wish, a Wedding*
*Surprise Heir for the Princess*

Visit the Author Profile page
at Harlequin.com for more titles.

With much love to Gerard, Chris and Chloe, who indulged me with that research trip to the Dolomites!

## Praise for
## Kate Hardy

"Ms. Hardy has written a very sweet novel about forgiveness and breaking the molds we place ourselves in...a good heartstring novel that will have you embracing happiness in your heart."

—*Harlequin Junkie* on *Christmas Bride for the Boss*

# CHAPTER ONE

'I LOVE YOU, HAN,' Sophie said, 'and I really appreciate the offer, but we both know I can't *really* stay as long as I like. Your spare room's going to be your nursery.' She indicated the bump under Hannah's maternity sweater. 'Which you're going to need in three months' time. So it's time for me to help you decorate it—and move out.'

Hannah folded her arms and glared at her. 'You're my best friend, Soph. I am *not* letting you be homeless.'

'I won't be homeless,' Sophie said, hoping she sounded a lot more sure than she felt. 'As soon as I get a job, landlords will see me as a viable tenant and I'll be able to rent somewhere.' Through the tricky bit, she thought with an inward shiver, was going to be getting a job in the first place. 'Hopefully the temp agency will find me something.'

'You've applied for forty positions, Soph.

Surely *one* of them will give you an interview.'
Hannah shook her head. 'You cook like an angel. Look at all the reviews your restaurant got. People love your food.'

Sophie believed in her own professional capabilities. But the black mark against her was so huge that she could see exactly why nobody had even offered her an interview. 'Would you employ someone whose business had crashed? Someone who might bring all that bad luck with her?' she asked.

'It wasn't your fault that you had to sell the restaurant,' Hannah said loyally.

Sophie wrinkled her nose. 'Yes, it was. You know those horror movies where someone goes to investigate strange noises in the basement on their own, and you know they're going to end up in trouble because of it, and you're shouting at the screen, "Don't do it!"? Let's be honest, Han. I'm on a par with *that*.'

'You,' Hannah said, 'were swindled, when you were trying to make the world a better place. Which is not the same as being a too-stupid-to-live horror movie character.'

'The end result's the same,' Sophie said softly. 'The restaurant's gone—along with my flat. And Mum and Dad must be looking down on me, wondering how I could've been so stupid as to let my inheritance fall through my fingers like that.'

'Your mum and dad,' Hannah corrected, 'would've been so proud of you. You put the money they left you into the restaurant, and you've built up the business.'

'And I trusted someone to look after the money side of it for me.'

'Blake swindled you,' Hannah repeated. 'And if he hadn't skipped off to a country that doesn't have an extradition treaty with England, he'd be in court right now for fraudulent appropriation of funds.'

And how stupid had Sophie been? Thinking that Blake wanted her for herself, that he loved her and he'd asked her to marry him because he wanted to settle down and make a family with her. The family she'd lost and missed so much. The family she'd wanted so desperately.

All the time, he'd quietly been planning to empty the restaurant's bank account; as the restaurant's admin manager, he'd been a signatory on the account. Sophie had trusted him to pay the bills, sort out staffing and supplies, and arrange everything so she could concentrate on the main business: making the best possible food for their clients.

She'd been doing well enough to consider expanding the business. Liking the idea of being able to do something in the community and give a chance to people who'd struggled at school, the way she had, she'd found a second premises. She'd even applied for a mortgage and was waiting for the building survey to come back to see if they could move forward.

And then, the day before month-end, Blake had called in sick, saying he'd gone down with the flu and she wasn't to come round with chicken soup or anything because he didn't want her to catch the virus from him. He'd stayed in touch on his mobile all day, texting her to apologise for not being in, and she'd been touched by his dedication.

The following day, her suppliers had started calling to say their bills hadn't been paid. Her staff had all come in, aghast, saying their wages hadn't gone into their bank accounts. And then, most horrible of all, the bank had called to say that she'd gone beyond the level of their agreed overdraft.

An agreed overdraft that was much, much bigger than she'd expected.

It seemed that Blake had stopped all the direct debits the previous day and transferred the money from the account—along with the amount of the overdraft she'd known nothing about—into some offshore account that was completely untouchable.

When she'd called him to find out what was going on, a recorded message told her that the number she was calling was unobtainable.

She'd gone to his flat; it was empty. And none of his neighbours had a clue where he was.

Blake had told her he had no family, but the police managed to trace his parents; it turned out they'd been estranged for years and they had no idea where he was.

He'd vanished.

Along with the money.

She'd had to sell the restaurant to repay the overdraft, settle the wages and pay the outstanding supplier bills. She hadn't even been able to sell her engagement ring to go towards the bills; when she'd had it valued, the solitaire diamond in its platinum setting had turned out to be cubic zirconia set in silver, with a resale value of practically nothing.

Luckily the business had been sold as a going concern, so her staff still had their jobs. She couldn't have lived with herself if they'd all lost out, too. But Sophie had lived in the flat above the restaurant. Selling up to pay her debts had made her officially business-less, jobless and homeless. And, with Blake having left the country, it was pretty clear she was fiancé-less, too.

The one good thing was that she hadn't been declared bankrupt. She could start again without *that* against her name, at least. But who would take a chance on her, after her appalling lack of judgement?

'Which brings us back to our very stupid horror movie heroine,' Sophie said wryly. 'I shouldn't have trusted him in the first place. But we'd been engaged for a year, Han. We'd been together for nearly two. I didn't think a swindler would wait that long?'

'If they were playing a long game, they would,' Hannah said. 'When Blake came into your life, you'd only recently lost your parents in that car crash. You were filling the gap with building up the business, and that meant you were vulnerable. And, instead of seeing the lovely woman with a big heart that you really are, I think he saw your inheritance money. He played you, Soph. I just wish you'd got me to check the agreement you had with your new bank.'

The change of account that Blake had persuaded her to make because she'd get a better rate of interest on her balance.

What she hadn't realised was that he'd applied for a larger overdraft at the same time. And she'd trusted him, as her admin manager, to get the details right.

She wished she'd run it past Hannah, too, but at the time her best friend had been undergoing IVF, and Sophie hadn't wanted to put any extra pressure on her. 'I can't change the past. All I can do is learn from it—and I'll never, ever let anyone be a signatory on my account again.' She sighed. 'Though it could've been worse. OK, so I've lost the business and my flat and I don't have any money, but I've still got Mum's wedding ring and Dad's watch. If I'd been made bankrupt, the court would've made me sell them, too.'

'And I would've bought them and kept them for you until the bankruptcy was discharged. Only you,' Hannah said, 'could see a bright side in this. Six months pregnant or not, if Blake was in front of me right now I'd punch him really, really hard. Break his nose, and possibly another couple of bits of his anatomy.'

Sophie smiled wryly. She could imagine Hannah—who could be very scary indeed—doing just that. But she'd resigned herself to the situation. 'I admit, I'm hurt and I'm angry and right now I'm feeling very stupid about trusting someone who lied to me, but what's the point in getting worked up over something I can't actually change? I'd rather spend that energy picking myself up, dusting myself down and starting all over again.' She lifted her chin. 'I know nobody's given me an interview so far. But I can kind of understand it. I'm either stupid or unlucky, depending on your point of view, and nobody wants their business tainted with that.'

Hannah coughed. 'If it had happened to someone else, *you* would've given them a chance.'

True. But Sophie knew that not everyone saw the world the way she did. 'Nobody's going to give me a junior position,' she continued, 'because I'm overqualified and they'll think I'm not likely to stay any longer than it'd take to find something more suited to my skills. So that rules out the permanent jobs. But, if I'm a temp, that takes out any potential recruitment or bad luck issues because I won't be there for long enough to have an impact. And Christmas is coming; everyone needs extra staff to cope with the office parties from around mid-November. The temp agency's my best chance. Then, once I've got some up-to-date references, I can start to find something permanent.'

And, as if on cue, her phone rang.

She glanced at the screen. 'It's the agency. Fingers crossed they're ringing with an interview.'

'Take the call,' Hannah said. 'I'll go and make us a cup of tea. Good luck!'

By the time Hannah came back with two mugs of tea, it was a done deal.

'You're looking at a proper chef again,' Sophie said, beaming.

'Fantastic!' Hannah, clearly delighted, hugged Sophie. 'Where is it and when do you start?'

'Ah. That might be the catch,' Sophie said. 'It's at a ski resort in the Dolomites. And they're flying me out the day after tomorrow—apparently the season won't really start until the end of November, but they like staff to settle in and do the training, and be there to look after the people who come just before it starts getting busy.'

'The day after tomorrow?' Hannah stared at her, looking shocked. 'You're never going to have time to arrange that!'

'Most of my stuff's in storage already, and it won't take me long to sort out the rest,' Sophie said. 'My passport's in date. It's Italy, so I don't need any extra vaccinations. All I really need are snow boots and a coat—and ten minutes in a sports shop will sort that for me.'

'But you can't ski,' Hannah said.

'I'm not going to be skiing. I'm going to be

the chef in a posh chalet,' Sophie said. 'Absolutely no skis required.'

'And you hate snow.'

'Because I'm clumsy and I fall over all the time.' Sophie shrugged. 'But I guess at least there the snow'll be deep enough that if I fall over I won't hurt anything more than my dignity.'

'You—and snow?' Hannah looked anxious. 'Soph, are you *sure* about this?'

'No,' Sophie admitted, 'but I think it's the best chance I've got. And maybe challenging myself a bit might help me to get my self-esteem back. I need a fresh start, somewhere nobody knows me.' And then maybe she'd stop feeling quite so useless and stupid. But the one thing she was clear on: no more relationships. No more putting her trust into someone who'd let her down.

How could one single day suck all the light out of the world? Josh wondered.

But today would always be his dark day of the year. The anniversary of the day his life had unravelled. He'd lost the championship and Annabel in very swift succession. Gone from being on top of the world to the bottom of a very deep and very dark hole: sixty miles an hour to zero in what felt like a nanosecond.

In the following months he'd focused on his

physio. Worked on his knee every single day. Forced himself through the pain. Blocked out the unfair and untrue media stories and tried to persuade his family—and the friends who'd stuck by him—that he was completely fine. He'd almost persuaded *himself* that he was completely fine.

And then, last month, his surgeon had sat down with him to discuss his future.

'It's up to you, Josh,' the consultant surgeon had said, leaning his elbows on his desk and steepling his fingers. 'The surgery was a success. You've done well with your rehab. But, if you go back to skiing competitively, it's not a question of *if* you're going to have another knee injury, it's a question of *when*. Next time you might do even more damage; I might not be able to repair it if you damage your patella tendon as well as your anterior cruciate ligament and meniscus. So you need to make a decision. What would you rather do: go back to competitive skiing now, or still be able to walk unaided in twenty years' time?'

What kind of choice was that? Josh had been horrified. 'Competitive skiing's what I do. It's who I am.'

And if he couldn't ski…

He was privileged, he knew. Born into a se-riously rich family so he'd been able to indulge his love of skiing—and his talent. For years Josh's father had wanted him to give up what he considered a seriously dangerous sport and join the family firm, with the aim of becoming CEO of the family software business. All Josh had to do was smile and agree.

Though, if he did that, Josh knew it would crush his big sister's dreams. Lauren had worked her way up through the company to become head of development. She'd be the perfect person to be CEO of Cavendish Software. She'd proved herself and she *deserved* the position. He absolutely wasn't going to shove his sister out of the way.

At the same time, Josh knew that the surgeon was right. He'd seen so many injuries happen on the slopes. He knew a few people who'd given up while they could still walk away; and he knew a few more who'd carried on until they'd had one injury too many and there was no way back.

The sensible decision would be to give up competing.

But the idea of never, ever having that rush again: it made the world seem flat and lifeless.

And, if he gave up skiing competitively, what would he *do*? Who was he without his skis?

'Think about it,' the surgeon had said quietly. 'It's your choice.'

'What would you do, if say you had an accident which meant you couldn't operate any more?' Josh had asked.

'Teach,' had been the prompt answer. 'Because then I'd still be working in medicine, still be making a difference. It'd be second best, but that would still be better than losing medicine from my life completely.'

Josh had thought about it.

And thought some more.

He could become a coach. Teach the next generation of elite athletes.

Or he could take a different path. Still teach, but bring the thrill of skiing to people who'd never done it before. Take them from rookie to…well, not reckless, but from being barely able to stand upright on their skis to enjoying something more challenging.

He'd ended up talking over the situation with his own coach.

'Don't rush into anything,' Angelo advised. 'Take some time out and think about what you really want to do. Moving from competing to coaching worked for me, because I still get the fun of being at a championship but without my wife worrying about me and without the risk to my middle-aged knees.'

He'd said it lightly, but that was the point. Josh wasn't middle-aged. At thirty, he'd thought he still had another five or so years left in competitive skiing.

'If you want to do a bit of teaching, to see if it's for you, you could work alongside me for a while,' Angelo suggested.

It was a generous offer, Josh thought, and one he appreciated: but he wasn't sure he could handle being at a championship on the non-competing side. Not yet.

Angelo raised an eyebrow. 'Or, if you want to try something different, there's my family's ski resort.'

Pendio di Cristallo, a private resort in the Dolomites. A luxury family resort, rather than the kind of place competitive skiers and their glamorous set hung out, which meant it wouldn't be full of people who knew or recognised him. Josh had stayed there plenty of times with Angelo's family, who'd always treated him as if he was one of them. There, he could be practically anonymous.

As if Angelo guessed at Josh's fears, he added, 'It's for families, not ski-heads. You could maybe spend a few months there. Get away from the pressure, teach for a couple of days a week, and build your strength up. Ski for fun instead of trying to beat the clock.'

'Stop and smell the roses?' Josh asked.

'Not on a ski slope,' Angelo said with a grin.

'But you know that poem. "What is this life if, full of care, we have no time to stand and stare?" There's an awful lot of truth in that.'

'I guess.'

And so Josh had done his teaching qualifications. He'd met people on his course who planned to work with disabled skiers, and in the back of his head a kind of lightbulb had flickered. He wasn't disabled—but he did know exactly what it felt like to have restricted movement, and to undergo surgery and painful physiotherapy. Maybe that was something he could explore: helping people with restrictions to ski and feel the thrill of hurtling down a slope. Assistive ski instructing.

At Pendio di Cristallo, there was enough snow even this early in the season that he'd been able to spend a couple of weeks skiing; though it had been on slopes that were kind to his knee but didn't make his heart beat fast, the way the freestyle aerial and mogul stuff always had. Giovanni, Angelo's older brother and the resort manager, had offered to help him sort out a small list of very select clients, and Josh was hoping that teaching would hold different pleasures. If he could give complete novices their confidence, and teach them how to handle themselves on a slope to the point where they could ski downhill and feel the magic for themselves, then it might remind him of his own first forays into skiing and bring back some of the joy he'd lost over the last year.

And if teaching meant that he didn't lose skiing completely, then he'd take the vicarious pleasure. His surgeon had been right about that. Having the snow in his life was better than cutting the snow out of his life completely; he'd already tried doing without the snow during rehab and it had just made him miserable.

He was still thinking about working with assistive skiing. Maybe that would be the answer to wiping out these lingering traces of restlessness. He couldn't go back to his old life. But he could make a better future: for others as well as himself. He'd give it until the end of the season, and then he'd decide where he went next.

It was snowing.

Big, fat, fluffy flakes, which floated down softly as a feather.

Here in the Dolomites, it wasn't like the tiny snowflakes in London which either melted swiftly or turned into grey sludge; here, the snow lay thickly and was a white so brilliant that Sophie could understand exactly why she'd been advised to pack sunglasses. She'd fallen in love with Pendio di Cristallo, with the jagged mountains and the pine trees and the amazingly blue skies. She'd fallen in love with the posh chalet she was working in—she still couldn't quite believe she actually had her own room in it—with its pitched roof, wooden flooring, log fire, mood lighting and the wall of pure glass with a stunning view over the mountains. Not to mention the spa pool, which she and Kitty, the chalet maid, were allowed to use when the guests were out and was utterly blissful. A good book, a mug of tea, the bubbling water and the view: it didn't get better than that.

And she'd really fallen in love with the sparkly, bright snow.

How had she ever thought she hated the stuff?

When it was falling like this, it was so pretty and she itched to be out in it; it was like being in a real-life snow-globe. And when it stopped snowing and the sun came out, the light glinted on the surface and made it look as if the ground was made of bright, sparkling diamonds.

Her guests wouldn't be up for another hour, and she'd already prepped everything. There was something she needed from the shop, so she might as well multi-task and enjoy the snow at the same time. Sophie grabbed the

snow boots she'd bought back in England—
boots with a thick rubber sole, fleece-lined
and made of bright pink waterproof material to
keep her feet warm and dry—and the matching padded jacket. She put on her sunglasses,
pulled up the hood of her jacket and slipped on
a pair of mittens, then headed out of the chalet.
It was so quiet here. There was no traffic, and
the snow dampened any noise. Walking in it
was magical. But she wanted something else.
She stopped where she was and lifted her face
up to the sky; the flakes drifted down in spi-
rals, brilliant white against a flatter white sky.
Utterly, utterly perfect. She opened her mouth
to let the snow fall in; it tasted crisp and clean
and fresh.

Her new beginning.

Starting now.

Smiling, she started to walk across the snow
again—and let out a scream as a man on a
snowboard materialised out of nowhere and
zoomed across the path just in front of her. A
skier screeched to a halt next to her and demanded, 'Are you *insane*?'

What the...?

When Josh had stayed here for weekends
before, he'd seen tourists not looking where
they were going in the resort, but was this one

completely crazy? Thankfully the fuchsia-pink jacket had made her visible. But she'd just wandered onto the edge of the piste and stopped dead; she was standing there without a care in the world, sticking her head up and staring at the sky.

OK, so it was early morning and there weren't that many people about, but surely she'd seen the skiers and snowboarders coming down the slope? He planned to drill into his pupils about rights of way for skiers and that joining a piste was like joining traffic on a road—but the woman wasn't skiing. She was looking at the sky. He was heading straight for her; a snowboarder just about missed her and whizzed in front of her, but he was at the edge of the piste and there was already someone skiing on his other side, so he couldn't simply turn to avoid her.

She was lucky he knew how to stop on a sixpence, otherwise he would've crashed into her and both of them could've been hurt. As it was, his knee protested at the sharp turn that brought him to a halt. He'd need to work on that later. And he just hoped this wasn't going to mean a setback. He'd worked so hard to get this far, and the worry made him snap with irritation at her.

'Are you *insane*?' he demanded.

She stared at him, one mittened hand clutched to her chest, breathing hard. 'Oh, my God! You nearly crashed into me. You *frightened* me!'

Good. Hopefully he'd frightened her enough so she wouldn't do this ever again. '*You* frightened *me*. And, for the record, I didn't nearly crash into you. You're lucky I have the experience to be able to stop.' Exasperated, he glared at her. 'What the hell are you doing on the piste?'

'Oh, my God—I didn't realise I'd wandered this way!' She looked shocked. 'I was looking up at the snow.'

'Which is *incredibly* dangerous.' He could barely believe someone could be this clueless. 'You need to keep more of an eye on where you're going. Is this your first time skiing here?'

'I haven't actually been skiing yet,' she admitted.

It sounded as if it was her first day in the resort, then. 'If you want to make it to the end of the week in one piece, or without putting someone else in hospital, take my advice and always check uphill before you walk anywhere,' he said dryly. 'Yes, it's early in the season and early in the day, but there are still some diehard skiers out.'

Her face—the bit he could see between her hood and the oversized glasses—turned a dull, embarrassed shade of red. 'Sorry. I just…' She gestured around her. 'The snow. It's pretty.'

'And it's *dangerous*,' he repeated, wanting to hammer the point home. 'You could've caused a serious accident.' And he knew all about the fallout from serious skiing accidents. It had taken long, miserable months to recover. 'Let me escort you safely to the side before someone crashes into you and ends up in hospital.'

'Thank you. And I'm sorry,' she said again.

He glanced uphill. Thankfully there was a gap in the skiers, and he was able to take her to the side of the piste without any further incident. 'Look where you're going in future, no matter how pretty the snow looks.' He gave a sharp nod, then disappeared down the hill.

So much for her new start, Sophie thought. She might as well have 'call me stupid' tattooed across her forehead.

She'd been so entranced by the snow that she hadn't been paying proper attention to where she was going. She'd thought she was heading away from the piste. Instead, she'd completely missed the fact that the fresh snow had covered the edge of the piste and she'd nearly caused an accident.

Maybe she ought to call off her skiing lesson this afternoon; but then she'd fail before she even started. This was meant to be challenging herself, forcing herself past the pain barriers and getting all of her courage and self-esteem back so she could make that new start properly.

This time double-checking her surroundings before she walked on, she headed into the town to pick up the blueberries she wanted from the supermarket. The teenage girl in her chalet's family had admitted to loving blueberries, and Sophie wanted to make some blueberry and lemon muffins for her. Particularly as tomorrow was their last day in the resort before changeover; it would be a nice way of saying goodbye.

She loved her new job. Every single detail: from calling the guests beforehand to check their dietary requirements, and whether there were any birthdays or anniversaries during their stay, through to planning the menus and discussing them with the guests. The plan was to prepare a full cooked breakfast six days a week and continental breakfast for her day off, to prep afternoon tea every day, and to make canapés and a three-course evening meal six days a week.

It was everything she enjoyed most at work: cooking, chatting about food, and delighting her customers. Here, she was essentially working as a private chef, providing a truly personal service rather than sticking to someone else's menus and recipes. It was almost as good as running her own business.

Plus sorting out the business side of things might make up for that huge black mark on her CV, because here she was responsible for purchasing supplies, budgeting, accounting, management and stock control.

And this time she didn't have someone like Blake to guide her through the numbers—or bring her crashing down.

Thankfully the supermarket had the blueberries she wanted, and she headed back to the chalet to start baking. She took a selfie in the middle of town to reassure Hannah, and sent it with a message saying she was loving every second out here.

I'm taking my first skiing lesson this afternoon. Will report back later. xx

Even though the idea of hurtling down a slope terrified her, she knew she needed to challenge herself. Prove that she could do it. And then maybe it'd give her the confidence to go back to England with her head held high and start all over again.

# CHAPTER TWO

ONCE SOPHIE HAD made the muffins, double-checked the contents of her backpack, and drunk a mug of coffee to sharpen her mind, she headed out to meet her skiing instructor.

The snow had stopped, and the sunlight made everything sparkle.

Her heart was thumping as she made her way to the beginners' area where they'd agreed to meet. The skis were surprisingly heavy, her boots weighed a ton, all the ski stuff she was wearing was extremely bulky, and she was carrying poles as well as her backpack. Had she maybe overreached herself? What if her habitual clumsiness kicked in and she fell over and made a fool out of herself?

But she wasn't going to back out now.

Apart from the fact that she'd promised herself she'd get past the fear, the private skiing lessons she'd booked were expensive. An indulgence she probably should've reined back, given the state of her finances. Although she was determined to try something new, she'd made enough of a fool of herself over Blake to feel that a beginners' class was still too much to handle. Thinking that it might help her pick up the skills more quickly if the instructor was focused on just her, she'd talked to Giovanni Rendini, the resort manager, and asked his advice. He'd been swift to recommend Josh Cavendish. 'He's not listed with the rest of the instructors,' Giovanni said, 'because he doesn't take many clients. This is kind of a trial season for him.' Sophie's doubts must've shown on her face, because he added quickly, 'But I can vouch for him. I've known him for more than a decade. He's a close friend of the family.'

That had reassured Sophie—a bit. But it would've been nice to be able to look him up and see his profile along with those of the other instructors, and know what to expect from him.

Josh Cavendish was a mystery.

She just hoped he would be kind.

Because meeting him in five minutes' time would be make-or-break for this whole ski-ing thing.

Josh recognised that coat. In-your-face fuchsia-pink. Teamed with oversized sunglasses that he also recognised, and with fluorescent yellow ski pants that clashed spectacularly with her coat.

Surely the clueless tourist he'd rescued this morning wasn't his new student? He couldn't imagine anything more horrifying. Introducing novices to the joy of skiing was one thing, but he really wasn't up for babysitting a walking disaster.

But she seemed to be making a beeline for him: as if following his directions to his new student to meet him under the clock, and she'd find him easily because he'd be wearing an orange-and-purple-striped beanie.

He saw the second that she recognised him from this morning, because her face bloomed with colour to match her coat.

'I'm...um... Sophie Harris.' She held one gloved hand out to shake his. 'You must be Josh Cavendish. And I apologise again for this morning.' She bit her lip. 'I feel very stupid.'

He knew he ought to be kind, even though he was still a bit annoyed with her for the near-accident this morning. And he really didn't want to have to babysit her on the slopes. It would be incredibly frustrating, working with someone so clueless.

But then Sophie pushed the sunglasses up on top of her head to reveal the fact that she had the most stunning blue eyes: a deep, cobalt blue, like the sky on a perfect skiing day. And a heart-shaped face. And the most perfect rosebud mouth.

His tongue felt as if it had been glued to the roof of his mouth. And all of a sudden there weren't any words in his head.

Not good.

*Really* not good.

He hadn't felt that zing of attraction towards anyone since Annabel—and that had gone so badly wrong that he didn't trust his judgement any more.

Gorgeous or not, Sophie Harris was his student. He needed to be professional, not gawking at her. What was wrong with him?

'Ms Harris,' he said, shaking her hand. And he was glad they were both wearing gloves. He didn't want to know how badly skin-to-skin contact with her might be able to distract him.

She looked nervous; he wasn't sure whether it was learning to ski that worried her, or the fact that he was going to be her teacher after their last encounter—when she'd done something unbelievably ignorant—had been awkward.

'I assume the ski hire place fitted your boots?'

She nodded.

'Good, but I prefer to check things myself.'
And focusing on a checklist might stop him
being distracted by the shape of her mouth.
What the hell was wrong with him? He never
let himself get distracted at work.

Well. He had. Once. When Annabel had announced that she was pregnant, then straight
away given him that ultimatum: marry me or
I'll have a termination. He'd let it distract him
from what he should've been concentrating on,
and the end result had been a disaster. Never,
ever again. That had been too hard a lesson
to forget. He shook himself mentally and went
through his mental checklist.

'Can you wiggle your toes?' he asked.

'Yes.'

'Good, otherwise your feet will be cold. Can
you move your foot around in the boot?'

'Only a tiny bit,' she said. 'Does that mean
they're too tight?'

'No—if your foot moves too much you
won't be able to control your skis,' he said.
'And your heels are flat on the sole of your
boot?'

'Yes.'

'That's a great start—but if your feet hurt at
the end of your lesson, you need to go back to
the ski hire and change the boots, OK?'

'OK.'

'And those ski pants are waterproof, yes?'

'Ye-es.' She grimaced. 'I know they don't go with my coat.'

'You're not here to be a fashion icon.' As soon as he heard them, he knew his words were too sharp. It wasn't her fault that his ex *had* been a fashion icon. 'Wearing bright colours is a good idea because it helps other skiers spot you on the mountain,' he said, trying to be kind. 'This is your first time skiing, right?'

'Yes.'

'You're in exactly the right place,' he reassured her. 'So. Gloves, helmet and goggles?'

She nodded.

'Perfect. We're going over to the beginners' area now, and we'll put your skis on.'

Sophie started to panic inwardly. She hadn't expected her skiing instructor to be so gorgeous. Tall, dark and handsome, with amazing grey eyes and the most beautiful mouth.

Thanks to their encounter this morning, he already thought she was completely ditzy and hopeless. She needed to get a grip. Right now. Prove to him that she was more than that. Especially because he clearly didn't like her.

*You're not here to be a fashion icon.*

He'd covered it up with another comment, but he was obviously impatient with her.

Which was yet another reason why she should make herself concentrate. What was wrong with her? Her mind kept wandering off and coming up with scenarios that involved softly falling snow, fairy lights, and Josh Cavendish in very close proximity—something that absolutely wasn't going to happen.

If she kept this up, she was going to make a total fool of herself and fall flat on her face.

'Everybody falls over,' he said.

Mountain, please open and swallow me now, she begged silently. 'I didn't mean to say that out loud.' And she really hoped she hadn't said the rest of it aloud, too.

'You didn't have to say it. It was written all over your face,' he said. 'But your ski pants are padded and waterproof, the snow's soft, we're not going on a steep slope and we're not going fast. When you fall over—and it's a when, not an if—you're not going to hurt yourself or slide off the edge of a mountain. You'll just land in a pile of snow. What you do then is get back up again, smile and shake it off.'

And now she had Taylor Swift singing in her head.

For pity's sake. Why was she letting herself get so flustered? She wasn't the sort to moon over handsome actors or pop stars, and she'd always managed to be polite and friendly to her customers and colleagues, whatever they looked like.

Well, except for Blake. She'd fallen for him like a ton of bricks. But that had been the biggest mistake of her life, and she needed to remember the lesson she'd learned. A very, very hard lesson.

To her relief, if Josh had even noticed her reaction to him, he simply ignored it. He talked her through putting her skis on, and helped her adjust her goggles. 'You'll find these useful today,' he said. 'We're protected from the storms here and get more sunshine than anywhere else in the Alpine region—and sunlight reflects on the slope, making it hard for you to see. Your goggles have pink tints, which means they'll let the light in but enhance the contrast, so you can see any irregularities in the snow.'

'Right.'

'So this is your first time on skis. How about ice skates?' he asked.

'No. I haven't been on roller skates, either.' Which made her feel even more foolish. What had she been thinking, challenging herself to ski when she'd never done anything remotely like it?

His expression was carefully neutral. 'That's fine. I just wanted to know what your experience was, so I know where to start. Everyone starts somewhere. And it's absolutely normal to feel wobbly and a bit awkward, the first few times.'

She gestured to the small children whizzing down the slopes further along. 'They don't look wobbly.'

'They probably ski all year. Ignore them. This isn't about them. It's all about *you*.'

She noticed then how intense his grey eyes were. And it made her knees feel even more wobbly.

She'd barely even finished thinking it when she fell over.

'That's good—just what I wanted to happen,' Josh said.

'What?' She didn't understand. He was meant to be her teacher. Why did he want her to fall over? 'Why?'

'Firstly, now you'll know from experience that falling over isn't going to hurt, so you'll relax, making you less likely to fall again,' he said. 'And, secondly, so I can teach you how to get up.' He smiled. 'Ironically, it's easier to get up when you're on a steeper slope. The boots stop you flexing your ankles, so on the flat it's hard to get your legs underneath you. But what

I want you to do is to get your feet downhill from you parallel to the mountain, use the poles and push yourself up in a squatting position.'

She tried a couple of times and failed dismally.

'Frustration is your enemy,' he said, 'so I'm going to help you up this time. But, by the end of this afternoon, you'll be able to do it yourself.'

Sophie wasn't so sure. But she really wanted to do this. It would help her in her real life, too. Prove that she could do something. That she wasn't the useless idiot she'd felt herself to be ever since she'd discovered how badly Blake had scammed her. That she could try something new and difficult, and she'd *succeed*.

Even though Josh was wearing gloves and her jacket was padded, she was sure she could feel the warmth of his hand as he helped her up. Again, it made her feel all quivery and weird.

She hadn't felt like this about anyone since Blake.

And that in itself should be a warning. She had terrible judgement when it came to men. Blake was absolute proof of that. Plus Josh was her teacher. She didn't want to come across like some kind of ski groupie. Be cool, calm and collected, she reminded herself. The Sophie you've promised yourself you'll be. *New* Sophie. Competent, confident Sophie who knew her own value.

'Thank you,' she said, proud of the way her voice didn't betray her attraction to Josh. Or the fact that his deep, gorgeous voice put butterflies in her stomach.

'We're going to walk sideways at first, so you get used to the feel of the skis,' he told her.

She followed his instructions, taking side steps along the snow. The incline barely even counted as a slope, it was that shallow. The more they stepped, the more confident she felt.

'You've got the hang of it. Good. Ready to try going forward?' he asked.

*No.* But New Sophie answered for her. 'Yes.'

'I'm going to teach you the snowplough.'

She'd read up on that. 'You point the front of your skis towards each other, right?'

'Not quite,' he said, 'because what happens then is your skis will cross at the tips, you'll get tangled up and you'll fall over. Think of your skis as being like the outside of a boat. Tilt them and keep pushing your knees together and your feet apart. The wider the plough and the more you tilt, the easier you'll stop.' He demonstrated, and stopped a little way away from her.

'Now you do it. Come towards me,' he said.

'What if I crash into you?'

'You won't. You're not going to crash and you're not going to fall. You've got this.'

It was maybe six or seven metres. Barely even a slope. She could do this.

She assumed the position he'd shown her, and went down the slope towards him. She was actually going slower than walking pace. Possibly even slower than a snail about to hibernate—did snails hibernate?

But she'd done it. Skied forwards.

He gave her a high-five, and that smile made her heart do a backflip. 'See? Now you're going to do it all over again.'

He walked back to their starting point. Feeling like a very ungainly and very ugly duckling, she waddled after him.

And then she repeated the slide, over and over again, until he was satisfied.

'Now we're going to add a tiny, tiny thing,' he said. 'You're going to turn.'

'Turn.' Was that really just a tiny thing, or was he jollying her on?

'What you do is shift your weight to your outside foot, face the way you want to turn, and lean your body in the opposite direction,' he told her.

Huh? He expected her to do *three* things at once? No way. Absolutely no way was she going to be able to do this. Tiny thing, indeed. It was huge. Scary. Out of her abilities.

But he talked her through it. He was kind, patient—and absolutely implacable.

Three things at once.

And, to her surprise, she managed it.

'I did it!' And her voice *would* have to squeak.

But there wasn't a hint of scorn in his face. He was just kind and encouraging. As well as gorgeous, though she'd have to stop thinking about that or she'd fall over again.

'See? You can do this,' he said.

They practised a bit more.

'I think you're ready for the magic carpet, now,' he said.

'Magic carpet?'

'It's a kind of conveyor belt—a quick way of getting you to the top of the nursery slope,' he said, taking her over to it. 'It works like the travelator you see in airports. Hold your poles in one hand, shuffle forward onto the magic carpet, and it will take you up and push you off at the landing area at the top,' he directed. 'And I'll be right behind you, ready to take you to the slope and guide you down.'

Adrenalin fizzed through her veins, and she wasn't sure whether it was from his nearness or from doing something unfamiliar.

But, to her surprise, everything happened exactly as he'd explained it.

'Ready? Remember—knees together, feet apart, and tilt. If I call "snowplough", that's what I want you to do.'

This slope was longer. And it felt as if she was flying, even though technically she knew she could walk faster than she was skiing.

'That was amazing,' she said. And then it occurred to her how naive and starry-eyed she must sound. How over the top.

But he was smiling. 'That,' he said, 'is precisely how it's meant to feel. Want to do it again?'

He sounded as enthusiastic as she'd felt. Not jaded or bored or supercilious. And it felt as if a weight had fallen off her shoulders.

He got what it felt like, to fly.

Of course he would. As an instructor, he'd be able to ski much more difficult things than this.

But, as he'd said, everyone started somewhere. Just as she'd started at the bottom at catering school, learning to make a simple *mirepoix* base for a soup and working her way up to producing something much more complex, complete with timing plans.

She nodded.

They went down half a dozen times more—

and, on the last run, he didn't have to remind her with a gentle, 'Snowplough.'

'I think you're ready for the next stage,' he said. 'Green slope.'

She looked at the slope he was indicating with one hand. 'That's terrifyingly steep,' she said.

'I promise you it's not,' he said. 'The point of this is for you to have fun, not be terrified out of your wits. I won't take you on anything that's outside your capabilities.'

Which meant she had to trust him.

The last time she'd trusted a man, it had gone very badly wrong.

But Josh had been good with her so far. Honest. So maybe she should take that little leap of faith. 'Green slope,' she said. 'So is there another magic carpet to take us to the top?'

'No, this time there's a button lift—which is a bit like the zip wire you'd see in a play-ground.'

The sort of thing she'd never go near because she'd fall off and hurt herself. Like when she'd fallen off a slide and a swing; or when she'd fallen off the beam in a gym lesson, one time, because the supply teacher had refused to let her have someone holding her hand for balance. As a child, she'd always had scabs on her knees and elbows.

*And it was moving.*

'You've got plenty of time to manage it,' he said. 'Hold your poles in the hand that's away from the lift, grab the lift-pole with your other hand and grip the pole between your legs. When you get to the flat bit at the top, just squat slightly and push the seat away.'

She watched six people get on the lift before she could summon up the courage to try it for herself.

'You've got this, Sophie,' he said. 'If I didn't think you were ready, I wouldn't suggest it.'

And this was his job. If he wasn't any good, he wouldn't have any clients, would he? Even though Giovanni Rendini had said something about this being a trial season as a coach.

She didn't want to let herself down. She wanted to feel capable again. The woman who'd built a career and had run a successful restaurant. Her parents had always encouraged her, telling her she could do anything she wanted if she tried. And she wanted that confidence back. Challenging herself to do something way out of her comfort zone was the best way she could think to do that.

She took a deep breath, braced herself, and went for it.

To her relief, she didn't miss or fall. And then she was at the top of the slope.

The views were amazing. The sun glinted off the mountains as far as she could see; the contrast between the brilliant white of snowy peaks, the dark pine trees and the wide cerulean sky was magical.

But there was a steep slope in front of her. A long slope. Much bigger than the one she'd skied down before. Intimidating didn't even *begin* to describe it.

'You've got this,' Josh said. 'And I'll be right by your side all the way down. If you're going too fast, simply tilt your skis and the resistance will slow you down. You've practised and you know how to do it.'

Learning to ski was the challenge she'd set herself, to prove to herself that she could move past the mess she'd made of her life.

'You're right. I've got this,' she said. She shuffled forwards. And then somehow she was going down the slope. Fast. Too fast. *Way* too fast. She was going to fall. She was going to crash. She was going to—

'Snowplough!' Josh called beside her.

Knees together, feet apart, tilt.

And all of a sudden she was back in control. Still going a bit too fast for her liking, but in control. She'd never felt an adrenalin rush like it: to the point where, when she came to a halt, she was actually crying.

She'd done it. Faced the challenge and proved to herself that she *could* do it. She was still standing upright. She hadn't made a fool of herself; she'd faced that terrifying slope and *done it*.

Thanks to Josh's guidance. He'd helped her rather than sticking obstacles in her way. His direction had finally helped her to move forward, away from the fear and the self-pity. She wasn't sure whether she was more grateful, relieved or excited. Maybe all three, in a weird kind of cocktail, but the end result was that tears were running down her face.

At the bottom of the slope she pushed up her goggles before they started misting up, and scrubbed at her face. 'Sorry.'

'Don't apologise. It's your first proper run,' he said. 'I remember how it felt. You're so thrilled you've actually done it, you don't quite know what to do with yourself once you've stopped.'

She mopped her tears. 'Are you telling me you cried your eyes out?'

'No. I was young enough to whoop my head off—as I couldn't exactly jump up and down when I was wearing skis. So I just stood there, feeling a bit lost and a bit ridiculous.'

Which was how she was feeling right at this moment, now the euphoria of achievement was wearing off.

'You're good at this,' she said.

'What?'

'Being empathetic. Teaching.'

He inclined his head. 'Thank you. Ready to go again?'

Yes, because she needed to prove to herself that this wasn't a one-off. She took a deep breath and nodded. 'Ready.'

All too soon, the lesson was over.

'So I'll see you the day after tomorrow,' he said.

And she could hardly wait.

Though she reminded herself that it was because she'd discovered that she liked skiing. It had nothing to do with the fact that Josh's smile made her heart skip a beat.

'In the meantime, I want you to practise a ski sit.' He talked her through the manoeuvre. 'If you want to practise skiing on your own tomorrow,' he said, 'stick to the nursery slope or the green slope.'

'How would I know I've got the right slope?' she asked.

'Because you won't need a chairlift to get to the top,' he said. 'You're not going to be quite ready for that on your next lesson, but

I'm pretty sure I'll get you safely on a blue slope before the end of your holiday.'

'I'm not on holiday,' she said.

Josh stared at Sophie, not understanding. 'You're not on holiday?' he repeated.

'I work here. I'm a chef in one of the chalets. I came here a few days ago.' She gave him a rueful smile. 'I'm rather better with a sharp knife than I am with skis.'

'A chef?' He looked at her. 'Forgive me for being nosey, but I don't understand why on earth you'd come to a ski resort to work as a chef when you've never skied before. This is the sort of job you'd take because you want to spend as much time as possible on the slopes when you're off duty.'

She wrinkled her nose. 'It's a long story and much too boring to take up your time. And, I hate to be rude, but I do need to get back because it's my family's last full day today.'

Which explained why she hadn't booked a lesson for tomorrow: with it being change-over day, she'd have no free time to go on the slopes. 'You're not being rude. Just practical,' he said. 'Well, practise that ski sit against the wall, and I'll see you the day after tomorrow.'

And funny how he was looking forward to it already.

# CHAPTER THREE

SOPHIE WAS SAD to say goodbye to her chalet family, the next morning: parents, grandparents, aunt, two teenagers and a cute ten-year-old. She'd really enjoyed cooking for them, and they in turn had adored her. She and Kitty were too busy getting everything ready for Sophie to give Josh more than a passing thought. But then the new guests arrived: a group of ten guys in their late twenties who clearly had too much money and not enough sense of responsibility, and who thought that booking the chalet meant they could do and say whatever they wanted. Including groping Kitty, the chalet maid, and indulging in the kind of 'banter' that bordered on bullying.

Anyone who'd behaved like that to her staff in her restaurant would've been asked to leave. Immediately. Politely, but very firmly, because she'd had a zero-tolerance policy and she always stood up for her staff.

Here, she was powerless. But this group had only booked for a week. Surely she could put up with them for a week? She'd do her job, be polite, and resist the urge to 'accidentally' drop iced water in their laps.

'We're only here to feed you and keep the chalet clean,' she said with a smile. 'I'm afraid anything else is completely off the menu.'

'Jealous because you're not as young and pretty as Kitz, you're flat-chested and we don't fancy you?' one of them, who seemed to be the leader of the group, sneered.

*No, you pudgy-faced idiot, and if you touch me inappropriately I'll 'accidentally' stand on your foot in spike heels.*

But she didn't say it. She simply smiled. 'More coffee and cake to soak up some of that booze, lads?'

'God, they're awful,' Kitty whispered to her in the kitchen. 'My mum used to work in a bar when she was a student. She said that's how people behaved towards the bar staff back then. Though they're not allowed to do it now—the bouncers would throw them out. It's the only reason she let me take a gap year to do this.'

'You'd think even *they* would've heard of *#metoo*,' Sophie said dryly. 'Don't worry. I'll make sure you're not alone with any of them.

And I'm going to have a word with the resort manager so he's aware of the situation and can step in if we need him to. It's not OK for them to behave towards you like that.'

'Can I spit in their coffee?' Kitty asked.

Sophie grinned. 'That's very tempting— but no. We'll smile sweetly and we won't give them the satisfaction of a reaction. Then, like any other bullies, they'll get bored and stop.'

She hoped.

The guests needled her all through the evening. Obviously their boredom threshold wasn't quite as low as their manners. But she did her job, and she did it well—even if they didn't really appreciate the food she made for them.

The next morning, Sophie was up early to prepare breakfast. Part of her was tempted to make as much noise as possible and cook things with scents that would make anyone with a hangover feel super-queasy; but then again she loved this time of day, and what was the point of spoiling her few moments of peace just to score a few petty points against people who didn't actually matter? So, instead, she made the batter for the waffles and then a mug of coffee for herself so she could sit by the glass wall overlooking the mountain.

Even though the sun hadn't yet risen, it was

still bright outside because of the snow. She could see the smooth whiteness of the snow on the ground, the dark spiky pine trees spreading up the mountain, and then the peak itself; the vertical nature of the cliffs meant the jagged peak wasn't covered in snow, and the stone turned bright pink as it caught the first rays of the sun. The sky behind the mountain shimmered from deep pink through peach up to the palest blue.

It didn't get any better than this, she thought, and the sight went a long way to restoring her temper.

But the lads were brash and braying all through breakfast, boasting about how fast they were going to ski all the black runs, commenting about Kitty's very demure outfit and how she should be wearing a skimpy black mini-dress and a frilly white apron instead, and generally being obnoxious.

When they finally left, Sophie made a chocolate and orange cake for the afternoon and prepped the veg for the evening meal; but even baking and the scent of chocolate didn't help. She was still in a thoroughly bad mood when she met Josh for her skiing lesson.

'If looks could kill,' he said, 'you'd be in the dock on a murder charge. What's up?'

She grimaced. 'The new guests. I wish the old ones were still here; they were so nice.'

'What's wrong with the new ones?'

'Rich boys,' she said. 'The sort who've never really had to work for anything. Let's just say they have a strong sense of entitlement. And it wasn't helped by the amount of booze they tipped down their throats last night.'

Josh winced inwardly. Rich and entitled. That was precisely his background; and, although he hoped he no longer behaved like a spoiled brat, he knew there were definitely times in the past when he had.

'Is it worth having a word with Giovanni Rendini?' he asked.

'Already done,' she said. 'I'm not bothered for myself, but I worry about the way they talk to Kitty. She's only eighteen.' She grimaced again. 'She's vulnerable.'

'If you're in any doubts,' Josh said, 'both of you lock yourself in your rooms and call Giovanni. You don't have to tolerate that sort of behaviour. There's a zero-tolerance policy at the resort.'

She nodded. 'I just don't want any trouble.'

'Your safety comes first,' he said. 'For now, they're not here and they're not worth the headspace. So forget about them and ski it out. I'm going to take you to a different ski run.'

'A steeper one?' She looked anxious.

'No. Just a different green run,' he said. 'You'll manage it just fine.'

And he was careful to stay right beside her on the piste, reminding her when to turn and when to slow down. He enjoyed seeing the way her expression changed from cross and anxious to peacefulness.

'Thank you,' she said at the end of the lesson. 'I needed that.'

Her eyes had cleared, and again Josh realised just how pretty she was. Weirdly, she didn't seem to know how lovely she was. 'The mountains always make it better,' he said, and realised that it was true: even though he hadn't been doing any of the elite skiing that had been his life before the accident, just being on the slopes in the snow was enough to soothe his soul.

'I think you might be right,' she said.

'Have you had a chance to try any of the après-ski yet?'

She wrinkled her nose. 'I'm not really one for partying.'

He smiled. 'This is more of a family resort than a party place, as the guys in your chalet might find out—and also skiing with a hangover isn't fun, so if they were hitting the booze last night they'll have found that out the hard way and they might not drink so much tonight. Which means they might behave better.'

'I hope you're right,' she said. 'They were going on about improving their times on the Val di Lungo today, whatever that is.'

'One of the black runs,' he said. 'Which means they're experienced skiers. Listen, I know somewhere that does the best hot chocolate in the Dolomites. Would you like to join me, to celebrate doing that green run?' he asked before he could stop himself.

'Sadly, I can't because I need to be back for afternoon tea,' she said. 'I'm hoping that good cake might sweeten their mood a bit.'

'You weren't tempted to stick salt or some super-hot chillies in the cake?'

'No, because that would be a waste of good food. I'm still hoping a charm offensive will work. If I treat them the way I want them to treat me, with courtesy, maybe it'll rub off. I've always found that if you're nice to people, they're usually nice back.' She wrinkled her nose. 'Or at least this lot will get bored if I don't react to their stupid comments.'

Sophie Harris wasn't a pushover, Josh thought. She was determined. He'd already seen that by the way she'd tackled the skiing lessons. And he approved. 'See you tomorrow, then,' he said.

'See you tomorrow.'

And funny how her smile seemed to make the snow sparkle that little bit more in the sunlight.

Josh couldn't get Sophie out of his head.

She wasn't his only student—but she was the one he looked forward to teaching most. Which probably meant he ought to let her work with a different instructor, or at least keep his distance.

Though his mouth clearly wasn't listening to instructions, because the next day after her lesson he found himself asking her to join him for hot chocolate again. This time, she accepted.

Better still, Sophie actually chose a slice of strudel from the display of cakes. So very different from Annabel, who would've insisted on consuming minimal calories, opting for green tea rather than hot chocolate and looking disapprovingly at the cakes. Sophie took absolute pleasure in hers, closing her eyes so she could concentrate on the taste of the very first mouthful; watching her as she tasted the strudel was the sexiest thing Josh had seen in years.

'Good?' he asked.

'Very. That buttery apple hit, with just the

right amount of cinnamon,' she said. 'The pastry's perfectly flaky. Did you know that if you've rolled out strudel pastry properly, you should be able to read a newspaper through it?'

No, he didn't. And Sophie seemed to be unfurling. Instead of the clueless, shy student he'd first taken onto the slopes, the day before yesterday, here she was in her element. Knowledgeable, but using that knowledge as a delight to be shared rather than to prove her own superiority.

The more he got to know her, the more he liked her. 'So are you enjoying the skiing?' he asked.

'Yes. The first day was really scary, but I'm getting over that now. I think I'm starting to understand why people love it so much.'

Joy shone from her face. Josh envied her; it was a long time since he'd felt that, and although the vicarious enjoyment was good, it wasn't quite enough.

She looked at him. 'I know I only booked three lessons with you—but do you have space to fit some more in, please?'

'Sure. Do you have your diary on you?'

She nodded. 'It's on my phone.'

'Snap,' he said, and flicked into his diary app.

It didn't take long to book in some more lessons. And Josh was surprised to discover how pleased and relieved he was that he still had a good excuse to see Sophie and get to know her better.

'Did you come to Pendio di Cristallo specifically to learn to ski?' he asked.

'No.'

'Then what made you come here?'

She wrinkled her nose. 'It's a long and boring story.'

She'd said that before. But this time, maybe, she'd talk to him. 'I have time.'

'I...' She sighed. 'I don't really want to dwell on it. The short version is that I trusted someone I really shouldn't have trusted—someone who let me down pretty badly.' She shrugged. 'So this is my new start.'

'In a ski resort. When you've never skied before.' He still didn't quite get that.

She nodded. 'I wanted to do something completely out of my experience. The idea was to challenge myself. Push myself past—well, the *past*. So I'd come out stronger on the other side.'

He knew exactly how that felt. Not that he was going to tell her. With her not being a skier, she clearly didn't know who he was. And he didn't want that to change; if she knew who he was and what had happened to him, she'd no doubt do the same as his family and friends and see him differently. Pity him, perhaps. He'd already pitied himself way too much over the last year. 'Sometimes,' he said carefully, 'you need a complete change.'

'Get out of your comfort zone,' she agreed. 'But it does mean that now I'm at a bit of a crossroads. What do I do when my job ends here?'

That was his dilemma, too. When the season had ended here, would he go back home to work for his dad? Maybe helping her talk through her own choices might help him get his own situation straight in his head. 'What are your options?' he asked.

'I'm still trying to work it out. I guess I need to find myself another chef job, back in London.'

'What made you decide to be a chef?' he asked.

'I'm dyslexic, so I struggle a bit with paperwork, and I knew I wasn't going to get great exam grades, no matter how hard I worked. But I discovered I liked cooking, and I made it through catering school. Since then, I've worked my way up from prepping to being the one who makes all the decisions.' She gave him a rueful smile. 'They say never trust a scrawny chef, but I assure you I do eat. I have a fast metabolism.'

'You're not scrawny. You're petite,' he said. A pocket Venus, though he didn't think she'd accept the compliment and he wasn't going to make her feel awkward by saying it. 'And you don't come across as one of these scary TV chefs who scream at their staff.'

'Because I'm not,' she said. 'That's not how you get the best out of people. You get the best out of them if they love what they do, and they won't do that if they're unhappy at work. In the best kitchens, you let your team share their ideas and you give them the chance to shine. I know this is going to sound a bit ditsy and flaky, but food made with love always tastes better than food made with fear.'

She still hadn't actually told him what had gone wrong, just that she'd trusted someone who'd let her down. And Josh didn't quite get why that meant she'd had to leave her job. Had she maybe fallen in love with whoever owned the restaurant where she'd worked, and he'd cheated on her? Obviously working together would be horrendous, after that, and it would be understandable why she'd left. Though there wasn't a way of asking that without either prying or stamping all over her feelings.

'Finding another job and working for someone else is one option,' he said. 'Have you thought about maybe working for yourself?'

Pain darkened her eyes.

He reached over to take her hand, but he didn't have a chance to apologise for treading on what was clearly a sore spot because the door banged open and a group of men who looked to be a couple of years younger than him came in, shoving each other and laughing uproariously.

'Oh, look, there she is! Sophie the chef!' one of them called.

'Having a cosy little drinkie-poos with the boyf?' Another of them made kissing noises.

'Your guests, I presume?' Josh asked.

She closed her eyes briefly. 'Unfortunately.'

'Love the skimpy top, Cheffy Soph. Been getting all hot and sweaty, have you?' another of them said.

'Watch you don't have too much cake. It'll make you fat,' another called.

'Mind you, she could do with a bit more up top,' another said, mimicking squeezing breasts.

'That's enough,' Josh said. 'Leave her alone.'

'Ooh! The boyfriend's getting all protective.'

Josh ignored the sing-song voice, knowing the man was looking for a reaction. He wasn't sure whether this lot were on their way to getting drunk, or whether they were just hyping each other up and acting like a pack of hyenas. Either way, the best way to shut this down was to ignore them.

Sophie clearly thought the same, but Josh noticed that she hunched over her hot chocolate and she'd quietly slid another layer over her strappy top.

When the group finally realised Sophie and Josh weren't going to engage, they went over to the counter to order drinks.

'Do you mind if we go?' Sophie asked, her voice low. 'I'm sorry for wasting the drink and the cake.'

'It's fine,' he said. 'Let's slip out now while their attention's on ordering their drinks.'

But, when she was safely outside the door, he said, 'I'll walk you back to your chalet, but I've just realised I left my wallet on the table.' It wasn't true, but she didn't need to know why he really intended to go back. 'Wait for me here?'

She nodded, her face pinched, and huddled into her jacket.

Josh walked back into the café. Sophie's guests had finished ordering and had claimed a table, where they were busy throwing sugar sachets at each other.

'Afternoon, lads,' he said. He wasn't smiling, and maybe something in the way he carried himself made them stop the raucousness and shut up.

'What do you want?' asked a pudgy, whey-faced, sandy-haired man—the one who seemed to be the leader.

'I want you to treat Sophie and Kitty with respect.'

'It's none of your business, *mate*,' the pudgy one said. 'We'll do what we want. We paid a lot of money for this holiday.'

'That's right, Gaz,' one of the others chipped in.

'Paying for a holiday doesn't give you the right to harass the staff in your accommodation. There's a zero-tolerance policy in Pendio di Cristallo.'

'What, you're going to throw us out?' Gaz scoffed. 'Are you the manager or something?'

'No,' Josh said. 'But, if you're looking to be asked to leave for unacceptable behaviour, it can be arranged.'

'It's not going to happen. Piss off and mind your own business,' Gaz said.

'Yeah. We're not interested,' one of his friends said. 'We're busy sorting out our black run for tomorrow.'

It was obvious Josh wasn't going to be able

to get through to them by appealing to their better nature. And they clearly weren't serious ski-heads or they would've recognised him. But they were talking about black runs: so maybe he could teach them a lesson in another way.

'You're all experienced skiers, right?' he checked.

'Yeah,' Gaz drawled. 'We did Val di Lungo today.' He named a time that was respectable enough for Josh to know they really were experienced skiers, rather than boasting, but slow enough that the plan forming in the back of Josh's head was likely to work.

'Here's the deal. Tomorrow morning, seven o'clock, we'll have a race.' And now to dangle the bait. Josh named the course.

Gaz's eyes widened. 'Hang on. That's the ski championship course.'

Josh inclined his head. 'Which means it's all set up for automatic timing and there will be no margin for error. The board will be very clear about who's the fastest. Who wins.'

'But you can't get lift passes to ski there,' one of the others said.

'*You* might not be able to,' Josh said softly, 'but *I* can.'

'At seven o'clock in the morning?' Gaz asked.

'It's half an hour before sunrise, so it'll be

light enough,' Josh said. 'If it's clear, the skies will be stunning.'

They just gaped at him. Which wasn't what he wanted; he wanted to teach them a lesson so they'd leave Sophie alone. Time to add some seasoning. 'Or aren't you man enough to compete with me?'

The goading had exactly the effect he wanted. 'So what are the stakes?' Gaz demanded.

'If I win,' Josh said, knowing there wouldn't be an 'if' about it, 'you leave Sophie and Kitty alone.'

They looked at each other and laughed.

'Plus each of you pays ten thousand pounds to a charity of my choice.'

That got their attention. Sophie had been right in her assessment: rich and entitled. This lot were heavily motivated by money.

'What if one of us wins?' Gaz demanded.

Josh shrugged. 'Then I'll match the payment to a charity of your choice.'

'There are ten of us.' Gaz's eyes narrowed. 'You'll match ten thousand pounds for each of us?'

'To a charity of your choice, for each one of you who beats me.' He shrugged again. 'Or for all of you. As you wish.'

Gaz blinked. 'You're serious?'

'Serious enough that the manager of the resort will be there to ensure it's a fair race.'

'How do we know you're good for the money?' Gaz asked.

'Have a little think about it. This wager means that either I'm very good at skiing,' Josh said, 'or I'm very rich.' Actually, he was both, but they didn't need to know that. 'In the meantime, I suggest you treat Sophie and Kitty with respect.'

There was a ripple of uncertainty from all of them now.

'And this,' he added, 'is strictly between us. Not a word to Sophie. I'll send a driver for you in the morning. Six-fifteen. Make sure you're ready.' Wanting to make absolutely sure they turned up, he added, 'If you're late, I'll consider it a forfeit because you're too chicken to face me.'

'All right,' Gaz said. 'You're on.'

'Good. See you tomorrow, *gentlemen*,' Josh said, making it very clear he didn't think there was anything gentlemanly about them, and left the café.

Sophie's face still looked pinched when he joined her. 'They didn't give you any trouble, did they?'

He'd taken too long about it. Of course she would've looked through the window and seen him talking to them. 'It's fine,' he said. The championship course wasn't easy. He'd skied it several times before and knew that some of the turns were seriously tight. If it was icy... He'd just have to hope his knee held up to the strain, or he might have made things worse for Sophie rather than better.

Once he'd walked her back to the chalet, he went to see Giovanni.

'Josh! What can I do for you?'

'I need a favour, Gio,' Josh said. 'Quite a big one. I need an escort for a party of ten to the championship course, for a seven a.m. start tomorrow—and I need you to be there.'

Giovanni raised his eyebrows. 'Why?'

Josh explained as succinctly as he could.

Giovanni winced. 'Sophie told me her guests were difficult, but she said she was dealing with them. Perhaps I should put her and Kitty in a different chalet and give this lot a male chef and a butler for the rest of the week.'

Josh shook his head. 'Then she'll guess I've said something to you as well. I think she needs to feel that she's handling this.'

'If she finds out what you've done,' Giovanni warned, 'it's going to blow up in your face.'

'She won't,' Josh said, 'because they're not going to admit they've lost the race, and particularly to losing all that money. But hopefully it will be enough of a shock for them to listen to what I say to them afterwards, and they'll learn to treat people better in future.'

'What about your knee?' Giovanni asked. 'Will it stand up to the run? Have you talked to your consultant about this—or to Angelo?'

Josh smiled. 'It'll be fine.'

'In other words, you haven't spoken to either of them.' Giovanni folded his arms and gave Josh a hard stare.

'What they don't know can't hurt them.'

Giovanni compressed his mouth. 'Angelo's my favourite brother.'

'And I've practically been your youngest brother for the last decade or so, since I started working with Angelo,' Josh said.

'Of course you count as family. That's why we put up with you.' Giovanni rolled his eyes. 'As the nearest you have to a big brother, I can tell you I'm not happy about this, Josh. At all.'

'The situation needs sorting,' Josh said, 'and sometimes you need an unorthodox solution to solve a problem effectively.'

Giovanni sighed. 'This is just a downhill race, right, not freestyle? And absolutely no moguls or aerials?'

'Promise,' Josh said. 'I'm not completely reckless. I know what the consultant said and

I want to be able to walk unaided in twenty years' time.'

'OK. I would've come with you even if you hadn't asked. I'll drive you to the slope myself.' Giovanni frowned. 'Have you secured access to the course?'

'No, but I don't think it'll be a problem,' Josh said with a smile.

'If it is, let me know and I'll get Babbo involved.'

Vincenzo Rendini—Giovanni and Angelo's father, and the owner of the resort—was a former world champion skier himself. 'If you tell your dad, he'll suggest taking my place,' Josh said. 'And then your mum would kill me. You and your dad, I'm not scared of. Your mum, on the other hand…'

'Everyone's scared of Mamma.' Giovanni grinned. 'Perhaps we should introduce her to Sophie's guests instead. She'd sort them out within seconds.'

'But then Sophie would definitely know I've interfered. This way, she won't.' Josh clapped his friend's shoulder. 'Thanks, Gio. I really appreciate this.'

'You're insane,' Giovanni grumbled, but he was smiling.

# CHAPTER FOUR

SOPHIE WAS DREADING the return of their guests. No doubt there would be more comments about her curves—or lack of them—and smutty suggestions. Maybe they'd all be bearable on their own, but together they were a pack who egged each other on. They'd made her feel so horrible in the café that she'd left instead of spending time with Josh.

Not that she should be thinking about Josh in that way. She wasn't looking for another relationship. Not after Blake. They might become friends, possibly, but that was the outer limit of any possible relationship between them. And she'd be back in England again in a couple of months, so what was the point of even starting something? Besides, for all she knew, Josh could be committed elsewhere. He'd held her hand today, admittedly; but that just confused things. Had he actually wanted to hold her hand, or had it just been a gesture of kindness and sympathy?

When they returned, her guests treated her as if she was invisible. Which suited her just fine. She was clearing up after dinner, when Pete, one of the quieter and nicer ones in the group, came into the kitchen. 'We're going skiing really early tomorrow. Can we have an early breakfast?'

'How early?' she asked.

'We're being picked up from here at quarter-past six.'

If they'd been like her last guests, Sophie would've offered to get up early to make them bacon sandwiches—and she would've made them granola bars to take with them. But with this lot she was playing strictly by the rules.

'I can leave you a cold spread,' she said. 'Cereals, rolls and fruit. You'll have to make your own coffee.'

'Cheers.'

While she was setting the table for breakfast, she could hear Gaz saying something about a bet and how he was going to win. She tuned him out and wrote a quick note to advise her guests that there was a platter of cheese and cold meat in the fridge, along with yoghurt and juice. Then she headed to her room for a shower and an early night with a good book.

* * *

At the championship course, the next morning, Josh had checked everything with the staff and was sitting in the car with Giovanni and Vincenzo, waiting for Gaz and his friends to turn up.

'It's a crazy idea,' Vincenzo said. 'But it's an elegant solution. Are you sure your knee will hold up?'

'No,' Josh admitted, 'so this could go spectacularly wrong.'

'It won't.' Vincenzo looked at him. 'So, Sophie's special.'

*Yes.* But Josh wasn't quite prepared to admit this. 'She's a nice woman and I don't like bullies.'

'She's special,' Vincenzo repeated, 'or you wouldn't take a risk like this.'

Oh, help. Josh had forgotten how perceptive Giovanni's father was. 'I barely know her. We only met a few days ago.'

'So?' Vincenzo shrugged. 'I knew the very second I met Maria that she was the one for me.'

Josh thought back to his very first meeting with Sophie. He'd been aghast at her cluelessness. But then he'd met her for her first ski lesson. The second he'd seen her blue eyes properly…

No, no and absolutely no. He wasn't looking for a relationship. He was still tending his wounds from the fallout of what had happened with Annabel, literally as well as figuratively. He didn't *think* Sophie was anything like his ex—she would never have given him such a shocking ultimatum in the first place, let alone dropped a bombshell with such vicious timing—but could he trust his judgement any more?

He didn't want to think about that right now. Thinking instead of focusing on the slope was what had wrecked his life. If he hadn't been distracted, he wouldn't have fallen and damaged his knee to the point where he'd had to give up the career he'd loved so much.

'It's not the case with me and Sophie,' he said.

'Hmm,' was Vincenzo's only comment.

A couple of minutes later, the minibus turned up and Gaz and his friends came to meet them.

Josh introduced them swiftly. 'This is Giovanni Rendini, the resort manager, and Vincenzo Rendini, who owns the resort.'

'You've got friends in high places, then,' Gaz said, raising an eyebrow.

'I have friends in a lot of places.' Josh shrugged. 'I learned long ago that you should treat people properly on your way up. It doesn't matter what level they are: treat people with kindness and respect and they'll do the same for you.' Even though what he was planning wasn't particularly kind, he could still be pleasant about it.

Gaz looked at his friends and scoffed.

'The staff here have come in early to sort out the lifts and the timers for us,' Josh said. 'Do you want a practice run, first?'

Gaz shook his head. 'Bring it on.'

Josh really hoped he'd never been as arrogant as that. 'As you wish. But watch the middle section of the course. It's tricky and the turns are tighter than you'd expect on a normal downhill course.'

'Listen to him.' Gaz addressed his friends and waved a dismissive hand at Josh. 'Anyone would think he's a world champion who's skied this a million times.'

Josh forbore to mention that the last time he'd skied here, he'd come away with two gold medals—for downhill as well as freestyle—and a world championship. They were clearly recreational skiers rather than the sort who followed the sport, because they hadn't recognised him. 'Did you bring energy drinks and bars?' he asked.

'Whatevs.' Gaz rolled his eyes.

'And Josh is right about the course,' Vincenzo added. 'Watch the turns.'

'So you're an expert, are you, old man?' Gaz demanded.

'If by "expert" you mean world champion three times running, then, yes, that would be my dad,' Giovanni said. 'Look him up. Vincenzo Rendini.'

Josh gave the tiniest shake of his head to warn his friend not to blurt out who *he* was, and Giovanni gave an equally tiny nod of acknowledgement.

'World champion?' Gaz suddenly looked a bit less sure of himself.

Good. About time, Josh thought. 'Want to toss for who's going first?' he asked. 'I'm happy to go last.'

'I'll go first,' Gaz said.

His time was good for an amateur; the next couple from the group did well, too. Then Gaz was back from the chairlift. 'Ha. *Knew* I'd be top,' he crowed, pointing at the board. The next member of the group knocked Gaz off the top spot, leaving Josh feeling pleased.

And finally it was Josh's turn.

He thought of Sophie. Hopefully what he was about to do would make life better for her. For her sake, he needed to get this right.

He stood at the top of the slope and looked

down. Today was the first time he'd skied here since his accident; but at least the accident hadn't been on this course, so he didn't have memories to flood into his mind and put him off.

But this was a championship course. He hadn't skied anything as difficult as this in the past year, because he knew his knee wouldn't stand up to it. Was he just about to make the second-biggest mistake of his life?

'You've got this,' Vincenzo said, standing beside him. 'Focus. Remember to look ahead. And their timings are way off what you can do, even without practice. You don't need to take any risks. Just enjoy the run and do what you know you do best.'

'Yeah. Thanks, Vincenzo.'

Josh took a deep breath. He closed his eyes for a moment; and then he was away, his body tucked in tightly for the aerodynamics. As he hurtled down the slope, he felt the adrenalin flood his body, and then the sheer joy of skiing and being at one with the mountain. He made a sharp turn, leaning forward. Another turn. And he was smiling, really smiling, as he looked ahead on the course, judging his speed and his angles.

This was what he was made for.

This was what he'd missed for the last year.

*This.*

He skied over the finish line, feeling at peace with the world, and took the chairlift back up to the top. As soon as he glanced at the board, he saw that he'd skied much, much more slowly than the last time he'd been on this course. But it was still twenty seconds faster than Gaz.

Guilt pricked his conscience. It was massively unfair for a professional to take on amateurs like this. What he'd just done made him almost as bad as Gaz. Maybe he shouldn't take the money; even though it was for charity, it felt wrong. The fact he'd beaten them so soundly should be enough to make his point and keep them from bullying Sophie—or anyone else—in future.

Gaz was waiting for him with narrowed eyes. 'How the hell did you *do* that?'

Josh shrugged. 'It's all in the turns.'

'Well, you've won.' Gaz looked furious.

'I'm not going to make you pay a penny,' Josh said. 'I simply wanted to make a point. The most important part of the terms of our bet was that you'll treat Sophie and Kitty with respect, and I'll hold you to that.'

Gaz shook his head. 'I'll pay the money we agreed. Nobody says I don't pay my bets.'

'That isn't what I'm saying,' Josh said

tiredly. 'And it wasn't the point of this. Just maybe you can start to think before you act. Treat people decently. Because you never know who they are or what they're going through. Kindness costs nothing and it makes the world a lot better.'

'He's got a point,' Pete, one of the quieter members of the group, said.

'I guess.' Gaz's voice was tight with resentment.

'You're a ski instructor, right? Can we book a coaching session with you?' Pete asked.

Josh shook his head. 'Sorry. I'm fully booked for the next month.'

'Can we at least buy you breakfast?' Pete asked. 'Because—I mean, even though we all lost, skiing here was *amazing*. And we'll pay for the booking fees.'

'No cost. I called in a favour to get the slot,' Josh said.

'The people who opened up, who did the ski lift and the timer—the least we can do is pay them for their time,' Pete said.

'You're right, Pete,' one of the others agreed. 'And we owe you an apology.'

'No, you owe Sophie and Kitty an apology,' Josh corrected.

Pete nodded. 'You're right. We'll apologise.' He looked at Gaz.

Gaz's expression was murderous, but eventually he nodded. 'Yeah.'

Maybe he could make a token gesture so their apology wouldn't stick in their throat and they'd be more encouraged to be nice to Sophie, Josh thought. 'It's not every day you get to ski at a run like this. Why don't we do it again—this time *without* the timers, so we can focus on enjoying the run?'

'Great idea,' Pete said.

Some of the others had dropped the aggressiveness of their stance, too, Josh noticed. Maybe they'd start standing up to their leader and it would make the rest of the week bearable for Sophie. He hoped. 'Let's go.'

Sophie had just finished making the lemon drizzle cake and scones when the chalet door opened and she heard their guests coming in.

Oh, no.

She'd been hoping they'd be out all day on the slopes, as they had yesterday. Or maybe she could sneak out the back way, so they wouldn't notice her...

Too late.

Gaz walked into the kitchen, carrying a box of chocolates. 'These are for you and Kitty.'

'For us?' She felt her eyes widen. 'Why?'

'To say sorry.' He stopped, clearly waiting for her to fill in the rest. *For being obnoxious.*

She didn't have a clue what to say. It was so out of character, given the entitled and boorish way they'd behaved since their arrival. From Pete, the quietest one, she might've understood it. But from Gaz—'gas-bag', as she and Kitty had dubbed him—it didn't ring true. 'Why?' she asked again.

'Let's just say your boyfriend showed us the error of our ways.'

'Boyfriend?'

'The skiing coach. The one you were holding hands in the café with yesterday,' Gaz clarified.

Definitely Josh. Who was definitely not her boyfriend. What had he done?

'We'll, um, watch what we say in future,' Gaz said.

'Thank you,' Sophie said, feeling utterly clueless. Josh was going to have a lot of explaining to do at her ski lesson, this afternoon.

He was already at their meeting place when she arrived.

'Had a good morning?' she asked sweetly.

'Fine, thanks.' He smiled at her. 'You?'

'Preparing dinner for my guests. Who just paid me a visit, when I thought they'd be out skiing all day.'

'Uh-huh.'

'What did you do, Josh?'

He gave her an innocent look. 'I don't know what you mean.'

Oh, yes, he did. She narrowed her eyes at him. 'They apologised. And they bought chocolates for Kitty and me.' She raised her eyebrows at him. 'You told them you were my boyfriend.'

'Actually, I didn't. They assumed it and I didn't correct them.'

'Which is the same thing. It's still a lie.' And she'd had more than enough of lies. Blake had trashed her life with his lies. She'd been lucky to be able to save her staff's jobs and stave off bankruptcy. Dishonesty was a huge red flag for her. She'd started to like Josh, to trust him and the way he was helping her to face her fears. But had she been as hopeless and naive about him as she'd been about Blake? Was he another man like Blake, a habitual liar who treated others cavalierly, using a veneer of charm and saying what he thought people wanted to hear so he could get his own way, and not caring about the effects his actions had on others?

'Sophie, you were upset and I wanted to make things better.'

'By letting them think you're my boyfriend?

I'm not even looking to date anyone.' She glared at him. 'And I'm perfectly capable of managing my own problems, thank you very much.'

'They were giving you a hard time. I was trying to make them back off. And it worked.'

'It wasn't just talking, was it?' Because she'd already tried that, and her efforts had been in vain. 'They said you showed them the error of their ways. What did you do?'

He winced. 'I took them down a black run, this morning.'

'Which I assume is the really difficult sort of ski slope?'

'Yes.'

So *that* was why they'd gone out so early. And hadn't she heard them saying something about a bet? 'There's more to it than that, isn't there?'

He blew out a breath. 'OK. I challenged them to a race. If I won, they had to apologise to you and behave better in future.'

She gasped. 'Do you have any idea how insulting that is?'

'It wasn't meant to be insulting.'

'You made me part of a bet!'

'I wanted to get through to them, and it seemed as if the only way to make them think twice about what they were doing was to challenge them.'

'To a *race*.' She shook her head with annoyance. 'Like a teenage boy boasting with his first car.'

'That wasn't the intention. I was honestly trying to help.'

'I didn't ask for your help,' she pointed out quietly.

'OK. I interfered. I apologise.'

But that wasn't what was really getting to her. It was the fact he hadn't been honest. 'How did you even know they could all ski well enough? How did you know they weren't just boasting to make themselves sound good, when they were really just as much of a novice as me?'

'They told me their times skiing Val di Lungo. That's something you can't fake. I knew from that they'd be able to cope with the run.'

'What if one of them had fallen and hurt himself?'

He flinched, suddenly looking haunted. 'Fortunately, they didn't.'

'You *hustled* them, Josh.'

'They deserved it.'

Part of her had to agree. 'Even so, it wasn't your place to step in. I wasn't looking for a knight on a white charger. Or a hero on skis.'

'I got it wrong,' Josh said. 'I won't do it again.'

'Too right, you won't.'

He coughed. 'It's possibly not a good idea to go skiing when you're angry. I don't want you to lose focus and fall.'

'What I want to do right now,' she said, 'is to smack you round the head with my skis.'

'I'm sorry, Sophie. I really did just want to help, but in future I'll trust your judgement and your client management skills.'

'Thank you.'

'So can we start today again? Plan for this afternoon: ski lesson, plus hot chocolate and strudel?'

Part of her wanted to say yes; but part of her was wary of getting too close. 'I'm still cross that you let them think you're my boyfriend.' Another lie, and it really grated. If Josh had asked her out before this had happened, she would've been tempted to say yes. More than tempted. But now he'd shown that lies came easily to him. Even though his intentions had been good, he'd still not been honest: and that wasn't something Sophie could overlook.

'How about,' Josh said, 'we drop the "boy" and I'm just your friend?'

Drop the 'boy'? There was nothing boyish about Josh, except perhaps for his smile. He was all man. Even as she thought it, she found it suddenly hard to breathe. 'You're my skiing teacher,' she said, more to remind herself than to tell him.

'Which puts me nicely in my place,' he said. 'But it doesn't change my offer of friendship. I like you, Sophie. Particularly because you're honest.'

'Which you weren't. You should have told them you're a ski coach and given them, I don't know, some kind of time advantage.'

'Then I wouldn't have been able to take them down a peg or two,' he pointed out.

'And who's going to take *you* down a peg or two?' she retorted.

He grinned. 'Are you offering?'

Part of her enjoyed the flirting; but his lack of honesty still worried her.

When she didn't reply, he looked serious again. 'I also realise now I'm in the wrong. But I'd like to make it up to you. And I'd like to be friends with you, Sophie.'

'Friends.'

'As you said, I know the area. You're new here. Maybe on your days off—or in the middle-of-day bit, when you're not looking after your guests and you have some free time—I could show you a few places.'

'You're my skiing teacher,' she said again,

needing to put that little bit of distance between them.

'So we'll operate with two sets of rules,' he said. 'When I'm teaching you, we'll have a professional relationship only. And when I'm not, we'll be friends.'

Sophie thought about it.

Friends with Josh Cavendish.

Defining their relationship would make him safe. She wouldn't be tempted to act on the attraction she felt towards him—and, more importantly, she wouldn't make the same mistakes she'd made with Blake. She wouldn't fall for someone who had such a cavalier disregard for the truth—though, to be fair, Josh had seemed penitent once she'd pointed out what damage his lies could've done.

'All right,' she said. 'We'll be friends.'

'Good.'

She ignored the fact that his smile made her heart give a funny little flip.

Even though she was still a bit cross with him, she enjoyed every second on the slopes—and she enjoyed going to the café with him afterwards, when he bought them both hot chocolate and strudel. If Gaz and his crew came in today, it would be very different; she could stay relaxed and enjoy her cake.

'So, tomorrow,' Josh said, 'would you like

to go to the Christmas market? It's in the next valley along and it's very pretty. If we switch your lesson to the morning, we could have lunch there.'

He'd offered her friendship; weirdly, this felt more as if they were planning a date.

She damped down the little flutter of adrenalin. It *wasn't* a date. And Blake had taught her that she was a rubbish judge of men. Friendship was the sensible option. 'Don't you have other students?'

'I do, but none of them are booked in for tomorrow,' he said.

'All right. A trip to the Christmas market sounds really nice. Provided I buy you lunch,' she said.

'OK. We'll drop your skis back at my place after the lesson,' he said, 'and then I'll make sure we've collected them and you're back at your chalet before afternoon tea.'

'Sounds like a good plan,' she said with a smile.

His answering smile made her heart feel as if it had done an acrobatic—and anatomically impossible—ski jump…

## CHAPTER FIVE

THE CHALET GUESTS weren't obnoxious that evening and, when Sophie served the cheeseboard with her home-made rosemary crackers and ran them through the local specialty cheeses, they actually asked her and Kitty to join them for a glass of wine and to share the cheese.

'Whatever your Josh said to them, it worked,' Kitty said to Sophie in the kitchen afterwards.

'He's not *my* Josh,' Sophie said with a smile. And she didn't have the heart to disillusion the younger woman by telling her about the downhill ski race and how Josh had hustled them.

'A guy only does something like that if he likes you,' Kitty said. 'And I mean *like* like.'

'We're friends,' Sophie said.

'Hmm,' Kitty said.

Sophie decided not to mention the trip to the Christmas market, not wanting Kitty to misinterpret it. But she was awake ridiculously early, the next morning, full of anticipation. Only because she'd be seeing more of the area, she tried to convince herself. Though, if she let herself face the truth, it was actually because she'd be spending more time with Josh.

She enjoyed her skiing lesson. 'I think I'm starting to get my ski legs, now,' she told Josh as they headed back to his chalet.

'Good. We'll get you on a blue run, next week,' he said.

'One of the ones where I have to take a chairlift to get to the top?' The idea was daunting. And what if she fell off the chairlift? At least the button lift meant she was close to the ground…

Maybe her fear had shown in her voice, because Josh said, 'Remember how you felt, the very first time you were on the nursery slope? But you managed that. When you went up to the green slope, that felt scary—but look how much you enjoyed it today. The first time you do a blue run, you'll worry because it's the unknown. But then you'll get to the bottom, realise you're OK, and then you'll be ready to do it all over again,' he told her. 'Trust me. I wouldn't let you do it if you weren't able to. I hate it when experienced skiers drag their novice friends into something they're not ready to cope with and scare them. I'd never do that to anyone.'

She could see the sincerity on his face. But, even so, could she take the risk of really trusting him with herself? What was the saying? Fool me once, shame on you; fool me twice, shame on me. Blake had fooled her. What if Josh turned out to be another Blake?

Or maybe she was being unfair. Paranoid. Apart from Blake, most people lived up to her theory that people were nice if you gave them the chance to be. Was she going to let Blake take her ability to trust from her, as well?

'I guess. Sorry.' She took a deep breath. 'Just being ridiculous.'

'Actually,' he said, 'I admire you. You were clearly terrified of the idea of skiing, but you've made yourself do it.'

To prove to herself that she could. To get her confidence and self-esteem back. It was that, or find herself inhabiting a smaller and smaller comfort zone every day. 'I'm trying,' she said.

When they got to his chalet, Sophie was surprised by how small it seemed. Did he live alone or did he share his space with another instructor? Though it felt rude to ask. He didn't offer to show her round; he simply propped her skis and poles in the rack next to his in the hallway.

'Christmas market, here we come,' he said with a smile, and drove her to the next valley.

'I'm not sure I'd be brave enough to drive, out here,' she said. 'It's not just because it means driving on the other side of the road. There's the snow piled up on the side, the fact the roads are so steep and with hairpin bends, and that sheer drop on one side.'

'You'd be surprised how quickly you get used to it,' Josh said. 'And they're used to dealing with snow here. It's not like England, where a couple of centimetres of snow makes everything grind to a halt.'

Maybe driving the roads here was a challenge she'd set herself before she went back to England. Once she'd conquered a blue ski run.

She caught her breath as they skirted the mountain and she saw the view of the valleys. 'That's amazing,' she said. 'I don't think I've ever seen anything so beautiful.'

'It's pretty spectacular,' he said. 'With any luck we'll catch the sunset on the way back to Pendio di Cristallo; the mountains and the snow turn pink.'

'That sounds wonderful,' she said. 'It was definitely a good idea to come here.'

'The mountains are a good place to think,' he said.

Once he'd parked, they walked together

through the streets. Evergreen wreaths were strung across the cobbled streets between the houses and the shops, twinkling with brilliant white lights; some of the streets to the side had strings of icicle lights rather than the evergreen swags, with white wicker hearts suspended every so often along the string.

'This is so pretty,' she said. 'I love the Christmas lights in London, but our snow turns to grey slush. Here—it's just what I imagined Christmas would be like in the Alps. It looks like a real-life winter wonderland.'

Just as she said it, she could feel her feet going from beneath her. Oh, no. She was going to make a fool of herself by falling over—and the snow wasn't as deep here as it was on the piste. This was going to hurt…

'Hey.' Josh caught her before she fell, and drew her close against him, anchoring her.

And it felt as if all her breath had suddenly left her lungs.

Josh had supported her before, on the slopes. But that was different. That was him acting as her skiing instructor. This felt like something else. Something that made her heart beat faster, her breathing shallow, and what felt like pure adrenalin fizz through her veins.

At the same time as thrilling her, it worried her.

Josh had suggested being friends. But what she was feeling right now was nothing like friendship. It was sheer, heady attraction. Not just physical; she liked him, too. Instinctively. He felt like the sort of man you could rely on.

Then again, hadn't she made that mistake with Blake? A mistake that had cost her her business, her self-respect and her confidence. She knew she'd never get her money back, but she wanted the rest of it back.

'OK?' he asked.

'Yes,' she fibbed. 'Sorry. It's a bit slippery underfoot.'

He didn't release her; instead, he kept her arm tucked through his. 'Hang on to me. If you feel your feet sliding, hang on more tightly.'

What if she pulled him over?

Either it was written all over her face or she'd said it aloud, because he reassured her, 'You won't pull me over.'

And oh, that smile.

It actually took her breath away.

She needed a large dose of common sense. Fast. To stop herself thinking how close he was, how easy it would be to reach up and touch her mouth to his...

Please don't let any of this show in her expression.

And she was really glad of her oversized

sunglasses. Hopefully they'd go a long way to hiding her thoughts. The last thing she wanted was for Josh to realise how attracted to him she was. He'd made it very clear that this was friendship only.

'Thank you,' she just about managed to mumble, and walked with him into the village; every fibre of her being was aware of his closeness. His strength.

Josh had noticed that, even though Sophie worried about things, she still just got on with it and did it—like the skiing. It had clearly been daunting for her, but she'd pushed herself out of her comfort zone. He liked that.

He liked *her*.

She was really easy to be with. And the way she saw things, the way she found delight in things he'd taken for granted, made him feel different. Alive. Connected.

He'd always liked the Christmas season in the Dolomites, but he'd been so jaded since his accident that last year had been a blur. This year, he was seeing things through Sophie's eyes. Instead of it being the commercial Christmas crush, with everything all lumped together, everything seemed bright and sparkly, with tiny details jumping out at him. It was all fresh and new, as if he was seeing it for the very first time.

'Oh, wow, just look at this!' she said as they rounded the corner into the town's main square, where the Christmas market was being held. The area was packed with wooden stalls, all festooned with strings of fairy lights.

'Even in the middle of the day, it's stunning. After dark, this place must really be a winter wonderland,' she said.

There were Christmas trees scattered about the market, and there was a particularly large one in the centre of the square, decorated with lights and huge red baubles. But the thing that seemed to draw Sophie most was the snow on the branches.

'Imagine that. Christmas trees decorated by nature with real snow.' Her face was full of delight. 'I've never seen anything so gorgeous. I mean, the wreaths at the Christmas markets and shops in London are pretty—but here it's so much more natural.'

Next to the enormous Christmas tree was a large reindeer made of lights with a red bauble on its nose. 'Do you mind if we stop so I can take a picture of this?' she asked. 'My best friend would love it.'

'Better than that, why don't I take a picture of you next to the reindeer?' he suggested.

'Thank you.' She beamed and handed him her phone.

He took the snap, enjoying her enthusiasm. Without her, he probably wouldn't have even bothered visiting the Christmas market. With her, he was seeing a lot more than he would usually notice. Shapes and colours and light: things that had always merged into the background for him. Through Sophie's eyes, they weren't just commonplace, everyday things. She noticed them, enjoyed them to the full, and drew them to his attention so he could enjoy them, too.

'This is wonderful,' she said. 'Look, there's a nativity scene over there.' They went over to take a closer look, and she oohed and aahed over the delicate work.

'You get that in most Italian towns,' he said. 'And there will be something like this in the windows of most of the shops. It's a tradition over here.'

'It's so perfect. The snow-globes, and the wooden ornaments, the gingerbread and the candles. And those wreaths over there, made from dried oranges and cinnamon sticks: they smell of Christmas, too.' She sniffed. 'Freshly baked cookies, roasted chestnuts…this feels like Christmas. Everything. The sights, the smells, the sounds…'

All the senses. The taste of Christmas foods and spiced hot chocolate. The soft feel of the Christmas textiles. The cool crispness of the air. Put together, they magnified the experience for him, too. Instead of being just another tourist attraction, the market felt *special*.

A guitarist, a singer, a keyboard-player and a drummer were set up in one part of the square, singing carols and Christmas pop songs in a variety of languages.

'Do you mind if I buy some Christmas presents?' she asked.

'Sure. I'll carry your bags for you,' he offered.

'Thanks.' She dawdled over the delicate lacy shawls, and the beautifully knitted scarves, hats and gloves.

The food stalls attracted her, too, particularly the one with all the Christmas cookies.

'I can't decide which ones to try,' she said. 'Maybe the glazed ones with rainbow sprinkles?'

'Those ones are usually flavoured with anise,' he said, 'which people either love or hate.'

'True. And look at those ones with layers: orange, white and chocolate. I need to get some of those, too.' She ended up buying a selection of cookies.

'You're seriously going to eat all these?' he asked.

She laughed. 'No, but I do want to try a bit of everything and see which ones I'd like to make or do my own twist on for afternoon tea for our guests. I know I could do traditional English mince pies, or American sugar and cinnamon cookies, but I want to do something local. You're probably right about anise not being the most guest-friendly choice, but I want to see what the texture's like. I could maybe do a vanilla version. Or cinnamon.'

'Let me take the bag for you,' he said, 'so you've got your hands free.'

'Thanks. That's lovely of you.' She rewarded him with a smile that made his heart feel as if it had done a backflip.

He tried to remind himself of the lines they'd drawn, but her enthusiasm was infectious and irresistible. And it was so good to *feel* something again, instead of being in an insulated box.

She was entranced by the stall selling panettone, and another with all kinds of flavoured oils, and one with various traditional sauces and jams.

And then they came to the stall selling *zelten*.

'What's this?' she asked, pointing to the

words on the board. 'Obviously it's some kind of cake. But my Italian's too basic to translate.'

'I don't know what *zelten* is, either,' he admitted. 'Though it sounds German; in this part of the Dolomites we're on the border with Austria, so the people here speak German as well as Italian. Some speak Ladin, which is the original language of this area.'

'Latin?' she asked.

'Ladin,' he corrected with a smile. 'Some of the resort staff speak it, so the Rendinis all speak it, as well as Italian, German, English and French. They taught me a little; you'd say *bun dé* instead of *buon giorno* or *Guten Morgen.*'

She looked at him with her head tipped slightly to one side. 'How many languages do you speak, Josh?'

'Four,' he said, 'simply because of my job. I did French and German at school, but I picked up Italian as I went along, and a smattering of a few others. It's nice to speak to people in their own language, even if I only know a few words; it puts them at ease.'

'In that case,' she said, 'would you mind acting as a translator for me, please, and ask the stall-keeper what *zelten* is for me?'

'Sure.' Josh spoke in rapid Italian, but the stall-keeper replied in English.

'It's a traditional sweet bread, made with yeast and dried fruits soaked in rum or brandy.'

'So a bit like a boozy English hot cross bun,' she said thoughtfully.

Josh stood by as she and the stall-keeper traded recipes and suggestions. Although the foodie talk mostly went over his head, he was fascinated by Sophie. By her intense focus and concentration, the way she'd switched so seamlessly from tourist to professional.

What would it be like if she focused on him? Touching, tasting, learning what made him groan with pleasure...

He shook himself.

No.

He was absolutely not going to have a fling with Sophie Harris, whatever his body might be urging him to do. This was about...

Actually, he didn't know what it was about. At all.

But it had been so long since he'd wanted to let anyone else into his life, he was beginning to think that he should go with his feelings. Sophie had talked about challenging herself, about pushing past her boundaries to get her confidence back. Maybe he needed to do the same.

Could he take a risk with her?

Annabel had left him feeling used. Miserable. And he'd realised that his ex had seen him as a way of providing the lifestyle she wanted. For her, he'd been a celebrity boyfriend—a trophy boyfriend, even—so she'd be invited to the right parties: the son of a billionaire, to whom money was no object. She hadn't seen him for himself, or wanted him for himself.

That realisation had hurt even more than the physical pain of his damaged knee. And, when it was clear that his future was going to be very different from the way things had been before the accident, Annabel had been quick to dump him—and to get her story out there first. By the time he'd realised what was happening, any denials would've been too little and too late.

So he'd melted quietly into the background, knowing that the best way to kill a story was to deny it oxygen. Yes, it hurt that people thought he'd be the kind of heartless bastard who'd dump his fiancée after a miscarriage; but sticking Annabel with a defamation suit would've made the situation even worse. People would've murmured about him trying to cover up the truth, buying his way out of a situation, and acting like a bully. None of which was true.

He was trying not to dwell on it. Trying not to let the hurt shape who he was. And he was beginning to think that maybe Sophie was the one who could help him move on from the past, because with her he felt different. With her, he could see the joy again. And maybe he could help her move on from the guy who'd let her down, too.

Sophie was talking rapidly into her phone, now; he tuned back in and realised that she was dictating a recipe from the stall-keeper, who was adding little bits here and there when she stopped, clearly enjoying sharing. She was lit up from the inside, shining just as brightly as the fairy lights draped over all the little stalls.

And she bought every single variation the shopkeeper was selling. 'This will be afternoon tea for my guests tomorrow,' she said. 'But Ruggiero's given me a recipe and some of his favourite tweaks, so I'm going to try making them myself as well.'

Josh smiled. 'I know you're a chef, but you're *such* a foodie.'

'Busted,' she said with a grin. 'I love my job. I love making food for people. And I want to extend my repertoire a bit while I'm here.' She looked at him. 'It's my day off tomorrow, so I'm thinking about trialling some recipes. If you're free, do you fancy being my guinea pig?' Then she added swiftly, 'As a friend.'

Of course. A stark reminder of the boundary he'd set and was starting to wish he hadn't.

'Your day off, and you're spending it cooking?' he asked.

'I love what I do,' she said. 'For me it isn't just my job.'

He knew how that felt—or how it had used to feel. It was something he missed dreadfully. Teaching novices had its own reward, but it wasn't the same as competing. He needed more.

'Your day off,' he said again. 'So does that mean you're free in the evening as well?'

'Yes.'

He looked at her. 'OK, how about tomorrow I'm your guinea pig, I do the washing up, and then I take you out to dinner?'

Her blue eyes looked huge. 'As friends?' she checked.

No. As a date. The idea made him feel hot all over, anticipation and excitement bursting through his veins, but the wariness in her expression meant he needed to hold back. For now. He'd spend tomorrow trying to get her to see him as something else. 'As friends,' he confirmed.

'That'd be nice,' she said. 'Thank you.'

They wandered through the market, and she

insisted on buying them lunch at one of the food stalls.

'Porchetta paninis are good and they're traditional here around Christmastime,' he said. 'Pork, stuffed with garlic and herbs, then slow-roasted.'

'Gorgeous,' she said after her first taste. 'Fennel, sage and rosemary.'

'It amazes me that you can work out what's in something so quickly,' he said.

'Practice,' she said simply. 'Just as I suppose you can look at a ski slope and know exactly what the snow's going to be like and how it'll affect the way you ski.'

'I guess,' he said.

'And I want to try these cookies,' she said when they'd finished their paninis, and nibbled a corner from one of the tri-coloured amaretto ones. 'Oh, now this is excellent. Try this.'

Before he realised what was happening, she was holding the cookie to his mouth in just the way that a lover would offer a taste.

His libido practically sat up and begged.

And he couldn't help watching her mouth. He noticed that her mouth parted slightly just as he opened his lips: almost as if she were offering a kiss.

He didn't have a clue what the cookie tasted

like, and mumbled something anodyne. All he could think about was how *she* might taste…

He just about stopped himself from wrapping his arms round her, drawing her close and kissing her properly. And to his relief she didn't seem to notice anything. 'Lovely,' he managed, putting on his brightest smile.

'I'm definitely going to find a recipe for these,' she said. 'Oh—and I want to stop here.'

It was a stall selling filigree cones that looked like stylised Christmas trees, decorated with various Christmassy shapes; underneath the cone, there was space for a tea-light, and the heat of the candle made the Christmas tree twirl round. 'I love this sort of thing,' she said. 'So pretty and Christmassy.' She chose a reindeer one, which the stall-holder wrapped for her.

Normally, Josh would barely have even noticed the stall; but now he could see the romance of it. A room lit by candles, looking out on snow. And the fantasy blooming in his head had Sophie firmly at the centre.

This was dangerous.

He'd told himself he didn't want to get involved with anyone after Annabel. And yet Sophie drew him. The more time he spent with her, the more irresistible she became.

At another stall, where they sold musical boxes, he couldn't resist one that played the Sugar Plum Fairy's dance from *The Nutcracker*. 'For my niece,' he said. 'Willow's three. She's just started ballet lessons. She'll love this.'

And Sophie found a wooden crib mobile which played 'Twinkle Twinkle Little Star', with a moon and stars hanging down.

'This is so lovely! I want to get this for Hannah's baby—my godson-to-be,' she said. 'Her due date's the end of January, so I'll be back in England just in time for the birth.'

'You're not staying for the whole of the season?' he asked, surprised.

'I have a three-month contract,' she said.

He was still processing that she'd be leaving sooner than he'd expected. But it also meant she'd be here on December the twenty-fifth. And Sophie loved Christmas. Something didn't quite feel right. Why would she spend Christmas miles away from her friends and her family? 'Given that you clearly love Christmas, won't it be hard for you, not seeing your family for Christmas?' he asked.

'Actually, it'll be the fourth Christmas I haven't seen my family,' she said quietly. 'My parents were killed in a car crash.'

He sucked in a breath. 'I'm so sorry.'

She gave him a sad little smile of acknowledgement. 'Me, too. They were the best parents I could've asked for. I loved them so much. And I have to admit I was raging for a while, afterwards; the way I saw it, if someone had to die, why couldn't it have been someone mean and horrible, rather than them?'

'That's understandable,' he said. 'Tell me about them—if it doesn't hurt,' he added swiftly.

'Mum worked in a museum,' Sophie said. 'I loved all the stories she could tell me about the exhibits. The people who wore the clothes or cooked with the pots, and what their lives were like. She made it all come alive for me.' She smiled. 'She used to take me for a proper afternoon tea, too, with sandwiches and cakes and scones.'

Josh had a pretty good idea where Sophie's love of food had started. 'She sounds lovely.'

'She was.'

'What about your dad?'

'He worked in insurance. My gran died from a heart attack, so he used to fundraise for a heart charity in his spare time. Everything from doing a ten k run to organising a bake sale in the office. But, even though they both had busy jobs and busy lives, they always made time for me.'

Just as his parents had, too. He'd grown up knowing he was loved.

'What about your aunts and uncles? Grandparents?'

She shrugged. 'Mum and Dad were both only children, born late, so I don't really have any family: but I'm lucky that I have good friends. Hannah always invites me to spend Christmas with her family.'

*I don't really have any family.*

That momentary bleakness in her face.

And Josh was guiltily aware that he took his family for granted, all their love and support. He made a mental note to ring his parents and his sister that evening, and tell them he loved them. Because he *did* love them. And he realised now he didn't say it enough.

'I'm sorry,' he said again. 'I really didn't mean to bring up difficult memories for you.'

'It's fine.' She took his hand and squeezed it briefly. 'You weren't to know. And I have only happy memories of my parents. I'm so much luckier than many people.'

She was amazing. Most people in her position would still have dwelt on the unfairness of the loss. Yet Sophie seemed to take it in her stride.

It made him wonder just what had happened

to make her come here to Pendio di Cristallo, so far out of her comfort zone.

'Come on. I have more shopping to do,' she said lightly. 'I saw a knitted hat back there that would look so cute on Kitty.'

What could he do but go along with her?

On the way back to Pendio di Cristallo, he stopped at another village.

'I think you'll like this,' he said. 'Every year, there's a snow sculpture exhibition here. The artists get a three-metre cube of pressed snow; they're allowed to use water, a saw, a shovel, and their imagination.'

And he loved the fact that she was so entranced by the exhibition: everything from Santa in his sleigh with his reindeer, through to a Christmas tree, a dazzling shooting star, penguins, a rose, and a dramatic lion with a huge mane.

'I assume this one's a Greek—well, Roman— god?' she asked by a winged statue. 'Who's the Roman god of winter?'

'I have no idea.' He looked it up on his phone. 'Apparently Boreas was the purple-winged Greek god of the north wind and winter. His Roman name was Aquilo.'

'We've both learned something new today.' She paused before a beautifully detailed geometric snowflake. 'This is gorgeous. I'd love a small version of this in a snow-globe, or as a pendant.' She looked thoughtful. 'That'd be a good theme for an afternoon tea. Snowflakes. Coconut's the obvious thing there—some kind of mousse cake made into the shape of a ball. Or a feathery glaze on a pastry, or a tiny snow-flake decoration made from white chocolate.'

'I love the fact you see things in terms of food,' he said.

She shrugged. 'A dress designer would see things in terms of fabric, and someone who makes jewellery would see things in terms of shapes, stones and metal.'

'True. But I think I've seen the Christmas market through different eyes today, thanks to you.'

'When you're showing someone round,' she said, 'you notice things all over again instead of taking them for granted.'

'I guess,' he said. 'But thank you anyway.'

When they went back to his car, the sun was beginning to set.

'I know you told me, but I still can't believe the mountains really do turn pink at sunset,' she said. 'They look so beautiful.'

'And sunrise. It's called *enrosadira*,' he said. 'There's a very elaborate story about it being because the king of the dwarfs kid-napped a princess and hid her in his rose garden; although he had an invisible cloak to hide him, the movement of the roses as he walked through them gave his position away to the guards who were looking for her. When they captured him, he cursed the roses for giving him away, saying they'd never be seen again by day or night—but he forgot to mention sunset and sunrise, and that's when the roses appear on the mountain.'

'Interesting story. What happened to the princess?' she asked.

'No idea.' He looked at her. 'What would you want to happen?'

'Justice for the princess,' she said promptly. 'I'd want her to be queen in her own right so she could order the king to do something to make up for kidnapping her.'

'Something to make the world a better place.'

'Exactly,' she said. 'The problem with most fairy stories is that the heroine is always feeble and has to be rescued by the prince.'

'So you'd want the heroine to rescue the prince?'

'No. I'd want them to rescue each other,' she said.

Rescue each other? That had never occurred to him before, and he rather liked the idea.

Rescuing her from Gaz and his friends had

definitely made Josh feel better. But Sophie couldn't rescue him. Not unless she changed careers completely and invented a new system for fixing knees. And that wasn't going to happen.

'So what's the real reason why the mountains look pink at sunrise and sunset?' she asked.

'The composition of the stone—calcium carbonate and magnesium—and the way it reflects the light.' He glanced at her. 'Maybe on one of your days off, weather permitting, I can take you skiing at dawn. Or at least somewhere you'll be able to enjoy watching the sun rising over the slopes.'

'I'd like that,' she said.

They picked up her skis and poles from his chalet, and he dropped her back at her chalet.

'Thank you for today. I've really enjoyed it,' she said. She leaned forward to kiss his cheek, but somehow her lips ended up brushing the corner of his mouth.

In response, his mouth tingled and his skin suddenly felt too tight. Josh was shocked to realise just how much he wanted to kiss Sophie properly; she was the first woman he'd wanted to kiss since Annabel.

Though he also knew Sophie was wary; if he did what he really wanted to do, hauling her into his arms and kissing her until they were both dizzy, she'd run a mile. He was pretty sure that she felt some kind of attraction towards him, because her pupils were huge and there was a bloom of colour in her cheeks, but he knew he needed to take this more slowly.

Please let his voice sound normal so it didn't make her back away.

'You're very welcome,' he said, relieved to hear that he sounded normal. 'I'll see you for your ski lesson at half-past nine, and then I'll be your kitchen assistant, and then we'll go somewhere for dinner?'

The whole day with her.

If anyone had suggested to him even a month ago that he'd look forward to spending the whole day with someone, he would've laughed.

But he was really looking forward to it. Getting to know her better. Finding out what made her tick. And maybe, just maybe, she'd start to let him closer.

'See you at half-past nine,' she said. 'And thank you again. Today's been utterly lovely. A proper winter wonderland.'

'My pleasure,' he said.

And with any luck he could talk a certain restaurant into squeezing in a table for him: because he really, really wanted her to love having dinner out with him tomorrow night. To the point where she'd agree to change the terms of their friendship into something else.

# CHAPTER SIX

'GET THE LETTERS in the right order,' Sophie told herself in the mirror. 'S-K-I-S, not K-I-S-S.'

But she couldn't stop thinking about last night.

What she'd intended as a friendly kiss on the cheek to say thank you had turned into something else entirely. She'd ended up kissing the corner of Josh's mouth, instead. And, for a moment, she'd thought that he was going to kiss her back.

But he'd drawn very strict lines, not to be crossed. They'd agreed that while he was teaching her, he was her ski instructor; and when he wasn't, he would be her friend.

Nowhere had either of them said anything about being lovers.

He hadn't mentioned a partner. But surely he wouldn't have taken her out yesterday if he'd had one? Because there had been definite moments when it had felt like a date. When he'd told her to hang on to him. When she'd fed him the cookie. When he'd taken her to the snow sculpture exhibition. When he'd pointed out the pink mountain peaks and told her that crazy story about the roses.

*When she'd accidentally kissed the corner of his mouth in the car.*

She really was going to have to get a grip.

If she didn't stop mooning about, she'd fall over and make a complete idiot of herself during the lesson.

They were absolutely *not* dating. She wasn't looking for any kind of romance. Josh was a nice guy—but Blake had seemed like a nice guy, too. And he'd let her down so badly. She didn't want to put herself in that position ever again. Her time here was meant to be about picking herself up and dusting herself off and getting her confidence back.

Even so, there were butterflies in her stomach and her pulse kicked up several notches when she saw him. Her mouth was tingling, too. What would it be like to kiss Josh properly? In the snow, with huge fluffy flakes falling gently around them? The idea made a shiver of pure desire ripple down her spine.

To make things worse, Josh was strictly professional with her throughout the entire lesson. He could hardly make it any clearer that he wasn't interested in her as anything other than a student and a friend.

'So do you still need me for kitchen assistant duties this morning?' he asked.

'If you're still free,' she said carefully, wanting to ask if anyone would actually mind him spending time with her—but holding herself back, because if she asked that it would be obvious that she was starting to have feelings for him. If those feelings weren't reciprocated, it would make everything super-awkward.

'I'm looking forward to it.'

As her friend. Nothing more than friends, she reminded herself as they walked back to her chalet.

Josh had kept himself under iron control during the lesson and hadn't let himself think of Sophie as anything other than a pupil.

Now they were back off that professional footing, supposedly in the friend zone. But he couldn't stop thinking of that kiss and wondering what it would take to make Sophie truly kiss him.

She'd seen him in his element, on skis; he was finally going to see her in hers. And he couldn't wait.

Everything was laid out neatly in the kitchen.

'So what can I do?' he asked.

'Make coffee?' she suggested. 'I like mine with a dash of milk, no sugar.'

'Got it.' And everything was in an obvious place—for the guests, he presumed—so it was easy for him to make them both a coffee. 'So what are you making?'

'*Zelten* and three types of cookie. Kitty, bless her, nipped to the supermarket this morning for the bits I needed.'

'Right.' He watched her measure things into a mixing bowl. 'No scales?'

'I measure by volume,' she said. 'It's not quite as accurate, but it's easier for me.'

'Because of your dyslexia?' he guessed.

'I'm OK with numbers, unless it's a tricky font,' she said. 'It's really certain letters. And you don't want to see my handwriting.' She smiled. 'Which is why I dictate to my phone rather than write. There's less chance of me getting it wrong.'

'I noticed you doing that yesterday, when the guy at the *zelten* stall was talking to you.'

'It just makes life easier.' She smiled at him, and his pulse ratcheted up a notch. 'Thanks for the coffee.'

'Pleasure. What else can I do?'

'Sit and chat to me.'

'You can talk to someone while you're making something for the first time? You don't have to concentrate?'

She grinned. 'I have two X chromosomes. It means I can multi-task.'

'You sound like my sister,' he said. And funny how he suddenly missed Lauren. He had a feeling she'd like Sophie, whereas he knew Lauren had never really liked Annabel.

'Willow's mum?'

She'd remembered that? He was impressed. 'Yes. Her name's Lauren.'

'Is she younger or older than you?' Sophie asked.

'Two years older,' he said.

'It must've been nice, growing up with a sibling.' She looked slightly wistful. 'Mum couldn't have any more kids after me, and she always said she felt guilty about me being an only one. But I had Hannah.'

'Yeah, it was nice. We've always got on well and Lauren looked out for me when I was little.' Not just then: she still did. She'd flown straight out to his hospital bedside after the accident to support him. And, when the surgeon had broken the bad news a few months ago, she'd sat him down and told him that if he wanted to work at Cavendish Software, she'd do whatever it took to help him be happy there—including stepping aside so he could run the place. He'd hugged her and told her he loved her, and no way was he shoving her out of the way because in his view she was the best one to take over from their dad. As for him: he just needed to work out what he wanted to do with his time, now he couldn't do his dream job any more.

He watched Sophie's hands as she measured and mixed. It was the first time he'd seen her at work, and he noticed that she shone from the inside out. This wasn't Sophie the student, who was scared of the snow but was absolutely determined to push herself past her fear; this was Sophie the professional, in her element, confident and secure in her knowledge. Strong.

An anchor.

He'd felt adrift, this past year. Was Sophie the one who could be his anchor, help him find out who he was, now he couldn't be a champion skier any more? And could he, in turn, help her push past what was holding her back?

He remembered what she'd said about fairy tales when they'd watched the mountains turn pink in the sunset. *I'd want them to rescue each other.*

Could they do that?

He looked at her. She was glowing. He wanted to be the reason why she glowed like that, too. And he really, really wanted to kiss

her. To find out how it would feel if she held
him close, matched him kiss for kiss. To find
out how those beautiful, capable hands would
feel against his skin.

To distract himself, he asked, 'So how did
you end up working here?'

'I signed up with a temp agency,' she said.

'OK,' he said, 'but how does that fit in with
what you said before about someone letting
you down?'

She sighed. 'All right. You might as well
know the depths of my stupidity, though please
don't judge me for it. I despise myself enough.'
She rolled her eyes. 'When Mum and Dad
died, they left everything to me. The owners
of the restaurant where I was working as head
chef wanted to retire and sell the restaurant. I
loved the restaurant, and I got on well with all
the staff, so I decided to take the leap and buy
it. I tweaked things a little bit, so I could put
my own stamp on it, but I was still the head
chef, and my team had stability.' She beat the
cookie batter a little bit harder. 'I had been
thinking about expanding. It wasn't just em-
pire-building. At catering college, one of the
tutors noticed I was struggling with the paperwork side and she was the one who taught me
a few workarounds. She made a real difference
to me. Just like the owners of the restaurant

who took me on, going by my references rather than by my exam results. I wanted to pay it forward and give other people a chance, too.'

He liked that. And maybe she was the one who could help him with the idea he'd been mulling over, about helping people with disabilities learn to ski. She might have an interesting take on how it could work.

Though right now wasn't about him. It was about her.

'So you were going to open a second restaurant?'

She nodded. 'I'd actually found premises I liked. But it didn't happen, because everything went wrong.'

'Someone gazumped you? The building had problems you only found out about when you started renovations—it turned out to be a money pit?' he guessed.

'No,' she said. 'As I said, it was my own stupid fault.' She took a deep breath. 'I didn't date that much at college. Nothing serious. I was focused on getting through my exams and getting my career off the ground. And then, after my parents died, I kind of buried myself in the business. It's how I met Blake. He was the restaurant's admin manager. We started dating after I bought the restaurant. I loved him and I thought he loved me. When he asked me to marry him, I said yes.' She looked away. 'A few months later, he got me to change bank accounts, to one that would pay me interest on my balance.'

Josh had a nasty feeling he knew where this was going. She'd said she'd trusted someone who'd let her down. He'd thought that maybe the guy had been unfaithful, but it was starting to sound as if it was a different sort of cheating.

'Blake was engaged to me. He'd been the restaurant's admin manager for a couple of years. Of course I trusted him,' Sophie said. 'You don't agree to marry someone you don't trust, do you?'

'No.' But clearly her trust had been misplaced.

She shrugged. 'He was a signatory on the restaurant's account because he sorted out the payments to suppliers and the wages. I hadn't realised there was an overdraft facility on the account—at least, not the size of the overdraft.'

'He emptied your account?'

'The day before the wages came out—and the day before all the suppliers should've been paid.' She blew out a breath. 'And that's when I found out about the overdraft. Because he took that to the max, too.'

'But—if he emptied your account and ran

up an overdraft without your knowledge, that
was fraud. You can get the money back.'

'The money bounced around a bit and
ended up in an offshore account that can't be
touched. And Blake himself has left the country. The police traced him to Spain, but then
the trail went cold. Hannah thinks he went
somewhere that doesn't have an extradition
treaty with England, so I can kiss the money
goodbye.'

'That's terrible. There must be something
you can do.'

She shook her head. 'Believe me, if there
was a way to get the money back, Hannah
would know—she's a lawyer—or one of her
colleagues would know and be able to help.
The only way I could pay all the money I owed
and wipe out the overdraft was to sell the restaurant. And who's going to employ someone who made such a huge mistake? Who's
going to lend money to someone to start up
another business when their last one crashed
so spectacularly? The only job I could get after
I sold up was a temporary one. *This* one.' She
shrugged. 'So there you have it. I made a bad
judgement and I'm paying for it now.'

Just as he'd made a bad judgement: letting
his fight with Annabel distract his concentration. A few seconds had changed his entire

life. 'I know what it's like to make a really bad mistake,' he said. 'I'm sorry your ex cheated you like that.'

'So am I.'

'Are you sure you were liable with the bank, though? You didn't know about the extent of the overdraft, and you weren't the one who emptied the account.'

'I signed the contract, he was a signatory, and nobody coerced me,' she pointed out.

'Who read the contract over for you?' he asked. 'I know you said your best friend's a lawyer, so she would know about contracts, surely?'

She winced. 'At the time, I couldn't really ask her.'

Josh thought about it. Sophie had said the baby was due at the end of January. He made a rapid calculation. Maybe when this had all happened, Hannah was at the early stages of pregnancy and things were complicated. 'So who read the contract over for you?' he asked again, his voice soft.

'Blake.'

'And he read out what you wanted to hear instead of what was actually in the contract?'

She narrowed her eyes at him. 'I'm dyslexic, not incapable.'

'Of course you're not incapable.' He

frowned. 'But you said yourself that certain letters give you trouble. I'm assuming you didn't get an electronic copy of the thing that you could run through your text-to-speech reader yourself?'

'No.'

'Then in your shoes I would've wanted someone else to double-check the paperwork for me. Someone I trusted.'

'Which is precisely what I did,' she pointed out. 'I trusted Blake. He'd worked with me for a couple of years. We'd dated for a year and we'd been engaged for another. Why would he ask me to marry him and then scam me?'

'Because some people aren't very nice?' Josh suggested. 'Think about how many people think they've fallen in love with someone they've met on the internet, help them out with money—and then discover it was all a con.'

'When I look back, I remember he didn't push me to set a date for the wedding. I thought he was being kind, being flexible and not putting any pressure on me when I was trying to expand the business. But now I can see it wasn't that at all. He never had any intention of marrying me, did he?' She shook her head. 'I *hate* this. Before Blake, I used to think everyone was nice until proven otherwise. It was the way I was brought up. Give someone a chance to be their best, and they will—but it's been hard to believe that since Blake. And I hate that he's taken that away from me. That I can't trust people, the way I did in the past. I suspect everyone's motives, and that's not a good way to live. It's not who I am.' She grimaced. 'As well as my inheritance, he took my belief in myself and my confidence. And I want them back.'

Now Josh realised why she pushed herself so hard on the slopes. To prove to herself that she could do something she'd thought herself incapable of doing. To give her back her self-confidence.

But one thing he didn't understand. Before she'd bought the restaurant, she'd been its head chef. 'Why didn't the new owners keep you on as chef?' he asked.

'They wanted to do their own thing. And, really, do you want the ex-owner hanging about your kitchens? I understand where they were coming from,' she said. 'They wanted a fresh start.'

'Couldn't you have got a loan to buy the other restaurant?'

'Not without a deposit. Besides, if you were a bank manager, would *you* lend money to someone who'd just lost her business because she trusted the wrong person?'

'Everyone deserves a second chance,' he said.

'It wasn't happening. And I was just lucky that Hannah had room for me to stay with her. But she's going to need her nursery back in a couple of months. Taking this job means I have somewhere to live and a bit of a breathing space. When I go back to England, at least there'll be something else on my CV that will push the stuff before into the background—and hopefully that means someone might give me a chance in their kitchen.'

His heart ached for her. 'What if someone was prepared to go after Blake for you?'

'You, you mean?' She shook her head. 'I know you mean well, and I appreciate the offer, but you're a ski instructor, not a lawyer. What could you do that Hannah and her colleagues couldn't?' Before he could answer that, she added, 'I can look after myself and I'm not looking to be rescued. I don't need rescuing.'

'But Blake cheated you.'

'It's not so much the money,' she said. 'It's how he made me feel: that the only thing that was worth anything about me was the money I inherited from my parents.'

That really struck a chord with Josh. It was how he'd discovered Annabel had seen him: not for himself, but as a billionaire's son and a media darling. She hadn't wanted him for his own sake; she'd wanted him for the money and the lifestyle he could give her. Which was why she'd given him that terrible ultimatum.

He knew exactly how it felt to be wanted for your money, and he hated to think that was how Sophie saw herself.

'No. That's not true at all,' he said. 'You've come out here, to a country where you don't speak the language, to hold down a demanding job—the level of cuisine the chalet clients expect is way above the level of even a really skilled amateur—and you're challenging yourself to do something that scares you. You're worth way, way more than any money.'

'Thank you,' she said. 'That's what I've been telling myself. What I need now is to stand on my own two feet again—and to know I'm capable of picking myself up and I don't have to rely on anyone else to do it for me. Life isn't a fairy tale and I'm not a princess.'

Josh could respect her point of view, even though he knew all he had to do was pick up the phone and make a few calls; a good private detective would be able to find Blake, having the time and resources that Sophie and her friends didn't have.

But Sophie had made it very clear that this wasn't Josh's fight—and he'd already got it wrong by stepping in with Gaz and his friends.

So, much as he wanted to charge in and rescue her, he had to do the harder thing: stand down and wait for her to ask for his help.

'So what about you?' she asked. 'How did you get to be a ski instructor?'

If he told her the truth, how would she react? As Josh the ski instructor, she'd taken him at face value. But he remembered what she'd said about the chalet boys, the other week.

*Rich boys. The sort who've never really had to work for anything.*

That was true of him, too. He'd had to train hard to get where he had in the world of skiing, but someone from a more modest background wouldn't even have had the chance to do that. He'd never had to earn a living. If she knew he was from a very wealthy family indeed, would she see him differently—as privileged and whiny, a 'poor little rich boy' who was sulking because his plans hadn't worked out and he didn't really know what to do with his life now?

Especially given that she'd worked so hard and she'd lost everything.

Maybe he could tell her part of the truth: just without telling her what his old job was or who he'd once been. The truth, and nothing but the truth: just not the *whole* truth.

'I've been friends with the Rendini family

for years,' he said. 'When my last job didn't work out, they offered me the chance to work here as a ski instructor. So I did my qualifications and came here. This is my trial season.'

'And are you enjoying teaching?'

'Yes,' he said. 'I like seeing my students blossom. You, for example: that first day, you were terrified of falling over and you could only see the danger and not the fun of skiing. And you've said yourself that now you're getting your ski legs you're enjoying it. And that's what makes the job feel worthwhile. Because I'm giving people the chance to know that joy.'

'Would you want to make it your career?'

He blew out a breath. 'Good question. Maybe.'

'What's your alternative?'

Sophie definitely had a business mind, he thought. She cut straight to the point. 'I've been offered an office job.'

'Would you be happy doing that job?'

'Honestly? I don't know,' he said. 'Very probably not.'

'So if you don't teach and you don't do the office job, what do you want to do instead?'

'That's the thing,' he said. 'I'm at a bit of a crossroads. Do I take a complete change of direction, or do I keep teaching?' Which in itself was a change of direction, too.

'For what it's worth,' she said, 'you're good

at teaching. If it makes you happy, then think about where it can take you in five years. Is it somewhere you'd want to be, or would your complete change of direction—even if you didn't enjoy the job at first—give you other opportunities that would make you happier?'

'I honestly don't know,' he said.

'Could you go back to your old job, but working for someone else?'

If only. 'No,' he said. 'My bridges are a bit on the burned side.' Crashed and burned, thanks to his knee.

'Maybe,' she said, 'you need a challenge. Something to make you pull yourself out of the hole you're in, so you can move on.'

'Like you and the skiing.'

She nodded. 'What are you most afraid of?'

Wrecking his knee again so he wouldn't even be able to walk, let alone ski. Having to rely on other people and losing his independence. Feeling trapped. 'Making the wrong choice,' he said.

'There's a theory that if you toss a coin, it'll help you focus. But that only works if you have two choices,' she said.

'How does it work?'

'If you're pleased or relieved at the result, then you know you've made the right choice. If you're disappointed, then you know that what you really wanted was the other option.'

'It's a good theory.' But he didn't have two choices. 'So, given the choice of doing absolutely anything you wanted in the world, what would you do?'

'Open another restaurant,' she said promptly. 'It'd be me giving myself a second chance—and I'd want to do that with my staff, too.'

Which might just fit in with his own ideas of what he could do in the future, with assistive skiing instruction. He knew first-hand what it was like to have reconstructive surgery and a gruelling programme of physiotherapy, so that would help him to understand the needs of his disabled skiing students. He almost asked Sophie there and then what she thought about the idea: but then he'd have to explain about his knee. About his past. And he wasn't quite ready to open up about that. The more he got to know Sophie, the more he thought he could trust her. She was a million miles away from Annabel.

But what if his judgement was still off? What if he got it wrong again?

So instead, he focused on her. 'That bet I had with Gaz and the lads,' he said carefully, 'involved a donation to charity.' A sizeable one. And he could add to that money. 'It'd be enough to get you a lease, stock and a few months of staffing, if you want to open that restaurant when you go back to England.'

'No,' she said. 'The offer's kind, but no. Apart from the fact that this would be a business, not a charity—so taking the money would feel dishonest and wrong, for me—I need to stand on my own two feet.

'Understood. But think about it before you reject it out of hand,' he said. 'The offer's there. Should you wish to take it.'

It was oh, so tempting to accept his offer.

But it would mean letting someone else rescue her.

With money that hadn't been obtained honestly, in her view. Plus she wouldn't be setting up a charity. It wouldn't be honest. And honesty was important, especially after what had happened to her. Her integrity wasn't for sale.

At the same time, she was relieved that Josh didn't seem to think any less of her now he finally knew the truth about the huge mistake she'd made.

And it seemed that he, too, was at a point where his life had to change.

Maybe they could help each other.

Though she had the feeling that he was holding something back. He'd been very cagey about his previous job. Or maybe he'd worked in financial services and didn't want to tell her, given the way she'd lost all her own assets.

By mutual unspoken consent they didn't talk any more about their jobs or their past. Sophie enjoyed working with him in the kitchen, getting him to try different flavours and textures.

'I've got a teaching session in half an hour,' Josh said when he'd finished doing the washing up, 'so I really need to go. But I'll pick you up for dinner at half-past six.'

'What's the dress code?' she asked.

'Smart,' he said.

She was glad that Hannah had persuaded her to pack a little black dress. But there was one teensy problem. 'I'm not sure I'll manage heels in the snow,' she said.

'Wear your snow boots outside, and whatever you like inside,' he said. 'Bring a bag for your boots. I'll carry it for you.'

'All right. Half-past six it is,' she said.

He kissed her on the cheek, and it felt as if little fires were dancing underneath her skin. 'See you later.'

'Have a good lesson,' she said.

Kitty came back from the slopes and fell on the goodies Sophie had made. 'These are so good,' she said.

'Thanks. I thought I'd start doing a couple

of Christmas-based afternoon tea things each week for our guests,' Sophie said.

'Great idea.' Kitty smiled at her. 'So what are you up to, this evening?'

'I'm going out for dinner.'

'With Mr Sexy Ski Instructor?'

'He's just a friend,' Sophie reminded her.

'If you say so,' Kitty said with a grin. 'What are you wearing?'

'A dress.'

'Show me.'

Sophie did so, and Kitty nodded her approval. 'What about jewellery?'

'I don't really wear much,' Sophie said. 'Just my mum's rings.'

'You need jewellery with that dress. Pearls would be good. Come with me,' Kitty said, and ushered Sophie into her room. 'Put the dress on.' She rummaged in her jewellery box. 'Right. Borrow these.' She handed Sophie a choker of creamy pearls. 'And I think you should wear your hair up.'

'I don't—' Sophie began.

'You do tonight. I'll do your hair and make-up.' Kitty grinned. 'I've already worked out that you don't wear much, so don't worry; I'm not going to make you look orange or put huge false eyelashes on you. Just a bit of foundation, mascara and lippy.'

At twenty-five past six, Sophie barely recognised herself in the mirror. Kitty had put her hair into a sophisticated updo with tiny curls at the sides, and the make-up was subtle but made her eyes look huge and her mouth look beautiful.

'You look amazing, Soph,' Kitty said with satisfaction. 'Almost as amazing as you are inside.'

Sophie felt tears prick her eyelids. 'That's such a nice thing to say.'

'It's all true. The cook here before you was a bit snooty and I didn't get on with her; you've already taught me loads and my mum's going to love you for ever because it means I'll be able to cook proper food at uni and won't just live on pizza.'

'You'll live on pizza because that's what students do,' Sophie said with a grin, 'but knowing how to cook means that if you decide to eat together in your flat, you'll get the fun of cooking and everyone else will do the washing up.'

'Perfect,' Kitty said. 'Now go and have fun with Mr Sexy Ski Instructor.'

'We're *friends*,' Sophie protested.

'He's taking you out to dinner somewhere dressy. That means more than friends,' Sophie said. 'And, from what I hear, he hasn't dated anyone for months.'

That answered one question; better still, she hadn't had to ask it.

The doorbell rang.

'All yours,' Kitty said. 'Have fun!'

Josh stared as Sophie answered the door while shrugging into her pink padded coat. He'd asked her to dress up, but he hadn't expected her to look this stunning. He remembered that kiss last night and felt as if his tongue was glued to the roof of his mouth.

But it was obvious that she expected him to say at least hello.

'You look…exquisite,' were the words that burst out of him.

She went very pink and her eyes glittered. 'Thank you. But it's all down to Kitty. She did my make-up and hair.'

'You're beautiful—it's *you*, not the way you're dressed. I'm not quite that shallow.' Well, he was, but he wasn't going to admit that.

She went even pinker, and changed the subject. 'Where are we going?'

'A place where the food is seriously good—because I wouldn't dare take you anywhere else,' he said with a smile.

'The food is always more important than

the surroundings,' she said. 'Antique furniture, the best linen and porcelain, and crystal glassware aren't enough.'

'Isn't presentation important?'

'Yes, but if it looks beautiful and the food doesn't live up to expectation, then it's a disappointment rather than a delight,' she said.

He thought about it. It was also true of people. Annabel was confident and beautiful outside, but hadn't lived up to the beauty inside; whereas Sophie... Sophie was beautiful inside and didn't have the confidence she deserved. He'd rather have one Sophie than a hundred Annabels.

Not that he could tell her that without a lot of awkward explanations.

So he simply drove her to the restaurant, getting her to glance out at the sky.

'The stars don't look like this in London,' she said. 'You're lucky if you can see half a dozen constellations. Here, without the streetlights, there's a whole sky full of stars I've never seen before.'

That was how she made him feel. As if a filter had been stripped away and everything was clearer. Brighter.

He parked outside the restaurant. The path had been cleared to the front door, so she changed from her snow boots to heels, but he tucked her arm through his so she wouldn't worry about slipping.

'This is lovely,' she said, gesturing to the wooden chalet with its pitched roof covered in snow. There were fairy lights draped around the edge of the roof and twined through the branches of the small spruce trees in pots either side of the door.

Inside, the tables were covered in starched white linen, and the plain silver cutlery was set very precisely; the table setting was simple, with a glass vase containing white hellebores and a plain white candle in an elegant silver holder.

The waiter showed them to a quiet corner table with a view over the mountains, and Josh made sure that Sophie was the one to get the view.

'This is lovely,' Sophie said. 'Elegant and simple.'

He wondered what her restaurant had been like, but he didn't want to hurt her by asking. Given what she'd said about presentation, earlier, he was pretty sure she'd gone for simple rather than fussy.

She took one look at the menu and then raised her eyebrows at him. 'How many stars does this place have, then?'

He blinked. 'You can tell just from the menu?'

She nodded. 'The fact there's a tasting menu pretty much gives it away.'

'Shall we go for that?' he asked.

'I'd love to,' she said, 'provided we go halves on the bill.'

He frowned. 'I'm taking you out to dinner.'

'Josh, I don't mean to be rude, but you're a part-time ski instructor. Paying the bill for both of us is going to put a bit of a hole in your budget.'

This was his cue to tell her who he was. Who his family was. Why he wasn't worried about the bill tonight.

But it stuck in his throat.

He didn't think Sophie was a gold-digger in the way Annabel had been, but he did think that telling her the truth about his background would change the way she saw him. He didn't want that. He wanted her to keep seeing him for himself. Just Josh.

'I have savings from my last job,' he said. As well as a trust fund that he'd come into when he was twenty-seven: old enough, in his grandparents' view, to be sensible. He'd invested some in property and the rest in a fund that was doing very nicely indeed, thank you.

'Even so,' she said. 'I don't want you to blow your savings on taking me to dinner.'

'Let me treat you,' he said softly. 'You can

buy me hot chocolate and strudel tomorrow after your ski lesson.'

She shook her head. 'There's a big difference between buying a snack in a café and picking up the bill for a tasting menu in a place like this.'

'Humour me. I wouldn't have brought you here if I couldn't afford it,' he said. 'This isn't about trying to impress you by taking you somewhere posh. It's about sharing some seriously good food with you—something I like and that I hope you're going to enjoy.'

'Then thank you, Josh,' she said. 'This looks amazing.'

The food was excellent, each course beautifully presented.

'This is perfect,' she said. 'There's one main ingredient that's clearly the star of each dish. The way it's put together, the colours and the textures…and for me the beetroot gnocchi is standout.'

'Good.' He smiled. 'It's lovely to share dinner with someone who enjoys it rather than picking at it.'

'It's impossible not to enjoy this.' She smiled back. 'Thank you so much.'

'My pleasure,' he said, meaning it.

She was relaxed with him, now, chatting easily. It was a long time since he'd enjoyed dinner out as much as this. If he could freeze time, he'd make tonight last for ever.

Well, if he could intercut it with that light kiss goodnight. The anticipation. The way desire had bubbled through his veins.

'I love the fact there's a pre-dessert,' she said when the waiter brought out a tiny moulded creamy dome on a plate, garnished with a crystallised violet and with a scribble of dark chocolate on the plate next to it. 'And if this is what I think it is…' She took one tiny spoonful and closed her eyes in bliss. 'Oh, yes.'

Her voice was as sexy as hell. Josh could imagine her saying those words as he touched her, caressed her. For a moment, he almost forgot where they were and leaned over the table to kiss her. But he held himself back. Just.

'Violet panna cotta,' she said, sounding delighted. 'This is sublime.'

*She* was sublime. And he really wanted her. But she'd notice if he didn't eat his pre-dessert. 'This is possibly a little too floral for me,' he said when he'd tried his.

'Violet creams—posh ones—are my favourite sweets in the entire world,' she said.

He stored that little nugget away for future use, and let her finish his panna cotta.

But the dessert, when it came, was more to his taste. 'Deconstructed apple strudel in a glass,' she said happily. 'I love the way they've done this. A sharp apple parfait, sweet zabaglione, spiced raisins and a cinnamon tuille.'

Even though they lingered over coffee and petit fours—a tiny lemon tart, a lush raspberry jelly and rich, dark gianduja—they reached the point where Josh knew he needed to take Sophie home. She'd need to be up early for her guests and it wasn't fair of him to keep her out late.

But he stopped at a viewpoint on the way back to Pendio di Cristallo. 'There's something I want to show you. You'll need your coat,' he said, and climbed out of the car. When he opened her door, she was wearing her coat and snow boots.

'Look up,' he said.

'That's amazing,' she said. 'I don't think I've ever seen so many stars in one place before.'

'New moon and dark skies,' he said. 'In summer it's even better because you can see the Milky Way. This time of year, sadly, you can't.'

'I'm going to add that to my bucket list,' she said. And then she pointed. 'Look! A shooting star.'

It was visible for only a few seconds, but he saw it streaking across the sky, a trail of silver and turquoise like a lone and silent firework. 'They're meant to be lucky. And you're supposed to make a wish when you see one,' he said.

'A wish.' She looked wistful.

Whatever she was wishing for, he'd make it come true. If she'd tell him what she wanted.

He knew what he wished for.

He wanted her to kiss him.

She looked up at him, and he felt his heart stop for a moment.

And then, at last, her mouth was touching the corner of his. Every nerve-end zinged with awareness of her.

'Sophie,' he said softly, and rubbed the pad of his thumb against her lower lip. 'Sophie.'

Those beautiful blue eyes were huge in the starlight.

And he couldn't resist her any more.

He dipped his head, and brushed his mouth against hers. Once, twice. The lightest touch, but it made his whole body ache with need.

And at last she was kissing him back, her arms wrapped round his neck and his wrapped round her waist.

That falling star had definitely done its work.

And he loved every second of it. The softness of her body against his. The warmth of her skin. The scent she wore. The silence of the snow at the deserted viewpoint. Just the two of them underneath the stars, surrounded by the snow…

Then, shockingly, she pulled away. 'I shouldn't have done that,' she said, not meeting his gaze.

It was his own fault. He'd been the one to set the parameters. He'd put himself in the friend zone.

'I'll drive you back,' he said.

It felt beyond awkward, in the car. He didn't know what to say. She clearly didn't, either. And the silence grew more and more awkward with every passing mile.

Eventually they reached her chalet. 'Thank you for this evening, Josh,' she said politely. 'I had a lovely time.'

So had he. He'd really enjoyed her company. 'Pleasure,' he said.

He needed to regroup, because she was clearly spooked by that kiss.

He'd have to stay stuck in the friend zone until he'd worked out how to change her mind. How to ask her to take a chance on him. 'I'll see you tomorrow for your lesson.'

'Tomorrow,' she agreed.

He waited until she was safely inside, then drove back to his own chalet.

That kiss had awoken so many things he'd thought were dormant. Desire. Need. Attraction.

The more he got to know her, the more he

liked her. And that liking was tipping over into something else. It wasn't something he was ready to name: something that had let them both down in the past and made them both wary. But could it be different for them, this time round? And, if so, how was he going to get her to change her mind—and take a chance on them?

## CHAPTER SEVEN

THE NEXT MORNING, it was snowing lightly.

Just like the morning when she'd first met Josh when she'd stood outside, catching snowflakes on her tongue, not realising she'd wandered onto the bottom of a piste.

Today, Sophie thought, she was a little less clueless.

Though she felt just as wary about meeting him. Last night—well, Josh wasn't the sort of man to assume that taking her out to dinner meant that she owed him sex. But she'd enjoyed sharing the posh, luxurious dinner with someone who appreciated good food as much as she did. She'd enjoyed his company. She'd loved the fact he'd stopped to show her the stars on a crisp Alpine night, the starlight reflecting on the snow-covered trees.

And that moment when she'd kissed him under the stars, when he'd brushed the pad of his thumb along her lower lip, making every nerve-end tingle, and then he'd kissed her… she'd wanted more. She'd wanted him to sweep her back to his chalet and make love with her.

But they'd agreed to be friends.

And she was a failure at relationships.

So she'd chickened out. Pulled back.

And how she regretted it. She wished she'd taken the chance. She could've said something in the car, instead of sitting in awkward silence. She could've leaned forward and kissed him goodnight when he'd parked outside her chalet, let him know without words that she wanted to be more than just friends.

But she hadn't.

And he hadn't made a move, either. He hadn't brought up the subject or said that he wanted to rethink their agreement. When he'd kissed her under the stars, she'd thought that maybe it was the first step to something else.

The fact he hadn't taken it further… Clearly he'd changed his mind and she needed to be sensible and stick to what they'd agreed instead of wanting more. They were friends. Strictly friends.

Josh was waiting for her by the lift to the blue run. 'Good morning.'

His smile made her heart skip a beat. 'Good morning. Can we actually ski in the snow or do we need to reschedule?'

'We can ski in the snow unless it's a blizzard. The weather forecast says it's going to stop soon—and fresh powder's lovely to ski on.' He smiled. 'Though it's also tiring. It's easy to catch an edge so your skis stop dead and you fall over.'

'And if I fall over, I pick myself up, smile and shake it off,' she said.

He grinned. 'Oh, good. A student who actually listens to what I say. Yes. Let's go.'

The snow seemed to muffle the usual noise on the slope. And it felt almost like skiing on a duvet. If she fell, it would be all cushiony and—

Yup. It was cushiony, she discovered when she fell.

And it was really, really difficult to get up. She tried once, twice, and just couldn't do it.

'Here.' He took her hand and pulled her to her feet. Except he was stooping, and pulling her up meant pulling her into him, and they ended up face to face. Just like last night. Except, instead of being surrounded by starlight, they were surrounded by soft, fluffy snowflakes.

As slowly as the huge flakes drifted down past them, his face lowered to hers. His lips brushed hers once, twice. Sweet and gentle and promising. Enticing. Asking, not demanding.

Persuading. Everything she'd wanted since last night.

What could she do but drop her ski poles and slide her arms round his neck, just as she had last night?

He'd dropped his ski poles, too, and his arms were tightly wrapped round her.

And all she could think of was the heat and sweetness of his mouth against hers, the softness and coolness of the snow. She closed her eyes, kissing him back, luxuriating in his closeness.

And then, shockingly, he broke the kiss.

'Sorry. I, um, crossed a line there.'

More than one. From teacher to friend to… something else.

But the snow had stopped as suddenly as it began, and all the glittering possibilities vanished with it.

'I'm sorry.' He rubbed a hand across his face. 'Actually, no, I'm not sorry for kissing you. I'm glad I kissed you. But I'm sorry for making things complicated. For not checking with you first.'

Oh.

And that made all the difference.

She leaned forward, holding on to him for balance, and kissed him.

When she broke the kiss, he pushed his goggles up.

She did the same, so she could look him properly in the eye.

'So what now?' he asked.

'I don't know,' she said.

'You're still getting over your ex.'

'No. I've had enough time to think about it. I'm not in love with him any more. But I don't quite trust my judgement in men now,' she admitted.

'I know how that feels,' he said. 'My last relationship went wrong. Badly.' He took a deep breath. 'But maybe we could take a risk. Together. See where this goes.'

'I don't know what I'm going to be doing when my contract ends,' she warned.

'I don't know what I'm going to be doing in a few months' time, either,' he said. 'Maybe we could treat this as just time for us and not worry about the future. We'll deal with it when the time comes.'

Which felt as scary as standing at the top of a steep slope, knowing that the only way you could reach the safety at the bottom was to conquer your fear and push yourself over the edge. 'So we're redrawing the lines?'

'When I'm teaching you,' he said, 'I'm your ski instructor.'

She coughed. 'That would be the ski instructor who just kissed me and crossed said line.'

'The ski instructor who is going to keep himself under strict control from now on and stick to teaching during a lesson. But, the second that the lesson ends,' he said, 'we cross back over the line.'

The line that they'd originally agreed was friendship. 'Except we're not going to be just friends?' she checked.

'Definitely not just friends.' His voice was slightly husky, sexy as hell. 'And I'm looking forward to being your lover. Finding out what pleases you, what takes your breath away, what turns you to flame.'

What could she do but reach up again and kiss him?

'That,' he said when she broke the kiss, 'was serious line-crossing, Sophie Harris. So we're going to ski down the slope now. And then we're going back to the top and practising it all over again. Without kissing.' He glanced at his watch. 'For another twenty-five minutes. And then…' He raised his ski goggles so she could see the intensity burning in his grey eyes. 'And then we're crossing that line. Together.'

She wasn't sure whether the anticipation was more delicious, scary or exciting. 'One more condition,' she said.

'Which is?'

He'd said his last relationship had gone badly wrong. 'We've both been hurt. So we should agree to be kind to each other.'

'Kind isn't quite how I'm feeling right now,' he said. 'It's more...troglodyte.'

'Troglodyte?'

'As in I'd like to carry you off somewhere warm and private.'

She got it, now, and grinned. 'Your cave. That would be acceptable.'

He kissed the tip of her nose. 'Good. And I agree. We'll be kind. We won't hurt each other.'

The anticipation grew with every trip they took back to the top of the run and down to the bottom.

At the end of one more run, Josh glanced at his watch. 'Lesson over,' he decreed.

Sophie's stomach swooped. 'Time to cross that line.' And suddenly it was really, really scary.

As if she'd spoken that last bit aloud, he said quietly, 'It doesn't mean we have to cross the line *quickly*. And I kind of liked the tradition we were setting of having hot chocolate and strudel after a lesson.'

'I need to be back at my chalet by four,' she reminded him.

'And I have a lesson at two. So we're not going to rush into anything today,' he said. 'We're going for a mini-date: hot chocolate and strudel in my favourite café. And we'll make a list of all the things you want to do while you're here in the Dolomites.' He raised his ski goggles again and his grey eyes were suddenly hot. '*All* the things,' he said softly, 'not just the places you want to visit.'

She was very glad of the ski poles she was hanging on to, because her knees had just gone seriously weak. 'All the things,' she croaked. His earlier words were burned into her brain.

*I'm looking forward to being your lover. Finding out what pleases you, what takes your breath away, what turns you to flame.*

She wanted that, too. She'd never wanted anyone so much in her entire life.

He stole a kiss, leaving her breathless. 'Strudel, first. We have all the time in the world.'

Actually, they didn't. She was due to leave Pendio di Cristallo at the end of January, only a few short weeks away.

But for now it was nice to pretend.

She insisted on picking up the bill for hot chocolate and strudel. 'You bought dinner last night,' she reminded him.

'And you're not a fairy tale princess,' he said. 'No rescuing, unless it's mutual.'

'I'm glad that's sorted.'

But she enjoyed sitting in the café with him, their legs entwined under the table and their fingers entwined above the table. Cute and cosy and fun. All the things she'd been missing and trying to tell herself that she could do without. Except she'd been so very, very lonely since Blake had duped her and left her without even saying goodbye.

'I know hardly anything about the area, really,' she said. 'The only thing I can think of that I'd really like to do is visit the Christmas market again when it's dark, so I can see the lights at their best.'

'We can do that on your next day off, so you don't have to rush back to make dinner for your guests,' he said.

'Thank you. What else would you suggest?'

'Walking round the lakes,' he said. 'Obviously it'll be too cold to swim in them—and some of them you're not allowed to swim in, anyway—but the views will be amazing. The colour of the water has to be seen to be believed.'

'Sounds good,' she said.

'We can have a look at some of the villages, because they're really pretty. I'm happy to drive you,' he said. 'And maybe we can take a sleigh ride through the forest.'

'Drawn by reindeer?' she asked.

'By horse,' he said.

She smiled. 'I'd love that.'

With his free hand, he made notes on his phone. 'OK. I'll text this to you. We can pick something from it each day, depending on the weather and how we feel. And maybe we can look up some touristy things online.' He smiled. 'If you like museums, we can go and see Ötzi the Ice Man. He was found by hikers in a glacier, and he's the oldest man ever found intact—he's more than five thousand years old.'

'Older than Egyptian mummies?' she asked, surprised.

'There are older mummies, but they'd had their organs removed during mummification. Ötzi didn't—he was preserved by the glacier.'

'How come you know all this stuff?'

'The Rendinis,' he said. 'Vincenzo's very proud of his heritage.'

'Then let's add visiting Ötzi to our list,' she said.

They wandered round the village together, hand in hand.

'There are plenty of other winter sports apart from skiing. We could go ice skating,' Josh suggested.

Sophie shook her head. 'Ice skates have

sharp blades. And I need my hands for work. That's a risk too far, for me.'

'How about snow-shoeing?' he asked.

'Maybe. How likely am I to fall over?'

'You're not. Unless I get you to do a snow angel—and that doesn't count because it's deliberate falling-over.'

'Got it,' she said. 'All right. Let's add it to our list.'

He walked her back to her chalet. 'Our list,' he said. 'We're not going to set a time for it. But the one thing I really want to do is make love with you. Touch you and taste you and explore you until I really know you.' He held her gaze. 'And for you to do the same with me.'

His goodbye kiss was scorching.

And Sophie was tingling all over as she walked into the chalet, with the simmering undercurrent of knowing that very, very soon they'd make love. Be skin to skin. Trust each other with themselves...

Over the next week, Sophie enjoyed going out with Josh after their lessons. As he'd suggested, they went for a walk round one of the lakes, their arms wrapped round each other.

'This is amazing,' she said. 'Even though there's ice on the surface of the lake and snow on the edges, you can see the water properly in the middle—and the reflections.' The snow-capped peaks and the forests surrounding the lake were reflected perfectly in the clear emerald water. 'And you were right about the colour. It's stunning.'

'There are others that are almost a milky turquoise, and others that are the same blue as the sky,' he said.

He took her to pretty Alpine villages with ancient churches covered with frescoes, cobbled streets and beautiful fountains in the central squares; everywhere looked incredibly gorgeous, dusted with snow.

He took her out on a morning when there was fresh snow everywhere, and taught her how to make a snow angel; and then he kissed her to the point where she forgot that she was cold because his mouth made her feel hot all over.

And, best of all, one afternoon, he took her for a sleigh ride.

'It's just like a real Father Christmas sleigh,' Sophie said with delight when he took her over to their sleigh.

It was drawn by a large black horse—a Noriker, Josh told her—who had tinkling bells on his harness. The driver helped them onto the seat and wrapped a fleecy blanket round them both, then sat on the front of the sleigh and gently urged the horse on.

All she could hear was the crisp sound of the sleigh sliding through the snow as they drove through the forest, and the tinkling of the harness bells. The air was so fresh and clear; but even more heady was the warmth of Josh beside her, his arm round her shoulders and his thigh pressed against hers.

'It's really like living in the middle of a Christmas song,' she said.

To her delight, Josh broke into an impromptu rendition of 'Sleigh Ride', his voice deep and clear and tuneful; and she found herself singing along with him and laughing.

This was so perfect, she thought. Life didn't get any better than this.

They drove round a lake similar to the one Josh had taken her to before, except this time the water was the same bright cerulean as the sky. The mountains and the forests were reflected in the lake, and Sophie had never seen anything so beautiful.

'This is utterly magical,' she whispered to Josh.

'I know,' he whispered back, and kissed her.

On her next day off, he took her to the Christmas market after sunset, and from the top of the Ferris wheel the whole village looked like a winter wonderland, full of fairy lights. Best of all, second time round, Josh kissed her all the way up the Ferris wheel, and all the way down again.

'Stay with me tonight?' he asked. 'I'll drive you back to the chalet before you need to get breakfast ready.'

Crossing their final line: from friendship to dating to being lovers.

Part of Sophie wanted to. *Really* wanted to. And part of her was terrified that this was where it would all go wrong.

'Or,' he said, 'you can just come back for a glass of wine. And I'll get you home before midnight.'

He meant it.

She could set the pace.

He wasn't going to push her into anything she wasn't ready to do.

'You don't have to decide now,' he said. 'We'll have dinner first.'

He took her to a tiny hut in the mountains, where the food was amazing: simple traditional recipes, freshly made and locally sourced.

When he pulled up outside his chalet, she said, 'I've decided.'

He kept his expression carefully neutral. 'Uh-huh.'

'I'll stay,' she said.

And the heat in his eyes was scorching as

he scooped her out of the car and carried her
through his front door and into his bedroom.

They worked their way through their list: the
museum, snow-shoeing, and a scary afternoon
where he took her tobogganing. And on Sophie's next day off Josh collected her well before dawn; he drove her into the mountains,
and together they watched the sun come up.

'The roses on the rocks again,' she said.
'And I can't believe that even the snow is pink.
This is amazing, Josh.'

'I hoped you'd like it. But I haven't finished
yet,' he said. 'I have plans with a capital P.'

'What sort of plans?'

'Ones I hope you'll like.' He refused to be
drawn on any of the details.

They spent the day skiing, and then he drove
her to a small cottage in the mountains.

'What's this?' she asked.

'I borrowed a cottage to make you dinner,'
he said.

'You borrowed a cottage?' she echoed.

'From the Rendinis. I wanted to have a kind
of early Christmas with you because we'll both
be working on the day.'

'That's such a lovely idea,' she said. 'So are
you telling me there's a full Christmas dinner
sitting in a cool-box in the back of your car?'

'No. I put dinner in the fridge here, yesterday,' he said. 'It's an Italian take on a traditional English Christmas dinner. It's kind of worrying, cooking for a trained chef, so I cheated a tiny bit and enlisted a bit of help; most of it, I just need to put in the oven. But I hope you'll like it.'

She smiled. 'Don't be intimidated, cooking for me. I appreciate you making a fuss of me and I'm not going to be all picky and score you on presentation or whatever. But if you need a sous-chef, let me know.'

He unlocked the cottage and they put their boots and skis on the rack in the hallway. She could smell spruce, cinnamon and orange. 'Whatever you've done,' she said, 'it definitely smells like Christmas.'

'I set most of it up last night, but I need to do a couple more things. Maybe you can boil the kettle for us and make coffee?'

'Sure,' she said, and let him usher her into the kitchen.

When she took the milk out of the fridge door, she tried very hard not to look at the rest of the contents, not wanting to spoil his surprise. Once she'd finished making coffee, she called, 'Let me know when you're ready for me to bring it through.'

'Now's fine,' he said.

She sucked in a breath when she followed his voice and walked into the living room. There was a real Christmas tree in the corner, decorated with twinkling lights and red baubles and gold stars; there was an evergreen wreath along the mantelpiece, studded with orange slices and bundles of cinnamon sticks; the room was lit by what must've been twenty or thirty candles; and there was a crackling log fire in the hearth.

It was the most romantic thing she'd ever seen in her life.

'This is absolutely lovely,' she said. 'The perfect Christmas.'

He looked pleased. 'That was what I was trying to do. Right. I'll be five minutes in the kitchen.' He handed his phone to her with a streaming app already open. 'Have a look through here and find some Christmas music you like,' he said.

She found a list of Christmas music for solo piano and had just set it playing when he returned.

'This is lovely,' he said. 'Dance with me?'

'I'd love to.' She glanced up. 'But where's the mistletoe?'

'You'll have to imagine it,' he said with a grin. 'Pretend it's right there above us.'

'Promises, promises,' she teased.

'I deliver on my promises,' he said, and kissed her.

And it was wonderful, dancing with him in a candlelit room, just the two of them, with beautiful music and Christmassy scents.

It would be oh, so easy to get used to this.

To fall in love with Josh.

She was more than halfway there already. She liked his warmth, his sense of fun, the way her blood fizzed whenever he kissed her.

And things had gone wrong for both of them, before. Which meant that this time maybe they could get it right...

His phone alarm chimed.

'Kitchen duties,' he said, and kissed her. 'Whatever you're thinking, hold on to that thought.'

'Can I help at all?'

'Nope. The idea is to spoil you,' he said.

Dinner was chicken fillet wrapped in prosciutto, with roast potatoes that were crispy outside and perfectly fluffy inside, tiny Chantenay carrots, and Brussels sprouts shredded and stir fried in butter, garlic and chilli, served with a creamy marsala sauce. He'd opened a bottle of champagne, too.

'I'll stick to one glass,' he said, 'because I'm driving. But I think tonight deserves proper bubbles.'

'This is all perfect,' she said. 'Thank you so much for spoiling me.'

She particularly liked the chocolate panettone he served for dessert with a large spoonful of mascarpone.

'I'm going to get some of this shipped to Hannah,' she said. 'It's fabulous.'

He smiled. 'I'll give you the name of my supplier. Tell them that I sent you, and they might throw in some of their lemon cookies—which are pretty spectacular.'

'I will,' she promised.

But when he went to make coffee, she heard him say, 'Uh-oh.'

'What's wrong?' she asked.

'Go and look out of the window,' he said.

Outside, she couldn't see anything but white. It was snow, but not like she'd seen it before. 'Is that a blizzard?'

'It's a whiteout,' he said. 'Visibility's not good enough to risk driving. We'll have to wait it out for a bit.' He grabbed his phone and checked the weather report. 'Ah. It seems the road to Pendio di Cristallo is closed for the foreseeable future.'

'So how are we going to get back to the resort?' She looked at him, aghast. 'I know I'm off tonight, but I need to be back there to make breakfast for the guests in the morning.'

'I think Kitty will have to do the kitchen duties for you,' he said. 'With conditions like these, and according to this weather report, we're going nowhere tonight.' He shook his head. 'I'm really sorry, Sophie. This wasn't on the weather forecast yesterday. I know how quickly weather can change in the mountains and I should've double-checked. Text Kitty to let her know where you are, and I'll call Gio and let him know we're snowed in here tonight.'

Sophie bit her lip. 'I feel terrible about letting everyone down.'

'It's not your fault. The blame's completely mine for not keeping an eye on the forecast.'

'You can't change the weather.' She sighed. 'Can I speak to Giovanni when you call him, please? I'd like to apologise.'

He nodded, and while she texted Kitty he called Giovanni; he spoke in rapid Italian, then handed the phone to her.

'I'm so sorry, Mr Rendini,' she said.

'It's not your fault, *bella*. These things happen. I'll arrange to get someone to help Kitty in the morning,' Giovanni said.

'Thank you. I'll swap my next day off for tomorrow, to make up for it,' Sophie added.

'Really, it's not necessary,' Giovanni said. 'Take care.'

She handed the phone back to Josh. 'I really hate letting people down.'

'It was my mistake, not yours,' he told her. 'There's nothing we can do about it until to-morrow. So either we can do this the English way and keep worrying about things we can't change, or we can remember where we are and do it the Italian way—make the best of the situation.'

'I guess.'

'Right now, I think you need a hug.' He wrapped his arms round her.

She leaned into him, enjoying his warmth and his strength.

They ended up dancing together again, and curled up on the sofa together in front of the fire. The combination of champagne, skiing and mountain air meant that Sophie ended up falling asleep in Josh's arms. He woke her gently. 'Let's go and get some proper sleep.'

It didn't matter that they had no night-clothes; the cottage was warm and the bed was comfortable. And Josh made love to her so tenderly that she almost cried.

In the morning, she woke in his arms, warm and comfortable and happier than she'd felt in a long while.

'I think,' he said softly, 'for once I'm glad the weather got in the way. Because waking up with you is the best thing that's happened to me since I don't know when.'

'Me, too,' she admitted.

It had stopped snowing during the night; Josh checked the weather report and drove her back to Pendio di Cristallo after a breakfast of coffee and leftover panettone.

'I'll see you later for your lesson,' he said when he dropped her at her chalet.

'Perfect,' she said, and kissed him.

# CHAPTER EIGHT

THE NIGHT OF the whiteout marked a sea-change in their relationship; after that, Josh and Sophie snatched every moment together that they could. Sophie felt more settled and happy than she had in months. Provided she could take time out to see Hannah and the baby at the end of January, she'd be happy to stay in Pendio di Cristallo for the rest of the season.

She didn't even mind that she took a hard tumble on the slopes, one particular morning, because Josh helped her to her feet and whispered to her that he'd kiss her better later.

And he did.

Life, she thought, was finally on the up again.

This Christmas, Sophie had secretly expected to be miserable: hundreds of miles away from London, in a temporary job, trying to get her confidence back.

Instead, it was turning out to be wonderful. Christmas in a winter wonderland. Yes, she'd be working—cooking a proper Christmas dinner for her guests of a smoked salmon mousse with crème fraîche, turkey with all the trimmings, Christmas pudding flambé, cheese, and petit fours—but she loved what she did out here. Better still, there would be time to see Josh. To make a snow angel with him, kiss him and make love. She could watch him unwrap the present she'd chosen specially for him; she'd secretly gone back to the Christmas market without him, and bought him a watercolour by a local artist showing the mountains at sunrise that she'd noticed had caught his eye. She'd made a proper English Christmas cake for her guests each week, and the last couple were maturing and waiting to be iced.

Everywhere she looked, there were Christmas trees. Everywhere she walked, she heard Christmas songs. And all the menus in the cafés and bars were distinctly Christmassy, offering eggnog lattes and stollen.

This was going to be the best Christmas since the last one she'd spent with her parents.

She wasn't quite ready to say it out loud, but she'd fallen in love with Josh Cavendish. With the man who'd helped her get her self-confidence back. With the man who was teaching her to trust again. Josh was definitely a good man. One who wouldn't let her down. One who could make her heart beat faster with a smile or a sidelong look.

Love.

Something Sophie hadn't thought she'd find again, after Blake.

And that made it all the sweeter.

How life could change in a heartbeat, Josh thought. A few short weeks ago, he'd been miserable and lost. And then Sophie Harris had walked in front of him and stood there, in her bright pink coat and gaudy sunglasses, and a moment of intense irritation at her cluelessness had dissolved into something warmer and fresher.

He actually looked forward to waking up in the morning, because most of the time she'd be waking in his arms. He looked forward to their lessons, seeing her gain in confidence and skills every single day. And most of all he looked forward to picking her up at her chalet after her guests had finished dinner, because that meant he could carry her to his bed and they could both lose themselves in each other. In pleasure.

The warmth and sweetness she'd brought into his life had melted every block of ice he'd stacked round his heart. And he was more than halfway to falling in love with her. Much more than halfway; because he knew he'd found the person he wanted to spend the rest of his life with.

Though what did she really want?

Would she stay here with him in the Dolomites, if he asked her?

Because he was beginning to work out what he wanted, now. To have his own resort, one which catered for skiers of all abilities and disabilities. And if he ran the ski school, maybe she could run the food side of the business. He was more than happy for her to hire people who needed a second chance, the way she'd wanted to do in London.

And he thought he knew the perfect time to ask her: under a sprig of mistletoe, on Christmas Eve. It was only a couple of weeks away. Maybe it was rushing it; but now he knew what he wanted from life, he wanted it to start as soon as possible.

But, a couple of days later, Josh woke to his mobile phone ringing. He looked at the screen, frowned and answered swiftly. 'Gio? Is everything all right?'

'No, it's not.'

'What's happened?' He went cold. 'Is Vincenzo ill? Angelo?'

'No, everybody in the family's well.'

'Then what's wrong?' Josh asked, knowing that his friend wouldn't normally call at such a crazy time of the morning.

'There's a story about you in the press.'

'Me?' Josh had kept a low profile for months. The world championships weren't for a few weeks yet, so there wouldn't be anything about past winners. 'What sort of story?'

'I think you'd better see for yourself. I'll text you the link. Call me back when you've read it.'

Josh's frown deepened when he clicked on the link to a gossip magazine. There was a photograph of him helping Sophie up from a tumble, captioned *World Champion to Novice?*

What?

He didn't understand. The only people who really knew who he was in Pendio di Cristallo were the Rendinis, and they treated him as part of their family. None of them would ever sell him out.

Then he skim-read the story and saw the name of the source.

Annabel Smethurst.

Oh, for pity's sake. Hadn't she made enough trouble in his life? Thanks to her bombshell news and that ultimatum blowing a hole in his concentration before the championship race, his career had literally crashed. She'd wiped out his reputation straight after, with her sob story in the media—a story which had been completely untrue, but he'd been in no fit state to protest until it was too late. Now he was starting to put his life back together again, and she was cutting the ground away from beneath his feet.

Scowling, he went back to the beginning and read the article properly, this time, knowing that whatever she'd written was going to annoy him, but wanting to know exactly what she'd said.

It was full of artfully composed photographs. Amazing scenery, a bottle of top-label champagne and fairy lights, big fat fluffy snowflakes falling in front of pine trees. Everything about it screamed luxury and aspiration.

And it was all embellished by little snippets of text with a giggly, confessional tone.

*A weekend skiing in Pendio di Cristallo*

What had Annabel been doing here? He'd thought this place would be way too quiet for her tastes. He'd always taken her to her favourite glitzy—and super-expensive—resorts: St Moritz, Gstaad and Courchevel. Places where the rich and famous mingled freely. Pendio was quieter and more family-oriented; it catered for all levels of budgets and experience, from the luxury chalet where Sophie worked through to a budget hostel. The rich skied here, too, but it tended to be the super-rich who didn't want publicity and parties and fuss.

Yet Annabel had clearly visited.

The idea of her staying in Sophie's chalet, being demanding and over-picky...

No. He would've known if she'd stayed at Sophie's chalet. If she'd been a guest, Giovanni would've known and given him a warning.

He was also surprised that Annabel had been anywhere near a blue run. Annabel had always liked to show off her skills. Or maybe she'd got up late one morning and ended up stuck with the less confident skiers in her party. If she'd been thoroughly bored by the lack of challenge, she would've started looking around—and maybe that was why she'd noticed him.

*Guess who I saw on the slopes? AJ Cavendish. How the mighty have fallen—from champion skier to coaching novices!*

It sounded gloating, and it left a nasty taste in his mouth.

*Has super-rich playboy—son of billionaire IT mogul Alexander Cavendish—gone from flying high to barfly?*

There was a picture of him from his championship days and another of him sitting at a bar with two drinks in front of him—the implication being that he was using alcohol as a crutch. Nothing could be further from the truth. He knew exactly which bar that was, and had a pretty good idea which day it was, too. He'd actually been having a quiet drink with Giovanni, who at that point had clearly left their table to go to the bathroom. But the angle of the photograph made it look as if Josh was lining up shots to drown his sorrows.

Josh was furious that Annabel had dragged Giovanni into what felt like a personal vendetta. Gallingly, he couldn't even slap her with a defamation suit, because the words were just on the right side of the law—posing a question instead of making a statement.

*Clearly he's not very good at coaching, either.*

That little remark was accompanied by a picture of Sophie after she'd taken a tumble and him looking slightly alarmed as he helped her up.

He could just about ignore the comments about himself and treat them with the contempt they deserved. But that little dig at Sophie wasn't on. Sophie was worth a million Annabels. Not in monetary terms, maybe—but Sophie was *real*, not a woman who put on a fake show half the time. She was warm and sweet and lovely. She wouldn't sneer at someone for not wearing designer brands or high-end cosmetics, the way Annabel did. Sophie saw what was really important in life, and she'd shown him that, too. It was why he'd fallen in love with her. No way was he letting Annabel drip her vitriol on Sophie. Not to mention the invasion of Sophie's privacy. He'd set his family lawyers on to this and make Annabel issue a public apology.

He sorted that out first, then rang Gio back.

'That…' Gio swore very colourfully and very inventively. 'Hasn't she done enough to hurt you?'

'Clearly not,' Josh said. 'I don't know what she thinks she's achieved by this piece of spite. It's not going to make me want her back or make anyone else think any better of her.' He sighed. 'I'd better go and see Sophie and warn her, before she finds out about it from someone else.'

'Does she know about Annabel?'

'No.' He hadn't told Sophie about an awful lot of things. Including his background. And he was going to have to tell her now, before she saw that story. 'No.'

'This isn't going to be pretty.'

That was an understatement. Sophie would be furious that he'd kept so much from her. He knew how much she valued honesty, and he knew how much Blake's lies had hurt her.

Josh hadn't actually *lied* to her. He'd simply omitted to tell her his background. But he was all too aware that she might see that as a form of dishonesty.

His gut turned to water. Hopefully she'd give him a chance to explain. He hadn't kept the information from her in order to hurt her; he'd kept his background from her because he'd wanted her to see him for himself, not as a poor little rich boy. And he hadn't told her about Annabel because he'd wanted to put that part of his life behind him.

But this was a conversation they needed to have face to face. 'I'm going to see her now. Thank you for the warning.'

'What do you mean, I'm in a gossip magazine?' Sophie asked, looking up from the waffle batter she was making.

'You're in *Celebrity Life*.' It was Kitty's favourite gossip mag, about the rich and famous; she read it avidly.

'Why on earth would I be in a gossip magazine?' Sophie asked. She wasn't even vaguely famous. She was just a quiet, unassuming chef in a ski lodge. OK, one with a past: but Blake wasn't famous, either.

Unless he'd been caught…

But that wouldn't have made the gossip pages. It probably wouldn't even have made the newspapers. Who cared about a con man who'd skipped the country with someone else's money?

'It might be someone who looks like me,' she said.

'Nope. It's definitely you and Josh.' Kitty handed over her phone.

Sophie stared at the photograph. 'That's when I fell over on the slopes, the other day.' And she hadn't been able to get up. Josh had had to help her.

She wasn't so bothered about being photographed looking a bit foolish—but her name was there, too, and that was enough to set up a little niggle of worry. What if the press dug further into her background? She'd been working so hard to repair her reputation. The last thing she needed was to become famous in the press as the woman so stupid that she let her fiancé empty her bank account and ruin her business. Then she'd never, ever get another job.

'Don't worry too much,' Kitty said. 'It's like that horrible model or whatever who took that picture of the old lady in the gym changing room and made nasty comments—it's just made everyone realise how vile she is.'

'But why me?' Sophie asked, looking at the name of the woman who was credited with the story. 'Annabel Smethurst? I've never even heard of her before. I definitely haven't met her. Why would she put a photo of me in the gossip magazine?'

'It's not you she's after. She's having a bit of a go at Josh,' Kitty said.

Sophie scrolled through the article: *World Champion to Novice?*

But Josh wasn't a champion skier...was he?

She read further. 'AJ Cavendish...that's *Josh*?'

'Seems so,' Kitty said. 'And he was world champion. In the skiing world, that makes him the equivalent of the guy who won a big award for best actor. You've been dating a superstar.'

Sophie brushed it aside. 'But, if he's a world champion, why is he here in Pendio di Cristallo, giving lessons to people like me? And who's this Annabel Smethurst?'

'I don't know,' Kitty said.

*Super-rich playboy...*

What? The Josh she knew was a part-time ski instructor.

But he'd taken her to a Michelin-starred restaurant. One where, now she thought about it, they'd treated him as if he was a regular customer.

*Son of billionaire IT mogul...*

Was that true?

And why hadn't he told her?

That picture of Josh in one of the resort bars, lining the drinks up in front of him—that wasn't the Josh that Sophie knew. He might have a glass of wine with dinner, sure, but if he was driving he wouldn't drink any more than that one glass.

Or maybe he was different when he wasn't with her. In the evenings, when she was working and maybe wasn't staying over at his, perhaps he really did sit in a bar and drink heavily. And perhaps Giovanni Rendini was recommending him to clients in the hope that it would give Josh something to do and keep him sober.

Well, that would certainly explain why Josh wasn't a world champion skier right now. If he really did have a drink problem, the way the article implied, then he needed help. She ought to be kind.

But right at that moment she felt numb and cold with fear. Because everything she knew had suddenly been turned upside down. She'd thought she'd been dating an ordinary man. A gorgeous man who turned heads, but still ordinary. A ski instructor. Not someone famous. Not someone from a super-rich, glamorous background that was a million miles away from her own.

'Can I...?' Sophie gestured to the phone.

''Course you can.'

She tapped Josh's and Annabel's surnames into the search engine. And then she wished she hadn't when the stories came up.

*Champion skier dumps pregnant fiancée.*

The photographs that went with the story were definitely of Josh, though the media called him 'AJ'. He'd changed his name, clearly. To cover his tracks? And maybe he thought the media wouldn't go looking for a world champion in a little family-oriented skiing resort.

There were pictures of Josh and Annabel together at swish parties with people that even

Sophie recognised; they had a very, very glamorous social set. Gstaad, where it was hinted that they'd skied with the royal family. And then there were other pictures with Annabel looking distraught, dabbing at her eyes with a handkerchief and with her hand resting protectively over her stomach.

Some of this didn't feel right. The Josh Sophie knew would never abandon his pregnant fiancée. He had integrity.

But then again, was the Josh she knew even real? The Josh she knew was a part-time ski instructor, whose old job had fallen through and he was trying to choose between a future in teaching and an office job.

What he hadn't told her was that his old job was being a world champion skier.

Or that the office job he was thinking about taking was being the CEO of his family's firm. Because AJ was the son of billionaire software developer Alex Cavendish, and some news articles were hinting that AJ was poised to take over from his father when Alex retired.

And to think she'd worried about her part-time ski instructor boyfriend putting a hole in his budget when he'd taken her out. With a family background that wealthy, he could probably buy this entire resort with his spare change.

She felt sick.

She'd been honest with him about the awful mistake she'd made.

In return, he'd kept something huge from her. He'd misled her about who he was. She'd thought they were getting closer, that maybe there was something special between them; but the man she'd believed she was getting to know, the man she'd fallen in love with, didn't really exist.

Had he been using her? Slumming it, to make himself feel better?

And why hadn't he told her the truth about himself?

No wonder he'd lied so easily to Gaz and his friends. His whole life here was a lie. She'd been furious with him for being dishonest with that bet, and he'd promised never to do anything like that again. No doubt he'd been laughing at her the whole time. Stupid Sophie, so easily duped. So easily lied to. And she hadn't learned from what Blake had done. She'd still trusted someone. She'd trusted Josh.

And he'd let her down.

'I can't believe this,' she whispered.

Kitty took the phone from her and skim-read the stories. 'That doesn't sound like the Josh we know. He's *nice*.'

But was he really? Was the Josh they knew

the *real* one? He'd lied to her, even though he knew how much she valued honesty and integrity. 'Right now, it feels as if I've just dropped into a parallel universe,' Sophie said. 'Where everything I thought was true isn't.'

The chalet doorbell rang.

Sophie and Kitty stared at each other.

'It's not delivery day,' Kitty said.

'Even if it was, they wouldn't be here at this time of the morning, before our guests are even up,' Sophie said.

'Supposing that's the press?' Kitty's eyes were wide. 'I'll go. If anyone's snooping around, looking for you, I'll tell them you're not here.'

Another lie. This had to stop. 'No,' she said wearily. 'I'll go. If it's the press, I'll face them and tell them there isn't actually a story. Josh is my skiing instructor, and that's all.'

He wouldn't even be that, in a few minutes' time.

Because she was going to call everything off, as soon as she'd dealt with whoever was at the door. And it was nothing to do with the desertion story: it was the fact he hadn't been honest with her. She'd had enough of lies with Blake.

Never, ever again.

Steeling herself—all she knew about the pa-

parazzi was what she'd seen in the movies, with camera flashes going off everywhere and a horde of journalists all talking at once so you couldn't make out a single word—she opened the front door.

There was no babbling horde, and no flashes. Just Josh.

Except he wasn't *just* Josh, was he? He was famous, he was wealthy, and he'd been playing games with her to amuse himself.

'What do you want?' she asked.

'To talk to you.'

She shook her head. 'There's nothing to say. You lied to me—and you know how I feel about dishonesty.' Even though it hurt to say it, and it meant her dreams were shattering all over again, this was the only course of action she could take. 'We're through.'

Oh, no.

It looked as if she already knew about the article.

'Sophie, please. We need to talk.'

'There's nothing to say,' she repeated.

The warm, lovely girl he'd fallen in love with wasn't standing in the doorway. Instead there was a stranger with cold eyes and a stony expression.

'The article. I'm sorry. You shouldn't have

been involved, and my lawyers are going to make her issue an apology.'

'I'm not interested,' she said. 'I don't care what it said about me. You *lied* to me, Josh. Or should I call you AJ?'

'My name's Josh,' he said. 'Officially it's Alexander, after my dad, but everyone's always called me by my middle name. I used my initials for work—for skiing.'

'Yes.' Her expression cooled even further. 'World champion. You knew I wouldn't have a clue who you are. So the article was right about that, wasn't it? You're a rich kid, slumming it and pretending to be someone you're not.'

'Sophie, I didn't lie to you.'

'A lie of omission is still a lie. You bent the truth to suit yourself, and that's as dishonest as what Blake did. It's not OK, Josh. Not OK at all.'

'Sophie—'

'No,' she said. 'I deserve better than this.'

'You do, and I'm sorry.'

'Too late,' she said. 'I told you everything about me. And you didn't even have the courtesy to tell me your real name, let alone who you are.'

Because he hadn't wanted her to see him as a poor little rich boy. He hadn't wanted her to pity him. He'd wanted her to see who he truly was, not through the filter of the media.

How had it all gone so badly wrong?

'I don't want to see you any more, Mr Cavendish,' she said. The formality in her voice felt as if she'd flayed him. 'I've had more than enough lies to last me a lifetime. No more. Goodbye.'

And then, to his shock, without even giving him the chance to explain, she closed the door in his face.

He stared at the closed door, wanting to hammer it down with his bare fists, but knowing that it would alienate Sophie even further. She'd made her position perfectly clear: she didn't want to see him again. She wasn't even going to give him the chance to explain.

He'd lost her.

And this felt worse than that terrible meeting with his consultant, the one that had forced him to face reality and see that his career was over. Everything he'd defined himself as was over.

Josh had managed to scrape himself back together since then. But this…this felt worse.

Because he'd lost *her*.

Just when he thought he'd found someone special. Someone who made him feel different. Someone he wanted to spend the rest of his life with.

She'd said it was over.

And all the sunshine seemed to have vanished from the world.

Everything around him felt cold and sterile. Unwelcoming.

He didn't know how he could even begin to fix this. Where to start. How to persuade her to give him five minutes of her time so he could tell her what really happened.

But for now everything felt so bad that the only thing he could do was pick up his skis and head for a black run. He'd once told her that the mountains made everything better; and he hoped to hell he was right.

Even though he didn't want to see anyone or talk to anyone, he knew that the first rule of the mountains was that you told someone where you were going—especially if you were heading out on your own. So he sent Giovanni a private message saying which run he was going on, and then turned his phone to silent so he could ignore any reply.

Gio would probably give him a hard time later for doing a black run and putting his knee at risk, but Josh knew that nothing less would sort his head out. He needed something where he'd get the buzz of skiing at high speed, whizzing down a mountain with just his skill to guide him. Something steep and scary to conquer.

He brooded all the way up on the chairlift.

He brooded as he double-checked the bindings of his skis.

He brooded as he got to the edge.

And then he pushed himself off, tucked himself in, and waited for the rush of skiing to clear his mind, the way it usually did.

Except he misjudged a turn, caught the edge of his ski, and tipped over.

At speed.

Christ.

He knew the drill of falls. Distribute your weight as evenly as possible. Land with a straight arm by your side and a straight leg, to avoid hitting your head or your hip. Then turn and dig your arms into the snow to reduce your speed. The last thing he needed now was to slide uncontrollably towards a drop and fall again.

But his knee caught something.

When he finally stopped, he couldn't put any weight on his knee when he tried to get up.

This was bad.

*Really* bad.

A skier came to a halt beside him. 'You OK, man?'

'No. My knee's...' Josh shook his head, unable to articulate his fears. Terror put a huge lump in his throat and blocked the words.

'Is anyone with you?'

'I'm on my own.'

'OK. Give me a second and I'll sort out help.' The other skier collected Josh's skis and stuck them, crossed, in the snow above Josh to warn other skiers there was an obstacle. 'Did you hit your head or black out at all?'

'No.'

'Well, that's something.' The other skier called the emergency services, giving all the details to help them locate him and Josh.

Was history repeating itself?

The last time he'd had a bad fall, it had been after his relationship had imploded. When Annabel had given him the news that she was pregnant—and then, before he'd even had time to absorb the fact that he was going to be a dad, she'd casually told him she would have a termination unless he married her.

He'd known at that moment how much he didn't want to marry her.

This time, his relationship had fallen apart for a different reason. He hadn't trusted Sophie with the truth. But he'd forgotten the hard lesson he'd learned from Annabel, and he was so angry at himself for not connecting it.

*Don't ski when your head's in the wrong place.*

He should've found a different way—a safer way—to clear his head.

But no.

He'd gone for the adrenalin rush to wipe out the pain and misery. Instead, he'd wiped out his knee. What if he'd done the rest of the damage his surgeon had warned him about? What if he wasn't able to ski ever again? That would mean he'd lost everything. He'd lost Sophie, he'd lost his new dream of opening an inclusive ski resort, and although adaptive skiing was a good alternative it would never give him the same rush as the kind of skiing that he really loved.

It would all be bearable if Sophie was there.

But he'd ruined that by not telling her the whole truth.

It seemed like for ever before the rescue team got there. And even longer while Josh was stuck in the ambulance. He hated having to be dependent, but he had no choice other than to text Giovanni to say that he'd fallen on the slope and was going to hospital.

By the time Giovanni met him at the hospital, the doctor had already told Josh the news wasn't quite as bad as he feared—he hadn't snapped his ACL again or damaged his meniscus—but he'd need more physio. More work to reduce inflammation and swelling, more exercises to restore full knee extension, and a repetition of all the work he'd done last year.

The worst bit was the doctor's unbreakable rule: no more skiing for the rest of the season.

'So are you going back to England?' Giovanni asked.

'Even if I can't ski—'

'There's no "if" about it,' the doctor cut in.

Josh acknowledged that with a wry smile. 'I'd still rather be here in the mountains.'

'No skiing, no snowboarding, no snow-shoeing, no ice skating, no tobogganing, and no other winter sport I haven't mentioned yet or haven't heard of,' the doctor warned. 'You don't even *walk* anywhere if there's the slightest chance you might slip on the ice and jar your knee.'

'I'll make sure he behaves,' Giovanni said. 'You're coming to stay with us, Josh.'

Josh shook his head. 'I don't want to be a burden on you.'

'You'll be more of a burden if you're on your own, because I'll be worried sick about you,' Giovanni pointed out.

'I'd rather be on my own,' Josh said.

'Wallowing in self-pity?' Giovanni demanded. 'Get over yourself!'

It stung, but Josh knew he deserved the rebuke. 'I'm not good company right now, so I'm really better off on my own,' he said. 'But I promise I'll check in with you every morning and every evening.'

'And every lunchtime.' Giovanni folded his arms. 'I'm tempted to let Mamma deal with you.'

Josh gave him a tired smile. 'I know my limits. And I'm not going to do anything stupid. Just work on my physio.' And work out what the hell he was going to do with his life, if he couldn't ski a black run ever again.

'All right. And I'll let Sophie know.'

*Sophie.*

What Josh would do right now to have Sophie's arms round him. To have her calm common sense whispered into his ear. To feel her warmth and sweetness.

But it wasn't going to happen. He'd ruined that.

'No need. Sophie and I are over.'

'But surely if she knows you're hurt, she'll—?'

'No,' Josh cut in. She'd already rejected him. He wasn't going to let that happen a second time. Or, worse, that she'd be with him out of pity. 'I have my pride.'

'And pride is a very cold bedfellow,' Giovanni said.

Right then, Josh didn't think he'd ever feel warm again. 'It's all I have, right now,' he said. 'Would you mind giving me a lift back to Pendio?'

'Only,' Giovanni said, 'if your doctor agrees.'

'Provided you stick to the conditions,' the doctor said.

'No winter sports of any kind,' Josh said dryly. 'I've got the message loud and clear.'

And he had a lot of thinking time coming up. The minutes stretched out emptily before him. Minutes, hours, days, weeks.

And it was all his own stupid fault.

It was a beautiful day. The sun was shining, the sky was impossibly blue, and it was the perfect day for skiing.

Though Sophie didn't plan to ski any more. She missed it—much more than she'd expected to—but no way was she risking going anywhere she might bump into Josh. She'd even asked Kitty to return her skis, poles and helmet to the ski hire place for her, to make doubly sure she didn't accidentally see Josh; and if she wanted any shopping outside their weekly delivery, she asked Kitty to pick it up for her.

She'd resolutely ignored *Celebrity Life*. Kitty had started to tell her something about

Josh that had happened a year ago, but Sophie had cut her short. 'I like you, Kitty, but we're going to fall out really badly if you take his side.'

'I'm not taking his side, Soph. But if you'll just li—'

'No ifs. No buts. Josh and I are history. I don't want to hear anything more about him.'

Kitty's shoulders had slumped, but thankfully she'd respected Sophie's feelings and stopped talking about Josh. Sophie had resisted the temptation to look up anything more about Josh's past. He was clearly a rich boy who'd been slumming it and wouldn't know what honesty was if it jumped up in front of him and shouted 'boo'; and she'd had a lucky escape from yet another poor decision.

Luckily Hannah wasn't a fan of the gossip magazines, either, so Sophie could avoid telling her best friend about what had happened and what a fool she'd been.

So much for thinking that this Christmas would be special. That it would mark the start of a new phase of her life.

Josh had tried to call her, but she'd rejected the calls. She'd deleted all his texts unread.

He'd sent her flowers, too. An enormous and hugely expensive display of roses.

She'd given them to Kitty and sent him a

note to say thank you for the flowers, but they hadn't changed her mind.

Although she'd made sure the chalet was decorated for the perfect family Christmas for her guests, she knew her smiles were fake and she wasn't even enjoying making Christmassy food for them. Though she had to stick it out and finish her job here in Pendio; she couldn't just leave and go back to England, because she needed the reference as well as the money. She'd get through this. One day at a time. One foot in front of the other.

But never, ever again would she allow herself to trust another man.

Josh didn't answer the video call. Just as he hadn't answered any of them since the day after the accident. He'd holed up in his chalet and spent all his time on physio and brooding, keeping everyone at a distance.

A few seconds later, a message flashed up on the screen.

Joshie, if you don't answer my call, I'll be forced to fly over to visit you. You wouldn't make me do that with morning sickness, would you?

He stared at the screen. Wait, what? Morning sickness? He was going to be an uncle again?

He called her back. 'Lauren? Are you all right?'

'Yes. Though I'm not using the Tube again until this phase passes. Rush hour crush and questionable personal hygiene isn't a good mix with morning sickness.'

'It's not a good mix, full stop.' He smiled at her. 'Congratulations!'

'It's still early days, so it's not public knowledge,' she warned.

'Got it. Mum and Dad know?'

'Yes. So does Willow. She's thrilled at the prospect of having a baby sister to play with and she's already picked out her favourite teddy as a present.' She laughed. 'She's been such a sweetie. I was throwing up yesterday, and she actually asked if I wanted Daddy to bring me some of the pink medicine to make the baby better.'

'That's lovely.' And suddenly Josh missed his family. His mum. His dad. His sister. His brother-in-law. His beyond cute three-year-old niece.

'So how are *you*?'

'I'm fine,' he fibbed.

'You don't look it,' she said, not pulling her punches. 'And you're in pushing-everyone-away mode, just like when you crashed in the race, so does that mean your knee's worse than last time?'

'We're not talking surgery—at least, not yet. Just intense physio.'

'Right.' She paused. 'So what actually happened?'

He gave her a condensed version of Annabel's article, Sophie's reaction and his fall.

Lauren rolled her eyes. 'That bloody woman. I wish she'd just leave you alone.'

Yeah. So did he.

'What are you going to do about Sophie?' Lauren asked.

'At the moment, there's nothing I can do. She won't talk to me.' And he wasn't brilliantly mobile, so he couldn't exactly chase after her to try and make her change her mind. She'd rejected his calls and ignored his texts; although she'd been polite and sent him a text to thank him for the flowers, she'd made it clear he was wasting his time because she wasn't going to forgive him.

'You should've been honest with her.'

'I would've been, if she'd given me the chance,' he pointed out.

'But you had plenty of opportunities to tell her before Annabel stuck her oar in,' Lauren said dryly. 'So what now? Are you just going to sit there stewing in self-pity?'

'Probably,' he agreed.

'Men!' She groaned. 'Josh, it's Christmas in a couple of days. I'll give you until Christmas Day to sulk, and then I'm pulling rank as your older sister. Either you find something you want to do with your life, or you're coming to work for me. And if you thought *you* were a slavedriver to yourself when you were training for the world championship, you'll find that I take it to the next level.'

His sister was the sweetest person he knew, besides Sophie. No way was she a slavedriver. Everyone in the company loved her. He couldn't help smiling.

'That's better,' Lauren said. 'Seriously, Josh, everything you've told me about Sophie makes it clear she meant a lot to you. Why don't you ask her to give you a chance to explain? And this time tell her everything. Including what Annabel did. I still think you should've sued that woman for libel.'

'I just wanted the whole mess to die down. Putting my side of the story out would only have raked it all up again, and some people would still have believed her anyway because she got her story in first,' he said. 'As for Sophie, I've blown it. I know dishonesty's a big thing with her.' He told Lauren what had happened with Blake.

'That's awful,' Lauren said, looking shocked. 'But you can do something to help her, Josh. We can pay a private detective to track the guy down. Even if he's spent all the money and she doesn't get a single penny back, at least we can find him and that'll give her closure.'

'She explicitly told me not to interfere.' He explained what he'd done about Gaz and his friends.

'Hmm. You should've handled that a wee bit differently.'

'Tell me about it.'

'So she told you not to interfere. She didn't tell *me* not to interfere, though,' Lauren said sweetly. 'And I don't like cheats and liars, either.'

He winced. 'I get the point. I screwed up. Big time.'

'And you're suffering for it.' She sighed. 'So what are you going to do, Josh?'

'Right now, I don't know. Work out how to get her to talk to me. And then work out what I'm going to do with my life.' He shook his head. 'Much as I love you, I don't want to work for you.'

'You're right. It'd be a disaster. We'd drive each other potty,' she said. 'And I don't think you'll settle for being a ski instructor. Not long term.'

'I have,' he said, 'been thinking about something else. Making the world a better place.'
Taking his cue from Sophie.

'That sounds good. What are you thinking?'

'I love skiing,' he said. 'It makes me feel free. Alive.'

She nodded.

'And I know I'm one bad fall away from disaster with my knee. Right now, and with what happened last year, I've got some understanding of how it feels to be restricted in what you can do physically.' He took a deep breath. 'So I've been thinking about adaptive skiing. Maybe I could set up a place where the whole family can ski together, regardless of injury or ability. We'd have trained instructors and the right equipment. Somewhere that makes the world a bit brighter for people with disabilities who've already had to struggle enough. Somewhere with a spa and massage therapy, and rooms that work for everyone.'

'That,' Lauren said, 'sounds brilliant.'

'But?' He could see the wariness in her face.

'But please tell me it's not going to be somewhere miles away from the family, so we never see you. You've spent the last ten years or so travelling the world. We miss you.'

'There's room for compromise,' he said. 'I want to set up a resort here—but in the summer months I'd be happy for someone else to manage it as a spa retreat, and I'll come back to England.'

'You *could* get snow machines and build a resort here, near Mum and Dad,' she said.

'It wouldn't be the same. There aren't any mountains near London,' Josh pointed out. 'And dry slopes just aren't like real mountains.'

Lauren sighed. 'Then your compromise sounds about the best thing. Dad's handing Cavendish Software over to me properly next month. As the new CEO, I'd be happy to offer some serious sponsorship. Not just helping you set up the place, but making it affordable for your clients. Assisted places.'

'That,' he said, 'would be amazing.'

'What's the point of being rich if all you're going to do is spend it on fancy clothes and partying?' she asked.

Which was what he'd done with Annabel. Wasted all that time and resources when he could've done something better: the complete opposite of what he knew Sophie would have done in the same circumstances.

'Sophie,' he said, 'would absolutely love you. And you'd love her.'

'Then you'd better fix things between you, little brother.' She smiled at him. 'Right. Nagging over. I'm going over to see our parents and reassure them that you're still just about in one piece. And you're going to talk to Sophie. In her shoes, I would ignore your calls and texts, too. You need to do this properly, face to face.'

'I will,' he promised. 'Not this evening, because she's working and it wouldn't be fair of me to go and demand attention. But tomorrow. I'll talk to her tomorrow after I've done my morning physio.'

'Good luck,' she said.

'Thanks. I'm going to need it,' he admitted.

# CHAPTER NINE

THE COFFEE SMELLED REVOLTING, and Sophie nearly gagged. No way could she drink this.

No way could she serve this to her chalet guests, either. It would be the worst Christmas Eve breakfast drink ever.

Except...the coffee had been fine when she'd opened it yesterday, and she'd stored it in an airtight container in the fridge: so it wouldn't have suddenly gone off.

Maybe she'd done something stupid. She couldn't think what, but then again she was finding it hard to think rationally at the moment. Worrying about the future. Worrying about what was going to happen when she left here in just over a month's time. Would she be able to find a new job, and quickly? Could she afford a room in a shared house in London?

Josh had been a distraction from that.

But Josh had lied to her. Toyed with her.

She tipped the coffee down the sink and made a fresh batch.

Only the new batch smelled vile, too.

Hannah had been like that six months ago, unable to bear the smell of—

She stopped mid-thought, breath frozen in horror.

Of course she wasn't pregnant.

OK, so she'd missed a period, but stress always did that to her. She'd missed three in a row after her parents' accident, and two when she'd lost the restaurant. This was just stress, she reminded herself. She'd be fine.

But the suggestion was in her head and it wouldn't go away.

Pregnant.

She and Josh had used protection when they'd made love, but condoms could fail. The chance was infinitesimally small, but it was still there. And it only took one sperm to fertilise an egg. Sophie knew from Hannah's infertility journey exactly when you could get pregnant: it wasn't just that little window during ovulation. Sperm could live for up to five days in fertile pre-ovulation cervical mucus. And...

No. She couldn't be pregnant.

Could she?

She managed to keep in professional mode

for her guests, making waffles, eggs Florentine and endless toast, but the cooking scents made her feel slightly ill.

Ill enough for Kitty to notice. 'Are you OK, Sophie?'

'Yes, sure,' Sophie said, brushing it off. She knew she needed to come up with a plausible excuse, so she added the fib. 'Just a bit of a headache. I'll be fine. And you go off skiing early. I'll clear up.'

'Are you sure?'

'Yes.' She wanted to be on her own to think things through.

By the time the kitchen was restored to perfect shining order, she'd come to the conclusion that she was probably being ridiculous, but buying a pregnancy test would reassure her that her missed period was down to stress and nothing more significant.

And please, please don't let her bump into Josh. It would be just her luck.

Thankfully there was no sign of Josh. She didn't know the person on duty in the pharmacy, and was able to buy a pregnancy test and shove it to the bottom of her bag without the risk of any gossip.

The walk back to the chalet seemed to take for ever.

She put her shopping away, then went to her

en-suite bathroom. Time to prove that she was worrying about nothing.

'It's stress, Sophie Harris,' she told herself firmly. 'Just stress. Do the test, and your period will probably start tomorrow.'

She didn't bother reading the instructions. Apart from the fact that she knew the stress of the situation would make her struggle more than usual with reading, and the letters of the tiny print would merge together, she'd been there enough times to hold Hannah's hand. All tests worked on the same principle. Pee on the stick, cap it, check the first window for a line to show that the test was working, wait a bit, look at the other window, and then there was either a line to say you were pregnant—or, in Hannah's case, month after month, a window as empty as her womb.

Her heart squeezed. Hannah was going to be such a great mum, yet she'd had such problems conceiving. It would be horribly ironic if Sophie, whose life was currently in a mess and who didn't have a partner, had fallen pregnant without even trying.

And, if she was expecting their baby, how would Josh react to the news?

'Don't overthink it,' she counselled herself aloud. 'It isn't an issue because you're not pregnant. You're just stressed, that's all.'

Just to prove it, she glanced down at the window.

Had she been holding the stick, she would've dropped it in shock. As it was, it lay where she'd set it on the side of the sink.

There was a line in each of the windows.

Meaning she *was* pregnant.

What now?

She'd thought about having children when Blake had asked her to marry him. She'd thought that she'd be able to combine motherhood and a career. That her children would grow up in a happy home, just as she had, safe and secure. She'd so wanted to be part of a family again.

Right now, she had no security. Her job here would end in a few weeks, and she didn't yet have anything lined up for her return to England—despite applying for several jobs online. She had nowhere to live. She'd saved her salary here and most of her tips, but those savings wouldn't last for long.

Her time in the Dolomites was supposed to be a way of getting herself back on her feet. Picking herself up and dusting herself down, just as she would if she fell over in the snow. Working out a plan for her life.

This had turned everything upside down.

A termination felt wrong, when her best friend had struggled so hard to fall pregnant.

And a baby would mean that she had a family again. Someone else in the world who was related to her by blood, instead of her being alone.

Though the baby wasn't just hers. It took two to make a baby. She couldn't just pretend Josh didn't exist. He had the right to know that he was going to be a father, even though she didn't intend to take a penny from him; she wasn't letting him back into her life, because she didn't trust him not to let her down again. Who knew what else he'd lied about?

How was she going to tell him?

Write to him? Even though she was angry with him for keeping her in the dark, for not telling her the truth about himself, she wasn't going to tell him by text or email. This wasn't the sort of conversation she could have on the phone, either. It would have to be face to face.

She grabbed her phone and texted him.

Need to talk to you. When's convenient?

More painkillers weren't the answer. The only way was to push himself through the pain.

Josh gritted his teeth and did the physio. It

hurt. It hurt *a lot*. But it was his own stupid fault. Hadn't he learned his lesson, last time? Don't ski when distracted. Especially don't ski a black run.

God only knew how far that tumble had set his progress back.

So much for telling Sophie that the mountains made everything better. This time, they had made things worse.

Maybe he should give up skiing completely.

What was it Sophie had said? Toss a coin and you'll know what you need to do. OK. Heads he battled on; tails he gave up.

He tossed the coin.

*Tails.*

Give up, then.

She'd said his reaction would make him know if it was the right choice. Be horrified, and he'd know he should carry on. Be relieved, and he'd know giving up was the right thing to do.

But what if you felt…empty?

He didn't feel anything. Anything at all.

It was like being stuck in a snowdrift, everything still and quiet and getting gradually colder, the change so gradual that he was barely aware of it happening. Chilled to the bone, the blood growing sluggish.

Just empty.

Because he'd lost her.

No way could he go to talk to her when he was in this mood. He was likely to say something stupid and make things even worse between them. Somehow he'd have to clear his head. Except what he always did to clear his head wasn't an option. No skiing. He couldn't even drive himself out to a forest somewhere.

Why would Sophie want to bother with such a pathetic specimen?

Well, she'd made it pretty clear she didn't want to bother with him any more.

Happy Christmas.

Not.

This was shaping up to be the most miserable Christmas ever. And he needed to shake off the self-pity. That wasn't who he was.

His phone beeped to signal an incoming text.

Probably a message from Giovanni to remind him that it was Christmas Eve and they were expecting him for dinner tonight. He definitely had to improve his mood before then; but even if he was still feeling this low, he was going to fake some Christmas joy, for their sake. Maybe playing with the kids would help.

But when he looked at the screen, he saw the message was from Sophie.

The person he most wanted to speak to; yet,

at the same time, the one person he knew he ought to avoid until his head was straight, so he didn't mess it up.

Need to talk to you. When's convenient?

Straight and to the point, which he expected from her. But, at their last meeting, she'd made it very clear that she wanted nothing more to do with him. What did she want to talk to him about?

Unless Giovanni had told her about the fall and his knee. If Lauren hadn't thought to tell the Rendinis that she'd staged an intervention, maybe Giovanni was under the impression that Sophie could get through to Josh when he was in pushing-everyone-away mode and had asked Sophie to get in touch with him.

He planned to deflect her—but his fingers clearly weren't agreeing with the plan, because he found himself texting back.

Whenever's convenient for you.

Oh, for pity's sake.

Disgusted with himself, he started a new message to say that he had a meeting—she didn't need to know that meeting was with himself to do his physio that afternoon—when his phone beeped again.

Now? Your chalet?

So she knew he wasn't teaching?
Well, duh. He wouldn't have replied to her text if he'd been teaching, would he?
Might as well get it over with.

OK.

On my way

That was her reply.
Then reality snapped in. The chalet was a pigsty. One glance and she'd know what a mess his head was in. So, if she'd been sent by the Rendinis in an attempt to find out what kind of state he was really in, she'd call them straight away.
Why hadn't he been sensible and suggested meeting at her chalet, or better still on neutral ground? Too late, now.
He needed to fix this.
Fast.
If he tidied the living room and kept her out of the kitchen, he might get away with pretending everything was just fine.

He scooped up the magazines and books he'd tried reading and had tossed aside, and dumped them on his bed. The pizza boxes and takeout cartons went in the bin. The empty coffee mugs and stray bits of cutlery went in the dishwasher, out of sight. He dragged the overflowing laundry basket from the bathroom—just in case she asked to use it—to his bedroom.

There was no time to vacuum or dust. But if he opened the kitchen window there would be some fresh air. It'd be cold—seriously cold—but that was a huge improvement on the stale warm air that was there now.

It was snowing, but not hard enough to mean he couldn't leave the window open.

He'd just put the kettle on and shaken ground coffee into a cafetière, hoping that the scent of fresh coffee would mask any lingering smells of pizza remains, when there was a knock at his door.

His knee was hurting, but he wasn't going to admit it. And he wasn't going to let her see him limp, even through the frosted glass of the door. He forced himself to walk normally, even though it hurt like hell, and opened the door to her. 'Come in. Coffee?'

'No, thanks.'

Her face looked pinched, he thought, but he

suppressed the urge to wrap his arms round her and hold her close. She'd made it clear she didn't want that from him. 'Can I take your coat?'

'It's a bit…' She gestured to the snowflakes. 'It's OK.'

'So what did you want?' he asked, knowing it sounded a bit abrupt and rude but not knowing what else to say. And scared that his mouth would run away with him and beg her to give him a second chance.

'I, um…you need to know,' she said. 'I missed my period. I did a test this morning. I'm pregnant.'

*Pregnant.*

There was a roaring in his ears.

He'd been here before.

All he could see was Annabel standing in front of him, that fateful day. The day of the championship competition. The day that had changed his life for ever.

*'I'm pregnant, Josh. I'm going to have a termination. Unless you're planning to marry me.'*

An ultimatum.

One that had clarified everything for him: yes, of course he had a responsibility to her because she was pregnant—but he didn't want to marry her. He didn't want to spend the rest of his life with her. They'd had fun together, but he'd started to suspect that she'd seen him in terms of his family background. The wealth. The lifestyle she wanted. The fact that he was world champion, so they were invited to all the glittery parties and events.

The way Annabel had told him the news— no discussion, just an ultimatum—had shocked him.

They'd had a huge fight.

And she'd stormed out.

He'd been thinking about it on that mogul run, instead of concentrating on what he was doing. Crashed. Wrecked his knee.

And Annabel had miscarried their baby.

At least, the press had said she'd miscarried. The story had been plastered across social media and the gossip pages. Photographs of Annabel looking wan and tearful. Annabel, who'd claimed he'd dumped her and broken their engagement—when they hadn't even been engaged.

The whole thing had felt staged. Maybe he was being unkind and she really *had* miscarried. But it didn't quite gel with the woman who'd given him the ultimatum *Marry me or I'll terminate the pregnancy.* That sounded like a woman who didn't care about a baby one way or the other.

And she'd certainly been happy enough dating the new world champion, a few weeks later.

Being stuck indoors had left Josh with too much time to brood. Too much time to wonder what the truth really was.

'You're pregnant,' he said, talking to Sophie but seeing Annabel.

'I thought you had the right to know,' she said. 'But I don't expect anything from you and I won't be claiming any kind of child support. We'll be fine on our own.'

He couldn't quite process this.

She was pregnant.

She wanted nothing from him.

She just thought he should know that he was going to be a father.

His mouth opened and closed, but there weren't any words. His head was as empty as his heart.

Before he could collect himself, she said, 'Clearly you're OK with that. Fine. Goodbye, Josh.'

And she walked out into the snow.

Closing the door quietly behind her.

What?

'Wait!' he called, and this time he hobbled to the door as fast as he could.

But she'd already gone.

Hell.

He couldn't rush after her the way he wanted to. Not when it was so icy and snowy outside. He couldn't risk slipping and doing even more damage to his bad knee. He couldn't drive, either.

What was going to be quicker? Limping to her chalet, or getting a taxi?

He called the local cab.

They were busy, but they could pick him up in twenty minutes.

Twenty minutes?

He couldn't wait that long. He wanted to talk to Sophie properly. Ask her to give him a chance. Ask her to let him explain. And he needed to do it now. The longer he left it, the less likely it was she'd talk to him.

When Sophie had told him her news, he'd been instantly transported back to the past. To Annabel. But Sophie was nothing like Annabel. She was honest. She wasn't going to run to the press and tell them a pack of lies to try and get what she wanted from him. Sophie had even said she expected nothing from him.

That wasn't what he wanted. At all.

What he wanted was Sophie—and their baby.

But first he was going to have to find her. And persuade her to talk to him.

He tried calling her, but the phone went straight to voicemail.

This wasn't something he wanted to do by voicemail message or text. She could ignore a phone call, but she couldn't ignore him standing on her doorstep.

Which left him with a choice. It was either wait twenty minutes for a taxi, or risk his knee on an icy path. And, given that the journeys would take about the same amount of time, this time he'd go for the sensible option.

He booked the taxi.

# CHAPTER TEN

IT DIDN'T LOOK as if the guests were in residence, Josh thought as he made his way up the steps to Sophie's chalet. Hopefully Kitty would be out on the slopes. And hopefully Sophie had come back here rather than going to a café in the resort.

He knocked on the door.

There was no answer.

He called through the letterbox, 'Sophie, I'm staying here until someone lets me in—whether it's you, Kitty or your guests. We need to talk. Please.'

Still no answer.

He texted her.

Sitting on the front step of your chalet. Staying here until you talk to me. Even if sitting here turns me into a snowman.

No answer.

He waited three minutes. He didn't care about the cold or the snow, but his knee was really starting to hurt. He texted her again.

OK. Going to borrow a megaphone and hold my side of the conversation very publicly.

That got him an answer.

She opened the door. 'What do you want, Josh?' she snapped.

Doing his best not to wince as he stood up, he said, 'We need to talk. I owe you an apology—and a lot of explanations.'

She shook her head. 'You don't owe me anything. We're done with each other.'

Oh, no, they weren't. 'You're pregnant with my baby, and we need to sort this out.'

'You can't dump me like you dumped Annabel, because I've already broken up with you.'

He winced. 'I guess I deserve that, though for the record there's an awful lot more to that story than what she told the press. But, first off, I want you to know that I'm not deserting you and I never would.'

Her expression was cold. 'I don't want you, Josh.'

He sighed. 'Please, Sophie. Let me explain. And then if you decide you don't want me in your life I'll walk away. But, regardless of anything else, I want you to know that I fully intend to support you and our child.'

'So that would be the son of a billionaire throwing money at a situation to make it go away?'

'No!' Oh, why did this have to be so complicated? 'I mean, yes, my dad's a billionaire, but I'm not trying to buy you off.'

'I thought you were a part-time ski instructor who had a bit of savings but you were thinking about taking another job. You let me believe that.' She shook her head. 'How many other lies have you told me?'

Technically, he hadn't lied. He *was* a part-time ski instructor thinking about his next job. He just hadn't told her that the savings were substantial. Or about his family background.

'I didn't set out to hurt you, Sophie. I know I've made a mess of things, and I'm sorry. But if you'll let me explain—let me be completely honest with you now—then maybe we can work our way through it. Please?'

She was silent for so long that he thought she'd say no, but finally she nodded. 'Come through to the kitchen.'

Then she frowned as he tried to walk normally beside her and failed. 'You're limping.'

'That doesn't matter right now. You're the important one. Are *you* all right? My sister had terrible morning sickness with Willow. How are you feeling?'

She stared at him. 'You're concerned about me?'

'Of course I'm concerned. You've just told me you're pregnant, you're in another country and you don't have family or close friends near—and it's Christmas Eve.'

'There's a thing called the internet. And another thing called a global mobile phone network. I don't have to be physically in the same place as my best friend to be close to her.'

He understood why she was angry with him. Hormones probably weren't helping. But his knee hurt and he was bone-deep tired and miserable. He didn't want to fight any more. 'Just answer the question, Sophie,' he said quietly. 'Are you all right?'

'Yes.'

'Good.' He took a deep breath. 'I'm sorry about the way I reacted when you told me about the baby. I was a bit shocked.'

'That makes two of us,' she said.

'I needed a few moments to process things,' he said quietly. 'I'm not here to fight with you. I'm on your side. Team Sophie.'

Her eyes filled with tears. 'How do I know that's true?'

'You don't,' he admitted. 'I can't prove it.

But maybe if we talk it through you might…'
He grimaced. 'I would say, start to trust me,
but I've already blown that one. You might
see it from a different perspective, perhaps.'

Her shoulders finally relaxed. 'OK.' She
glanced at the way he was standing. 'You'd
better sit down and take the weight off your
knee.'

Did she know about either of his crashes?

'What happened?' she asked, gesturing to
a stool in the kitchen.

He sat down, grateful for the pressure to be
off his knee. 'The quick answer is that it's an
aggravation of an old injury. Entirely my fault.'

'And the slow answer?'

'That would be part of my explanation,' he
said.

'All right.' She paused. 'Do you want a cup
of tea?'

The English answer—or perhaps the chalet host's answer—to everything. 'No. Just to
talk,' he said.

She nodded. 'I'm listening.'

'I was never engaged to Annabel,' he said.
'She was one of my set, and her background's
similar to mine. I dated her, yes—but I never
asked her to marry me. I think deep down I
knew we weren't right for each other.'

Sophie said nothing.

'What you said, about your only value to Blake being your money—that, and my position in the media, was precisely my value to Annabel,' he said softly.

Sophie flinched.

'She liked dating a world champion, having access to swish parties and skiing invitations that might not otherwise have come her way. And it suited me at the time to have someone beautiful and glamorous as my partner.' He paused. This might upset Sophie, but then again she already knew some of it from the media stories. 'I don't want to hurt you or give you the wrong idea. I'm just telling you the facts,' he said carefully. 'Annabel told me she was pregnant.'

Sophie still said nothing, but her eyes were huge and full of wariness.

'Not like the way you told me,' he said. 'Annabel told me if I didn't marry her she'd have a termination.'

Shock flittered across Sophie's face. 'That's—' She shook her head. 'I don't know what to say.'

'Her timing wasn't great,' Josh said dryly. 'I told her I didn't have the headspace to think about the situation until after the competition. I was racing that day. Freestyle.'

At Sophie's blank look, Josh explained, 'It's

the thing where you do acrobatics. Jumps, turns, spins, that sort of thing. You ski on moguls—the bumps made when people do turns. I loved doing that, more than anything else in the world.' He paused. 'Anyway, I had some time to think before the race. I tried to imagine myself settled down with Annabel and a baby, the way my sister was with her husband and Willow, or my parents had been with Lauren and me. And I just couldn't see it. I couldn't imagine her cuddled up with a toddler and a book, reading a story. She wouldn't tolerate sticky hands on her designer clothes, or risk her hair being mussed or her make-up smudged. She would've had a team of nannies and insisted on boarding school.' He shook his head. 'That wasn't what I wanted. At all. I realised then I didn't want to marry her. I was attracted to her, yes, but in a really superficial way. I didn't love her. Obviously I had responsibilities to her and the baby, and I would never have shirked them. Of course I would've supported them. But I didn't want to marry Annabel and spend the rest of my life with her.' He dragged in a breath. 'Normally, when I raced, my mind would be completely on the course. That day, all I could think about was Annabel and the baby, and her ultimatum. If I married her, we'd all be miserable. If I didn't...

she'd terminate the pregnancy. I wasn't paying enough attention to what I was doing and I crashed. Wrecked my knee. My surgeon said I had a choice: I could go back to doing what I loved, but it was highly unlikely I'd still be able to walk in twenty years' time. Or I could be sensible and stop competing.'

Sophie winced. 'So you had to give up what you loved most in the world. I'm sorry.'

'It wasn't your fault. It was mine, for letting myself be distracted at the wrong moment.' He frowned. 'Annabel realised I didn't have a future in professional skiing any more, so she wouldn't get the invites to all the parties and all the things she enjoyed most. She broke it off between us.'

Sophie narrowed her eyes at him. 'The papers said you dumped her.'

'I guess the "heartbroken dumped fiancée" was a better spin for her than "disgruntled girlfriend dumps injured champ who'll never race again while he's still in hospital"—and she broke the story about my knee, too,' he said. 'Which meant all my sponsorship deals were terminated pretty quickly.' He grimaced. 'I understand why they dropped me from their campaigns, but it wasn't her place to tell them.'

'Why didn't you tell everyone the truth— that she was the one who dumped you?'

'At the time, I had other things to think about,' he said. 'I was coming to terms with the end of my career. Plus she got her story in first. If I'd protested a few days later, people wouldn't have believed me. Plus their minds were already made up by then.' He looked away. 'Annabel didn't want to marry me for myself. I'm not sure whether she just wanted the glory of being with a champion skier, or whether she wanted to marry a billionaire's son so she could carry on with the lifestyle she enjoyed. As I clearly wasn't going to be forth-coming on either front, she decided to cash in and sell her story. Even though it wasn't true.' He shrugged. 'It took a few weeks, but the story died down eventually.'

'What happened to the baby?' Sophie asked.

'She told the papers she had a miscarriage. Maybe she did; or maybe she had a termina-tion. Your guess is as good as mine.' He spread his hands. 'Either way, I don't think she was as devastated as she made out to the press. Apart from the fact she'd given me that ultimatum in the first place, it wasn't very long before she was dating the new world champion skier.'

Sophie digested this.

All was becoming horribly clear.

No wonder Josh had reacted with silence

when she'd told him about the baby. He'd been here before and it had turned his life upside down: not in a good way.

'Let me get this straight. You'd had an accident, you'd really hurt yourself, you weren't going to be able to do what you loved most any more—and Annabel not only told everyone lies about you, she did a hatchet job on your career and your reputation as well.' Blake had cheated her and lied to her, but what Annabel had done was on another scale entirely. She'd really rubbed salt in Josh's wounds.

'Looking back, I know I had a lucky escape. We would have made each other seriously unhappy and ended up with a really messy divorce. Though I would've made sure I had custody of the baby so my child could at least grow up feeling loved.'

She believed him; the way he'd talked about his family, he'd grown up loved and he'd do the same for his child.

'So why did she make up this new story?'

'My best guess is that it was because she was unhappy and I'm an easy target for her,' he said. 'I hear on the grapevine that her latest guy dumped her recently. Maybe she was lashing out to make herself feel better. Although Pendio's a family resort rather than the kind of glamorous party place where she'd normally ski, someone had obviously invited her here for a break. Unfortunately she saw me—saw *us*—and it was one of those things where she couldn't stand to think I was happy when she wasn't. I'm sorry she dragged you into it. My family lawyer's arranging that she makes a public apology to you.'

Sophie shook her head. 'It doesn't matter about me. To be honest, I'd rather you left it. I don't want her digging and finding out about Blake. I really don't want the story spread everywhere.'

'Then we'll do it the other way,' he said. 'I'll get my lawyer to tell the gossip magazines I don't have a drink problem and remind them about the laws of defamation. She won't get any more airspace because they won't want to risk having to pay damages.'

It was a good solution. 'I can live with that.' But there was something else worrying her.

'You weren't limping, the last time I saw you,' she said. 'So what happened?'

'After the accident, you mean? I had a lot of physio, before I came here,' he said. 'Racing's completely off the cards for me now. Angelo—my coach, and Giovanni's younger brother—suggested I tried coaching, because at least then I could stay on the slopes. I did my teaching qualification and the idea was to spend this season here, to decide what I want to do. This isn't the sort of place that people who follow skiing championships would come to, even though Vincenzo—Angelo and Giovanni's dad—was a world champion in his day. But, even so, using my name instead of my initials gave me a little bit of anonymity. Space to think.'

'That wasn't what I meant. Why are you limping *now*?'

'Ah. That. Pure stupidity,' he said. 'You know I told you that the mountains make everything better?'

She felt her eyes widen. 'What did you do?'

'Went as fast as I could down a black run,' he said. 'I took a tumble. And I hit my knee when I was trying to come to a halt.' He grimaced. 'It's the second time I've ever been taken off a mountain by the rescue teams. There won't be a third.'

'How bad is it?'

'Not as bad as last time,' he said. 'But, when they found out what I'd done, my coach shouted at me, my surgeon shouted at me, my parents shouted at me, my sister shouted at me, Gio shouted at me…' He moved his hands in rueful circles.

Did he expect her to shout at him, too? For taking a stupid risk? But there was always a reason why someone behaved in a certain way. And she remembered what he'd said about his original accident. It had happened because he wasn't concentrating, because he was thinking about the baby and his fight with Annabel.

This time, had he been thinking about *their* fight?

She needed to know.

'Why did you fall? Was it because…?' Guilt made the words stick in her throat.

'Of the fight I had with you?' he finished, clearly guessing her thoughts. 'No. It was my own fault. I wasn't paying proper attention.'

'Because you were thinking of the fight.'

'I should've had more sense than to go out in the first place,' he said, 'so do *not* blame yourself. This one's all on me.'

'How long will it take to fix?'

'I don't know,' he said. 'I'm doing the physio, even though it hurts like hell. And that's probably another reason why I wasn't as receptive to you as I should've been this morning. Physio always leaves me in a filthy mood.'

'I'm sorry.'

'So am I,' he said. Then he looked her straight in the eye. 'So where does that leave us?'

'I…' She shook her head, not knowing what

to say. Did they have a future? Or had she messed it up? 'I'm sorry I didn't give you the chance to explain about Annabel.'

'I understand why you didn't. I lied to you—mainly by omission,' he said. 'Because I thought you'd see me in terms of my background.'

'You thought I'd be a gold-digger?' It hurt even more that he'd thought she could be like Annabel.

'No. I thought you'd see me as a poor little rich boy. Spoiled and entitled, like Gaz and his friends.'

She frowned. 'You're not like that.'

'But I have been in the past,' he said, 'and you were pretty scathing about rich boys who'd never done a day's work in their lives. I didn't want you to see me as one of them.'

She could understand that.

'Given the damage Blake did to you by lying, it's not surprising you were angry with me when you found out who I was. I knew how you felt about lying, and I should've told you the truth sooner. A lie of omission is still a lie.'

She could sugar-coat it and say everything was OK. But it wasn't. 'Yes, it is, and yes, you should have,' she said. 'It hurts that you didn't trust me.'

'I pretty much lost my trust in relationships and I didn't want to get involved with anyone, after Annabel. The same way as I'm guessing what happened with Blake made you lose your trust in relationships.'

'Yes.' She hadn't wanted to get involved with anyone again, either.

He looked at her, his grey eyes very clear. 'Then I met you. And everything changed. I'd started enjoying working with my students, but you were different. There was something more. You were like sunshine making everything sparkle, and I couldn't wait for our lessons. You gave me a different perspective, and I started seeing the world through your eyes. Seeing the magic of the Christmas market, with the fairy lights: I think that's the moment when I really fell in love with you.'

She stared at him. 'You fell in love with me?'

He nodded. 'I never intended to. And all that stuff I said about just taking things as they come—I think I was trying to convince myself as much as convince you.'

He loved her.

Or did he? Had he changed his mind, since she'd ended things between them?

'So,' he said. 'We're having a baby. And I'm telling you now that I plan to be a hands-on dad. My dad worked ridiculous hours when I was growing up, but he never missed anything at school—from sports days to the awful concerts where Lauren and I played one or two shrieking notes over and over on a recorder. That's the kind of dad I want to be. Not just the fun dad who does afternoons in the park, but the one who changes nappies, gets up in the night when the baby's teething and fractious, reads a bedtime story and coaxes a toddler to eat more veg.'

'That's what my dad was like,' she said.

'And I want to be your partner,' he said. 'Your husband, if you'll marry me, or living with you, if not. I want to support you, Sophie. That dream of having a restaurant that gives other people a second chance—I can make that happen. Anywhere you want it to.'

Her dream. Handed to her on a plate.

It was tempting.

But was it what Josh wanted from life? She'd thought he wanted to stay out here in the Dolomites. Even after his accident, he'd chosen to be in the mountains rather than England. The last thing she wanted was for him to feel trapped and end up resenting her. 'What about you?' she asked. 'What are your dreams?

'Short of getting someone to invent a new kind of knee replacement, I'm not going to get my old job back,' he said wryly. 'I didn't lie to you about that. No more championship skiing.'

'But you love the snow. Surely you want to stay in it as much as possible?'

'I do, and I have ideas of what I want to do here,' he admitted, 'but I love you more. If it's a choice between you and the snow, then you win, hands down.'

'There must,' she said, 'be some room for compromise. Or are you planning to work for your dad, after all?'

He shook his head. 'Lauren's the one who's worked for it and deserves it. She'll be a brilliant CEO—way better than I ever could be. She understands the business and she's great with the staff. I'm not shoving her out of the way. Ever.' He took a deep breath. 'Actually, this last tumble has done me a favour.'

'How?'

'It's focused me,' he said. 'It's made me realise what I want. You know your coin challenge?'

'Ye-es.'

'I tried it. It seems I don't want to be a ski instructor and I don't want to be a world champion skier any more, either. What I want is to make the world a better place.' He looked at her. 'I want my own ski resort.'

His own ski resort. She frowned. 'That

means snow. I mean—I know we sometimes get snow in England, but nothing like it is here. You couldn't have a ski season in, say, London.'

'Technically I could, with a snow machine and dry slopes; but it's not the same. It's not the mountains.'

'So what are you thinking?'

'There's a place in the next valley from this one. The owners are looking to sell,' he said. 'Except I'd want to make a few changes. With the injuries I've had over the last year or so, the limitations I've had to face, it's made me realise I want to do something with adaptive skiing.'

'Adaptive skiing?'

'For people with disabilities,' he said. 'And their families. So they can have a break together and all of them can enjoy the thrill of going down a slope. Nobody's left out. I'm thinking a hotel, self-catering chalets for families, a ski slope, specially trained disability instructors and physiotherapists, and a spa.'

Which all sounded amazing: but it didn't fit in with her dream of getting another restaurant in London. They couldn't spread themselves that thinly. She'd have to give it up.

Either it showed in her face or she'd accidentally said it aloud, because he said softly,

'You don't have to give up on your dream. I was thinking maybe we could spend snow season here, and the rest of the time in London with someone else managing the resort. So either you could have a restaurant as part of the resort, or you could have a place in London with a manager during ski season. Whatever works for you. We can do both. Work together. You could work with me at the resort in snow season, and I could work with you at the restaurant in summer. A waiter, perhaps.'

'A billionaire's son—a former world champion skier—working as a waiter in a restaurant?' she asked.

'A husband,' he corrected, 'supporting his wife's business and helping her make a difference.'

'You haven't actually asked me to marry you,' she pointed out.

'Because I'm terrified you'll say no,' he admitted. 'And I'm also terrified you'll say yes, in case I don't live up to what you want from a husband.'

She blinked. 'How could you ever think you wouldn't live up to what I want?'

'I quote,' he said, '"I deserve better than this." And you're right. You do.' He shrugged. 'Plus I'm pretty sure I can't get down on one knee. Though I wish I could, because it's snowing—just like it was the first time I met you.'

'I remember. When I wandered onto the edge of the piste.'

'It was too early for many skiers to be out, and the snow had obscured the edge of the piste,' he said. 'And you were looking up at the snow.'

'Thinking that this year I'd see a proper white Christmas with proper snow, not just a tiny dusting in some corner of London that was miles away from me,' she said. Then she looked at him, her blue eyes piercing. 'It's Christmas Eve.'

'It hasn't felt like it,' he admitted. 'All the magic of Christmas I had with you, from the market and the sleigh ride and the snow angel—and it was gone, wrecked because I didn't tell you the truth about myself soon enough.'

'You've explained now,' she said. 'And I understand why you didn't want to tell me earlier.' She reached out and took his hand. 'It's snowing. Like it was when I first met you.' She took his hand and drew him outside to the deck, where they were sheltered from the wind and the snow was falling in huge, slow, fluffy flakes.

'Look at it,' she said. 'This is pure magic. The mountains and the trees and the snow. And the way you got me to wish upon a falling star, that night... Do you know what I wished for?'

He waited.

'I wanted to fall back in love with life. Leave all the bad bits of the past behind,' she said. 'And I think even then I wanted to feel safe enough to fall in love with you.'

'It's safe,' he said. 'I might have a dodgy knee, but you can always lean on me.'

'You taught me,' she said softly, 'to trust again. To hurl myself down a slope on two tiny bits of wood or whatever skis are made of, and know that I'm not going to fall and hurt myself. You gave me my confidence back. And I've realised now that what I want for Christmas is for you to feel the same.'

'Safe enough to fall in love with you?' he asked. 'Yes. I love you, Sophie. But do you feel safe enough to fall in love with me?'

She pretended to think about it, then dropped down on one knee. 'I love you, Josh Cavendish. With you, I've got my confidence back. I feel safe. I don't care how much you're worth and I really don't care about skiing in posh places or partying with celebrities. I just want to make a family with you and our baby—and to work with you to make the world a better place. Happy Christmas, Josh. Will you marry me?'

'In a heartbeat,' he said, drawing her back up to her feet. 'Happy Christmas, Sophie.'

And then he kissed her as the snow fell softly round them.

# EPILOGUE

*Christmas Eve, two years later*

OPENING DAY.

Josh had worked incredibly hard on setting up the resort, spending his entire trust fund and savings on it, refurbishing all the accommodation so it was suitable for all guests and their families, no matter what their physical abilities. Cavendish Software had given them an extensive sponsorship package to fill in the gaps, and although they'd been up and running properly for a month today was the day that Josh's sister Lauren was going to cut the ribbon and open the resort officially. Christmas Eve: a day special to all of them.

Sophie had worked by Josh's side all the way, creating menus that could be easily adapted to their guests' needs; she worked on training the seasonal chalet staff, too, doing the interviews herself and giving people a chance to turn their lives round.

Today, the resort was in full Christmas mode. A Christmas market, sending out the gorgeous smells of Christmas food; Christmas trees dotted around the resort; Christmas songs being played by a local band; and Father Christmas in his sleigh, ready to hand out presents to everyone.

'Ready?' Sophie asked.

'Yes. No.' Josh took a deep breath. 'This is scarier than standing at the top of a championship freestyle run. Right, Lex?'

Little Alexandra Louisa—named after Josh's dad and Sophie's mum—who was comfortably sitting on her father's shoulders, pulled her father's hair, kissed him and laughed. 'Dada!'

Josh grinned. 'Just like her mum. Keeping me in line.'

Sophie laughed. 'She loves you to bits. Just like I do. Just like we all do.' She stole a kiss. 'I'm so proud of you. And I'm prouder still that you're not going down the slope as a champ but as an assistive instructor.' And Josh's student Mia—an eight-year-old girl with cerebral palsy—was going to be the star of the show, proving that a girl the doctors had said at birth might not ever be able to walk could beat the odds.

'This isn't about me,' he said. 'It's about making the world a better place. Giving people chances.' He kissed her. 'Just like you've done with me. You rescued me.'

'We rescued each other,' Sophie said. 'Now go and ski.'

'Me ski,' Lex said hopefully.

'Later, princess,' Josh promised.

'Go and make sure Mia's all right,' Sophie said, taking Lex off her father's shoulders and settling her on her own. 'We'll be waiting for you both at the bottom, with Mum and Dad.' Josh's parents had asked her to call them that even before the wedding. Lauren had welcomed her instantly as a little sister. And Sophie had been drawn straight into the heart of the Cavendish family as one of their own.

'The woman I love, our daughter, our family and our community. And doing a job that actually means something and makes a difference to other people's lives,' Josh said. 'It doesn't get any better than this.'

Oh, but it would.

Though Sophie wasn't going to tell him that particular piece of news until he was safely at the bottom of the slope again, with his skis off. He didn't need the distraction of a positive pregnancy test.

So she just smiled. 'I love you.'

'I love you, too,' Josh said.

'Dada ski,' Lex said, patting the top of her mother's head.

'Yes, Dada ski,' Sophie agreed.

She went to stand with the Cavendishes and watched as Josh met Lauren and Mia at the top of the slope, Lauren made a short speech and cut the ribbon, and Josh helped guide Mia down the slope. She made sure all the waiting staff were circulating with drinks and nibbles and had the support they needed in the kitchen, the journalists had all the background they needed, and posed with Josh, Lex and Mia for photos.

And then, when everything was in full swing and Lex was with her grandparents, she whisked Josh off to a balcony for a private moment.

'Happy?' she asked.

'Ecstatic,' he said. 'Today's been perfect.'

She grinned. 'There's always room to add a cherry on top of a Christmas cake.'

'How?' He looked intrigued.

'I have a Christmas present for you.'

Josh looked intrigued. 'A present?'

'Not something to unwrap right now. But your hospitality manager would like to give you advance warning that's she's taking leave in July.'

'July?' He looked confused. 'Are we going on holiday somewhere, Soph?'

She laughed. 'Not quite. It's a particular kind of leave. Which I'll need to take in about—ooh—seven months' time. Hence July. And that's why you can't unwrap your present now. You'll have to wait until July.'

She rested both hands on her stomach and watched as the penny dropped.

'Sophie Cavendish! Are you telling me we're going to be parents again?'

'Yup.'

His face filled with delight. 'That's not just an extra cherry on top of a Christmas cake. It's one of those cake fountains.' He picked her up and whirled her round. 'So when did you find out?'

'This morning,' she said. 'I've been dying to tell you all day. But I'm not giving you news like that before you go down a slope—even if it's not a black run and you're teaching. That's a distraction too far.'

'You're right,' he said. 'But it's the perfect bit of news to end a perfect day. In the perfect place. With the perf—'

'I've got the message—you don't have to say that word again,' she cut in with a grin, and kissed him. 'Happy Christmas, Josh.'

\* \* \* \* \*